D0406019

SAVING ROOM FOR DESSERT

NOVELS BY K. C. CONSTANTINE

SAVING ROOM FOR DESSERT

K. C. CONSTANTINE

Published by Warner Books

An AOL Time Warner Company

Mysterious Press books are published by Warner Books, Inc.,
1271 Avenue of the Americas, New York, NY 10020.

Visit our Web site at www.twbookmark.com.

 An AOL Time Warner Company

The Mysterious Press name and logo are registered trademarks of Warner Books, Inc.

Printed in the United States of America

First Printing: August 2002

10 9 8 7 6 5 4 3 2 1

Library of Congress Cataloging-in-Publication Data

Constantine, K. C.
    Saving room for dessert / K. C. Constantine.
       p. cm.
    ISBN 0-89296-763-3
       1. Balzic, Mario (Fictitious character)—Fiction.   2. Police—Pennsylvania—Fiction.
3. Pennsylvania—Fiction.   I. Title.

PS3553.O524 S38 2002
813'.54—dc21   2002020096

This book is dedicated to world peace.

SAVING ROOM FOR DESSERT

1993

AFTERWARDS, RAYFORD couldn't remember exactly when he'd gotten the feeling, and he wanted to remember because he knew this wasn't just some good feeling. This one was serious. This one was going to make a difference. He knew it came during the run, the mile and a half he had to do in under twelve minutes, which he did in 9:04 and could have done faster if somebody had been pushing him. If somebody had really been pushing him he could've done it in eight, but when he passed the mile mark he also passed the last of the strung-out apps, and that was when he figured it was safe to take a look back. That's when he saw that the closest app was more than two hundred yards behind and losing ground and he knew he wouldn't have to do it in anywhere near eight.

And the feeling he got, so clear he could almost see it as well as feel it, was of total indifference. He didn't care where he finished among this bunch of apps; he was just going to run, and to hell with everything. In the last five years he'd done so many sit-ups, so many chin-ups, run so many mile-and-a-half runs in under twelve minutes, taken so many written tests, so many oral tests by committee, he just felt fuckit. He didn't say it. The words never formed in his mouth. But it was like they were printed in big black letters on glass or clear plastic, out there about twenty or twenty-five yards in front of him for the rest of the time he was running. Fuckit, William. Just run, man, and fuckit.

And after he saw the words and felt them as clearly as anything he'd ever seen or felt, the other words did form in his mouth, and he said them aloud and didn't care who heard him.

"They don't want me, they don't want me, I don't care, but long as I'm here I'm goin' run their asses into the ground. They might not hire me, but they're never goin' forget this nigger turned their vanilla asses into tap-ee-oh-ka."

And with those words in his mouth he glided the last hundred yards or so, vowing not to breathe so the sergeants with the stop-watches and clipboards could hear him when he crossed the finish line. And he hadn't. Hadn't doubled over either, the way every other app did when they came in—long after he'd come in. He remembered walking around, putting on his sweats, and starting his stretches before the next app even made it across the finish line, about two minutes after he'd crossed. He noticed the looks he was getting from the two sergeants, but he didn't acknowledge them. He just noticed them and thought, that's right, go on and look. Look at the nigger done whipped all these vanilla apps' asses. By a whole long time. Just like I whipped their asses in sit-ups. And chin-ups. And if you'da had a push-up test I'da whipped 'em in that too. Y'alls goin' remember William Rayford. You might not hire me, but fuckit, I don't care, I'm the best y'alls seen today. Or any other day. Make you out a deposit slip on that.

And he'd had the same attitude the following morning when, just as the Rocksburg Safety Committee chairman was telling him he was excused and thanks for coming in, that funky dago council-man with the birdy voice chirped up, "Just a minute, Mr. Chair-man, I got a question."

Rayford had started to thank everybody for their time and the courtesy they'd extended him and had already taken a step toward the door, but he stopped where he was and waited for the question.

The councilman, who'd been quiet until then, said, "Suppose

you got called to a robbery at, uh, say like a convenience store, a Sheetz or a 7-Eleven or somethin'. And while you're doing what you're supposed to be doing, you know, asking questions and getting everything ready for the detectives, suppose you see another cop, you know, one who answered the call just like you, maybe even your partner in the car, suppose you see him put a pack a cigarettes in his pocket, coupla candy bars maybe. What would you do?"

Rayford saw that clear plastic with the black letters on it again, and the feeling swept over him like the gentle drizzle he'd felt as he walked from the parking lot into council chambers before this oral exam. Fuckit, the sign said. Hire me, don't hire me, either way it's not goin' touch me.

He didn't sit back down. He talked while he draped his raincoat over his left arm. He said, "If there was no doubt in my mind he took the stuff?"

"No doubt," the councilman said.

"Then I'd go ask the clerk how much for a pack of cigarettes or the candy or whatever. And I'd pay him what he said, tell him the money was for what my fellow officer took, and then, after the detectives got there, I'd take my fellow officer aside and very politely I'd tell him, next time you take somethin' don't belong to you, and I see you? I'm goin' write you up. That's what I'd do, sir."

The funky dago councilman threw back his head and laughed, but quietly. He didn't make a sound. But he sat there laughing with his head back for maybe two seconds, and Rayford thought, there, see? Least he's goin' remember me.

"Is that it?"

"That's it, Mr. Rayford," the chairman said. "Unless Councilman Figulli has another question. No? We'll be in touch, one way or another. Thanks again for coming in."

"Thanks for giving me the opportunity," Rayford said, and went out to his Toyota in the soft rain and felt good. He didn't have the words to say how good it felt to not care how things were going to turn out. Now all he'd need to feel better was for the Toyota to start. Nothing wrong with the Toyota. Best car he'd ever owned. But the battery was dying, and he was broke and maxed out on both his Visa and his MasterCard, and payday wasn't till Friday. He put the key in, closed his eyes and was saying a little start-the-Toyota prayer when he heard somebody rapping on the window.

"Rayford?" It was an older man, with grayish whitish hair sticking out around his ears from under a white Kangol cap.

Rayford easily recognized the face but the name wasn't there. And he knew he should know the name.

Rayford wound down the window a couple of inches and tried to fake it. "Hey, man, hya doin'?"

"What, you don't remember me? Huh? I can see you don't. Balzic. How'd you do in there?"

"Oh oh, yeah yeah, hey, I knew it was you, I just couldn't remember whether we were first name or what, you know? Hya doin', Chief?" Rayford wound the window all the way down and held out his hand. "Good to see you, yeah. Hey, thanks, you know? Really appreciate you talkin' me up, man, really."

Balzic shook hands and said, "You're welcome. But I didn't do that much, believe me. So how do you think you did, huh? Pretty good? Nowicki told me you killed 'em on the physical stuff yesterday. Said he never saw numbers like yours before. Like what, you come in a minute and fifty-five seconds ahead of everybody in the run? Is that right?"

"Something like that, yeah."

"Yeah, well, you know, personally, I think it's a lotta bullshit myself. I mean I understand you gotta be in shape and all that, but puttin' all that emphasis on the physical stuff? See, I think they all do that 'cause they're scared to death to interpret the psychological test. That's where I'd be lookin'. I mean, nothin' personal here, I'm glad for you you're in good shape, you know, stay that way. For your own health I mean. But what I'd wanna know is, so you can run the thief down, what're you gonna do after you tackle him, huh? See what I'm sayin'?"

"Absolutely," Rayford said. "And I agree. But I still wanted to do my best, you know, just for me. And I did. Those were my best numbers ever. And I think I did okay in there just now. Never know, but, uh, I didn't stutter, I didn't hesitate, I looked 'em in the eye. I knew what I was talkin' about or else I told 'em I didn't know. Course, hey, you know, up to them, right? Hey, whyn't you get in, man, you're goin' get soaked out there."

"Nah, this jacket's, uh, my daughters bought it for me. It's Gore-Tex, you know? Guaranteed waterproof. Nah, I'm alright. So, uh, you think you did alright, huh?"

"Yeah, I think. Hey, lemme buy you a coffee or somethin', huh?"

"Huh? Yeah, okay, I could go for that." Balzic walked around the car and got in as Rayford, eyes closed, turned the key. The only response from the Toyota was a dead click.

Balzic had opened the door and dropped onto the seat in time to hear the click. "Oh-oh. Deadsville, huh? Hey, no problem, my car's right over there, c'mon, we'll go in mine."

Rayford winced. "Yeah, but I gotta get home sometime, gotta be on the job at four."

"You still workin' at the mall here?"

"Not anymore, uh-uh. One in the South Hills. Century Three?"

"Woo, that's a long way from here. Belong to Triple-A?"

"No, uh-uh, that's sort of a continuin' problem I got. My mother-in-law, got-damn woman, all she got to do is eat, do her business, sleep, go to the store once in a while get some milk or coffee, go to the mailbox end of the block, drop some envelopes in. Keep tellin' my wife don't let your momma mail no bills, 'cause she get short, she tries to cash them checks."

"What, the ones you're payin' bills with?"

"Yeah. Exactly. Go 'head, laugh. I know you want to. If everybody's brain is a thousand molecules, that woman got seventy-nine. Three months ago—yeah, you're laughin', go 'head—but no shit, man, she tried to cash a check I wrote to Ma Bell. Woman walk in the got-damn Giant Eagle, told those people the check's made out wrong, somebody made it out to Ma Bell 'stead of Mrs. Bell. Tried to tell 'em that's who she was, Mrs. Bell, and here the check made out to AT&T. She heard me say it was made out to the phone company, and she still thinks Bell owns all them companies. Go 'head, laugh, it's okay."

Balzic was laughing, shaking his head.

"Had to go down the station house, man, bail her ass out. That's what ain't funny. Told my wife, said, this ain't this woman's fault, this is your fault, she don't know no better, you the one lettin' her mail them checks. You got to mail them bills your damn self, you can't be lettin' her do that. Woman got a history of stupid shit long as her legs, you know, and she used to be six feet tall before she got osteoporosis. I mean the woman got some long legs."

"Cut it out," Balzic said, "I got a crick in my neck, it hurts when I laugh. So, uh, what, she try to cash your Triple-A dues?"

"Yeah, man, tried to cash that too. Told 'em her name was Ahmed Aman Amal or some Muslim shit like that, told 'em some dummy made it out to three As—you think I'm makin' this up, it's the truth. Yeah, and if you talk to the woman, she sounds intelligent. And she will try to make you think she's smarter than she is. But see, she can't read, and she fronts all the time. Sit with a newspaper in her lap watchin' the TV news, try to make you think she just read somethin' when what she did was hear it on the TV. It's pathetic. If she wasn't my wife's momma I could maybe work up some kinda feelin' for her, you know? But the woman has seriously fucked up my life. I probably told you, I musta, 'cause I tell everybody, so I musta told you, but she's the reason I had to get out the air force. I was an E5, man, with four years in, all set to re-up for six, makin' damn near eleven hundred a month, all those benefits, goin' get maybe a three-grand re-up bonus, and what does my wife say? No, William, uh-uh, we goin' give all this up, yeah, 'cause we got to go back to Pittsburgh, man, take care of Momma."

"Yeah, you told me."

"Been a money cripple ever since, man. Workin' three jobs to get sixty hours, you believe that? And sixty hours, that's a good week. And no health insurance, no commissary prices, no PX prices, no vacation—I used to get thirty days paid leave a year, man! From day one! But since I got out? Six years, man, every vacation day I've had is unpaid sick time. 'Cause of this woman thinks she's Mrs. Bell. Or Mrs. Triple-A."

"C'mon, let's go, you're hurtin' my neck," Balzic said.

"What am I goin' do with my car?"

"C'mon, we'll figure somethin' out."

Balzic drove to Muscotti's, where he ordered and paid for coffee and pointed Rayford to a table against the wall so they wouldn't have to put up with Vinnie ragging everybody at the bar. Loudly.

"Man, whyn't you let me pay, I wanted to buy."

"Well then you'd have to deal with the bartender, and I was already in here once today and he's pissed 'cause his gums are shrinkin', he gotta get a new set of choppers, and he doesn't have dental insurance, and he doesn't wanna spend the money, so he's takin' it out on everybody. He's alright, I just didn't know if you were ready for him or not. You can't pay him too much attention, that's all, or he'll drive you nuts. So, uh, listen, you know if you get this job, they're gonna tell you you gotta move here within six months, you do know that, don't ya?"

"Well nobody told me that exactly, but I figured. Pretty S-O-P, right?"

"I don't know how it is everywhere else, I just know about here. So, uh, how's your family gonna deal with that?"

"Don't have the job yet, Chief."

"No no, no Chief. Mario, okay? And if you don't get the job, I'll be the most surprised guy in America. Nowicki's been takin' heat from the NAACP about no black cops ever since he became chief. So when he was talkin' about your numbers, your written score—"

"Wait wait, he told you my written score?"

"No, not the number, I didn't ask him that. Asked him where

you finished, that's all I wanted to know. Told me you came in first—"

"First on the written? No shit?"

"First, yeah, that's what he said."

Rayford started to whoop but saw the sign go up in front of him again. Fuckit. Don't care, man. Do not care. Allow yourself to smile maybe, but do not allow yourself to care.

"Anyway, what I started to say before was, uh, as much heat as Nowicki's been takin'—and not just him, the whole council too, they all been catchin' hell about no black cops. So hey, now? You know, anybody starts bitchin', Nowicki's got your numbers to show 'em. Makes it easy on him."

"So what you're sayin', if I'm hearin' you right, you're sayin' even though I'm first in all these tests, except the orals which we're not goin' know about for a while, right?"

"Yeah, coupla days probably. And the psychological too, don't forget. Course they won't say anything about that."

"Yeah, okay. So despite all that, I'm goin' get the job because I'm black?"

"No, you're gonna get the job because you were the best app they had. But when somebody starts bitchin'—and somebody will—'cause that's just the way people are—oh what's this look you're givin' me?"

"What look, I'm not givin' you any kinda look."

"The hell you're not. You're lookin' like you're pissed 'cause they're gonna give it to you for the wrong reason."

"No, man, no, uh-uh. I'm just sayin', you know, I work my ass off to stay in shape, and to keep up with what's happenin'. I go to the library two, three times a week, I do my homework. And to get the job 'cause I'm black?"

"You're gonna get the job 'cause you came in first in all the tests—the ones they can measure, okay? Like I said, nobody's gonna talk about the psych test. All I'm tellin' you is, from Nowicki's point of view, that you happen to be black with the best scores means down the road there ain't gonna be any suits landin' on his desk from pissed-off white guys who came in ahead of you on the tests, okay? 'Cause no white guys did. So that just makes his job easy. And believe me, there's nothin' a boss likes better than an employee who makes that happen. So stop givin' me that look."

"I'm not givin' you any look, I'm just . . ."

"Just what? C'mon, what? This I gotta hear."

"Okay," Rayford said, rubbing his palms together, bopping his head. "What I'm tryin' to do is teach myself not to care how things come out. I been workin' on it for a while now. Like years and years. But it's not easy, okay? It is definitely not easy. Thing is, I been through so many of these things, you know, and it's such a got-damn comedown when it doesn't happen? I'm really workin' on tryin' to keep myself separate from the result. Am I makin' any sense?"

"Yeah, you're makin' lotsa sense. But, you know, I'm havin' a little trouble understandin' why you're havin' so much trouble hookin' up with any department. I don't get around anywhere near as much as I used to, but still, I hear all the time about departments all over the place lookin' for good apps."

"Yeah, right, me too. But my wife still got her momma. And every time I go through the drill, I mean, most of the time I know goin' in I can't take the job 'cause that got-damn woman won't move and my wife, no matter what I say, she ain't about to leave her."

"Well that's what I was askin' you earlier about movin' here."

"I know. And I don't know how I'm goin' work it, but I'm goin' work it somehow. 'Cause I told my wife, if they offer me this one, I'm takin' it, I'm sick a this bullshit scufflin' around from one lame-ass job to another. I've had to turn down six jobs, man, 'cause my wife wouldn't move. So you're right, man, no question, the jobs are out there. Went through the whole got-damn drill six times—well a lot more than that—I'm just talkin' 'bout the times I actually got an offer and then I had to say no and tell 'em why. And that shit gets around, don't think it don't. Before this one here, the last three departments? Soon as I told him my name they said they weren't takin' any more apps. So I said, nooo, uh-uh, no more, man, they offer, I'm takin', this is it!"

"You must really love your wife."

"Huh? Hey, I ain't pussy-whipped, man—"

"Didn't say anything about pussy. I said love."

"Yeah, okay, so you did. Well. I do. Sometimes I love her so much it . . . it pisses me off. I didn't know love was supposed to be such a got-damn problem. I mean, that's why I'm workin' so hard at not givin' a got-damn. 'Cause all the times I did good and I had to say no 'cause my wife wouldn't move? That shit will break you down, man.

"But it's not just her. I mean everybody in this got-damn country, they're always talkin' this bullshit 'bout how you have to work hard, and if you do work hard, then you're goin' get the result, the job, the goal, the prize, the raise, whatever.

"See, this martial arts teacher I had in Alabama, he's the one started me thinkin' about it, about how you have to separate yourself from the result of what you do. He used to drum it into me, every class I took from him. And for the longest time I didn't know what the hell he was talkin' about, thought he was crazy, tell you the truth. I mean I tried, 'cause I liked the dude, I really respected him, you know? He had his shit together. And he was old too. Sixty somethin'—"

"Woo that's old," Balzic said, laughing.

"Yeah, I know, I know, but I was eighteen when I met him. And sixty was ancient to me then, you know? And I figured 'cause he was so old and so together, the man must know *somethin'*. So I tried, I mean I could get it in my mind, you know? I could intellectualize it—that's what he said was the first trap. And that's what I did for years and years, all I did was think about it, but I never really got past that, you know? Thinkin' about it? I could never really keep what I was doin' separate from what I was hopin' I was gonna get as a result, you know? Not until yesterday.

"Then yesterday, man, for the first time, I actually got the feeling, I mean I could see this sign, I know this is goin' sound like some serious bullshit, but I could actually see the words out there in front of me, like they were printed on glass or a piece of plastic or somethin' clear like that. Big black letters. Fuckit. Just fuckit. Just run. Don't care where you come in, it don't matter where you come in. And after all these years of thinkin' about it and thinkin' about it, it finally happened—I mean it happened over my whole body, it wasn't just happenin' inside my mind, you know?"

"So this was good, right?"

"Yeah, man, it was like this huge weight fell offa me. And then today, when I was in front of that committee, I had it again. I was givin' it my best shot and not carin' how it was goin' come out."

"But then I tell you how you're probably gonna get the result you want but maybe not for the right reason—"

"Yeah, man, right, exactly, you tell me that, and I lost it. That fast, man, I was back all twisted up again. That just funked me out. Shit. Now I got to start all over."

"Yeah, well, you know what the Buddhists say."

"The Buddhists? Don't take this wrong, man, but anybody ever look like a dago Catholic, man, it's you," Rayford said, laughing despite trying not to.

"I know, I know, but yeah, the Buddhists. My one daughter, she got me started with them after my heart started playin' games with my mind. They say life is a series of moments, the Buddhists, so you have to approach each one like it's brand-new. And believe me, nobody knows more than me how hard that is. So I got some idea what you're talkin' about. All I'm sayin' is, don't let yourself get all tied up over that. If the result happens, you know, then that's your karma. If you lived each moment as fully as you could, you were makin' karma—least that's my take on it. But don't quote me, okay, 'cause I'm king of the backsliders. I'm always draggin' this, uh, this wagon around with all my bad memories and prejudices and so on. So approachin' anything like it's brand-new, for me that's no sure thing, believe me. Hey, c'mon, let's go see what we can do about your battery."

"Told you, man, I'm broke. And maxed out on all my plastic."

"I'm not. C'mon."

On the way to Tony Finelli's Garage, Balzic said, "I'm gonna say somethin', and I want you to think about it. I know you got the makin's of a good cop or else I wouldn't've done any talkin' for you, alright? But even if you get this thing with your mother-in-law straightened out, and you're able to move here? It's not gonna be any picnic for you here, you know that, right?"

"Yeah I know that."

"Well from my own experience I'm gonna tell you somethin'. The worst is domestics. Inside the residence? They're fire, man. You say the wrong thing, you may as well be spittin' gasoline. But the next worst—and it's really gonna be tough for you if you don't think 'em out before you get outta the car. That's the ones between the neighbors. T-D-K-P-S. Trees, dogs, kids, parkin' spaces, man, I'm tellin' you, they're dynamite lookin' for a fuse. And when you show up? You? All these hunkies and dags, especially the old ones, what they're gonna see first, before they see the uniform, what they're gonna see is your skin. And if you don't come on super cool, calm, and collected, they're gonna turn on you, no matter what the beef was that prompted the call."

"I know that."

"Yeah, but I don't think you know why."

"I think I know why."

"No, excuse me, but I don't think you do, you're too young. This goes back to when the unions were startin' to organize, way before my time, but not before my father's time. The steelworkers and the miners, when they were tryin' to organize in the early part of this century, whether they walked out or got locked out, it didn't matter which. 'Cause if it went on for too long, the owners, they'd bring in the scabs. And guess what color most of them were. They also brought in the immigrants too, the new hunkies and the new wops.

But the immigrants, eventually they could blend in. Not so with the blacks. And that shit? That old resentment over them bein' scabs? That's still here, man. Even though those unions are dead. 'Cause the owners, that animosity between the old union guys and the scabs? The owners worked that, man, they worked that to their benefit for years and years. Decades. And it's still here, don't think it isn't. I swear I think sometimes it got passed down through the genes."

"I do know that," Rayford said. "I have read my history."

"Yeah? Well good. But knowin' it is one thing. Havin' to deal with the results, that's somethin' else again. What I'm tellin' you is, you gotta be real careful how you get outta the car. Be real careful how fast you walk up on people. And especially be real careful to keep your distance, three steps at least, and if you gotta get physical with somebody, unless it looks like somebody's gonna get hurt bad or killed, don't even think about doin' it without backup. And even with backup, you be absolutely sure you don't let anybody get behind you. These things over trees, dog shit, parkin' spaces, I'm tellin' ya, people come outta the houses with everything you can think of in their hands, every tool they got in their cellar, everything they got in their kitchen. So you make sure their hands're empty when they're comin' to see what the noise is about.

"And don't forget the spectators. Worst beatin' I ever took on the job was from a woman I coulda picked up with one hand. And all because I didn't think she packed the will or the gear. Big mistake. She hit me with a metal servin' spoon, caught me in the throat with the first one, second one right under the nose, third one I managed to get my arm up, that's when I saw the knife in her other hand. Look here." Balzic pulled his sleeve up and nodded to the scar on his left forearm.

"Twenty-three stitches to close that up, and what fooled me was she never said a word. Had her hands behind her, just walked up and started swingin'. Turned out the guy I was cuffin' was her son. God only knows why she swung the spoon first, 'cause if she'da swung the knife first? She'da laid my throat open, I never saw it comin'. That was the first time I ever pulled my piece on anybody. 'Cause I did everything wrong. Didn't call for backup, never challenged her, never looked at her hands, and soon as she caught me with the spoon, he started kickin' at me, her son, so I had to resort to usin' my piece. I'm backin' up, blood flyin' everywhere, I'm tryin' to get my piece out, they're both comin' at me, I finally clear my piece, I'm screamin' get on the ground or I'll kill you both. And thank God, they did.

"But from then on, buddy boy, nobody walked into my space they didn't show their hands, I didn't care who else was there or what else was goin' on. Fuckin' pope himself, he walked up on me, he'da had to show me what he was holdin'. What I'm sayin' is—and you can't ever forget this—their animosity for you goes a lot deeper than it ever did for me. And you can't forget that. Not for half a second. Not for a tenth of a second. 'Cause nobody's reaction time is as fast as somebody else's action time. Burn that into your brain."

Balzic got out, and went and talked to somebody standing under a lift using a hammer and chisel to take a rusted exhaust system off a Nissan.

Rayford got out and went and stood beside Balzic.

"What year's your Toyota?"

"Eighty-seven."

"Twelve-volt, right?"

"Yeah."

"So whatta ya say, Tony? Got somebody go up City Hall, put a battery in this kid's car?"

"Soon's I get this thing off. Sent my kid out to get a whole new system for this forty-five minutes ago, he still ain't back. Which means either he's makin' it himself or else he thinks I forgot where the Nissan garage is. Eighty-seven Toyota, huh? Whatta ya want, three-year, four-year, five-year, what?"

"Best you got," Balzic said, ignoring Rayford's protest that he couldn't afford the best. "Put it on this," Balzic said, taking a Visa card out of his wallet and holding it up first for Finelli to see and then for Rayford, who continued to protest.

"Aw stop it. You can pay me back a buck a week for the next two years."

"Buck a week? Man, how much you wanna make on this deal?"

"What's it gonna cost me, Tony?"

"With tax, seventy-four nineteen. Just sold one, that's how I know—holy Christ, finally, you're back. What the hell you doin'?"

A teenage boy who bore a strong familial resemblance to Finelli shuffled up, shrugged, and said, "They were busy."

"Busy? They were so busy it took you forty-five minutes to go one mile there and back, is that what you're tellin' me?"

"Yeah, right, they were busy."

Finelli gave the tailpipe one final whack and ducked out of the way to avoid the rust as it clattered to the floor. "Hey, Albert, your mother says I gotta put you to work, so I lay off a guy worked for me for three years to do that? And you're gonna disappear for forty-five minutes at a time? Don't ever do that again. Where is it?"

"Where's what?"

"Where's what—Jesus, what did I send you to get, huh?"

"Oh. Out in the truck."

"How's it gonna get on this car if it's out there? I'm s'posed to carry it in? Hey, I don't care what your mother says. This is the last time I'm tellin' you, you pull this crap again I'll take you down the recruitin' office myself, I'll enlist you in the goddamn marines for four years, see how you like that. What, you forgot Bill was sick? You forgot I'm here by myself?"

"They were busy I'm tellin' you."

Finelli wiped his hands on a rag and disappeared into another part of the shop, calling out, "I gotta go up town, put a battery in this guy's car. You better be here when I get back, you hear me? You walk outta here like last week, you're not gonna be livin' in my house tonight, and that's not a threat, Albert, that's a promise."

"Jesus, whatta you want from me, I can't help it other people ain't on your schedule."

Finelli came back out wheeling a battery on a dolly. "What do I want, huh? I just told ya: be here when I get back, okay?"

"Yeah yeah. Where'm I gonna go on what you pay me?"

Finelli stopped short wheeling the battery outside, causing Balzic to bump into his back. Finelli started to say something else to his son, but Balzic held up his hands. "Hey, Tony, fight with your kid later, okay? Please? Better yet, talk to your wife."

"Yeah, yeah, right, let's go. I'll follow youse up there, go on. City Hall, right? Where am I gonna go on what you pay me, fuck me. My son's a fucking load, he don't wanna work, my wife's been babyin' him since the day he was born. Ah fuck's the use."

Balzic waited until he and Rayford were in his car before he said, "Think you got family problems, huh? Wanna trade yours for his?"

"I'll keep mine, thanks, but listen, about this battery, man—"

"Don't worry about it. See, from now on, every time you see me you'll have to listen to my stories. You try to escape, your conscience'll bother the shit outta you. I know what I'm doin'."

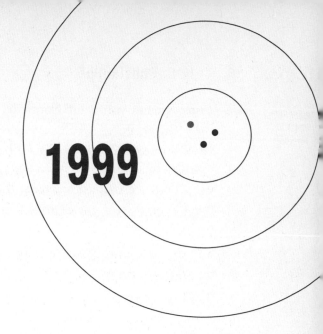

1999

RAYFORD HUNG up from talking to his wife more disgusted and discouraged than he was Monday in the marriage counselor's office. The third marriage counselor. In six years. Right before their hour was up Monday Rayford said, "Charmaine? You remember I told you I passed the sergeant's test? Well, baby, they goin' give it to me, you hear?"

"Been sayin' that for how long now? They give it to you yet?"

"They goin' to, that's what I'm sayin'. And you know what that means? Big raise, huh? You hear what I'm sayin'?"

"You hear what I'm sayin', William? I'm not movin' my momma to no got-damn Rocksburg, I don't care how much raise you get. I been tellin' you that for six years now, when you think it might sink in, huh? And how many times do I have to remind you Pittsburgh got a large po-lice department? They lookin' for apps all the time."

On the phone today it had been a rerun. That's when he'd said, "And when you goin' understand they haven't put a class through their academy in more'n four years, how many times I got to tell you that? You say I don't listen to you, you cap all over my ass to that counselor—who was your choice, remember that? This one was your choice, you picked this one—"

"I know whose choice she was, why you keep remindin' me?"

" 'Cause the first two was mine—"

"And they were both men!"

"Well now you got you a woman!"

"Both men, both Jews. You know I ain't goin' listen to no Jew tell me how to act, bad as they treat their women."

"So now this one's yours and she keep askin' the same questions them Jews did—"

"Oh she does not, what you talkin' 'bout?"

"—don't interrupt me—"

"Oh listen to you, you the king, right? Don't interrupt me, don't interrupt me, that's all you say. All you *can* say."

"See how you do? And yet you just shut your mind to that one fact I keep tellin' you every got-damn time we talk—talk, shit, we don't talk. I talk, you look out the got-damn window—"

"And I talk, you look at your got-damn shoes!"

"Oh why we doin' this mess, Charmane, can you tell me? And if you can't tell me that, tell me why do I love you, can you tell me that? Least tell me that much, shit!"

"I don't know if you don't know."

"Aw bullshit, Charmane, this is bullshit, baby. I love you, you know that. I love you like the first day. More. Worse. Love you worse than the first day, I didn't get sick that *first* day. I got sick that night, yeah, right, if I'm lyin' I'm dyin'—"

"And I'm sayin' good-byein'." And she hung up.

Rayford growled at the phone and wanted to bite it. That's me, he thought. Po-lice dog. William Milton K-9 Rayford. Growlin' and wantin' to bite, I need to be on a leash, need a motherfuckin' handler, that's what I need, don't need no got-damn marriage counselor. And I'm not even no grown-up K-9, I'm a motherfuckin' puppy! Puppy motherfucker, that's me. Baby, why do I let you do that to me? Ten years! Ten years of this bullshit and I'm still as crazy for you as the first night, what the fuck is wrong with me? Am I ever goin' get over this shit?

Aw shut your mind up, William, get your gear on, get your duty face on, man, get to gittin', it's time to go to work.

But in the middle of putting on his summer-weight black trousers, it all started again. Got-damn you, Charmane, be so easy to get me a lawyer, file the papers, send you a copy, do the drill, wait it out, get on with my life. Why can't I do that? Why can't I love somebody else? Every woman I'm with, get 'em in the bed, all I see is you, can't stop my mind from showin' home movies of you, can't stop my body from feelin' you under me, beside me, on top of me— is this all this is? Pussy? Is this what I'm crazy about? 'Cause nobody fuck like you? Is that what all this mess is? . . . Got-damn counselor ask me am I unfaithful to you? Shit, I ain't unfaithful to you, I'm unfaithful to every woman I jump, can't fuck none of their sorry asses without thinkin' how much I'd rather be with you. Be better off polishin' my knob than be with these women, all they do is remind me how much they ain't you.

Aw, go on, man, listen to yourself, what are you, thirteen? Thirty years old, just passed the sergeant's test, they're goin' make you a detective, and here you are actin' like some got-damn thirteen-year-old boy woke up think his dick is broke just 'cause he had a wet dream. Least you can still put a crease in your pants.

Separate yourself from this woman, William, get her out your head! Stop thinkin' like some got-damn pussy-whipped boy!

Rayford managed, briefly, to calm his mind while he put on his socks and shoes. He checked his watch against the Weather Channel's. Theirs said 2:48, so did his, which meant twelve minutes to finish dressing and get to City Hall. He watched the local weather to see whether he might need rain gear. Sunny and warm, high of 66, low of 50, no rain predicted till Saturday. Too got-damn warm for April, too got-damn dry too. Where these April showers? Need some storms keep these honky motherfuckers out their backyards and in their houses.

He put on his white V-neck Commander T-shirt, then slipped into his Second Chance Monarch body armor and hooked up the

Velcro tabs. Then he put on his short-sleeve black shirt, tucked it in, went to the front door, and checked himself out in the full-length mirror he'd hung the day he'd moved in. He put his cap on, squared it, put his heels together, saluted, and inspected himself up and down, from black cap to black safety-toed oxfords, all cloth cleaned and pressed, shoes polished to a high gloss.

He got his duty belt from the bedroom closet beside his bed and put it on, adjusting his duty-belt keepers to his buckleless trouser belt, then checked out his duty belt, sight and feel, from left to right around his back: key holder, baton holder, pepper spray, cuffs, glove pouch, flashlight holder, SIG-Sauer 9mm pistol in holster, and double-magazine case. He took out both magazines, made sure they were full, then replaced them in the case and snapped both snaps. Then he drew his pistol, eased the slide back far enough to make sure he had a live round in the chamber, then reholstered it and adjusted the retention strap. He made sure his PR-24 baton and four-cell MagLite flash were still in their holders on top of his black nylon gear bag, checked his wristwatch one last time against the Weather Channel's clock, turned the TV off, picked up his gear bag and briefcase, gave himself one more inspection in the mirror, and went out, locking the door carefully behind him, ready for Mrs. Romanitsky to bless him.

After pulling his door shut, he turned around and there she was, peeking out her door opposite his. She came out, eyes dancing as usual, her palms together briefly, and then she made a cross in the air between them. "I'm gonna pray for you today, Officer William. You gonna be safe 'cause God will look out for you."

"Thank you, ma'am. As always, I appreciate your prayers. I know they're keeping me safe. Now is there anything you need today? Anything I can get for you while I'm out and about?"

"Oh no, no no, you just watch out, you be good, God will be good to you, okay? I don't need nothing, no thank you very much, you such a good boy, your mother's very proud, I know."

"I'm sure she is too, ma'am, wherever she is. I have to go now, okay? Anything you need, you call the station, tell 'em to tell me and I'll get it for you, okay?"

"Ouu, thank you, God bless you, you're so nice."

Every day, for nearly six years, it was the same exchange, almost word for word, since the first afternoon he came out of his apartment in uniform and startled her as she was coming back from the grocery. She'd dropped one of her bags of groceries at the sight of him, quickly asking what was wrong. He'd said nothing was wrong, he'd just moved in that morning and would be living there for just a while until he could find a larger, more suitable place for his wife and child. She put her other plastic bags of groceries on the floor, crossed herself, put her palms together, and rocked back and forth from the waist, saying thank you repeatedly while looking at the ceiling.

"Is there a problem, ma'am?"

"That man," she'd said, pointing at the ceiling, "he plays his music so loud, till one, two o'clock in the morning, I can't sleep, could you maybe ask him, please, not so loud, okay?"

"You talk to the owner about it?"

"I tell him, I ask him, please, but he don't do nothing."

"Alright, I'll check it out when I come home tonight, okay?"

"Oh, please, would you? I would be so happy, thank you."

When he came off duty that night, his first on the job, as soon as he got out of his car, Rayford heard the music, some white-boy blues, some Stevie Ray Vaughan wanna-be. He listened for a moment on the sidewalk, then went inside and listened by Mrs. Romanitsky's door. Then he went upstairs and had to knock three times before a grunge-ball with a fish belly hanging over his sweatpants opened the door. He had a vacant grin and was gnawing on one end of a foot-long stick of pepperoni. As soon as the door opened Rayford smelled the pot. It took considerably longer for Grunge-Ball's grin to dissolve as the uniform registered in his brain.

"Whoa."

"Almost right," Rayford said. "Woe is you is more like it. Got a complaint about your music, but my nose tells me I got probable cause to look for controlled substances, namely marijuana, which I can smell all over you."

Grunge-Ball tried to close the door, but Rayford put the side of his left foot and left forearm against it. When he did he happened to catch a glance through the living room into the kitchen, and his jaw dropped and he started to laugh.

"Oh-oh, what's this I see? Are those grow lights I see? In your kitchen? You got grow lights in your kitchen?!"

"Uh, no."

"Oh now what you goin' say, you growin' tomatoes in there, is that what you goin' say?"

"Uh, no. Huh? Tomatoes? Fuck you talkin' 'bout?"

"Oh man, step back inside, turn around, put your hands behind your back—let go that pepperoni." Rayford snatched it out of Grunge-Ball's hand and tossed it into the room onto a couch with a broken right leg.

"Hey, man, that's Armour brand, man, you don't throw that around, that's primo."

"Well listen to you, my man the pepperoni connoisseur, huh? Do what I tell you, pep con, and the only problem you're gonna have is with a judge, you hear me? Turn around, I said, put your hands behind your back."

"Oh man, you just can't come in here," Grunge-Ball said, but he got into a laughing jag from the pot and then, still laughing, tried to push his way past Rayford into the hall. Rayford spun him around, grabbed his left wrist and twisted it back and down, got that wrist cuffed, stepped on Grunge-Ball's left toes while pushing his right shoulder down and pulling his left wrist up, and before Grunge-Ball knew it he was on his knees, saying, "Man, somethin' bit me on the toes. Fuck was that? You got a dog?"

"You don't stop squirmin', it's goin' bite you again."

"That ain't right, man, siccin' a dog on people. Where the fuck'd it go, man, you got a magical dog or somethin'? Where's it at?"

"Magical dog? You're trippin' out. You need to stop smokin' your own product, my man, you're growin' some mutant weed."

And so, on his first day of duty with the Rocksburg PD, Patrol-man William Rayford made his first drug collar, arresting John Har-rold Walinski in apartment 3C at 335 Detmar Street, Rocksburg, and charging him with violations of Act 64, the Controlled Sub-stance, Drug, Device, and Cosmetic Act, Section 13, paragraphs 1, 12, 30, 31, 32, and 33, possession, possession with intent to deliver, and use of paraphernalia for the purpose of planting, propagating, cultivating, growing, harvesting, etc., etc., a controlled substance, namely marijuana in excess of thirty grams. This arrest led to the confiscation of fifty marijuana plants at various stages of cultivation, most about six inches tall under the grow lights in the kitchen but five of them nearly four feet high in a closet. Also confiscated were three cookie sheets full of marijuana leaves and buds drying in the oven, several boxes of Baggies, a carton of Top cigarette papers, and two scales.

The arrest, detention, prosecution, conviction, and subsequent incarceration of John Walinski also led to the daily gratitude of Mrs. Romanitsky in 2A, who ever since had greeted Rayford as soon as she heard his door open if she sensed he was beginning a watch, at seven, three, or eleven o'clock. If he opened his door at any other time, she did not appear, but at the beginning of each of his watches, she never failed to appear and bless him with her prayers.

For a long time Rayford thought she was just some lonely old honky woman, half nuts from living alone for so long, but the more it became clear his wife and son were not moving to Rocksburg to be with him, the more easy it became for him to slip into relying on Mrs. Romanitsky's prayers. Nobody else was praying for him that he knew of, and even though in his private heart he thought religion was just the way rich folks kept poor folks satisfied with their poverty, he knew in his bones he wasn't big enough to turn down anybody's prayers. He'd take all the prayers he could get, even though he believed that as long as all you were worrying about was your immortal soul, you were no threat to stake out a corner of what might be yours in the here and now. And if Balzic was right about how rich folks had played with the emotions of early union organizers in the mills and mines by hiring blacks as scabs—and Rayford had no doubt of that—then religion was just the hammer on that nail in the coffin of poor folks, white, black, brown, red, or yellow.

Still, after nearly six years in this apartment building—and he'd never signed a lease for longer than a year at a time—Rayford had had no choice but to reassess who was half crazy from loneliness, Mrs. Romanitsky or him.

Social life for blacks in Rocksburg was nonexistent. He'd heard that at one time there had been a black American Legion post, but that had closed long before he'd arrived. There were two black churches, Bethel AME and Rocksburg Baptist, but Rayford had no interest in church or church socials. It was true that if his mood was right, a good gospel group could get him off his behind and onto his feet, the operative word being "good," but if you didn't go to church, the only place you could find good gospel was on the radio or the TV, and given the state of radio and TV ownership in Pittsburgh, the chances of that were slim.

Still, early on, within a month after moving to Rocksburg, Rayford heard about a black club in Knox, Freeman's Club and Barbecue, fronted by two blacks for a mafioso with the unlikely street name of Fat Buddha. It wasn't much. Just a bar, a grill and barbecue pit, a tiny dance floor, a jukebox, a couple dozen tables, and every Saturday night, an open mike for any local musicians who wanted to jam, mostly the blues and rock 'n' roll but occasionally jazz. Freeman's was where Rayford had met the women he was unfaithful to, every one he managed to bed doing nothing for him as much as magnifying his memories of Charmane and intensifying his hunger for her.

Somehow, to his irritation and annoyance, every woman he'd met in Freeman's who'd looked clean enough to take out into daylight had managed to find his phone numbers, home and cell, even though he'd never taken any of them back to his apartment and had given each one a different misspelling of his last name, Reyford, Raiferd, Reyfird, Rayfer. He thought that should have been enough to protect himself from their prying minds, but the fact that he had a spotless red '97 Toyota Celica, decent clothes, and a steady income seemed to put a serious jump in their curiosity about him.

He also never discussed his job with any of them. That was his first rule; he never told anybody he met socially outside of Rocksburg that he was a cop. Too many brothers had been through the system with God only knew what resentments for him to open himself up to any of those possibilities. And the last thing he wanted was any sister to have that information to trade to any resentful brother.

So he was perplexed that not only one but all four of the ones he'd been seeing off and on had found out his unlisted phone numbers and called him constantly. He had a machine and caller ID and never took any calls without screening, but every day that he came home from work or shopping or eating he would find at least one message from one of the sisters and sometimes one from each of them, and sometimes many more than that.

On his way to City Hall, he was trying once again to recall if he'd slipped and told one of the bartenders in Freeman's his numbers after too much Wild Turkey one Friday night. He couldn't fully convince himself not to worry about it, even though what was done was done and even though he knew it wasn't like him to slip about things like his numbers. More and more lately he'd been thinking that one of the sisters had a relative or an old boyfriend who was a cop and had run his plate through DMV, then got his insurance carrier off the title, and got his phone numbers from his insurance agent while making up some jive about an accident mix-up. Had to be. Or more likely it was some dude who wanted to be the new boyfriend.

So either it was time to change his numbers and stop going to Freeman's for his social life, or else start motoring to Pittsburgh to find a new one. Or maybe he'd just go on a woman fast, no women for thirty days, no pussy and no booze, just eat veggie stir-fries and drink green tea and do yoga and lift and run. Yeah, right. The running and lifting and yoga and stir-fries and no booze he could handle, but thirty days without a woman? Hey, why not, he asked himself as he pulled into the parking lot on the south side of City Hall. Didn't have a woman the whole time I was in air force basic. Didn't die or go blind. Just did what I had to do. Why can't I do that now?

Stop bullshittin' yourself, William, he thought. You know what you want. You know what you've wanted for five years. You want to make another baby with Charmane, that's what you want, you ain't bullshittin' nobody, man. You want to fill that black hole in your black heart where William Junior used to be. Before that got-damn woman let that boy crawl up on the back of that couch and get up on that got-damn windowsill. That's what you want, William. And none of those women from Freeman's is good enough to do that with, none of 'em got the looks or the body or the laugh. That boy looked like Charmane from the day he was born, same velvet chocolatey skin, same healthy body, same perfect fingers and toes, same brown eyes, same laugh comin' up outta their bellies . . . great God almighty how they could laugh. And you're never goin' hear it again, William. Not in this life. So separate yourself from it. Get it out of your mind, get it out of your heart. Go to work. Do your job. Every second a new one. Every breath a new one. Just do them one at a time. . . .

Rayford parked his Celica in one of the slots against the chain-link fence that separated City Hall's lot from the one used by the businesses in the South Main Commerce Building. He collected his gear bag and briefcase, locked his car, and checked his watch once more as he headed for the door into the station. It was 2:58. At 2:59 he was hustling into the duty room just as Chief Nowicki was coming out of his office, clipboard in hand, to begin the watch briefing. Rayford nodded and exchanged greetings with Patrolman Robert

"Booboo" Canoza and Patrolman James Reseta, the two other patrolmen who'd be in the mobile units this three-to-eleven watch.

Nowicki waited for Rayford to set his gear bag and briefcase on the floor and then said, "Afternoon, gentlemen. Not much happening today, but we're still lookin' for the mope that tried to take off Leone's Pizza yesterday. Detective Carlucci thinks it's the same one that's been takin' off pizza joints in the townships. State guys gave us this Identikit mug shot from the three previous."

Nowicki handed out copies of the mug shot and said, "Details of physical description, as you can see, are pretty crappy, the kids were too scared to take more than a glance at anything but his face. But all these kids're sure about three things, and that's the gun and the black ski mask and that he's on foot. No vehicle. So you see anybody on foot near any pizza joint, convenience store, gas station, et cetera, with a black watch cap or black knit cap or anything you think could turn into a ski mask, tell him get on the ground and call for backup, okay?"

Nowicki paused there and studied Patrolman Canoza. "Booboo, you don't have your vest on, do ya?"

"It chafes me."

"Aw don't even start with that chafes-me shit, I don't wanna hear it, okay? You don't have that vest on by the time I'm through talkin', don't even reach for the keys, you hear me?"

"It chafes me, I'm tellin' you."

"Cornstarch, baby powder, then the Commander shirt, then the vest, that's the drill—fuck's the matter with you?"

"It scares me to wear that thing, just reminds me how many crazies there are out there."

"Oh man, now there's perfect logic for ya, Boo, I mean it, there're crazies out there, so what you do in all your smartness? Huh? You keep your vest in your gear bag. And why? 'Cause it chafes you. Don't chafe nobody else, just you. I'm tellin' you, Boo, you don't put it on, you're sittin' down for ten days, no pay, I swear. I love you like a brother, you know that, but I'm not jokin' around with you anymore about this. Put it on. Now. Or go home. Up to you."

Canoza blew out a sigh from deep in his enormous torso. It sounded like somebody had cut the valve on a truck tire. Rayford glanced over at him, all six feet five and two hundred and seventy or eighty pounds depending on what he had for breakfast, and shook his head, but not so Canoza could see. Rayford knew better than to let Canoza see that. During Rayford's first month on the job, he'd backed up Canoza at a call to a bar which the owner feared was being taken over by bikers as their favorite hangout. He'd seen Canoza yank two bikers off bar stools by their belts and carry them outside, one in each hand like they were gym bags, and slam them headfirst into the side of his mobile unit just because they laughed when he said the bar's owner said their presence was costing him business. So it was true they only weighed about one-fifty, one-sixty apiece. Still, one in each hand wasn't something Rayford would ever allow himself to forget.

"C'mon, Boo," Nowicki said, folding his hands over the clipboard and rocking on his heels and toes, "get it outta your bag and get it on. I can't understand you. You paid two eighty-three thirty-four for that thing. The feds paid a third, the city paid a third—why wouldn't you wear it just to get your money's worth out of it, huh? I don't get that. Cheap as you are?"

"I'm not cheap. I'm frugal. Frugal is not cheap."

"Frugal is not cheap, huh? What's 'at mean—oh I know what that means. You took it outta your clothing allowance, huh? So it didn't cost you anything. How frugal is that? Is that what you did? Say you didn't, I wanna hear you say you didn't do that, c'mon."

"So what if I did?"

"So it didn't cost you a penny then, you chinchee motherfucker—put it on! You take it off ten minutes after you're out there, I don't care, but you get shot there's gonna be two witnesses said you were wearin' it when I handed you the keys to an MU. Nobody leaves till he puts it on, you hear me? James? William?"

Rayford and Reseta both nodded and mumbled their assent. Neither one wanted Canoza to think they were piling on.

"My ass is gonna be covered here," Nowicki said. "And you better be wearin' it when you come back in tonight, Boo, understand? And every day from now on, you hear me? Come in again without it on, you're sittin' down for ten days no pay, I'm not gonna go through this shit with you again, enough's enough, you got me?"

"I got you. Yes sir, Chief Nowicki, sir."

"Cut the bullshit, just get it on, c'mon, everybody's waitin' here. Boo, no shit, could your head be any harder? You get one of the best fuckin' vests money can buy, and whatta you say? It chafes me. Jesus Christ, Boo, I knew you wouldn't spend your own money, I knew if anybody in the department would take it outta their clothing allowance it would be you."

"Aw c'mon, lotta guys took it outta that, you kiddin'?" Canoza said, taking his duty belt and shirt off, draping them over the back of a chair, and getting his vest out of his gear bag and putting it on. "Two eighty-three's a lotta money, man. We ain't all makin' forty-five somethin' a year like some people, right, guys?"

Rayford and Reseta threw up their hands, shook their heads, and started backing away from Canoza as though choreographed.

"Uh-uh, ain't touchin' that one."

"Not a chance, Boo, not one chance in one and a half, man."

"Oh right, like I'm s'posed to call you pussies for backup."

"Well see there, there's your problem right there, Boo."

"What?"

"Where the fuck's your Commander shirt? No wonder you're chafin', Jesus. What? Oh don't tell me—you didn't buy any of them?"

"What Commander shirt?"

"We told you—oh listen to him, what Commander shirt? I told you, you gotta have 'em, they're what keeps you dry, no wonder you're chafin'. They let your sweat evaporate—c'mon, what the fuck, I got you guys a good deal on 'em, and look at you, that's just a regular cotton T-shirt, you fuckin' jaboney. Where's your Commander shirt—in a fuckin' drawer I bet, right? What am I gonna do with you?"

"You could sit on somebody else's back for a while, Chief, sir."

Nowicki threw up his hands. "Hey, Boo, what're you doin' here, huh? You lookin' for a vacation, is that what you're doin' here? 'Cause no pay ain't no vacation, my friend, and a suspension W-O-P ain't no day at the beach either. My friend."

Canoza shrugged into the vest, hooked up the Velcro, and held out his hands. "Look at this thing," he said, looking down at the vest and then at Nowicki. "It don't cover nothin' below my belly button, it don't cover my intestines or my genitals, it don't cover my neck, it don't cover my face or my head, you think the bad guys don't know that? You think they're nuts enough to shoot me, they're gonna aim for my heart? Or my lungs? That asshole that used to work for Nixon, how many times did he say on the radio, hey, everybody, aim for their heads? You think that ain't all over the Internet, huh? Every nutso out there knows we wear these things and they know how high they go and how low they go, and I just think it's . . . it's just givin' us all a false sense of security when we put these on, that's all I'm sayin'."

"Oh. So it's not about chafin' anymore, huh? So now it's a philosophical protest, is that what it is?"

"Maybe. Maybe that's what it is."

"Okay. Okay. Duly fuckin' noted. Now that you got it on, Boo, here's the keys to thirty-three. Reseta, you got thirty. Rayford, uh, thirty-one. And since Rayford had so much fun with the United Nations, I figured why change the lineup, so, uh, same sectors as yesterday. So go. Remember: nothin' without backup."

Reseta and Rayford left first, shaking their heads at each other over what they'd just witnessed. Rayford was shaking his for another reason. The United Nations. Depending on his frame of mind, he also called it Belfast, though there were no Irish there, or Palestine, though there were no Jews or Arabs there either, or Rwanda, though there were no Tutsis or Hutus there either. It was in the Flats, down by the Conemaugh River, four houses at the end of one block, separated by what had once been an alley now overgrown with stunted and mangled maple and walnut trees, grass, shrubbery of a dozen different varieties, and in one backyard, a rusting truck camper. There were also six dogs, three in one house, two in another, one in another, and none in the fourth. And no garages. Lots of tree branches, lots of leaves, lots of dog droppings, and only so many places to park.

Yesterday, Rayford thought he was going to have to shoot somebody, a possibility that had never come up in his four years in the air force or in his first five years and eleven months in this department.

Yesterday had started with the session in the marriage counselor's office, and had ended with him dancing backwards and drawing his nine, shouting at Nick Scavelli, "Stop where you are! You move again, I'm goin' shoot you and your wife both!" Today had begun with that phone call to Charmane. Normally Rayford did not put much stock in omens or portents or signs or predictions. Normally he believed that every moment in this life was as different as every breath he took. You breathed from the time you were born and you were dead when you stopped breathing, but in between, once you had breathed a breath, you were never going to breathe that one again. So even though this was a different watch on a different day, and he was breathing different breaths, he didn't like the way today had begun because it was starting to look like how yesterday began. And he really did not like the way yesterday almost ended.

Even worse, it was a beautiful afternoon, perfect summer weather, not April weather at all, the humidity was down, the temperature was in the high 60s, no rain was predicted by the Weather Channel till the weekend, which meant the United Nations would be out and about again, barbecuing, tending their seedlings, washing their dogs or their cars, doing something outside because it was too nice to be inside.

What I need tonight, Rayford thought, is a good thunderstorm, one to rattle every got-damn window in the Flats, and I ain't goin' get it. Shit.

Rayford hustled across the narrow drive and opened the passenger door of Rocksburg Mobile Unit 31, a black-and-white Ford Crown Victoria, and set his gear bag on the floor and his briefcase on the seat. He wedged his flash and baton behind the briefcase, closed the door, and went around the other side, in time to see Reseta disappear downward on the other side of his MU. Then, just as quickly Reseta was back up. Rayford knew what he was doing: Reseta was going down on one knee, making the sign of the cross, saying a quick prayer, and popping back up as though he'd dropped his keys. Rayford knew better. He'd seen Reseta kneeling and crossing himself too many times now to think this time was any different.

What was different about it was that until right after last Christmas, Reseta had never done it at all before. Right after Christmas, Reseta had changed, that was all anybody knew. And until last week, that was all Rayford knew. Then Reseta told Rayford what had brought the change about. And now all Rayford seemed able to do was ask himself why he kept forgetting to tell Mrs. Romanitsky about him. If anybody needed her prayers it was Reseta. A whole damn bunch more than me, Rayford thought.

Just then Canoza came down the steps from the station, across the parking lot, humming loudly, bellowing would be more like it, in da-da-dit-dat fashion, "Stars and Stripes Forever," interrupting his humming to mock-whisper at Rayford, "Remember, you African-American asshole, nothin' without backup."

Rayford mock-whispered back, "I call for backup, you Italian-American asshole, you better have that vest on, that's all I know."

"And the monkey wrapped his tail around the flagpole, to see his asshole," Canoza sang back at Rayford as he tossed his gear into his MU and then squeezed himself in, interrupting his furious humming to howl, "What the hell's so hard about pushin' the seat back when you get out? Bastards never push the seat back."

Oh Jesus, Buddha, Allah, who's ever out there, please don't make me need backup tonight, please. Not that those two dudes ain't the best backup a nigger could have, but please just let me keep my black ass in this motherfuckin' vehicle all night. Except when I need to pee.

Rayford started the Crown Victoria, hooked up his seat belt and pulled out onto Main, heading south for four blocks before turning east on River Way and heading for the Flats.

And Momma, Rayford thought, if you see Junior, tell him I miss him so bad I could cry. Tell him just 'cause he never seen me cry don't mean I don't want to. Tell him everything be cool, all he gotta do is listen to you. And I miss you too, Momma. Wherever you are.

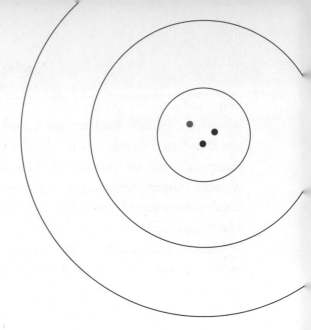

Patrolman James Reseta turned north on Main and eased into the curb lane and stayed there through three traffic lights until he got to the intersection of Park Street. On the west side of Main, across the street from Rocksburg Middle School, were St. Malachy's Roman Catholic Church and Elementary School. All of St. Malachy's buses, five full-size and six vans, were lined up on the west side of Main from the church and back into the school playground. Reseta turned right on Park, waving and nodding at the crossing guard working that corner. On the opposite corner, another guard was working the intersection of Park and Maple, which ran parallel to Main. Rocksburg Middle School students who walked home used the doors on Main while all those who rode the buses used the doors on Maple, where twelve buses were parked on the west side of that street and lined up around the block and into the middle school's parking lot.

Before Chief Nowicki convinced City Council to let crossing guards handle those two intersections, it had been the duty of a patrolman to handle both corners because one patrolman was all that was available at the beginning of the second watch. Whenever Reseta caught that detail, it made him nuts because there was no way one man could handle it. It was the kind of situation guaranteed to piss everybody off, the school bus drivers most of all. They had to live with the pigheaded wrongness of council's not understanding the fact that one cop was needed on each corner. Fact was, while some Catholic buses were turning left to go east on Park, some middle school buses were turning right to go west on Park at the same time normal traffic was going north and south on both Main and Maple. Two schools, two intersections, twenty-one buses, hundreds of kids, and normal traffic in good weather was mess enough; toss rain or snow into the pot and what you had was traffic stew.

So Reseta was more than happy just to cruise the one block of Park to make sure the ladies in the goofy white hats and orange vests with their whistles and portable stop signs were on the job. What made him smile was how serious they were about their job, so serious they wouldn't even return his waves. The most they would do was give him a slight toss of their heads or a raised brow. This made him smile because he knew they weren't armed; if they had been he wouldn't have been smiling. He believed in his heart that people who took their jobs that seriously shouldn't ever be armed with anything more than a citation book and a pen.

He turned north on Maple, barely moving when he made the bend, 10 mph at most, but had to stomp the brake to keep from hitting two kids who sprinted out from behind the first bus in line, one chasing the other. When they got to the other side of the street, the second kid caught the first by the neck of his shirt, pulled him to the ground, grabbed his book bag and threw it up onto the porch of a house. When the kid who'd been pulled down got up and tried to retrieve his bag, the first one stuck out his foot, tripped him, and sent him sprawling face-first into the concrete steps of the porch.

Reseta jammed on the foot brake, put it in park, jumped out and sprinted to the fallen boy's side, saying, "Don't move, son, stay right where you are. You!" he shouted at the tripper. "Get on your knees, put your hands behind your head, and don't move."

Reseta bent over the fallen boy's back and said, "Don't move, you hear me? Stay right where you are, okay?"

"Why?" the boy mumbled, lifting his head and blinking up at Reseta. He was bleeding badly from the nose and less badly from the right cheek. His nose looked broken, but Reseta couldn't be sure because it might've looked that way before the dive into the steps.

"Don't move I said. Put your head down," Reseta said, turning on the radio attached to his left epaulet. He called the station, ID'd himself, and said, "Ten-forty-seven Maple Avenue by the middle school. Young male, Caucasian, facial injuries, possible fractures, extensive bleeding, result of an assault."

He got a 10-4 back while the tripper started to get up while whining, "Hey, I didn't assault him, he tripped."

"Shut up," Reseta said. "I'll get to you in a minute—I told you don't move, who told you to stand up? Did I tell you stand up? Get back on your knees or I'm gonna put a stick across one of 'em." That's when he remembered that he'd left his baton and flash on the passenger seat. That's how fast crap like this happens, he thought, and that's how fast you forget even the basics. He reached around in back on his duty belt faking a move he hoped would make this kid think he had a collapsible baton back there. He didn't. But the kid didn't know that and the move worked. The kid knelt back down, but continued to whine that he hadn't done anything, the other kid was clumsy, couldn't walk and chew gum at the same time, was always tripping over himself, fell down every day, twice before lunch.

"Didn't I tell you shut up?"

"Yeah."

"Then who's makin' that noise? Not me. Not him either, he's not sayin' a word, so it must be you, and I just told you shut up. What, the connection between your ears and your brain, you unplug it or somethin'?"

"Huh?"

"Don't talk, just nod your head if you understand me. Don't say another word unless I ask you somethin', you hear me?"

Tripper nodded, but Reseta could see he was bursting to whine and weasel his way out of what he'd done, so Reseta said, "I saw you chase this boy across the street, saw you grab him by his collar, pull him down, take his bag, throw it up on that porch, and I saw you trip him when he tried to get it, so if I were you, I'd shut my mouth and keep it shut."

Reseta turned his attention to the boy crumpled half on the sidewalk, half on the steps. "How we doin' here? Can you breathe alright? You feelin' any pins and needles anyplace, your arms or your legs, huh?"

"Uh-uh."

"Okay. That's good. Now let me see you move your fingers. Don't move anything else, don't try to roll over, just move your fingers, that's all I wanna see."

The boy wiggled the fingers of his right hand. His left hand was under him and he told Reseta that.

"Okay. That's good. Now if you can move your left hand without movin' your neck, take it out slow and move your fingers on that one, okay?"

Reseta switched on his radio again and said, "Where's my 10-47, huh? C'mon, guys, my bleeder's still down here, I'm not lettin' him move till somebody else decides he doesn't need a body board. Still bleedin' from the nose and cheek. Awright, 10-22 that, I hear the siren . . . and there he is, I see him now."

The Mutual Aid ambulance, siren winding down, eased around the corner from Park and stopped in front of Reseta's MU.

To the boy, he said, "Don't move, you hear? You wait till they ask you questions, but you don't try to move until they say so, you understand? I wanna be sure you didn't hurt your neck here, the way you went into these steps, okay? Just talk, don't move your head up and down like that—what're you doin', what's wrong with you? You tryin' to make me crazy? Don't move I said."

Three EMTs spilled out of the ambulance. Reseta briefed them and then got out of their way. He went to the tripper's side and lifted him to his feet by his right arm and led him to the MU, where he told him to put his hands on the roof and spread his feet.

"Oh what, you think I'm holdin'?"

Reseta had started to pat him down but stopped and thought, *you think I'm holdin'?* What, am I in some kinda bad movie here?

"I told you shut up how many times now? You special ed maybe? Slow learner? Last time: shut up!"

Reseta continued his pat-down until he was satisfied the boy wasn't holding any kind of weapon. He opened the back passenger door and told him to get in, sit down, and put his hands on the back of the front seat and to keep them there.

Reseta leaned in and spoke very softly. "I'm gonna ask you some questions now, but before you answer 'em—"

"When you gonna read me my rights?"

I *am* in some kinda bad movie, Reseta thought. I'm standing here in the middle of a beautiful sunny afternoon with a kid probably doesn't even have hair on his balls, the kind of hairless prick likes to beat on people smaller than himself 'cause that's how he makes himself feel big.

Reseta flashed back to the days when he was this tripper's age, when he was the kid who got his books thrown all over the street, the one who got tripped, shoved from behind on the steps, the one whose homework got taken off him and who, after the smart-asses copied it, had to watch while they laughed and tore his up and threw it down a storm drain. It was smart-ass pricks like this tripper who made him want to be a cop when he grew up, made him dream about having his own mobile unit just like this one here, so he could put pricks like this one here in the backseat, take them for a ride to someplace where nobody was, maybe cuff them to a fence, maybe go to work on their hands and shins with his baton, ask them how they liked feeling helpless, friendless, small.

Reseta put his craziest face on, his wildest eyes, and glared at the tripper until he blinked and swallowed. "Whattaya think? You ready to answer my questions now?"

"Yes." Tripper's voice was suddenly quivery.

"What's your name?"

"Joseph."

"Joseph what?"

"Maguire."

"How old are you?"

"Thirteen."

"Maguire, huh? Irish, right, huh?"

"So what?"

Reseta had to step back, take a breath, count to ten. Because all he had to do was hear the word *Irish,* and a wagon full of bad memories suddenly appeared behind him, full of Guinnan brothers taunting and tormenting him. Little dago boy, scrawny little wop, macaroni arms, spaghetti legs, guinea head, garlic head—those were just the names he could bring himself to tell his mother when she asked him why his shirt pockets were ripped or why he had to have another new tablet or why his nose was bloody or his elbow raw or his knees scraped and his pants torn. He couldn't tell his mother what they said about her husband, that he didn't have a dick and balls, he had a pepperoni and a couple heads of garlic and that she didn't have tits, nah, what she had was fuckin' eggplants, all saggy and purple, that's what they used to say, laughing with their heads back, all three brothers, like they were the funniest people God put on this earth. But when he was in Nam, when the VC and the NVA Regulars were trying to kill him and he couldn't figure out any other reason why he should be trying to kill them, he found his thoughts turning more and more to the Guinnan brothers and the more he thought of them the less doubt he had about why he should be shooting at people whose country he was in, people who had done nothing to him.

And when he came home from Vietnam? Only Teddy Guinnan—the youngest one, the one who'd been in his class at St. Malachy's Elementary and later at Rocksburg High—was still living at home with his parents. So Reseta bought an eggplant and let it get so squishy rotten he had to surround it with plastic wrap to hold it together. And when Teddy Guinnan came staggering up the street that night, drunk as usual, Reseta stepped out from beside his mother's house, unwrapped the front of the foul purplish mess, tapped Teddy on the shoulder, kicked him in the nuts when he turned around, and then shoved that rotten eggplant in his face, as hard as he could up his nose and in his mouth, and then watched him squirm on the sidewalk clawing at his face and gasping for breath and groaning. And then Reseta leaned down and said, "There's a little bit of my mother's milk for you, you piece a Irish shit. . . ."

Joseph Maguire had summoned up some reserve of defiance and was trying his best to lock on to Reseta's gaze, but he started to tremble in spite of his best effort to brass it out, suddenly trembling violently as though he were wet and cold even though it was sunny and in the high 60s.

"Where you live, Joseph? Wanna give me the address?"

"No," the boy said, his whole head shaking, but especially his lower jaw and lip.

"Okay, I'm sure somebody in the school has it."

"One twenty-three Elm Street," he blurted out. "In Maplewood."

"Ohhhh, Maplewood. That's where a lotta doctors live, huh, right? Your father a doctor, Joseph?"

"Yeah. And my mother's a lawyer."

"Oh. Impressive. She Irish too?"

"Yeah. So what? Why you keep askin' me that?"

"Doctor father, lawyer mother, wow. And both Irish. A winning combination. I have no doubt you'll be in the U.S. Senate before you're forty. Put your hands behind you."

"What for?"

"What for? I'm gonna put my handcuffs on you, Joseph. 'Cause I'm arresting you. And then I'm gonna take you down the station and book your little Irish behind. Then I'm gonna take you down the juvey center and file a petition against you for assault and aggravated assault. In case your mommy hasn't explained this to you, that second one's a felony. And whenever I make an arrest I have to follow department procedure to restrain the arrestee, which means I have to put cuffs on you, so I can take you to the station in safety. And after I book you, then of course you'll be allowed to call your lawyer, or in this case, your mommy."

The boy put his hands behind him but suddenly stiffened his legs, shoving his back against the seat. Reseta quickly grabbed the boy's lower lip, twisted, and pulled. The boy instantly came away from the seat, his eyes filling with tears.

"Last warnin', kid. Don't do anything like that again, you hear me? 'Cause if you think that hurt, that was nothin'. If you understand me, just nod your head, don't say nothin', okay?"

The boy struggled to stop his tears. He nodded, his lower lip quivering.

Reseta put the cuffs on, then shut the back door, went to the front seat and got a nylon leg restraint out of his gear bag. Then he went back, opened the rear door and said, "Alright, Joseph, do exactly what I say. Put your feet and knees together and swing your legs out."

"What's that for?"

"Gonna say it once more. Pay attention. Put your feet and knees together and swing your legs out."

"You gonna hit me with that? You can't hit me, you ain't allowed."

"Oh believe me, Joseph, nothin' I would love more than to give you the beatin' you deserve, but what I'm tryin' to do is restrain your legs with this strap so, number one, you don't hurt yourself or, number two, you don't damage any part of this vehicle on the way to the station. Now we gonna do this easy or hard—which?"

"Why you have to do that?"

"Because, my little son of a lawyer, City Council got tired of havin' their vehicles in the shop because fellas like you get to thinkin' how much fun it is to kick the seats and the windows and the door handles, and things get broken and have to be repaired, which takes the vehicle out of service. So the Safety Committee of City Council issued a policy directive that says anytime a person's in custody in police vehicles, officers shall, in addition to restraining their subject's hands, also restrain their legs with the appropriate device, which the city bought for this purpose, and that's what this strap is here. You satisfied with that explanation, or would you like to read the policy directive yourself?"

What Reseta wouldn't allow himself to say was that if he had to get in his briefcase to get that policy directive, when they got back to the station he was also going to get his baton and whack his current arrestee across the shins so hard he wouldn't need to use a telephone to call his lawyer, she'd be able to hear him even if she worked in Pittsburgh.

"You know you ain't allowed to hit me. My mother says you ain't."

Little prick's a mind reader, Reseta thought. More likely, he's taken this ride before.

Joseph Maguire continued to try to glare defiantly up at Reseta, but it wasn't easy with tears on his cheeks and mucus bubbling at his nose. After a moment he tried to rub his nose on his shoulder, then put his knees together and swung his legs out. Reseta stood to the boy's right, pushed against the boy's right knee with his left hand and used his right hand to loop the nylon strap over the boy's Nikes and work it up his legs to above his knees, where he cinched the loop tight and told the boy to swing his legs back in. Reseta then positioned the other end of the strap so the door could close on it, thus pinning the boy's thighs to the seat. As far as Reseta was concerned, these leg restraints were worth a hundred times the eleven bucks apiece they cost the city.

"We better be goin' to the station, you better not be takin' me anyplace else," the boy said when Reseta returned to the car after checking with the EMTs and getting the victim's name, age, address, home phone number, and his mother's name.

"Must be true what they say about the luck of the Irish, Joseph.

No thanks to you, that boy's able to move all his extremities and he's not havin' any trouble breathin'."

"Where you takin' me? It better be the station."

Reseta got behind the wheel and started driving, easing slowly around the ambulance and making two left turns to head south on Main toward City Hall.

"You know, Joseph, the more you talk the more you sound like you been in the backseat before, am I right?"

"Juvenile records are private."

Juvenile records are private? Reseta looked in the mirror at the jailhouse lawyer, all of maybe a hundred twenty pounds. "You're right, Joseph, juvey records are private. So are juvey proceedings. But who'd you think all those other people were the last time, huh?"

"What last time?"

"Hey, stonehead, all those adults who were in the room the last time you went through the system, who did you think they were?"

No answer.

"Suddenly can't talk now, huh? You don't remember those grownies standin' around in Family Court? Or maybe you had your hearing in front of a master, huh? If there was no judge in a robe, there had to be an acting judge. You don't remember somebody called a master?"

No answer.

"Don't talk, that's alright, I'll talk. There had to be an assistant DA, a deputy sheriff probably, at least one cop testifyin' about why he arrested you, a stenographer takin' down every word everybody says—what, you think when it was your turn they all went deaf, dumb, and blind? You think when you walk in there this time none of them's gonna be allowed to read what happened the last time? Or they won't remember you? Mommy must not've explained that part, huh?"

The boy said nothing and pretended to look out the window.

"Still no answer? What am I gonna read, huh? Other assaults? Aggravated assaults? I get to read that stuff too, you know. And look at you. Those Nikes you got on I bet cost more than all the clothes that kid was wearin'. Bet your parents make more in one week than that kid's parents make in a year. What's his name? You even know his name?"

"Who cares?" the boy said with a sneer. "Misco-somethin'. He's stupid, he smells, he falls down all the time, he's a poster boy for abortion."

Reseta pulled into the lot beside City Hall, shut the MU off, and hustled around to open the passenger back door. He reached down, grabbed the strap that had been held by the door and jerked up on it hard, sending Joseph Maguire sprawling onto his left shoulder.

"Ow! Hey! That hurts!"

"Excuse me, my foot slipped. There's some oil here or somethin'. Did that hurt? I'm awfully sorry, won't happen again, I promise. Swing your legs out, so I can get this strap off, I know it's uncomfortable. Then we can go inside, take care of the paperwork. Won't take long."

After Reseta removed the nylon strap, the boy started to stand, and Reseta said, "Watch your head. Here, let me help you out," and he reached behind the boy, grabbed the links between the cuffs and jerked upward hard, while faking another slip on the imaginary oil.

"Ow! You're doin' that on purpose, you . . . you . . ."

"On purpose? Me? Oh no, I swear," Reseta said. "It's this oil here, I slipped."

"There's no oil there, you're makin' that up, I know what you guys do—"

"*You guys?* Oh no, it's a dangerous condition here, I'm gonna have to report it to my superiors. Somebody could get hurt. Accidents happen, you know? Like when we get inside I could slip again. My shoes, you know, they could just, with this oil on 'em, they could shoot straight out on me, and we could both fall. Me on top, you on the bottom. I read about accidents like that all the time, don't you? Or maybe you think that only happens to other people, huh? Like Timothy Miscovitz, you know? Stupid people? People that smell? Clumsy people, people that trip and fall a lot, you know? Poster boys for abortion? But I'll try to be real careful from now on, I promise. I'll wipe my shoes real good on the mat by the door there. C'mon, Joseph, let's take care of this paperwork, then you can call your mommy—I mean your lawyer."

"I'm gonna tell her everything you did and everything you said, all you fuckers're gonna be workin' for us—"

" 'Cause of what you're gonna tell her? Oh no, Joseph, see, we already work for you—you didn't know that? Yeah. We work for you, we work for your mommy, your daddy. We also work for Timmy Miscovitz's family. We're public servants—you didn't learn that in civics class? C'mon, watch your step, I don't want you goin' face-first into these steps out here."

"Ow! You're hurtin' my arms pullin' 'em up like that!"

"Ooh, did that hurt? And here I was just tryin' to make sure you didn't fall. I think I'm gonna have to discuss this with my training officer, Joseph, we might have to come up with another way to assist people like you up steps, you know?"

Inside the station, Reseta spotted Chief Nowicki going down the hall to his office. "Hey, Joseph, you're in luck, c'mon, I'm gonna introduce you to the chief. I want you to tell him how all of us are gonna be workin' for you and your family. I think that's somethin' he should know about, and I think he should hear that right from you, whattaya say?"

Reseta led the boy into the chief's office and said, "Chief, I know you're busy, but whatever you're doin', it's gonna have to wait, 'cause I have some really important news for you."

"Oh yeah? What's that?" Nowicki said. He'd been dialing the phone but dropped it back into its cradle and gave Joseph Maguire the once-over.

"First, I want to introduce Joseph Maguire here. Joseph, this is Chief Nowicki. He'd be happy to shake hands, Chief, except he can't right now 'cause he's wearin' my cuffs. And the reason he's wearin' them is because I arrested him for assault and aggravated assault against a fellow student in the Rocksburg Middle School, for which I have brought him to the station here to book him."

"I see," Nowicki said.

"But first, I wanted you to hear from his mouth how we're all gonna be workin' for the Maguire family—we bein' you and me and everybody else in the department, right, Joseph? You did mean everybody, right?"

The boy looked for a moment as though he was going to spit on Reseta. Apparently something made him think better of that.

Nowicki folded his arms and rocked back in his chair. "But, Patrolman, we already work for his family, all of us, so what's the lad tryin' to say—that we have to assume other duties? Just for his family? Obviously, I'm missin' somethin' here, there must be unusual circumstances—which you're gonna tell me about, right?"

"Yes sir. Seems young Joseph here believes I was somewhat too strenuous in my arrest and detention and restraint of his person. Did I mention his mother's a lawyer?"

"No, Patrolman, you were remiss in that. Interesting. Your mommy's a lawyer, huh, Joseph?"

"And his daddy's a doctor."

"Oh really? Say, that is impressive. But I have to tell ya, Joseph, not that I know all the lawyers in town here, or all the doctors either—but, uh, I don't believe I've had occasion to do any legal or medical business with your parents, but maybe, just to be on the safe side, maybe the patrolman and I should, I don't know, say tomorrow maybe? Whattaya think, Patrolman, tomorrow, we go to the young lad's house—where would that be, Joseph?"

"Lives in Maplewood. One twenty-three Elm."

"Ohhhh, Maplewood. Very nifty part of town, very classy. I'm familiar with that street, very spiffy houses there. Well, Joseph, I'm sure your father and mother have at least two cars, probably more, and they probably need to be washed, maybe need the tires rotated, the oil changed—whattaya say, Patrolman? Tomorrow we go out

SAVING ROOM FOR DESSERT • 47

there, we wash the cars, cut the grass maybe, trim the hedges, clean the gutters—'bout that time of year, right, spring cleanup? You up for that?"

"Yes sir, I am. Be only too happy, I mean since we already work for the family."

"Absolutely." Nowicki leaned back in his chair and gave the boy a large smile. "But first, I think you probably need to book the lad, and then maybe you should take him down the juvey center, file the proper petition—what was that you said he did again? Violate the statutes prohibiting assaults against other persons, is that what you said?"

"Yes sir."

"Well then by all means we need to follow the rules of criminal procedure exactly. I mean the last thing we want, we wouldn't want his mommy to think we'd been lax in our duties—in our normal duties as their employees, certainly not in a matter as serious as the arrest and detention of her charming son. And now if you'll excuse me, Joseph, I have some calls to make. But while I'm at it, I'll be happy to call your mommy the lawyer, or your daddy the doctor, just give me their numbers. I'm required to do that, you know, but, hey, it'd be my pleasure, I'd be happy to do it."

The boy dropped his chin toward his chest and said under his breath, "Kiss my ass." It was loud enough so that both Nowicki and Reseta heard him.

"Ah, the lad's got a great future," Nowicki said.

"I told him he'd be in the U.S. Senate before he was forty."

"Absolutely. Couldn't agree more. But maybe you should interrupt his career long enough to book him, huh?"

"Be my pleasure, sir. Come along, Joseph, we need to get your fingerprints, take a couple pictures, make sure you're properly logged in to our humble facility here. If you want, you could think of it as just a sort of an orderly room for the servants on your, uh, on your parents' plantation."

Reseta led the boy into the duty room, parked him in a chair next to a desk, unlocked one of the cuffs and locked it to the arm of the chair, then put his pistol in a gun safe in the desk, and sat down and logged on to the computer on that desk. He filled out the booking sheet on the computer screen, then printed several copies, folded one and stuck it in Joseph's shirt pocket, and put the others in a new manila folder in the bottom desk drawer.

"I love computers, don't you, Joseph? Make everything so much easier, so much quicker. Jeez, just six years ago, this would've taken, I don't know, probably a half hour. I could never get the typewriter to line up right with the forms, you know? And the copyin' machine was broken more than it worked, but no more, uh-uh, now it's hit a coupla keys, and bingo, there's your bookin' sheet."

"Okay, Joseph, stand up," Reseta said, hauling the boy up by his arm but stopping suddenly when the boy cried out. "Oooh, did that hurt? Man, I don't know what's the matter with me, I forgot you were still cuffed to the chair there, how could I not remember that, huh?"

"You didn't forget, you bastard, you did that on purpose, you wait till my mother gets here, you just wait."

"Well, while I'm waitin', c'mon, let's take some pictures, and then we'll take your prints, and then we'll check R and I—or maybe I should check that first, maybe we already got real recent pictures of you. Sit down, take a load off," Reseta said, pushing the boy down hard in the chair.

"Oh did that hurt? Woo, I'm sorry. See, I slipped again. I knew that oil was gonna be a problem. Apparently I didn't get it all off. And you know what else? I forgot to report it to my chief. Oh, he's not gonna be happy with me about that. But you just sit tight here, Joseph, I'll be right back."

Reseta started to walk toward that part of the duty room where the paper files were kept, but stopped and called to the civilian dispatcher working the radio, former sergeant Vic Stramsky.

"Hey, Vic, wanna do me a favor?"

"What's that, James?"

"If this young lad here tries to steal that chair or those handcuffs that are attached to it, you be sure and call nine-one-one for me, okay?"

"Absolutely."

Joseph Maguire squinted at Reseta and then rolled his eyes and groaned.

"Little police humor there, Joseph. See, couple years ago that wasn't even funny, that was serious, 'cause we weren't hooked up to the nine-one-one system. We just got hooked up into it, like what, Vic, I don't know, three years ago, right?"

"Right."

"The lad's not laughin', Vic. I guess you have to be us. Did I mention, Vic, the lad's mommy is a lawyer? And she'll be comin' in soon, you'll get to meet her, I'm lookin' forward to meetin' her myself, 'cause he thinks when she gets here, we're all gonna be workin' for her and him and his daddy, the doctor."

"You mean we ain't all workin' for 'em already?"

"Apparently not. Or if we are, we're doin' a crummy job."

Reseta found nothing on Joseph Maguire in the paper records. He came back to the computer and made a show of slapping his forehead. "What am I thinking, Joseph, you know? Do you know what I'm thinking, huh? Sometimes, I swear, if my butt wasn't attached to the bottom of my back it'd fall off and I'd lose it. You couldn't've been busted before you were ten, were you, Joseph? I don't believe that. And since we've only been usin' e-records since '96, I gotta believe I'll find you right in here."

Reseta typed in the boy's name and hit Enter and waited. Nothing. "Entry not found."

"Something's not right here, Joseph. I would've bet a month's pay you'd been through the system before. You wouldn't be givin' me a phony name, would ya? You that crafty?"

Reseta typed an e-mail to the Pennsylvania State Police Registry, asking for ID confirmation, photos, and fingerprints of Joseph Francis Maguire, but received no response.

"Hey, Vic, you know anything about the state computers? I'm tryin' to confirm an ID here, I get nothin'. Last time I got nothin' like this, they were down for a whole weekend."

"I didn't hear nothin'. Call Troop A, that's all I know."

Reseta picked up a phone, called Troop A, and got the news that the state police computers were indeed down for routine maintenance and would be down for another twelve hours at least.

Reseta hung up and glared at the boy. "I'm gonna ask you again. What's your name?"

"Told ya."

"Tell me again."

"Joseph Maguire."

"What's your middle name?"

"Francis."

"What grade are you in?"

"I forget."

"Who's your homeroom teacher?"

"I forget."

"What's your father's first name?"

"I forget."

"Now you know the state computer's down, you lost your memory, didn't ya?"

"Never had a memory."

"Alright, wise guy, let's get your pictures, get your prints, get you outta my life—at least till tomorrow."

Reseta unlocked the cuff attached to the chair, stood the boy up, backed him against a bare, white wall and made him stand there until he got the booking information on the photo board, then used a Polaroid to take front and profile mug shots. After the photos developed, he put them in the same folder he'd put the booking sheet. Then, always keeping the boy in his view, he went looking in several desks until he found a print pad and forms, filled out a form, and took the boy's prints, putting that form in the same file folder in the same drawer as he'd put all the previous. He dropped the print pad on top of the folder, shoved the drawer shut with his foot, and took the boy to the john and watched him wash the ink off his hands.

Then he cuffed the boy's free wrist to the other one and took him back into the duty room, where he retrieved his pistol from the gun safe, holstered it, and hustled the boy toward the door.

"I'm takin' this one down the juvey center, Vic. Maybe somebody there knows him."

"Hey I wouldn't dawdle, Rayford's havin' more fun with the U.N."

"Already? Jesus. Those people made him crazy yesterday. Good God . . . c'mon, whatever-your-name-is, let's find out if anybody knows you."

Whatever-his-name-was was suddenly acting as though he didn't have a care in the world.

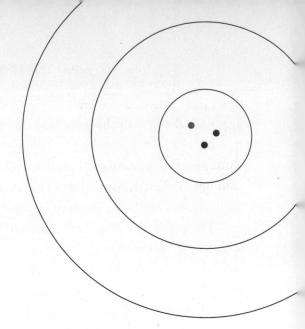

Uₙₜᵢₗ ₕₑ'D poured and drunk his first coffee from his own vacuum bottle, Rayford didn't even drive within two blocks of the United Nations, staying off the entire lengths of Bryan Avenue and Jefferson and Franklin streets. Then he waited another half hour before driving past the Scavellis' house on Franklin.

In the meantime, he'd been listening to B.B. King's latest CD on his portable Sony and checking out the radio traffic, such as it was, between Reseta and Canoza and civilian dispatcher Vic Stramsky. Reseta had caught a kid fight at the Rocksburg Middle School, and Canoza was trying to pop the lock on some lady's Toyota in the Giant Eagle lot. Canoza'd need some good luck. Toyota locks were tough. Rayford had stood next to a locksmith for twenty-two minutes once while he tried to pop the lock on his '87 Toyota. Watched him use about a dozen different Slim Jims before one worked.

But otherwise, it's beautiful so far, Rayford thought. Let's let it stay this way, people. Let us aaaaall remember a slightly different version of the immortal words of the prophet Rodney King: let us aaaaaall continue to get along. Lock your keys in your cars, tha's awright. Beat on your little school buddies, that's awright too. Bend some fenders, the babies of bodymen need shoes too. But let us do no real harm, people, Polish, Eye-talian, Russian, Ukrainian, whatever your flavor, let us looooooove one another, every-got-damn-body say a-men and hal-ay-fuckin'-lu-ya, awwwwright. . . .

Now why'd Nowicki put me down here again? Didn't I have enough grief yesterday? He knows I did, the man knows I had enough grief with these people to last me two careers. Had enough last night to last me the next ten years.

These people. She-it. Niccola Scavelli and his seriously ugly wife, Mary Rose. Occupants of 101 Franklin Street on the corner of Bryan, yessir, if ever there were two people fit the description of "occupants" these two were it. These two people were not the work of amateurs, no thank you ma'am; these two were seriously fucked up by some heavyweight pros. Been to this house twice a year—at least twice—every year since I've been in this department. And when they hand me that piece of paper says I have been promoted to sergeant, and that other one says I have been promoted to detective, I am still goin' be comin' to this address till these crazy mother-fuckers kill each other or go into a nursin' home, whichever comes first, a-men. Motherfucker oughta be in Mamont right now, many times as I carried his sorry ass up to Mental Health? Catch the dago by the toe, eenie meenie minie mo, hold him a month and let him go, eenie meenie minie mo. She-it. Three times now. Motherfucker is stone craaaaa-zy. But not at his hearings, oh no. At his hearings he's cool as Johnnie Cochran. But yesterday? The man stone topped out. With all that fries shit? . . .

"Sir, did you smear dog crap all over Mr. Hlebec's doorknobs?"

"Do you want fries with that?"

"Excuse me?"

"I said do you want fries with that?"

"Sir, try to answer my question—"

"I'll answer your question when you answer my question—do you want fries with that or not?"

"No, sir, I do not want fries with that. Or with anything else either."

"Alright, now we're goin' places. Hey, Mary Rose? Hold the fries!"

Mary Rose, hold the fries, Jesus Christ. And last month it was let me take this blow-dryer and go sit in my truck and point it at Mr. Matthew Hlebec and Mrs. Ann Hlebec when they come home from work, and shout how they're exceeding the walkin' speed limit when they get out their cars and walk up on their porch. And write everything down, oh yeah, get it all recorded, absolutely, in my little notebook here, times, days, dates, speed of feet on the radar blow-dryer and how many times have they changed lanes without putting on their turn signals and how many times has she tailgated, walked too close to her husband for conditions . . . aye-yi-mother-fuck-ing-yi, where do these people come from? More important, where they goin' go? Lord, please say they ain't goin' be with me forever. Please say they ain't my special honky hell. I need to get Mrs. Romanitsky down here, have her pray for these motherfuckers, maybe she knows somebody do an exorcism or some shit, 'cause Lord, you got to know ain't nothin' else worked. Worked, workin', or goin' work. Lord, when it comes to these two, you got a ton to answer for.

Ohhhh man, look there, now why didn't I stay off this street, what's that motherfucker goin' do now? What's he carryin'? Oh shit. A shovel? Motherfucker got a shovel? Oh mannnnnn!

Rayford pushed the button for his PA. "Mr. Scavelli, put that down, sir! Don't go there, sir."

Oh man, here we go again, sure as God made dog shit, that motherfucker got a shovel full, ohhh got-damn. . . .

Rayford jammed the foot brake and rammed it into park, hustled out to get in front of Scavelli, who was walking sideways with the shovel angled out to his right and behind him, getting ready apparently to hurl its contents onto the front porch of the Hlebecs' house.

"Stop right there, sir! Don't do that!"

"According to the prophecy, to the ass from where it came out, it shall go back."

"Sir, put the shovel down, sir. I'm orderin' you to stop. Sir, if you throw that over my head, and some of that fall on me? I'm goin' be really upset, sir. I'm goin' be seriously disturbed. I washed this uniform and pressed it myself, I do not want even one molecule of that crap on it, you hear? Sir? Stop right there, and put that down!"

"According to the prophecy, the coloreds will not tell the Italians, the Italians will tell the coloreds, that's the way it was in the beginning, that's the way it shall always be."

Ohhhh God, here we go with the coloreds again.

"Sir, I have told you before and I'm goin' tell you again how we are all brothers and sisters, how we all came out the same tribe in Africa, some of us headed north, some of us headed south, some east, some west, but we are from the same mother and father—"

"According to the prophecy, the coloreds will wash out their mouth with soap when they tell lies—"

"Aw enough with this prophecy noise—gimme that shovel! Now, sir! I'm orderin' you, give me that shovel!"

Scavelli screwed up his face haughtily and tried to hand it over blade end first.

"Aw that's cute," Rayford said, recoiling from the stench. "Turn it around, sir. Please?"

Scavelli turned sideways, sidled up to Rayford, and handed it over without further fuss.

"There. Now that wasn't so hard, huh? Was that so hard?"

"According to the prophecy, the coloreds will carry dog shit for the Italians," Scavelli said, turning and shuffling back toward his house.

Rayford carried the shovel, a third full of fresh dog droppings, to the storm drain on the corner and hurled the contents into it. He took the shovel back to Scavelli's house, pushed it into the strip of grass between the curb and the sidewalk a couple of times to clean it as much as possible and then tried to hand it up to Scavelli, who was now on his porch. Scavelli closed his eyes, crossed his arms over his bony chest, and thrust his chin upward.

Rayford slid the shovel past Scavelli's feet and turned around in time to see Matt Hlebec attempting to park his maroon Chevy Beretta in the space between the MU and Scavelli's multicolored Ford pickup. There wasn't enough room so Rayford hurried to his MU waving to Hlebec and indicating to him that he was going to move. Just as he got in, he saw Scavelli coming down the porch steps with his blow-dryer pointed at Hlebec.

Oh shit, here we go with the blow-dryer again, Rayford thought, backing up and out into the street so Hlebec could park and then getting back out to be ready to intervene as soon as these two started in on one another.

Hlebec came out of his Chevy yelling and gesturing first at Rayford and then at Scavelli. "Well good, I don't have to call you guys, you're already here, now you can see what I'm talkin' about—"

Rayford couldn't help noticing that as soon as Hlebec spoke, his dog came alive inside his house, jumping up on a wing chair in the living room, shoving aside the curtains with his snout, and barking, then bounding away. In a moment he was back on the chair, his paws on one wing, barking again, and then bounding away again.

"Just go in your house, sir, please?" Rayford said, watching the dog pushing the curtains around with its snout.

"My radar gun is new and improved. Not only measures speed, now it measures noise. When he talks he's louder than a chain saw—"

"Oh shut the hell up!"

"I'm not the one with the big mouth, that's you. I'm not the one with the dog runs loose all over my yard, craps in my yard—in violation of the city ordinance."

"My dog's in the house all day, he never runs loose, how many times you think I have to tell him before it finally sinks in, huh? I walk my dog on a leash, my wife walks the dog on a leash, you been seein' us do that for ten years, you maniac—"

"Mr. Hlebec, sir, just go inside, please?"

"This is a public street, I'm comin' home from work, I'm allowed to walk into my house without bein' hassled by this asshole—"

"Sir? How many times have we been through this? Go inside, sir. Please!"

"Oh yeah, with the hunky, yeah, please this, sir that—what do the Italians get, huh? *I'm orderin' you*—that's what we get! The coloreds give us orders! But the hunky gets pleeeeeease, please please please, pretty please, oh yeah!"

"Mr. Scavelli, go inside, please, I don't want a repeat of yesterday, sir. Please? Go inside, sir."

"According to the prophecy, I'm on my property, I'm allowed to be right here, right where I am."

"Yes sir, according to *your* prophecy, that's true. But according to *my* prophecy, you're not allowed to stand out here and instigate a fight, verbal or otherwise, so go inside please."

"Coloreds don't have no prophecy. All you got is jungle music. All you people know how to do is scratch records, you don't even know how to play 'em." Scavelli tried to imitate a rapper scratching an LP record on a turntable while huffing and grunting and jiggling from side to side.

The man looked so ridiculous Rayford had to turn his face away to keep from laughing.

"I can't tell you how happy I am you're here to listen to this yourself."

"Heard it all before, Mr. Hlebec, you know that—"

"No no, uh-uh, what I mean is you're hearin' him right from the start, not from when you get here after my wife calls you—"

"Been respondin' to these addresses, sir, for six years now. I've taken Mr. Scavelli to Mental Health three times myself, and you've testified at all three of his hearings, Mr. Hlebec, let's not forget the facts, okay? So now whyn't you go inside, sir, please?"

" 'Cause my wife's comin' home, should've been here already, I don't know what's keepin' her, but I don't want him harassin' her. He starts in on her as soon as she gets outta the car—"

"If you went inside, sir, it would help considerably, okay?"

"Help you maybe. Not her."

Rayford took a deep breath and blew it out and watched the curtains being shoved aside once again, this time with only the tip of the dog's snout showing. The dog barked four times in a row, then apparently stopped and jumped down again when he couldn't toss the curtain aside.

How long were these people goin' stand here? How long am I goin' stand here? She comes home, shit's really goin' fly—and, aw motherfucker, here she comes now. How'm I goin' get these two assholes inside now?

Rayford stepped carefully, unobtrusively, between Hlebec and Scavelli, while remaining at least three steps away from Hlebec. Scavelli had moved to the bottom step of his porch.

Hlebec was a large man, six feet two, two-forty, maybe two-fifty, who'd been a defensive lineman in high school and college and who coached the defensive linemen at Rocksburg High while working as a supervisor in a food warehouse. He'd never been violent in any of these confrontations, but Rayford was absolutely convinced everybody has a cracking point, so he never failed to maintain his reaction distance from Hlebec, no matter what Hlebec's history.

"Sir? Mr. Hlebec? Please go inside before your wife gets here, okay?"

"Tell *him* go inside, don't tell me! He wants to know whose dog craps in his yard, all he has to do is go in the back and look that way, he knows whose dogs are runnin' loose. He knows it's not ours. But we're the ones suffer for it. Go ask the Hornyaks they ever had shit smeared on their doors. Ask the Buczyks. Five dogs they got between 'em. They're the ones don't keep their dogs tied, they're the ones just open the door and let 'em run, I walk my dog on a leash—"

"Sir, I know all this—"

"If you know it, why don't you arrest 'em? They're the ones violatin' the ordinance, not me. You wanna see it? I got a copy inside. All you gotta do is write 'em a ticket, hand it to 'em. Three-hundred-dollar fine. Plus costs! That's what it's supposed to cost 'em. But it never does 'cause you guys never write 'em up. They had to pay a coupla times, maybe they'd tie their dogs up, huh? You think? And maybe he'd stop hasslin' us. Ask him why he don't hassle them, go 'head, I wanna hear what he has to say—"

"Sir, we did that last night, remember? And where'd it get us?"

Mrs. Hlebec parked her Chevy Cavalier, got out shaking her head, and hurried toward her husband with her hands over her ears. "I don't wanna hear it, old man, don't you start with me, I'm telling you. If he starts with me with that blow-dryer again, I'm gonna scream!"

Rayford sniffed and licked his lips. "Please, Mr. Hlebec, take your wife inside, please—"

"Exceeding the walking speed limit by two miles an hour—"

"C'mon, Annie, don't pay him no attention, c'mon—"

"How much proof you need she's a reckless walker, huh? Can't you coloreds see the evidence? What, it's only evidence if Johnnie Cochran says so? If it don't acquit, you must convict."

"It's if it don't fit, you must acquit, asshole," Matt Hlebec said. "Can't you get anything right?"

"Tell me he didn't do the doorknobs again. Please tell me I don't have to do what I did last night, please tell me that."

"No no no, he didn't do that, huh? Rayford, he didn't do that, did he? Why you here, Rayford? Who called you?"

"Nobody called me," Rayford said. "I'm here because I saw him with a shovel headin' for your porch and I stopped him, okay?"

"A shovel? He had a shovel? What was he gonna do with a shovel?"

"Ma'am, please, you and your husband just go inside and let me do my job here, okay? I can't handle him if you two stay out here jawin' at him, okay?"

"What, we're not allowed to be on our own sidewalk? In front of our own house?"

"Yes you are, ma'am, but I can't get the man off a boil if you're standin' here agitatin' him."

"Oh *we're* agitating him now. Right? Us? I guess we're the ones smeared crap all over our own doorknobs, is that right?"

"No ma'am, what I said is, your presence out here is enough to agitate him and as long as you're out here I can't get him calmed down, so I'm askin' you once again, please go inside."

"Well excuse me but that is *not* what you said—"

"Well that's what I meant, ma'am, even if it didn't come out that way, that's what I meant, okay?"

"Well you ought to say what you mean, especially if you're gonna start accusing people."

"Ma'am, I am not accusin' you of anything—"

"Well it sure sounds like it—"

"According to the prophecy, the coloreds and the hunkies, even though they join up together they will be defeated—"

"Will you stop with that prophecy noise? And stop callin' names!"

"According to the prophecy, I calls 'em the way I sees 'em."

"Did he just say what I think he said? Did he call me a hunky?"

"Mr. Hlebec, for the last time, I'm askin' you, sir, please take your wife and go inside."

"He called us hunkies, didn't he? I know he did, you don't have to answer that—why you scrawny old prick, you were half a man I'd throw you down the goddamn storm drain—"

"I got no chance of calmin' him down—oh man don't make threats, please, this is bad enough already, don't be threatenin' the man, just go inside, will you please?"

"Nobody calls me a hunky, I don't care if you are seventy-five, you scrawny old prick, c'mon down here, c'mon, I'm sicka you— twenty years of your bullshit, c'mon! What're you waitin' on, huh?"

"Mr. Hlebec, last warning, go inside now!" Rayford stepped in front of Hlebec and put his hand on his pistol. He turned quickly and shouted at Scavelli, "Mr. Scavelli, get inside your house!" Then he danced off the sidewalk into the street so he could see them both. "Mrs. Hlebec, go inside, please, ma'am. And take your husband with you."

"I will not! You heard what he called us."

Up to that point, Rayford had been forceful but controlled. Authoritative, commanding, but not overly loud and certainly not emotional. But when this woman defied him—this woman he was trying to protect—something cold rippled up from his stomach and he sensed that everybody was slipping and staggering wildly toward a sharp edge here. And inside the house, the dog's barking became more intense.

"How 'bout what he called me? What he's been callin' me for six years? I ain't colored, ma'am! I'm black. He calls me colored, that don't bother you at all, does it? But it sure bothers me. So whatta you think I oughta do 'cause he calls me that? You think maybe I should spray him? Or maybe you think I oughta shoot him—is that what you think? Tell me what's that goin' accomplish, huh? That goin' solve everybody's problem here? C'mon, answer me! C'mon, Mrs. Hlebec, tell me, I wanna hear what you think about that."

"No," she said, suddenly very sheepish.

"No what, ma'am?"

"No I don't think you should shoot him."

"Good. Excellent! I'm glad you think that. But then I have to ask, what's wrong with you people? You and your husband, look at you, both educated people, both got jobs, two cars, your house is paid for, why you wanna throw all that away 'cause a fool call you out your name?"

"Now look who's callin' names? You lousy colored, I ain't no fool."

"Hear that? Did you both hear that? Now will you look around, please? And will you tell me where we are? We in Jerusalem? Huh? Maybe we're in Belfast. Maybe I'm the fool here, 'cause I keep thinkin' we're in Rocksburg, and y'all oughta know better. But that's what I thought last night. And that's what I'm wonderin' every time I come to this address—where am I? Who am I dealin' with here? Am I dealin' with two educated people or not? And why do these two educated people have to act like this fool? Huh? This man plays you, you don't know that?"

"We've put up with his bullshit for twenty years, he oughta be in Mamont—"

"The people in Mental Health do not agree with you, sir. Every time I commit him, the longest they have ever kept him is thirty days, now you know that as well as I do, but every time he starts up, you let him play you! Why do you react to him? Why you lettin' him play you right now? Why you still standin' here? Why won't you go inside and let me do the job your taxes pay me to do? Just let me do my job, that's all I'm askin' you! But I can't do it while you're standin' out here woofin' at him, challengin' him to come down off his porch! Go inside. Please!"

"Let's go, Matt, c'mon, honey. He's right, let's let him do his job, okay? C'mon, honey, we don't wanna do this again, Mother of God, I'm gonna have a stroke we have to do this again."

"Scrawny old dago prick."

"Big-belly hunky! Go on a diet!"

"Oh that's it, I'm gonna break your goddamn neck—"

Scavelli bent down and grabbed the shovel and held it out like a lance. "C'mon, I'm waitin'!"

Shit! Rayford dropped into a crouch and drew his nine. "Stop! One more step, Mr. Hlebec, you're under arrest!"

"Arrest?! You gonna arrest me? The hell for?"

"You move toward him, I'm goin' charge you with riot, failure to disperse, and disorderly conduct—you hear me?"

"Riot?!" Hlebec said, his eyes going wide and his mouth dropping open. But at least he'd stopped moving. "What the hell you talkin' about, riot?"

"You're makin' threats, sir. And there are three of you here, and

I've ordered you to disperse and you're makin' threats to commit an assault, that's riot! And you've refused my order to disperse. And you're disorderly, all three of you!"

"You didn't say nothin' about arrestin' *him!*" Hlebec pointed at Scavelli, jamming his finger into the air furiously. "Just me!"

"I can't say everything at once! If y'all don't shut up and go inside, you're all under arrest! You know what that means? Huh? Felonies, misdemeanors, second degree, third degree. That's years in the joint, y'all! You listenin'? That's thousands of dollars in fines, plus costs, plus lawyer fees, plus you get convicted you're goin' lose your jobs, you're goin' lose your house, who you think's goin' pay your taxes while you're locked up? Y'all that stupid? Y'all sure act like it! I promise you, you make me call for backup here, I will arrest y'all, I promise you, you will be callin' a bail bondsman tonight. Is that what you want? I can make it happen! Just don't go inside, keep makin' threats, see whether I make it happen."

"C'mon, Matt, c'mon, honey, he's not worth it, c'mon, please?"

"C'mon, honey," Scavelli mocked her.

Rayford pointed his nine at Scavelli and said, "Last warning, sir, put that shovel down and go inside. You got three seconds to obey my order or I'm goin' arrest you—last warnin'."

"Me? For what? What for you gonna arrest me?"

"Failure to disperse, disorderly conduct, harassment, ethnic intimidation—that enough? I got the Crimes Code in my briefcase, I'm sure I can find somethin' else that fits. Terroristic threats, reckless endangerment, I'll let the judge figure it out. Three seconds, sir . . . two . . . one."

Scavelli dropped the shovel and it bounced wildly off his porch step, coming to rest at Rayford's feet. Then Scavelli turned around and stomped up the steps and into his house, trying to pull the storm door shut behind him; the pneumatic cylinder resisted his effort and he stood there yanking on it and muttering under his breath. His wife could be heard telling him to let go and get out of the way, she'd shut the door. "Go watch TV, get outta here, I'll close it—let go!"

Thank you, Jesus, for keepin' Mary Rose inside, Rayford thought, and then turned toward the Hlebecs. "I got some disorderly conduct and failure to disperse for y'all, if that's what y'all want. Do ya?"

"Oh you're going to threaten us now?" Mrs. Hlebec said.

"Ma'am, when I say it, it's not a threat, it's an official warning, and I've given it to you and your husband for the last time tonight. Shoulda arrested y'all last night. Every one of you. You should all be payin' a bondsman right now. Maybe that's what it's goin' take to wise y'all up, I don't know. To grow y'all up. Worse than a buncha junior high school kids. I just wish there was some way I could get a PFA against y'all. Wish I could get some judge to write an order sayin' y'all had to stay a thousand feet away from me at all times. But I can't do that. But believe me when I tell ya, I go to sleep at night prayin' somebody could make that happen. Now get inside, both of you. And don't y'all make me come back here tonight or I swear y'alls goin' to jail."

Hlebec pointed at Rayford and started to say something, but Rayford swung his nine at him and said, "One more word, you're under arrest—just one!"

Mrs. Hlebec caught her husband's arm and tugged and pulled it down. She leaned close to him and began talking to him. It looked to Rayford like she was pleading, but pleading, rationalizing, signifying, he didn't care what she was saying or how as long as she got him inside and kept him there.

Rayford holstered his nine and closed the retention strap. Then he went back to the MU, got in, and slumped forward, exhaling hard, then pulled his shoulders up and back, inhaling, filling his belly and then his chest, doing a complete yoga breath. He did five more complete breaths, feeling his heart slowing with each one as he held his breath for a few seconds at the end of each inhale and each exhale. Then he put his seat belt on, released the foot brake, put it in drive, and eased south on Franklin, noticing for the first time all the people milling around on the opposite sidewalk. There were four or five clusters of people, two or three in each cluster.

He switched on the PA and said, "That's it, folks, that's all there is. Go on inside now and be safe. Have a good evening."

He didn't wait to see what they did. He went to the end of the block, turned west on Miles Avenue and kept going for a couple of blocks until he ran into parking lots for the Pittsburgh and Lake Erie RR repair yards against which all the avenues in the Flats abruptly ended on the west. On the east, the avenues ended near the bank of the Conemaugh River.

Rayford turned at the end of Miles Avenue and parked parallel with the fence outside the P&LE lots. He engaged the foot brake and put it in park and tried to remember when daylight saving time kicked in. Suddenly that was the most important thing in the world: knowing when he turned his clocks forward. Spring forward, fall back. Yessir, now that was some serious shit. When did that happen? Had to've been last week. No. It was the week before that. Why can't I remember that?

He switched on the radio and called the station.

When Stramsky responded, Rayford asked him to switch to Channel 3, the channel they used to defeat the eavesdroppers.

"What's up?" Stramsky said.

"When did daylight saving time kick in?"

"First Sunday in April, 2 A.M. Same time as always. Why?"

"First Sunday? Damn."

"I repeat, why?"

"Couldn't remember, that's all. Seemed important."

"As important as you drawin' your piece?"

"Now how you know that?"

"How many civilians you think saw you do that? More to the point, how many you think called in tellin' me they saw you did it?"

"Aw I just had to get the motherfuckers off the street, that's all. How many?"

"Four."

"Four? Is that all? I'm losin' my star power, man. Used to be, when I drew my nine, everybody on the block called. Thought there was goin' be a race riot."

"Two nights in a row, same address, you got those people all shook up."

"They oughta be shook up. They oughta get their pitchforks and torches and chase the Scavellis down the river and drown their asses."

"Hey hey, wash your mouth out with soap. If it wasn't for people like the Scavellis, people like us'd have to find real jobs. So if you did see anybody come outta their houses with pitchforks and torches, it'd be up to you to stop 'em."

"Easy for you to say, Victor, my man. You're just sittin' there doin' finger push-ups on a coupla buttons."

"Hey. I was respondin' to bullshit with the Scavellis before you got outta diapers. Before they lived down in the Flats, Franklin Avenue there, they used to live up on Norwood Hill. And they were just as big a pains in the ass up there as they are now, believe me. Worse. You know they had a fire?"

"A fire? Kinda fire?"

"A fire fire, what kind you think? Lost two kids."

Something cold hit Rayford in the middle of his stomach and spread upward over his chest and outward through his arms. He'd had the air conditioner on low, but now he had to turn it off, had to rub his hands together and blow on them.

"You jivin' me? They had two kids die in a fire?"

"No, I'm makin' this up. The old man got drunk, fell asleep smokin', woke up, the chair was on fire, got his wife out, by the time he came back in the livin' room, the curtains were on fire, the walls, it got into the wiring, inside the walls, it was an old wood house, they never got the kids out. Boy and a girl."

"Oh man," Rayford said, wincing, rolling his neck from side to side, rubbing his hands and blowing on them. "Both of 'em?"

"Both. Boy was six, the girl was four."

"Got his wife out, but he couldn't get his kids out?"

"I'm just tellin' ya the way I remember it. You wanna ask some-body about it, ask Balzic. He worked it. Him and that asshole fire marshal we used to have around here. But you want details, ask him. Those people, hey, there's no doubt they're fucked-up, but they've had some shit, believe me. People used to holler at 'em, you killed your kids, you killed your kids. How'd you like to hear that every time you stepped out your front door?"

"Oh man," Rayford said again, the cold in his stomach spread-ing to his back and legs. "Oh man."

"Yeah. Oh man is right. I don't know, but I've been told, ain't nothin' worse than buryin' your kid. Kids. Can't imagine it. Hey. That's life. That's death."

"Oh man."

"So you 10-7 or what?"

"Huh? Yeah, I'm goin' fill out the report. Then I'm goin' make a sandwich, have some coffee."

"What's your 10-20?"

"Washington Street, beside the P&LE parkin' lot, end of Miles Avenue."

"Don't forget to 10-8 me when you're done."

"Who you talkin' to, me or Canoza?"

"Alright, alright, base out."

"Thirty-one out."

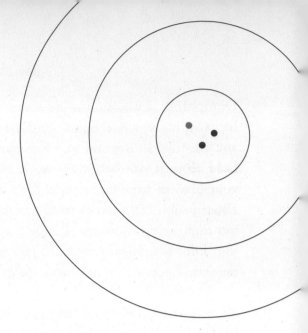

CANOZA WAS tasting his breakfast for the second time, the orange, the banana, the rolled oats, the can of sardines with the jalapeños, the garlic toast, the mocha java. Fucking Toyotas. Fucking Jap cars. People who bought them deserved to lock their keys in them. Permanently. Only someplace else. Like Harrisburg. That would be a good place for this lady to be. An excellent place. And she doesn't stop yakkin' at me pretty fucking soon, she's gonna get a fifteen quad-E up her ass, see if she can fly there without callin' a ticket agent.

"Well I've read, I can't remember where right now, but I'm sure I read it somewhere, probably the paper, car thieves would rather steal anything else except Toyotas because the locks are so good."

"Yes, ma'am, I'm sure you did read that somewhere."

"Well you don't have to say it that way."

"What way was that, ma'am?"

"The way you said it. Just because you can't get it open, you don't have to get snippy with me."

"I wasn't bein' snippy with you, ma'am."

"All I said was I read somewhere that car thieves don't generally try to steal Toyotas, that's all, because the locks—"

"And I was agreein' with you, ma'am, I wasn't bein' snippy.

Don't know how you got that idea," Canoza said, thinking if you had any brains, geezer bitch, you'd be drivin' a Chevy or a Pontiac, and when you came out of your cage every day and you put your head up your ass where you usually kept it and locked your keys in your car you wouldn't have to call us 'cause you were too fuckin' cheap to join Triple-A so this would be their problem instead of mine. . . .

"I don't understand why it's taking you so long. You do this all the time, I'd think by now you'd be an expert at it."

Canoza had to take a moment after the pain started behind his right eye and snaked up behind his brow and into the right side of his head. He reminded himself about the first half of the oath he took, what was it, twenty-four years ago? Yes. Twenty-four years and six months. Exactly one week from today. And in six more months from that I won't have to try to make polite conversation with people who're too cheap to get another set of keys to carry around on their person for occasions such as this when they have an acute attack of Asian fucking brain fever where they can remember to lock the door of their fucking Jap car but they can't remember to remove the keys from the ignition before they lock the fucking door.

Easy, Robert, easy, easy, 'cause if you don't ease up you're gonna slip and say something wonderful, something that might become part of your legend. And you don't want that. Your legend, while impressive, is what's gonna get you voted into the Fuckups Hall of Fame. So be careful what you actually let outta your mouth. And remember: you were the one raised your right hand and swore an oath to serve, nobody held a gun to your head, nobody was holdin' anybody you loved for ransom. You did that all on your own, completely and totally voluntary, don't try to say you didn't just 'cause this lady oughta be strangled. Slowly. With razor wire.

"No, ma'am, I am not an expert at this, I mean we really don't go to classes on this, you know? I mean all I know about it I sorta picked up on my own. Just like these Slim Jims here."

"Just like what?"

"Slim Jims." Canoza nodded and looked down at what he was holding in both hands and jiggling around to try to catch the nub of the lever that would pop the lock. This was Slim Jim number six in his bag of fifteen, which he'd acquired over the years from various retired cops, bodymen, and car boosters.

"I thought that was some kind of dried-up sausage you men eat with your beer. Never could understand why they were called that. I see them in the checkout line at the Phar-Mor. My husband's brother used to eat them all the time. His breath was just awful. And you know what he died of? Stomach cancer. And his doctor told his wife it was probably caused by all the preservatives they put in those things. And the smoke too. You know, that smoke, that causes histamines. In the meat. Those are terrible for you. Grilling ought to be outlawed. Why do they call them that?"

Histamines? In the Slim Jims? So why didn't he just take a Benadryl after he ate 'em? Don't say it, Robert. Don't fucking say it, man. But histamines in the Slim Jims? What the fuck, Jesus Christ, save me, Father, for I must've fucking sinned big-time. Please shut this fucking woman up, I swear, you shut her up I'll fly to Rome, I'll walk from the airport to St. Peter's on my knees, without fucking kneepads I'll do it, I promise, just please shut her the fuck up.

"You didn't tell me why they named those things after a sausage. Aren't you going to tell me? I mean as long as I'm here, I might as well try to learn something. If that's possible."

"I didn't say they named these after a sausage. You said that."

"I did not."

"You said you thought Slim Jims was the name of a sausage—"

"I never said that. I said I *thought* that's what it was. I was asking you why you called that thing that. That thing you can't get my door open with. A whatever. Slim Jim."

"I don't know why they call 'em that, ma'am, okay? Been callin' 'em that as long as I been tryin' to learn how to use 'em, okay? They could call 'em elephant for all I care—"

"Oh now you are getting snippy. Obviously, you think I'm stupid. Or senile. Well I'm not! I'm not senile *or* stupid."

"No, ma'am, I don't think nothin' of the kind. And I'm not bein' snippy here, okay? Just frustrated, that's all, just . . . this is very tedious stuff, you gotta catch this little hickey down there and you gotta do it with the right tool 'cause with the wrong one it keeps slippin' off, and don't ask me why, okay, please? I already went through six of these things here, see? And now I'm gonna put this one away and I'm gonna try number seven here. See that? See, this is Slim Jim number seven slidin' down the window here. And I'm hopin' this one does the trick." Please, God, make this one do the fucking trick.

"Well you can try to pretend you're not being snippy with me, young man, but I know when people are snippy. I may be old, but I'm not stupid. I'm not senile, and I don't have Alzheimer's either. So you can stop thinking all that stuff, I know what you're thinking."

"No, ma'am, I promise you, you do not."

"Do not what?"

"Know what I'm thinking. I promise you, you don't." What I'm thinkin' is I'd like to stick number seven down your throat and rip your tongue out, that's what I'm thinkin'.

"There! Ha! Got it!" Canoza leaned his head back and stuck out his tongue at the door as he opened it with a flourish and a little bow. Then he looked at his watch. It had taken him only twenty-one minutes. Last fucking Toyota took him twenty-eight. Yes! A personal best. Canoza takes the gold for popping the lock on a Toyota in a personal-best time of twenty-one minutes, give or take a coupla seconds. Canoza is wavin' to the crowd as he takes his victory lap, yes. . . .

He turned to the woman and bowed once again, deeply from the waist. "Don't have to thank me, ma'am, no no, don't even mention it. 'Cause see? I took an oath to serve and protect, and this is the service part here, what I just did for you."

"What's your badge number?" she said coldly.

"Huh? What do you want that for?"

"Why do you think? I'm going to report you, that's what for. You forget, young man, if you ever knew, I pay your salary. Me and people like me. People living on fixed incomes. Which people like you working for the government wouldn't know anything about. All you know how to do is spend our taxes. And then you get snippy with us. I don't have to take that. And I'm not going to take that. I know where City Hall is. And I remember the chief's name too. It's Nowicki."

"Well, ma'am, you're very welcome. Right. That's just the cherry on top of my hot-fudge sundae. But here's what, ma'am, okay? Next time you lock your keys in your car? And you call us? We'll have to respond because that's our job. But I promise you we won't be in any hurry. 'Cause in order to report me you'll have to give the chief your name and address, 'cause he doesn't respond to anonymous complaints. He's good that way. And after I got your car open for you here? So you didn't have to pay a locksmith? You know what they charge, huh? Call one. Ask him. You'll find out how much money I saved you here today. And go 'head, tell the chief on me, that's okay. But just remember, he's gonna ask me for my side of it, alright?"

She started to cry, and to whimper. "All I have is my school pension . . . my Social Security . . . both of them together don't add up to seven hundred and sixty dollars a month . . . I wasn't able to work long . . . I had to quit teaching to take care of my mother-in-law . . . my husband wouldn't put her in a nursing home . . . wouldn't even discuss it! But then what did he do? He died first. And what did he do, the stupid son of a . . . I'll tell you what he did. He forgot to sign me up for his survivor benefits . . . and she lived ten more years, his mother . . . and you can talk all you want about how you took an oath to serve, but I never took any oath to wait on her hand and foot for nine years before the county took her in . . . nine years! So don't you talk to me about how you took any oath, you big bully . . .

get snippy with me, must make you feel real big, doesn't it, huh? Pick on an old lady."

"Aw, lady, c'mon, don't cry, please?" Canoza sucked in his breath and threw his head back and then dropped it on his chest and sighed and said, "Hey, I didn't mean none of that, c'mon. Here, take my hanky, take it, c'mon, don't cry, okay? What I said, huh? I was just blowin' smoke, huffin' and puffin' there, that's all, I shouldn't've done that, I was wrong. Listen, you lock your keys in again? Huh? We'll come right away, we have to, that's our job. Don't cry, okay, please?"

"That's right," she said, sniffling. "You shouldn't have said that. But I don't want your hanky. I have Kleenex in the car. I don't need you at all anymore, you . . . you big boob!"

Oh now I'm a big boob, huh? Swell. "Okay, okay. Then here, let me help you get in—"

"I said I don't need your help anymore." She crept close to him and peered intently at his shield and started to whisper his number to herself.

"Okay, okay, you don't want me to help, I won't help. Sorry, okay? Really didn't mean to make you cry—"

"Oh yes you did. I was a teacher. I know a bully when I see one. It was a long time ago, but bullies don't change."

"Aw Jeez, see there? I'm not a bully, ma'am, okay? I'm sure I said some things I shouldn't've said, but I'm no bully, ask anybody in the department. I never had one complaint against me for excessive force. Sometimes I don't have a lotta patience maybe, I'll admit that, but . . . ah crap, I'm real sorry you feel that way."

"Oh stop saying you're sorry, you don't mean it," she said very loudly. "I can tell by your eyes you don't. You just wish I'd go away. That's what everybody wishes. You'll find out. You get old, people just want you to go away. It'll happen to you too. Well I'm old alright, but I'm not stupid. I memorized your badge number."

He bit his lip and thought, well then go already, fuck you still here for? You're drawin' a fuckin' crowd here. Maybe I should let you use my PA. Give you a hundred fucking watts of Street Thunder, you could tell the whole fucking world you think I'm a bully. Fucking great. People that drive Jap cars deserve every shitty thing happens to 'em. Fuckers.

"Have a good rest of the day, ma'am," Canoza said, giving her a half-wave, half-salute, then collecting his roll-up bag of Slim Jims, and taking them back to his MU before she could say anything else. Or before he did.

In the MU, he switched on the radio, said, "Thirty-three here. I'm 10-24 on that lady's keys."

"Roger that, thirty-three," Vic Stramsky said.

"Hey, Vic, 10-91."

In a moment, Stramsky came back on Channel 3, the one that couldn't be picked up on any citizen's police scanner.

"What's up, Robert?"

"No more fucking Toyotas, Vic. I want thirty days off from Toyotas. That's the third one I caught already this year, and it's still April. No more, you hear? I don't get what the fuck it is with old ladies and their fucking Jap cars, no shit, but I'm done with 'em, you hear?"

"Oh-oh, you pissed another one off, huh? Nowicki's gonna love that. You tell this one your right shield number, or'd you lie again?"

"I did not lie."

"Still stickin' with that, huh? How you were only off by one digit? I gotta tell ya, Boo, I never saw Nowicki laugh that hard in all the time I've known him."

"Oh what, you don't make mistakes, huh? Somebody asks you for your Social Security or something, you never stutter or stumble around? Always get it right? The first time, every time? Bullshit."

"Hey, Booboo, it's only three digits. And you only been wearin' it for what now, twenty-five years? Huh?"

"Twenty-four six next week. Which is neither here nor there."

"That's right, it ain't. Only two reasons for givin' a citizen a wrong shield number, Boo, and the first one is you're so stupid you shouldn't be a cop. I have to tell you what the second one is?"

"Stop changin' the subject, which is no more Toyotas for me, I mean it, Vic. Next one goes to whoever ain't named Canoza. I won't respond, I'm not kiddin' around, that lady took my balls out, she put 'em on the blacktop, and then she jumped up and down on 'em with her pointy little shoes."

"Oou you made her cry, didn't ya?"

Canoza didn't respond.

"Ohhhh, you bad boy you, you made her cry. I'm tellin' you, she files a complaint? Chief calls you in, you better be wearin' your vest is all I know."

"Huh? How'd you know about that?"

"God, Robert, how do you think? Listen, I'm givin' you fair warnin', man. Nowicki's really pissed about you not wearin' it. You come in again without it, he's gonna make you sit, two weeks no pay, I'm tellin' ya. Which also means somebody else is gonna have to pick up your slack, and you know how you love it when you have to suck it up for somebody else, right?"

Canoza said nothing.

"I know you're still there, Robert. Tellin' you, man, this was Nowicki's project. He waded through paper shit up to his elbows to get that grant. And then he had to get council off their ass to come up with their end. And then he got you guys the best possible deal for one of the best ones made—and you won't wear it? Not a good move, Robert, especially not now since you're makin' these old ladies cry. What's with you, what'd you say to this one?"

"I didn't say nothin' to her. She just took it the wrong way."

"Ohhh, she *took* it the wrong way. Oh, that's always good when you *give* it the right way but they *take* it the wrong way. What'd she take the wrong way?"

"Hey, ask her, I don't know. My attitude I guess. Body language. My body language was probably screamin', hey, what the fuck's wrong with a Chevy, you can't buy a Chevy? Chevys I can pop in thirty seconds—I don't know, what the fuck, I'm 10-8. Out."

"Roger that. And remember the vest, Robert, you been warned."

"Yeah, yeah, warn this," Canoza grumbled to himself, switching the radio back to the open channel.

"I heard that, Robert," Stramsky said, laughing.

As loud as he could, to the melody of "Stars and Stripes Forever," Canoza started singing,

> "Oh the monkey wrapped his tail around the flagpole,
> To see his asshole, yes he did.
> And the monkey saw the people that were up there,
> With their numbnuts, yes he did.
> So the monkey took a dump beside the flagpole,
> To clean his asshole, oh yes he di-i-id . . ."

He couldn't think of the next line. He always had to stop when he came to this part. He was starting to wonder if he'd ever known the next line. He'd been singing these goofy words since he was in grade school, and now he was beginning to wonder if there had ever even been a next line.

"Maybe I am stupid," he said aloud. Then he thought, maybe I am a bully. Maybe it's time for me to quit singing this stupid fucking song. I'm forty-six fucking years old, for Christ sake, and I'm still doin' somethin' the first time I thought it was funny I was in the third grade. Or maybe the second. Shit. Why'd she have to cry like that? What'd I do so bad she had to cry, Jesus Christ, I didn't say anything that bad. Second one this month. Man, Nowicki's gonna be pissed, sure as Japs make fucking Toyotas, he's gonna shit a hat and make me wear it. Man. Whyn't Rayford or Reseta catch that call? Why me? I gotta take this fuckin' vest off, it's drivin' me nuts. . . .

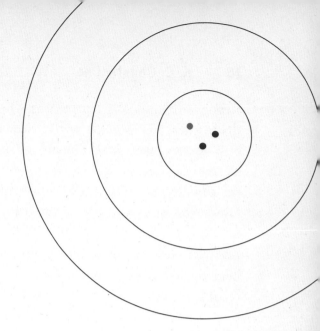

RAYFORD WAS trying to get a grip on the information Stramsky had just given him about the Scavellis and their two children dying in a fire. He was also trying to fill out the unusual incident report, trying to find the words that would justify drawing his piece, but every time he had to write Nick Scavelli's name he would hear children crying and coughing and see flames and smoke pouring out of windows and out of that smoke would come William Junior falling, tumbling head over feet. . . .

The cold that had started out in the middle of Rayford's gut was now spread over his whole body, so intense he had to turn the heater on. This was crazy, he kept telling himself. This was emotion out of control. Crazy or not, he was getting colder.

Man, what was James E. always sayin'? Emotion starts with a thought, and if you can control what you're thinking, you don't have to be a prisoner of your mind. And he didn't care what any brain-strainer wrote or said. . . .

James E. My man. My martial arts man. "E" for Eberly. So white he had twice the shit to ride. Because he steady refused to pass. Said in order to do that he would've had to move, and in the nineteen years and six months he served in the army, he'd moved more than enough for any man. Korea, Okinawa, Japan, Vietnam.

Said Montgomery, Alabama, was where he was born and raised, that's where his momma was buried, that's where he took care of business, and that's where he intended to live out his life and damn all the black people said he was a fool for refusing to pass when in their minds he could have done so with no sweat. Used to tell him, James, you white as the governor, man, with eyes as blue as the Gulf of Mexico on a sunny day. James E. listened to it but wouldn't allow himself to hear any of it. Walked the streets of Montgomery with his head up and his eyes front and damn anybody tried to tell him what color they thought he was supposed to be.

"Why should I let any man tell me that?" James E. would say in his soft voice. "I did not ask for my body, my height, my gender, the color of my skin, my hair, or my eyes. I am what I am because I am that. I have no need to advertise it falsely. My life advertises it truly. I have trained my mind to think its own thoughts, not the thoughts of others, no matter what group they would have me be part of or not be part of. I have trained my mind to respond to the world I inherited, no matter where it is or what it is. Because my body, no matter what its shape or color, is of no consequence without my mind and my mind accepts all shapes, all colors, all sounds, all smells, all tastes, all textures.

"Remember, William. An emotion starts with a thought, no matter how fast that thought enters your mind-body. As fast as it enters your mind-body, you have to learn how to change that thought just as fast. And with that change of mind, you can change your body. We are all locked in our bodies, William, for however long we don't know and we can't predict, but only fools are locked in their minds. Are you a fool, William? Do you want to be locked in your mind? Do you want your body reacting to every little breeze that blows through your brain? If that's what you want, then walk away now, I have nothing to teach you. Walk away from me and walk away from yourself and you'll never learn what you're capable of."

Rayford could hear James E. now as clearly as he had ever heard him in his studio in Montgomery, that voice so calm, so smooth, so soothing, so measured, so controlled. An emotion starts with a thought. A-men. I'm freezin' here 'cause I hear about the Scavellis' kids and a hurricane blows through my mind. William Junior blows through my mind. So motherfuckin' cold I can't even write. Frozen in time, that's what I am. Drove around the corner and saw that ambulance and Charmane's got-damn mother blubberin' in the street how it wasn't her fault, the boy wouldn't listen, the boy was a disobedient child, a disrespectful child, a child who would not pay attention to his elders, beatin' on her chest, throwin' up her hands to the heavens, screamin', wailin', this ain't my fault, this ain't my fault, in everybody's face with that bullshit. Worse than bullshit. Ain't a word for what bullshit that was. He was a child, that's all. A child with a child's energy and a child's curiosity. He was strong and inquisitive and agile and he had to be watched. You couldn't watch TV and pretend you were watching him, you had to watch him. When he was awake and moving, he had to be watched because he wanted to go everywhere, see everything, touch everything, taste everything, you could not pretend you were watching him if what you were really watching was Jerry Springer or Ricki Lake or Jenny Jones or any of those motherfuckin' freak shows.

But you're here now, William, my man. You are here! You're the one sittin' here freezin'. Right here, right now, you're the one sittin' in this MU with the motherfuckin' heater on in the middle of a spring evening. So stop this shit right now! You are here, it is now, get warm! You have work to do and you can't do it while you're shaking with cold from a mind four and a half years old. William Junior is dead. You know he crawled up on that windowsill by himself, you know that, there's no question about that. You know she wasn't watching him, you know she was lookin' at one of those got-damn freak shows, which one don't make no difference, you know she wasn't payin' attention to that child no matter how many times she said otherwise. You know the boy fell. And you know the result. Ain't no point in goin' over the motherfuckin' details in your mind once again. Get it out your mind, get your mind back on the Scavellis and fill out this got-damn UIR. Do it, man! Do it now!

Do the fire breath. Inhale and pump your belly out ten times, c'mon, do it!

He did. He filled his diaphragm, straining against his belts, then pumped his diaphragm in ten times, hard with each exhale. It changed the cold in his belly. Started to warm it. So he did it again, ten more times, and got warmer still. Then he inhaled deeply, filling his belly, thinking warmth, saying warmth, feeling warmth, and exhaled that warmth to his fingers, hands, arms, toes, feet, shins, knees, thighs, butt, belly, back, and chest, and repeated that inhalation and exhalation again nine more times until finally he was no longer cold. Finally he was warm enough he could turn off the heater. Warm enough that he could finish filling out the UIR. Warm enough, when he was done with that, that he could open his gear bag, get his Little Playmate cooler out, and take out the makings of a sandwich.

First thing every morning after breakfast, he put into separate plastic bags some variation of greens, cheeses, pickles, mustards or tofu spreads. This morning he'd packed Romaine lettuce, low-fat Swiss cheese, dill pickle slices, and a small jar of Nayonaise along with two small pita breads. He opened each bag and arranged them on top of his briefcase. He sawed the pita open with his tomato knife, then laid on the Romaine first, then the cheese, then two long slices of dill pickles, finally spreading the Nayonaise over the top half of the pita. He poured another coffee from his vacuum bottle, and settled back to eat, all the while repeating silently the word *warmth* until he opened his mouth to take the first bite.

Then he thought about eating. That's what James Eberly had tried to drum into him: do one thing at a time. Do it with full attention. Focus. Concentrate. Eliminate distractions. If you're eating, eat. Sleeping, sleep. Going to war, go to war. Making love, make love. When your mind wanders, bring it back. If it won't come back, ask whose mind it is that's wandering. Is it yours? Or somebody else's? If it isn't yours, ask how it got inside your head. Who allowed it to be there if not you? Whose ever it was, if it's in your head, it's yours now. Meet it, greet it, take possession of it. Be here with it, be now with it. Pay attention. . . .

Yeah, James, I hear you. I know all the words you said. Wish I could do it, man. But my sorry-ass brain just don't work that way. Just keeps on keepin' on with all the stale, stupid shit and debris pourin' through there like a got-damn white-water river, 'cept it ain't white, it's brown. Color of shit and sorry desperation. Six years' worth of Miss Paige. Miss Leontine Paige. Miss Paige and her got-damn itch to know the future. If it ain't some voodoo bitch on the kitchen floor with chicken parts, it's some got-damn psychic hot line, two dollars and ninety-nine cents a minute, and Charmane think I'm s'posed to pay that motherfuckin' phone bill like it's mine. Day I pay for nine-hundred-number calls is the day I turn into Denzel Washington, b'lieve that, James. I may not be able to control my mind, but I damn sure ain't goin' pay for no psychic bull-shit come out a nine-hundred number.

Rayford chewed his sandwich. Drank his coffee. Brought himself back as best he could to the here and now. Zipped closed the plastic bags, put them back in the cooler, put it in his gear bag, washed his hands and mouth with a Moist Towelette, balled it up and put it in an empty plastic grocery bag he used for garbage. He always carried a bunch of those as well as several large green garbage bags to spread out on the backseat in case he had to transport some pukey drunk or somebody who had little or no interest in personal hygiene. It was a lot easier to toss the bags than to get the funk out of the upholstery.

There were a lot of things that smelled worse than puke: one was somebody who was still alive and had lost control of his bowels, another was a corpse that had a full bowel when its temperature started falling fast. Thank Jesus, Buddha, and Allah I don't have to transport the dead. Ain't nothin' get that stink out of cloth. Might as well have a dog got wrong with a skunk jump up in the bed lickin' your face, trying to get you up. Stick that skunked-up nose in your face? Lick you with that skunked-up tongue? Damn, that's some nasty shit—now what am I thinkin' this nonsense for? Call Stramsky and 10-8 yourself, man, this unit s'posed to be mobile, so make it move, man, git to gittin', what the fuck. . . .

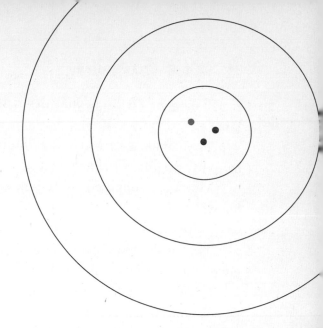

WHEN RESETA led what's-his-name into the Conemaugh County Juvenile Center on the rear of the grounds of the county's home for the aged and infirm, he waited by the reception desk until the intake officer showed up. The intake officer came out of the john adjusting his belt just as the phone on his desk started to ring. He answered it, identified himself, and then listened and nodded several times. Then he took the phone away from his ear and said, "You Officer Reseta? Rocksburg PD?"

"Yeah."

"It's for you. Your boss I think."

"Okay, soon as I lock this one down." Reseta turned the boy around, unlocked the right cuff, steered him around in front of a heavy metal chair, pulled him down, then locked that cuff around the left arm of the chair. He moved around to the opposite side of the desk and took the phone.

"Reseta. What's up?"

"Somethin's not right with your juvey. I called the county bar association, the medical association, all I got was one Maguire and he's a lawyer and never been married. So then I checked the crisscross file, which by the way you shoulda done, you know? Why didn't you do that?"

"I thought I'd bring him down here, see if somebody knew him."

"Hey, James, after you booked him, your next call's supposed to be to the parents, you know that."

"How'm I supposed to call somebody whose name I don't know?"

"Why didn't you call the address—like I did?"

"Hey, if the kid's givin' me a wrong name, he's also gonna be givin' me a wrong address, so I didn't see the point."

"Okay, so if you'da called the address, you know? In Maplewood? One twenty-three Elm? That was the address, right?"

"That's the one he gave me, yeah."

"Well when I called it, I got a woman with a maid service answered, said the name on her worksheet is Feeney, not Maguire. And there's no Maguire in the white pages on that street at that number. So I'm waitin' on a callback from one of the school guidance counselors, got him at home, says he has to go back in, check his files, 'cause that name doesn't ring any bells. Meanwhile, James, I hate to say this over the phone—matter of fact I was gonna bring it up when you brought the kid into my office and I forgot—but lately, you know? You been walkin' around in a little bit of a fog, you know that? You thinkin' about retirement—is 'at what you're doin'?"

"No no, uh . . . I don't know. A fog? I don't think so."

"You don't *think* so? That's weak, James. Not like you at all. Drink some coffee and see what you can get outta the kid. Meantime I'll see what the counselor comes up with—hey, James?"

"What?"

"I'm serious, James, drink some fuckin' espresso or somethin'. Don't go to sleep out there, you hear? You got somethin' on your mind, bring it in here, I'll listen. You hearin' me?"

"Yeah, I hear ya," Reseta said. "Okay. I'll see what I can get out of him. If you get anything, we didn't get started yet, just got here." Reseta hung up, staring hard at the boy but thinking about what Nowicki had just said about his being in a fog lately. Was that true?

Am I thinking about retirement? I'm not thinking about that, that's crap. So what *am* I doing?

He continued to stare hard at the boy, who was trying hard to stare back. The intake officer's eyes went from Reseta to the boy and back. "Is there a problem here? I mean aside from the usual?"

"Kid's a criminal mastermind apparently. Boy of at least two names. You wouldn't happen to know him, would ya?"

"No. Why?"

"I know he's been through here before, that's all. I mean I knew it before we found out he was gamin' us on his name and address. Now there's no doubt. But I'm also feelin' this vibe he wants to be in here. So you sure you don't know him, huh?"

"Positive. What's the state registry say?"

"Can't say anything for at least eleven, twelve more hours. Got maintenance geeks in their computers. So okay, what's the drill here now? Been so long since I collared a kid, last time I was down here, I had to fill out the petition with a pen. Please tell me you have forms in your computer, huh?"

"Here. Lemme get you on, then type 'Control P' and it'll come right up. Just fill in the blanks. So just so I'm clear about this, okay? Nobody's talked to his parents, guardians, or custodians, right?"

"Can't talk to people you don't know, my friend," Reseta said, sitting down at the intake officer's desk after the officer had opened the computer to the petition program.

"Where'd you make the arrest?"

"Outside his school. Rocksburg Middle School."

"And you didn't take him inside to get a solid confirmation on his ID?"

"Hey, look, okay? We all have our days. So, so far today hasn't been one of my better ones, alright? But I'm tryin' to make it so it's not a total waste. Just let me type this up, and then you wanna do a performance evaluation on me, be my guest. My boss's already done one, what the fuck, you might as well jump in while the water's still the right temp—"

"Hey, I didn't mean anything, you know? I know I couldn't do your job, so, uh, you know, forget I said anything."

"Yeah yeah, it's forgotten. Well, this is gonna be quick. In the Court of Common Pleas of Conemaugh County, Pennsylvania, Juvenile Complaint, date April 16, 1999. Name John Doe. Address Rocksburg. Telephone unknown, Social Security Number unknown, Sex male, Race white—you are male and white, right? Date of birth unknown. Father's name, address and phone number unknown. Mother's name, address and phone number unknown. Act and Section Violated—finally somethin' I know—18 Pa. CS Section 2701(a)(1) and Section 2702(a)(1). Date, Place, Time of Offense, 4-16-99 1510 hours approx., 300 block of Maple Avenue, Rocksburg.

"Description of Incident: John Doe did attempt to cause or intentionally, knowingly, or recklessly caused bodily injury to another, namely Timothy Miscovitz, 13, of 709 O'Hara St., Rocksburg, in violation of 18 Pa. CS Section 2701(a)(1) of the Pennsylvania Crimes Code, Act of Dec. 6, 1972, 18 Pa. CS, Section 2701(a)(1) as amended, and did attempt to cause serious bodily injury to another, namely the aforementioned Timothy Miscovitz, and did attempt to cause such injury intentionally, knowingly or recklessly under circumstances manifesting extreme indifference to the value of human life in violation of 18 Pa. CS Section 2702(a)(1) of the Pa. Crimes Code, Act of Dec. 6, 1972, 18 Pa. CS, Section 2702(a)(1) as amended. To Wit: During the midafternoon hours, John Doe pursued Timothy Miscovitz into traffic on Maple Avenue, pulled him to the ground by his clothing, removed a book bag from Miscovitz's shoulder, threw it onto the porch at 305 Maple, and when Miscovitz attempted to retrieve his bag, John Doe willfully extended his foot tripping Miscovitz and causing him to fall face-first into concrete steps leading up to that porch, causing facial injuries that required Miscovitz to be hospitalized.

"Complainant's Name, Address and Phone No.

"Ptlmn. James M. Reseta, Shield No. 356

"Rocksburg Police Dept.

"City Hall

"115 S. Main St.

"Rocksburg, PA 15889-1867

"724-830-7799."

Reseta hit the print key and then looked at the intake officer. "I forget—how many copies I need to make here?"

"At least six. Me, you, him, the DA, the judge, the parents—if they ever show up. I always make eight."

"Then eight it is," Reseta said, hitting that number and standing and waiting for the printer to catch up. When it did, he kept one for himself, gave one to John Doe, and the rest to the intake officer.

"Now what?"

"Now I read this and play judge." The intake officer sat down, read the petition, and after a minute said, "Well, John Doe, it looks like you're gonna be here at least until tomorrow."

"Then I get my hearing, right?"

"See," Reseta said, "I knew this prick's been here before."

"We don't call names here," the intake officer said softly. "Not on my watch."

"Okay. Your watch, your rules, doesn't matter to me. You need my testimony, you got my name and number. I'm outta here. Just let me get my cuffs off him and he's all yours."

Reseta unlocked the cuffs and put them back in their pouch on his duty belt. "See ya, John Doe. Good luck. You're gonna need it."

"You're the one's gonna need it, fuckhead."

"You threatenin' me? Huh? Easy for me to type up another count of simple assault, kid. That what you want?"

"That hardly qualifies," the intake officer said.

"Read your Title 18, pal, that qualifies, believe me."

"Excuse me, but I'm the one who decides that."

"That you are. I stand corrected."

"And the only reason he's stayin' is 'cause I don't know how to reach his parents, otherwise he'd be gone."

"I know, I know," Reseta said. "But before you get all gooshy on me here, maybe after you get off tonight or whenever, you could take a ride up the hospital and check out the other kid, okay?"

"Officer, the next one that comes in that hasn't been banged around will be the first one I've seen. They've all been banged around by somebody."

"Hey, I see 'em before you do. Anytime you wanna compare nightmares, gimme a call. Bye."

Reseta walked quickly outside, got in the front seat of his MU, called the station, and said, "Thirty here. I'm 10-24 at the juvey center."

"Ten-four," Stramsky said.

Reseta started up the MU and headed back toward Rocksburg, thinking, well, there's another one of God's shop projects gone kaflooey. Everything's upside down, I swear. Been to God knows how many classes on how to make war, never been to one yet about how to make love. Spent a thousand hours practicing how to subdue violent people, nobody yet ever taught me the first thing about how to keep a kid from becoming violent. Listened to all these experts about how to recognize all the different drugs and drug reactions, never had one yet say why anybody would want to take the damn things in the first place. James, my boy, it's way past time you started writing that thesis, way past time you started looking for another line of work. This stuff is starting to get old faster and faster.

Never do anything till something happens. We don't act, we react. I know there are departments where people are talking about anger management, peace negotiation, we should've been working on that years ago. Why the hell don't we? Is anybody in the schools talking to these kids about controlling their temper, talking about how to avoid a fight? Oh listen to me. Ain't I wise all of a sudden? How exactly would I know? When was the last time I was in a school building here to do anything but collar somebody? When did

I ever go to a school board meeting, try to find out what's up? When did I ever go to a PTA meeting? Who the fuck am I to talk about what other people aren't doing? And how exactly would I explain this to Nowicki? Who thinks I'm falling asleep out here. Thinks all I need is a cup of fucking espresso. . . .

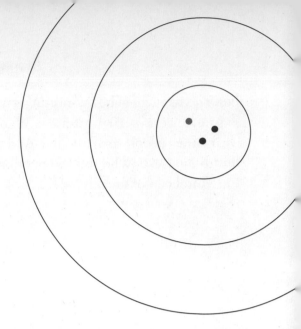

CANOZA PULLED into the strip mall on the east side of the Amtrak lines, looking for a parking slot near Jimmy's Suds and Subs, where for the last six years he'd taken his meal break whenever he caught the second watch. He passed Annie's Launderette, which used to be a branch office of Rocksburg Savings and Loan; Domino's Pizza, which used to be Monte's bar; Larry's Flooring, which used to be Lukow's Floor and Wall Coverings; ABC Cleaners, which used to be Al's One-Hour Martinizing; and Rite-Aid drugstore, which was closing because its stock was being moved into the new Eckerd's building at the corner of Mercury Avenue and Pittsburgh Street.

Jernevich's Beer Distributorship, which used to take up the back half of the building behind these other businesses, had moved into the store where B&T's Freight Liquidation used to be, before it was itself liquidated in Bankruptcy Court. Jernevich's former space in the back was now occupied by Jimmy's Comedy Club, the Jimmy Abrigatto of Suds and Subs having branched out on Friday and Saturday nights into showbiz. On the other side of Jernevich's was Maytag Appliances, which used to be Rocksburg TV and Appliances; Joan's Videos, which before the divorce was to be Jack's Videos; Advance Auto Parts, which used to be Al's All-Auto Warehouse; Lonnie's Hairport, which used to be Lou's Barbershop; and finally Jimmy's Suds and Subs.

Canoza found a slot in front of Jimmy's, parked, and called in his location and himself out of service at 1800 hours.

"You keep eatin' at Jimmy's," dispatcher Stramsky said, "one of these days you're gonna look like a meatball sub."

"Maybe so, but no matter what I eat, I'll never look like a Polak," Canoza said back, signing off, locking up, and going inside Jimmy's. He went straight to the john, where he took off his duty belt, shirt, and his Second Chance Kevlar vest, and gave his belly, ribs, and back a good scratching as far as he could reach. Then he put his shirt and duty belt back on, went out and found himself a seat at the bar, folded up the vest, and put it in his lap.

Jimmy, as usual, was behind the bar haranguing his waitresses, all three of whom were in their late twenties or early thirties and wore red satin short-shorts and tight white T-shirts with "Eat At Jimmy's" printed atop the words "Suds" on their left breasts and "Subs" on their right breasts. If it were up to Jimmy, his waitresses would be wearing nothing but tattoos, but since he'd already tried that and caused such outrage among the members of the Rocksburg Council of Churches that he'd almost lost his liquor license, he'd gone back to having his waitresses dress like the ones at Hooters on Route 22 West halfway to Pittsburgh.

To Jimmy, Hooters represented everything he wanted out of life: TV sets continuously showing sports, so many brands of draft beer he'd never heard of half of them, cheeseburgers with yellow mustard and grilled onions, french fries as thick as his thumbs, and young women with big breasts serving his beer, burgers, and fries with such sunny sincerity he believed they actually would go home with him if only they didn't have to care for their crippled mother, cancerous father, retarded sister, unemployed brother, son, daughter, puppy, kitty, canary, ferret, or iguana.

Jimmy's dream to own a Hooters franchise had been quashed when he applied for the license himself. He thought the suits from

Hooters' home office wouldn't be nearly as diligently interested in his past as either the Pennsylvania Liquor Control Board or the county Health Department had been when he got the required licenses and permits to open Suds and Subs, though even Jimmy had to concede that neither the LCB nor the HD really had a chance to examine his past, because their investigations were directed at his mother, whom Jimmy had hired to apply for those licenses by paying for her monthlong vacation in Italy. Since Mrs. Abrigatto, unlike her son, had never been convicted of a felony, she had no trouble getting LCB and HD licenses and permits. And as long as Jimmy continued to pay her way to Italy for a month every year and bought her a new Chrysler New Yorker every two years, she didn't care how he ran the businesses that were in her name. The only times she ever went into Suds and Subs were to tell Jimmy he was late with her car payment.

Aside from Jimmy's near fatally clumsy attempt to have his waitresses work in the nude—the morning after he did, the Rocksburg Council of Churches gave him twenty-four hours to get his waitresses dressed or they would petition the LCB to revoke his license on the grounds he was running a "nuisance bar"—his only other glitch on the road to his entertainment empire occurred when a group of bikers, aspiring to membership in the Pagans, started using the Suds and Subs as their hangout. At first they seemed just harmlessly rowdy, a bunch of guys who, after Jimmy's own heart, wanted what he wanted: many TVs showing different sports continuously, draft beer in frosty mugs, half-pound cheeseburgers, thick french fries, and busty young women in tight T-shirts waiting on them with parted lips, oily hips, and a consuming desire to know how many different parts of Harley-Davidson engines could be chromed.

But then, of course, bikers being the same as any other humans inclined to club membership, different cliques began to form among these Pagan wanna-bes, one clique calling themselves the Animals and the other the Undertakers. For a while their disputes were strictly vocal, but then they started showing up with different colors on their jeans jackets, and the louder their vocal disputes became, the more Jimmy's regulars tended to stay away. It didn't take Jimmy long to figure out that on the nights when the bikers didn't show up, his beloved Suds and Subs had become a place for him to stand around and harangue his waitresses while they pretended to listen to him. In Jimmy's mind the only way the situation could've been worse was if his bar had been invaded by fags.

Since Jimmy Abrigatto's grandparents and Robert Canoza's grandparents had come from the same village in Italy, and since Jimmy's mother and Robert's mother were both members of Mother of Sorrows parish in Norwood, and since Jimmy and Robert had gone to Mother of Sorrows Elementary School together, Jimmy thought he'd have no problem reaching out to Robert to solve his problem with the bikers.

"You always said I wasn't smart enough to walk and chew gum at the same time," Canoza had responded to Jimmy's outreach.

"Hey, I was a kid, you know? Kids say things."

"Oh is that what it was, huh? You were a kid. I get it."

"C'mon, you're not gonna hold that against me now, are ya?"

"Well what happened—you got older and dumber? And I got older and smarter—is that what you're sayin' now?"

"Whattaya mean?"

"Hey, genius, ever hear of nine-one-one? Next time they start some shit, pick up your phone and push those numbers. Coupla cars'll show up, they'll bust some heads, kick over a few bikes, that'll be the end of that."

"Yeah but how will I know you'll be workin'?"

"Whattaya mean, how will you know I'll be workin'? You askin' me to do this? Me specifically? What's goin' on here, Jimmy? You wouldn't be solicitin' an aggravated assault, would ya?"

"No no no no no, nothin' like that, c'mon. I'm just sayin', you know, I don't want a coupla little guys showin' up, I mean what the fuck, you know? You show up, that would be like, uh, impressive, you know? You're a big guy, Booboo."

"Don't call me that."

"Hey, sorry. I forgot."

"I'm a big guy, huh? No kiddin'. Nobody ever told me that before."

"Hey, you know what I mean—oh, you're pullin' my chain now."

"Me? Robert Canoza? I'm pullin' your chain? The guy ain't smart enough to pass the sergeant's test? The guy ain't smart enough to get out of a car and behind a desk?"

"Hey, I never said that about you, man. Anybody says I said that is a fuckin' liar, man."

"Yeah? Well maybe you should have a little talk with your mother, 'cause that's who told my aunt. And guess who she told, huh?"

"Nah, whoa, c'mon, Bobbie. My mother said that? Never. Never fuckin' happen she said that."

"Yeah? First off, not even my mother calls me Bobbie. Second, this better be on the square, Jimmy, 'cause I find out you're usin' me to solve a problem? After I bust their heads I'll bust yours, you got that?"

"Yeah, hey, Robert, I got ya, man. I understand. Absolutely."

"Good. 'Cause, uh, obviously your memory's goin' bad."

"Huh?"

"Yeah. What you apparently can't remember is how you been raggin' me since we were kids. You think I forgot that, huh? Back in Mother of Sorrows? Then, you were the skinny good-lookin' one, the one with the wavy hair and the fast mouth, and I was Quasimodo, remember? King Kong? Mighty Joe Young? Now you're just another bald guy can't see his dick when he pees. Another bald, fat guy with a problem he thinks I'm supposed to solve just 'cause I'm on the city payroll. I'm gonna say this once more, Jimmy. If this ain't what you say it is, I'm gonna be on your payroll long as you own this bar, understand?"

"Absolutely. No question, man—Robert. I know exactly what you're sayin'. But I swear on my mother, these guys are ruinin' my business, man, they're worse than a buncha fags. They don't show up, I'm empty here."

Three days after that conversation, the leader of the Animals got loud with the leader of the Undertakers, and Jimmy thought he saw a knife. Then he thought he saw another knife, and then he started hollering he was dialing 911 before he even started for the phone.

By the time Canoza and Rayford showed up a few minutes later, the Animals and the Undertakers were all charm; their behavior could not have been more congenial. Canoza looked around for a minute or so and then asked who their leaders were. Nobody answered. Canoza stepped quickly behind two of the Undertakers who happened to be sitting with their backs to him, cracked their heads together, and then slammed them facedown onto the bar, breaking both their noses.

After their screams turned to muffled sobs, a strange silence fell over Suds and Subs, exaggerated by the hum of the beer coolers and the sizzle of frozen potatoes in the deep fryers.

"One more time, who's in charge here?"

At the other end of the bar, the two who had been in each other's faces provoking Jimmy's 911 call held up their right hands.

Canoza approached them, bent between them, put his hands on their shoulders, and said, "We got a report this place is becomin' a nuisance bar. Know what that means? The LCB is gonna be sendin' its agents here. Know who they are? Case you haven't heard, LCB regs are now enforced by the state police. If you fellas don't want the state cops on your case, you'll find someplace else to hang out, understand?"

The leader of the Animals looked at the leader of the Undertakers and they started to laugh and turn around.

Canoza cracked their heads together, quickly slid his hand down their backs until he found their belts, then jerked them backwards off their bar stools, and started carrying them, one in each hand, toward the front door, telling Rayford to open it. Then, banging their heads off every surface he passed, Canoza carried them, gasping and coughing, outside, where he rammed them, first one and then the other, headfirst into the side of his MU. Then he dropped them, barely conscious and bleeding profusely, onto the macadam.

He turned around, looked at the double line of Harleys, eleven in a line closest to the door and nine in the second line, dropped into a crouch beside a bright red one on the end of the second line, put his hands on the seat and gas tank, and with a guttural roar, shoved it into the next one, toppling all nine like dominoes. Inside, he made the same announcement as before, much louder this time, to the rest of the bikers, who were scurrying to put tables between them and him.

No one was more impressed with Canoza's display of courage and power than William Rayford, who'd only been on the job six months and knew he didn't have the vocabulary to say how happy he was that Canoza arrived on the scene about ten seconds before he had and not only was first through the door but had never hesitated about taking the initiative. As Rayford described it later, and he would describe it many times to any of his fellow officers who wanted to listen, he stressed that Canoza had never even asked him if he wanted to handle it. "It was like I wasn't even there," Rayford would say. "But I'm tellin' you, man, my chin was on my chest, I ain't lyin'. I had to tell myself to swallow or I would've been droolin' all down my chin."

Second most impressed, of course, was Jimmy Abrigatto, who, the moment the last Undertaker ran out his front door, shouted, "Man, Robert, long as I own this place, you eat here, you drink here, you don't pay for nothin'. I swear on my mother, anything you want, anytime you want it, it's on me, man."

"And that's the only time ol' Boo acted like I was even there, man," Rayford would say. "He looked at this Jimmy and then he pointed at me and he said, 'I got a witness, Jimmy. You heard that, Rayford, right?' And I told him yes sir I surely did. And that's why Boo eats there all the time. Man, you shoulda seen those bikers scatter. Left their wounded behind too, man. Buncha chickenshits. . . ."

Even before Canoza found the one empty seat at the bar, Jimmy was working on a meatball sub for him, while one of the waitresses reached around the corner of the bar, got a frosty mug and filled it with ginger ale. She brought it around the bar and set it in front of Canoza with her most genuine smile while pushing into his right arm with her breasts.

"Hi, Robert," she said.

"Save that for the tourists," he said, leaning away from her.

"Gee, you're welcome," she said, acting hurt. Or maybe she was hurt, Canoza couldn't tell.

"Why do you always do that?" she said.

"Do what?"

"Pull away from me like I'm some kinda . . ."

"Some kinda what?"

"Hey, you know what I mean. I'm just doin' my job, okay?"

"And you do that to do it better, right?"

"Hey, it's a job, you know? I got a kid, okay?"

"If that's part of the job description, you oughta sue the prick."

"What prick, who's a prick?" Jimmy said, delivering the meatball sub.

"Who do you think? You."

"Me? I'm the prick? Fuck'd I do now?"

"Tell your waitresses shove their boobs into me every time they bring my ginger ale."

"Hey, that's bullshit, Robert, I don't tell 'em do that. They do that all on their own. What you don't understand is they like you."

"Yeah, right," Canoza said, taking a bite of his sub. He chewed for a while, closed his eyes, and said, "Good sauce. Good meatballs. Had it all together when you made these."

"Same way I always make 'em."

"Nah, uh-uh. Some days you make 'em you leave your dago soul in the parkin' lot. Those days they're like sawdust and porch paint."

"What're you talkin' about, sawdust and porch paint, that's my mother's recipe. Get outta here with that bullshit."

The waitress was back, looking genuinely hurt. She tapped Canoza on the shoulder.

"What?"

"I'm tired of you really hurtin' my feelings."

"Gimme a break. You said it yourself, it's just a job."

"You think you don't have feelings 'cause it's your job?"

"Hey," Jimmy said, "if you don't have tables to work you can always clean the ladies' toilet, you know? Do somethin', Jesus."

"If I had tables, I'd be workin' 'em, okay? God knows, that's the only way I make any money around here."

"What's she mean? You don't pay 'em?"

"Whattaya think—I'm nuts? Much as they make they oughta be glad I don't take a cut."

"Oh please, much as we make."

"No joke—he doesn't pay you?"

"He just said it, didn't he?"

"You don't pay them *anything? Nothin'?* How do you get away with that? You can't do that."

"Who says?"

"Get outta here. You can't make people work for nothin'."

"They don't work for nothin', they work for tips. You think tips are nothin', you kiddin'? How much'd you make yesterday, Lois, huh? Tell this fuckin' gorilla."

"Sixty-three and change. Only had to be here from eleven till midnight."

"Wait wait wait—what'd you call me?"

"Huh?"

"You said tell this effin' gorilla."

"No I didn't."

"I ain't deaf. Hey, Lois, what'd he call me, huh? You heard him, what'd he say?"

"I didn't hear anything, honest."

"You're both fulla crap. I heard what you said, Jimmy." Canoza jumped up, stretched over the bar, and grabbed Jimmy's right ear and squeezed. "I'm tellin' you for the last time, Jimmy, you ever call me gorilla again? Or anything like it? You'll spend the next nine months in rehab learnin' how to write with a pencil in your teeth, you got that?"

"I got it, Robert, I got it, let go my ear, man, that hurts!"

"Not half as bad as it's gonna hurt you ever call me that again. Or I ever hear anybody tell me you called me that again, you got that?"

"I got it, man, I got it, let go, please!"

Canoza let go of Jimmy's ear and sat back down. Jimmy rushed away to put some ice in a plastic bag and hold it to his ear.

Canoza turned and said to Lois, "I'm tryin' to stick up for you with this prick and whatta you do? You go deaf. You wanna work here for nothin' but tips, that's your problem. Don't ever complain to me about it again."

"I wasn't complainin' to you about that. I was complainin' 'cause you hurt my feelings."

"Aw please, hurt your feelings, Jesus."

She took a deep breath, started to say something, but couldn't.

Canoza saw tears running down her cheeks and swung around on his stool. "Okay okay, look, I'm sorry, alright? Don't cry, okay? C'mon, don't! I didn't mean to make you cry, aw Jesus—here, take my napkin, c'mon, take it, here."

She started to take the napkin and they both saw the red stains from where he'd wiped sauce off his mouth. He folded the paper napkin so that the stains were on the other side and tried to dab her cheeks, but she pulled away.

"C'mon, Jeez, I was tryin' to stick up for ya, you know? What, you havin' your period or somethin'?"

"No! Jesus, you think the only reason I might be cryin' is if I'm havin' my period? Screw you, Robert, okay? Just screw you."

Canoza's shoulders sagged as he watched her hurry away. Jesus Christ, he thought. Come in here, all I'm askin' for is a little peace to eat my sub. And what the fuck do I get? Grief. Everywhere I go today, I'm in a fuckin' grief storm. Fuckit. I'm outta here.

Canoza picked up the rest of his sub and walked out the door, taking another bite and chewing as he walked.

"Hey, Jimmy, look at me," he called out over his shoulder. "I'm walkin' and chewin' at the same time."

He finished the sub in the MU, and was starting to call himself back into service when he noticed that he'd slopped sauce on his shirt and tie. "Fuck," he said. Then he remembered he was out of Moist Towelettes. "Double fuck."

He started to drive to the Giant Eagle out on Route 30 in Westfield Township but thought he better go to the Foodland up on Pittsburgh Street, even though the last time he went there they were out of Moist Towelettes. So he'd had to go to the Giant Eagle in the township, but some piss-and-moaner from the city spotted him and called the station. Chief Nowicki had just relieved the dispatcher so he could take a piss break, and Nowicki took the ear assault from the P&M about city cops being in the township when they were supposed to be patrolling in the city.

The geopolitical fact was the city was one large land island and two smaller ones surrounded by the township, so city cops were always driving through parts of the township to get to other parts of the city, a geographical fact complicated by the political fact that the township had no police department of its own and was supposed to be patrolled by state police from Troop A Barracks, which was located in the city, two blocks east of Pittsburgh Street. But since Troop A—like the entire state police since the early 1990s—was pitifully undermanned because nearly a third of the force took early retirements offered by the state legislature to balance a budget at that time, Rocksburg PD was called to respond to incidents in the township more often than the state police. Troop A dispatchers were in fact doing most of the calling. Because it irritated and annoyed Chief Nowicki to repeat these geographical and political facts to every caller who pissed and moaned about city cops wasting their taxes shopping in township supermarkets, he appealed to his officers to try to avoid doing so.

"Fine," Canoza had reminded him. "What are we supposed to do when they want an escort to the bank, huh? Sit outside and blow the horn? We ain't allowed to go in and tell 'em we're there? And I can't buy somethin' while I'm waitin' for the manager to get his shit together? Always waitin' on 'em, they're never ready. This is stupid. The P&M can shop there but he gets pissed 'cause *I'm* there? Tell *him* to shop in Foodland. They never have Moist Towelettes. And they never have any spicy V-8 either."

"You can't put Red Hot in the regular and spice it up yourself?"

"That ain't my point."

"Hey, forget your point, okay? *My* point is, avoid it whenever possible, that's all I'm askin'. I know these people are fulla shit, but it's how it looks, you know? How many times I gotta tell ya, it ain't the reality, it's the perception of the reality, c'mon."

"Hey, how'm I supposed to know how other people perceive what I'm doin'? I ain't no mind reader."

"Booboo still can't understand those ladies perceivin' that he's a big meanie. Makin' 'em cry all the time, Boo, you oughta be ashamed of yourself."

"Aw fuck you, Mr. Personality. Next one locks her keys in her Toyota, it's all yours."

So Canoza, with that conversation still in mind, drove to Foodland and tried but failed to find Moist Towelettes. He knew that if he didn't find something wet soon, the sauce stain was going to set and he'd have to buy a new shirt and tie, and nothing annoyed him more than spending his clothing allowance on clothes. He went in the public rest rooms near the office and tried to get the stains out with wet paper towels. He couldn't tell whether the stains were coming out or whether he was just spreading them around. Fuckit, he thought, screw the P&Ms. I'm goin' to Giant Eagle.

He went back out to his MU, hoping that, even though he hadn't called himself back into service yet, nothing was happening so dispatcher Stramsky wouldn't start squawking about where he was. He loved Stramsky like a father, and Stramsky loved him like a son, but sometimes that relationship got too real to suit Canoza. Sometimes Stramsky acted like he was, if not Canoza's actual father, then his police rabbi, which had been more than okay when Canoza first joined the department. Stramsky had had ten years in by then, and he'd been Canoza's training partner.

Back then, when Mario Balzic was chief, rookies rode with training partners for six months before Balzic would let them take an MU out by themselves. He didn't care what their experience was, or how well they did in the Municipal Police Education and Training classes or where they ranked when they graduated. Balzic was obstinate: there never was a book written or a class taught that could substitute for on-the-job training. If you didn't know how to do it when it mattered, he didn't care how well you could write or talk about it in response to a tester's question.

The thing about Stramsky was that sometimes he acted like he was still Canoza's training partner, a relationship that had ended more than twenty years ago. Enough was enough, Canoza thought, and tried a dozen different ways to tell Stramsky to lighten up. But every time he felt like he'd thought of exactly the right way to approach Stramsky, he'd remember the times Stramsky had saved him from making an ass of himself, and Canoza couldn't do anything but give Stramsky some jokey put-down, like telling him that no matter how much pasta he ate he'd always be a Polak. Or that no matter what part of Poland the pope came from, he still had to move to Italy. No matter what the Polaks thought, the Vatican was never going to be in Warsaw. It was always jokes. Funny put-downs. The stuff that passed for conversation among men.

There were times Canoza wished Stramsky *was* his real father.

And sometimes he wished even harder that he could leave the jokes behind and sit down with Stramsky and have a real conversation. About real shit: courage, manhood, life, death, the fear of getting your balls shot off by some idiot crackhead who was just passing through on his way to Pittsburgh and thought Rocksburg might be a good place to boost a car. . . .

By the time Canoza pulled into Giant Eagle's parking lot off Route 30, he had the uneasy feeling that something was wrong. He'd made up his mind he wasn't going to call himself back in service until he got the Moist Towelettes, but he knew he was pushing it just being at this Giant Eagle. Even though he hadn't been in Jimmy's more than twenty minutes at the most, it was now 1729 hours and if he didn't call Stramsky right now, he was going to get his balls busted real good. But that wasn't what was bothering him. Something wasn't right, he just didn't know what it was exactly.

He hustled into the Giant Eagle, found the Moist Towelettes, bought two containers, had to wait behind only two women in the express line, and made it back out to the MU by 1732 hours. He'd purposely not turned on his shoulder radio until he was back outside, but as soon as he did Stramsky was squawking at him.

"Repeat, thirty-three, you 10-8 or what? What's your 10-20? Repeat. Hey, thirty-three, what're you doin'?"

"Thirty-three here. I'm 10-8. My 10-20's Route 30 West."

"Thirty-three, 10-91."

"Roger that." Canoza switched to Channel 3. "I'm here, Vic, what's up?"

"I'll tell you what's up, you fuckin' meatball sub you. You missin' anything?"

"Huh? Missin' anything? What?" Canoza looked around on the seat. "Oh shit." Now he knew what hadn't felt right.

"Oh shit is right. You better get down there fast, you hear?"

"Aw man, Vic, it was just one of those things—"

"Don't aw-man me—and don't give me that one-of-those-things shit either, just get your ass down there and get it. And go light a candle I wasn't takin' a dump. 'Cause Nowicki woulda answered that call? Man, Boo, you really push it sometimes, no shit you do."

"I'll get it, I'll get it, don't worry."

"What should I be worried for? You're the one should be worried. Fuck's wrong with you—what'd you take it off for anyway? We just talked about that, man, remember?"

"C'mon, Vic, get up, alright? It musta slipped off my lap when I grabbed Jimmy."

"When you did what? Grabbed who?"

"Jimmy."

"Fuck you grab him for?"

"Never mind, it was personal."

"Hey! You're in uniform, you got a shield on, it's crowded, it's never personal—"

"How'd you know it was crowded?"

"Oh for crissake—it was 1700. What do people usually do at 1700, Boo, huh? Honest to God—hey, enough! Get down there and get it, you hear me? And put it on!"

"Alright, I hear ya. Can't make a mistake with you anymore, Jesus. You ain't my TP anymore, Vic, you know that?"

"Hey if I was, you wouldn't be pullin' this kinda happy horseshit, believe me."

"Well you ain't, okay? So get up. Startin' to weigh about a ton more than I wanna carry, okay?"

"Ohhhh so that's how it is, huh?"

"Yeah that's how it is. I ain't been a rookie for twenty-four years, which you can't seem to remember."

"Oh I remember alright. I remember plenty. You're the one havin' the trouble with his memory, buddy boy. Booboo."

"Hey, Vic, don't use that tone when you call me that."

"Tone? I used a tone with you? Oh excuse me, Booboo."

"Hey, Vic, knock it off, man, I mean it."

"You knock it off! I saved your big dago ass so many times,

Jesus—I saved your fuckin' job for you. Your fuckin' career! You wouldn't've had one it wasn't for me."

"What're you talkin' about?"

"Oh you don't know what I'm talkin' about? End of your pro period, everybody wanted to cut you loose."

"What're you sayin'?"

"You heard me, I ain't stutterin'."

"I know I heard you. Spell it out, man, draw me a picture."

"I'll draw you a picture alright. How's this? Everybody, Balzic, everybody senior to you in the department, the Safety Committee, they all said the same thing—let him go. He ain't worth the trouble he gonna cause. Me, I'm the only one talked for you. I talked my ass off for you. I convinced 'em. All of 'em. Wasn't for me you'd've been gone. Is that enough of a picture for you, you fuckin' meatball you."

Canoza didn't know what to say. He felt a terrible, queasy feeling in the middle of his stomach. It spread downward, upward, and outward. He felt humiliated. Embarrassed. Exposed. Shamed. He'd been driving the whole time he'd been talking to Stramsky, but suddenly he didn't know where he was going or why. Then he saw the overpass, the one for the Amtrak lines, and he knew as he drove under it that he was on Pittsburgh Street. Then he saw the L-shaped strip mall ahead, and the red and yellow sign for Jimmy's Suds and Subs, and he knew where he was going. But for the life of him, at that moment, he couldn't have said why.

He pulled into the first open slot he came to, turned off the radio and the ignition, and just sat there. He thought for a second he was going to start bawling. He almost wished he could. He couldn't, but he wished he could because he thought if he could he might be able to get rid of this awful queasy feeling spreading over his whole body. The queasier he felt, the more he tried to comprehend what Stramsky had said.

Everybody? The whole Safety Committee? Everybody who was senior to me in the department? Fuck, man, there wasn't anybody who wasn't senior to me. Even Balzic? Jesus, I thought Balzic liked me. He never said anything, he never told me he didn't like me, never told me I shouldn't be doing this or that or whatever. Did he tell me somethin' and I just can't remember? 'Cause I don't want to remember? Or am I too fuckin' stupid to remember? Not Balzic, I can't fuckin' believe that. He's the last guy would've fucked me around like that. Uh-uh. Never. He was too stand-up to fuck me around like that. That would've been really chickenshit, and if there was one thing he wasn't, he wasn't chickenshit. He would've called me in and told me faceup. I don't believe this. So why's Vic saying it? Man, that is really a ball-bustin' thing he did, sayin' that. Jesus Christ, why the fuck'd he do that? He didn't have to do that. That fucking hurt, man. That was chickenshit. . . .

Somebody rapping on the window startled him.

"Yo—what? Oh. It's you."

Lois the waitress stood there holding his vest, saying, "Well I can't give it to you if you don't roll the window down."

Canoza pushed the power button. Looking toward the dash, he said, "I could've come in for it, you didn't have to bring it out."

"Jimmy made me bring it out. He was scared you were gonna come in and blame it on him that you forgot it. He says he's gonna have to go to the emergency room, you almost tore his ear off—"

"Aw what's he talkin' about, almost tore his ear off, Jesus, he's so fulla crap sometimes. All I did was squeeze it, I didn't twist it. What's he care anyway, it ain't like he uses it to listen to anybody."

"Well you gonna take it or not?" Lois said, shifting from one foot to the other. "Why don't you—I mean, ain't you supposed to be wearin' this thing?"

"What're you—on the Safety Committee now? I got enough people bustin' my hump about that—gimme that thing."

"Okay okay, here, that's what I been tryin' to do, sheesh."

Canoza took the vest and tossed it on the seat beside him.

"Ain't you gonna put it on?"

"Hey. You delivered it, okay? So thanks. Now go back inside, go back to work for that creep. For nothin', go on."

"Well that's none of your business, who asked you anyway? You don't have to get all huffy."

"If it's none of my business, why'd you bring it up in front of me, huh? Sure sounded to me like you were tryin' to make it my business. And who's huffy? Not me."

"Well you just happened to be there when he said somethin', I wasn't bringin' it up in front of you!"

"Hey you don't want certain somebodies to know your business, you don't talk about it in front of those somebodies."

All this time Canoza had been staring out the windshield. Now he turned to her and said, "Hey, Lois? What're you doin' here, huh? You got somethin' you wanna discuss with a cop? Or with me in particular? 'Cause if you don't, I don't understand why you're still here. You brought me my vest, I thanked you, you're still here. What's up?"

She looked around, looked at her Keds sneakers, looked at him, and said, "Um, this is not official, okay? I mean it's not about me—"

"Yeah yeah, okay, it's about your girlfriend. Okay, what?"

"How'd you know it was about my girlfriend?"

"Just psychic, I guess. So, uh, she in the middle of a divorce, custody battle, what?"

"No. Nothin' like that. It's this guy, he keeps comin' to where she works. She never led him on or nothin'. And she never went out with him. She was just nice to him like everybody else, 'cause, you know, that's like, part of her job. They're not married, he's not anything to her."

"Yeah? So?"

"Well, he just, uh, I mean, he's like he's followin' her around."

"Does he touch her?"

"No. He's just, like, I mean, everywhere she goes, she looks around and there he is."

"That's harassment and stalking. Tell her file a complaint, that's all. She doesn't have to put up with that."

"Well she's scared if she does that, he's gonna really do somethin', you know?"

"I'm just tellin' you what she can do, that's all. Nobody can predict what anybody else is gonna do because of what she does. Tell her go to the courthouse, go to the DA's Office, tell 'em what's goin' on, they'll give her a PFA, they'll give him one, they'll file copies with the local cops—"

"Give her a what?"

"—protection from abuse order. And they have to file copies with the local PD, wherever she lives, and also with the state cops. Long as there's a copy of that PFA, that order, if they got a copy in their offices, whatever the PD, they gotta respond if she calls."

"Well isn't like there anything else she can do?"

"Like what?"

"Like get some kinda spray thing, tear gas, or whatever."

"You mean pepper spray?"

"Yeah, or Mace or whatever you guys carry—don't you carry Mace? Tear gas?"

"Nah. Pepper spray. OC. That Mace, there was a lotta problems with the wind."

"Oh. Or like, Jimmy was sayin', like maybe some kinda stunner gun."

"*Stunner* gun?"

"Isn't that what you call it? Or did Jimmy make that up?"

"No no, there's a thing called a stun gun. You touch somebody with it, it sorta paralyzes 'em. But you don't wanna mess with that."

"Why?"

"Coupla reasons. Like, for instance, your friend, uh, she any bigger than you? Or stronger? No offense, but does she lift weights, work out, run, study martial arts or somethin' like that, you know?"

"Uh, not much, no—I mean she tries. She just don't have a lotta time for that, you know, with her job. And her kid and everything."

"Uh-ha. Well, first, those stun things, they cost a lotta money. Second, say she gets one, and this guy decides to get handsy one night. He takes her by surprise, overpowers her, which ain't outta the realm of possibility, right?"

"Oh right, yeah."

"So whatever she's carryin', he takes it, he uses it on her. So the thing she thought was gonna protect her now winds up hurtin' her, you follow? Course that's true with any kinda weapon, you gotta know how to use it, and you gotta have your mind right to use it. Easy to shoot at paper targets, lotsa people do that. They get a gun, they get a permit to carry, they go waste a lotta ammo on paper, comes time to shoot somebody 'cause they're in danger, hey, suddenly it's a whole different story. Their body's in full fight or flight, their pulse is up to about a hundred and eighty a minute, two hundred maybe, not exactly the ideal conditions to be makin' those kinda decisions, whether you should shoot somebody, you know? Best thing for her to do is turn it over to the people in the DA's Office, let the pros handle it."

"Yeah, well sometimes those pros don't handle it so good."

"Yeah, granted, sometimes mistakes get made, I'm not gonna argue that. But see, the mistakes, everybody hears about those. The things that go right, you don't hear about them so much, those things, they don't get in the papers. Believe me, in cases like this, things go right a lot more than they go wrong, I'm tellin' you. Tell your friend go to the DA."

"You really think that's the best thing?"

"Yeah, I really do. I'm no expert, understand? I mean you listen to Jimmy, all I am is all muscle and no brains, but I've dealt with a lotta these things. Your friend's way better off lettin' the DA and the cops handle it than tryin' it herself. Unless, uh, your friend would maybe like me to make a personal appearance with this guy, you know? Whattaya think? Think she might prefer that instead?"

"Oh I don't know, you know? I don't know if, uh, if she'd think that was such a good idea."

"Well, that's all the advice I got, Lois. Except for one other thing. Your friend, she gets one of these pepper sprays?"

"Yeah?"

"Make sure she buys a new one, what she doesn't wanna do is borrow one's been layin' around in somebody's drawer five or six years. Especially if she also gets a stun gun."

"Why?"

" 'Cause those old sprays, they used to have alcohol in 'em, along with the OC."

"What's that stand for, OC?"

"Ah, that stands for oleoresin capsicum, that's the stuff that burns ya, the stuff they extract from the hot peppers. But that ain't my point. Those old sprays, the ones with alcohol in 'em? You spray somebody with one of those, and then you hit him with the stun gun? They catch fire. Just go poof, their face just practically explodes, that's why nobody makes 'em with alcohol anymore. So what I'm sayin' is don't let your friend, you know? Don't let her wind up with some old spray, especially if she's listenin' to Jimmy talk her into buyin' a stun gun, you understand me?"

"Yeah. I think so."

"Somethin' else too. They're illegal, you hear? Both those things. In this state they're prohibited offensive weapons. They're not listed in the statute exactly, they sorta come under the catchall phrase in that part of the statute, you know what I'm sayin'? I mean nobody comes down too hard on a woman for carryin' a spray—if that's all she does. Nobody's gonna do a stop-and-search on her, but she sprays some guy 'cause he gets handsy? And then she zaps him? That could get sticky in the DA's Office."

"Woo. This is a lot more complicated than I thought."

"Yeah. It usually is. Listen, talk to your friend, tell her what I said about maybe me just goin' to see the guy, give him some information. Some people, they're just ignorant, you know? They find out what's what, sometime the problem just goes away. Never know."

"Yeah. I'll tell her that. Probably. I mean I should."

"Yeah, and then lemme know what she says. Okay? We done here?"

"Yeah. I think."

"Well thanks for bringin' my vest out, Lois. Appreciate it."

"Oh don't mention it. Thank you. I mean it."

"Sorry I hurt your feelings. Didn't mean to, you know?"

"Oh that's alright. I know you didn't. You're just . . ."

"I'm just what?"

"You're just . . . you're just you, that's all."

"Whatever. Listen, like I said, some guys, you know, they get the right information from the right person, that's all they need. Don't need to go through the whole paperwork thing. Not everybody's nuts. Or deaf. There are some guys, you can talk to 'em."

"Is that what you'd do? Talk?"

"Hey, I know how to talk."

"The way you, uh, way you talked to Jimmy? Little while ago?"

"Well, see, Jimmy's a special case. He's always overestimatin' his brainpower. Been doin' that since we were kids. Hey, I gotta go, Lois. Your friend wantsa talk to me, you know my number, right?"

"Nine-one-one?"

"No, Lois, that's only for emergencies. Didn't I ever give you my card?"

"No. You cops have a card? You mean like a business card?"

"Yeah, Lois, a business card. We're in the information business, the cops. People call us all the time."

"You're puttin' me on, right?"

"Whatever, Lois. See ya tomorrow probably."

Canoza gave her one of his cards, then left her, arms folded across her chest as though she was suddenly chilled. In his side mirror, he could see her starting to run back into Jimmy's. He shook his head. She ran just like a girl. He hoped she didn't do anything stupid like listen to Jimmy about that stun gun. Skinny as she was, she wouldn't last ten seconds with any guy put his hands on her. Why'd all the good-looking ones wind up working for assholes like Jimmy? That was something else God was going to have to answer for. . . .

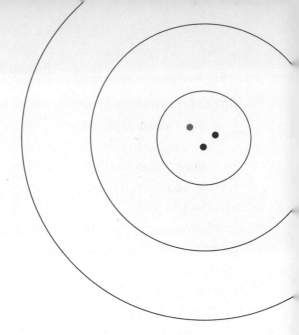

Reseta got back in his MU with the same disgusted feeling he always had after he'd delivered a juvenile to the detention center. No matter how many times he'd done it, there was always something sour about locking up a kid. Whether they gave him a lot of trouble or none—and this Maguire, or whoever he was, had been no worse than many of the rest and not nearly as bad as some—Reseta couldn't get over his own psychological hump about how young the kid was. Probably still fascinated by his reflection in mirrors, of fuzz on his upper lip, of hair sprouting in his armpits and in the middle of his chest or below his navel. Probably just beginning to puzzle out how to look like he was with a girl so he could brag to the boys.

Reseta knew what his disgust was about. He'd discussed his own childhood many times with a shrink. His "counseling" had lasted for a year, starting a week after his probationary period when he'd turned what should have been a straightforward arrest into an inexcusable assault and then-chief Mario Balzic had "strongly suggested" to Reseta that counseling was not negotiable: if he wanted to keep his shield, he'd not only make the weekly appointments but at least once a month would submit a written summary of his sessions. Balzic told Reseta, "Everybody's got axes to grind from when they were kids. Last thing I need in this department is somebody doesn't even know he's carryin' an ax."

It had started when Reseta was cruising the alleys in the Flats at the end of the first week he was in an MU without a training partner. He happened on a father beating his son with a piece of garden hose, and he came out of the MU with his baton like a lance and rammed it into the father's back without a word, not so much as a "Stop!" "Freeze!" "Police!"—nothing, according to the kid who was taking the beating, who was the worst witness against him when the lawyers were taking depositions for the civil suit.

The father wound up in Conemaugh General with a ruptured kidney; the city solicitor, upon council's unanimous recommendation, settled the suit with sealed results; the city wound up with a higher deductible in its liability insurance, and Reseta served the next six months on administrative probation, and the next twelve in counseling with Abe Stein, the psychologist of Balzic's choice.

Fortunately for Reseta, and despite all of his prejudices and all the ragging he took from the rest of the members of the department, he'd hit it off with Stein from the beginning. Plus, he was powerfully motivated to see the counseling through to the end for two reasons: one, of course, was that it had been "strongly suggested" to him by Balzic, and two because Reseta had wanted nothing else in life but to be first a soldier and then a cop. At eighteen he'd enlisted in the army and served his year in Vietnam from October 15, 1967, to October 15, 1968, with the mechanized infantry in the 25th Division. He was wounded four times, twice in one firefight. A piece of mortar shrapnel still floated in the soft tissue of his right buttocks. He kept telling himself he was going to have it removed, but after the pain of its occasional stab went away, he'd forget about it until the next time.

What had most interested Abe Stein was what he called Reseta's "psychological algebra" that equated the Viet Cong and North Vietnamese Army regulars with the Guinnan brothers. Stein was fascinated by that almost more than by Reseta's accounts of the continual harassment he'd endured from the Guinnans from first grade through his senior year in high school.

"And you understood this transference, this projection onto the Vietnamese? There was no doubt you knew what you were doing?"

"Oh no, uh-uh. I knew exactly what I was doin'. Absolutely."

"So you never saw yourself there as a patriot, a man serving his country in a time of war?"

"Patriot? Nah. That word never crossed my mind."

"You simply—if such a thing is possible to be simple—you wanted to be a soldier, is that it?"

"Yeah. Probably would've been one if I'd been born in Hanoi."

"Interesting. So, despite your existential participation, you were, uh, totally unconcerned with the politics of this war."

"I didn't know what the politics was. And wouldn't've cared if I did. I never heard one guy, my whole year there, never heard any enlisted man, any grunt, say one word about politics—except, and there was always this one exception—every time we got an FNG, there would always be—"

"A what? An F-what?"

"FNG. Fucking new guy."

"Oh. Go on."

"Uh, well, yeah, I mean, every time one of them came into the platoon, some guys, not me, 'cause I didn't care, but some guys would always pump him, you know, ask him what was goin' on back here. So you would hear about these protests and the marches and all that stuff, but I never paid any attention to it. I mean I'd listen to it, you know, but it didn't make any difference to me."

"And why was that, do you think?"

"Didn't apply to me. I wasn't goin' anywhere else. I was there. Didn't make any difference to me what was happenin' back here."

"But surely in your training, you must have received some indoctrination, some motivational training, for lack of a better phrase, about why you were going there, and what you were going to do when you got there, no?"

"Look, highest rank I made was sergeant, E5—and that was only the last month I was there. I'd been actin' squad leader for like two months, and they finally gave me the stripes and the raise. But all I ever heard from our platoon leader, either from a lieutenant when we had one, or from the platoon sergeant, was, uh, this is where we're goin', this is what we're gonna do when we get there, either set up a base camp, or go on ambush patrol, or be the anvil for the hammer—"

"The what?"

"Search and destroy. You were either the anvil, you set up an ambush, and another unit did the sweep, they were the hammer, or vice versa, and the idea was the one unit was supposed to push the VC or the NVA your way and you were supposed to take 'em out. Most of the time it didn't work, I guess 'cause we were in the APCs, we sorta figured they always heard us comin', I don't know—"

"The AP-what?"

"APCs. Armored personnel carriers. That's what mechanized infantry was. Is. They had tracks like a tank, they could hold a squad, you know, thirteen guys—but we never had a full squad the whole time I was there. And it doesn't have a cannon like tanks. Biggest weapon was a .50-caliber machine gun. In a turret on top. But one RPG could take you outta action real fast. Hit the turret, it'd blow it right off—"

"RPG?"

"Yeah. Rocket-propelled grenade. Some of those slopes were pretty good with those things, man. Put a lotta tracks outta action. Lotta guys too. Between them and the mortars, sometimes it was NFF."

"No fucking fun?"

"You got it. None whatsoever."

"But, uh, you don't seem to have ever been really all that distressed by this."

"I wasn't. I liked bein' a soldier. I think maybe—no maybes

about it, I'm sure—if I hadn't wanted to be a cop, I would've stayed in. Been a thirty-year man."

"So are you sayin' you were never afraid?"

"No, that's not what I'm sayin'. Nah, there were times, I mean I was afraid real bad a coupla times. Once we caught hell for—I don't know how long 'cause I was unconscious for most of it—but I heard like six, seven hours. They musta had two battalions. They weren't supposed to be anywhere near us, I mean, we were lookin' for 'em, but this lieutenant we had at that time, he told us they were like maybe six clicks northwest of where we were. Six kilometers. And we were goin' down this road through this, uh, rubber plantation. I guess at one time it was French. So there are these rubber trees on both sides of the road, meanwhile, dead ahead of us, I could see this tree line, you know, dense, about maybe two hundred meters in front of the lead APC, just jungle, you know? Like a green wall. I was in the turret in the fourth one back, I could see that whole tree line, man, it just, I don't know how to describe it, it just went from trees to smoke, like that! One after another, so close together they sounded like some giant wooshy machine gun, all these RPGs were comin' at us, man, one went by my head, missed me by less than a foot. And the first three APCs, I mean, I couldn't even blink it happened so fast, tracks were flyin', turrets were flyin', guys were flyin', somebody's hand hit me in the chin, like a thumb and three fingers, and I just bailed, just dove outta that turret, and I'm on the ground, runnin' back, all I got's a .45, I managed to get behind I think it was the sixth track in line, sixth, seventh, I don't know, but I knew we stayed there, we were all dead. It was just flat. Open. No dikes, no ditches, no canals, nothin' to get down into.

"There were twelve APCs in all. First three were done in the first five seconds. But at the end of the column, this FNG was drivin' the last one. I didn't know him except his nickname was Hog, 'cause he would eat all the C rations nobody else would touch. And he couldn't see anything but the APC right in front of him, so he didn't know what was goin' on, and the asshole wouldn't believe us, the guys that were runnin' back, all the guys that could move, they bailed just like me, and here comes the lieutenant walkin' back like he's on the beach lookin' for seashells, just amblin', you know? And his right arm is gone, blood's spurtin' out like a hose, man, and obviously he's in shock, and guys're screamin' at him to get down, and he makes it all the way back to where I am and just keels over, you know, face-first. So I knew he was dead. Which was lucky for me 'cause he was still carryin' his M-16 in his good hand. So then I had somethin' to shoot with.

"But those slopes, man, they had us out there in the open—and I'll never understand this—if they would've just spread out along that tree line? They would've got us all. They would've got us all in the first five minutes—if it had taken that long. Man, the only cover we had was the first three, the ones they blew the tracks off of. If they'd've spread out, they could've got the rest easy, 'cause when we stopped we closed up, we were way too close together, we were only like ten, twelve meters apart.

"And the worst part was we couldn't convince this Hog asshole to turn his track around and get outta there. He kept sayin', where's the lieutenant, where's the lieutenant? I ain't movin' till the lieutenant tells me, and I'm tryin' to tell the jagoff the lieutenant's dead, and the captain, the company CO, I figured he had to be dead too, 'cause he was in the second track, so I'm screamin' at him, you know, turn this thing around and get outta here, you're blockin' everybody, nobody can move, and the idiot just sits there. So I did get scared when I shot him. A little bit. Afterwards."

"You shot him?"

"Yeah. He wouldn't turn his track around, and he wouldn't get outta the driver's seat, so . . ."

"So you shot him?"

"Yeah."

"Uh . . . dead?"

"Yeah dead. He wouldn't move. Kept hollerin' he was only takin' orders from the lieutenant, I kept tellin' him the lieutenant was dead, he wouldn't believe me, I tried pullin' him outta the seat, he pulled his .45, told me to get away from him, meanwhile, we're takin' RPGs fast as they can load 'em, he's wavin' his .45 at me, then somethin' hit the turret, I didn't know what, but it made him turn around, take his eyes off me for a second and, uh, when he did I shot him. I mean, he might as well've been sittin' there with both his tracks blown off—except they weren't. And on both sides of us are all these rubber trees, I mean those APCs are powerful, but they couldn't flatten trees thick as those rubber trees. So how were we supposed to get outta there if we didn't move the last track in line? It was a narrow road. Couldn't go around him."

"Well obviously you did get out."

"Yeah. But not right away. Not for six or seven hours we didn't. We got turned around, the ones that could move, eight of 'em, but we only got, I don't know, maybe eight hundred, nine hundred meters back that road and I guess we got hit with a hand grenade or maybe a satchel charge, I don't know what, I just know we lost our right track, and then we were stuck again. And started takin' fire. Broadside. I found out later, it was a small unit of VC, maybe twenty guys, maybe not that many, and for some reason, after they blew the track on our right, all they had was AKs. I mean, they didn't have any rockets, which believe me . . . man, if they'd've had them, we would've been slaughtered. 'Cause the goofy thing, I mean, the NVA behind us? Who were the ones in front of us when they opened up? I mean we were only like a thousand meters from them. They should've been nailin' us. But after the first couple seconds they never hit another one of us. Either we were farther away from them than I thought or else they must've used up all their RPGs in the first couple minutes. 'Cause after that it was just the ones on our right givin' us hell, they had us pinned there for, I don't know, hours. I took one in the arm, and then another one, it hit me in the helmet, bounced off my skull, knocked me out, for I don't know how long. When I finally woke up, we were on our way back to the base camp. Which was really strange. We never did get any artillery support, and when we finally got air support, they were already cuttin' out—that's what I was told anyway. I mean . . . it was just all fucked up. Which was the way everything was there. But anyway for the most part, I was just, uh, you know, unconscious. But we really got shot up. I mean we weren't at full strength by anybody's count, but we started out with what was supposed to be a company, and there was only like, I don't know, maybe thirty guys made it back in one piece."

"But if I understand you, the only time you were afraid was when you thought about shooting this driver, this Hog."

"Yeah."

"Why?"

"Why? Well if somebody wanted to make somethin' of it, I mean, hey, that was murder. I mean even I knew that. In the army that's a capital offense. They hang you."

"And that's what you were afraid of? Hundreds of enemy soldiers firing at you for hours and that's the only thing that frightened you, is that what you're saying?"

"Yeah, pretty much. I knew I could get hung for that. And if I got hung I was never gonna be a cop."

"Are you being facetious?"

"You mean am I jokin'? No. Uh-uh. That's the way I used to think when I was there. See, let me explain somethin'. When I first got there, I knew that none of the training I went through back here, none of that was gonna make any difference. I mean it was all blanks, you know? There was only this one time they had us crawlin' under barbed wire while they were firin' live rounds over us with a couple machine guns, but even an idiot knew that as long as you kept your belly on the ground you weren't gonna get hit. I mean, c'mon, they weren't gonna kill any of us to prove a point, that's ridiculous.

"But I knew once I got over there, anybody shootin' at me if they saw me crawlin', they weren't gonna be aimin' two feet above my butt. So I made up my mind, I was gonna find the sharpest guy in my unit, the one who'd been there the longest and who everybody looked up to, and I was gonna follow him around like tan on sand till I learned everything he knew."

"So you didn't consider, uh, the randomness of death in combat?"

"Randomness? You mean luck?"

"Yes. That no matter what you did, you couldn't protect yourself from the, uh, utterly hit-or-miss aspect of life or death there."

"No. And I'm not stupid. I didn't think I was immortal, or unkillable, or whatever. But the whole time I was flying over there, the whole way across the Pacific, I kept tellin' myself over and over, learn as much as you can as fast as you can, don't be a hero, dig fast, keep your weapon clean. I know it sounds like so much bullshit, but that's the way I thought. I wouldn't allow myself to think that no matter what you did or didn't do you could still get killed. That was too . . . I couldn't live with that . . . I had to believe that I was gonna survive because of what I learned . . . and I knew that fear would keep me from learnin' it.

"I mean fear is fear, everybody's afraid of somethin'. I mean the noise . . . Jesus, the noise of war, man, it's . . . it's unbelievable. But no matter what, the thing you can't allow to happen is that you get so afraid you get paralyzed. 'Cause you . . . I mean, you get panicked, you get your heart bangin' so hard you think it's gonna bust right out your sternum, I mean, that is not the way to control your body. And you gotta control your body when you're under that kinda . . . extreme stress like that. That's what I learned from Jukey Johnson."

"The smartest man in your unit?"

"Oh absolutely. Smartest, most observant, coolest, most experienced. We'd go on patrol, or go set up an ambush, he was always out front. I asked him why he did that. He was the platoon sergeant, senior NCO in the platoon, he didn't have to do that. Half the time he was there he was our platoon leader. All those lieutenants, they didn't last too long. But he said he didn't trust anybody to see what

he could see, or could hear, or could smell, or just, you know, sense
it. That's why he was out front. So I just attached myself to his back.
He didn't like it at first, didn't trust me at all. But that was his third
tour there, I mean I never met anybody else had been there more
than two. Only him."

"So was he a lover of war? Combat? Death? Killing? A seeker of
extreme stimulation? A stimulation addict perhaps?"

"That's a dumb question."

"Oh? Why?"

"'Cause that's what I asked him, and that's what he said to me."

"Surely he said something else to justify himself. Or to explain
himself, to rationalize his behavior."

"Well, among other things, he was from Mississippi. Same town
where they killed those three Freedom Riders, remember? Those
two Jewish kids and that colored kid?"

"Yes, I remember."

"Well he said the army was the only place where crackers had to
treat him with respect because of his rank and the ribbons on his
chest. He'd been in fourteen years and was on his third tour in Nam
when I met him—I said that before, right?"

"Right."

"Plus, he'd done somethin' like seven, eight months in Korea before the armistice got signed there, so he'd seen a lotta shit hittin' a
lotta fans, and when he finally started trustin' me, he told me everything. Said I was the first cracker he ever trusted. Last two months
he was there, we used to take turns on point, that's how much he
trusted me."

"And you thought what he told you would keep you alive."

"It did."

"If you think it did, then I suppose it did."

"There's no supposin' about it. It did."

"It's not for me to say whether your beliefs were founded in reality. If you believed they were real, then for you they were."

"What you're sayin' is there's a difference between what's real and what we perceive as real. Lotta people say that, even Balzic says that."

"Oh I'm sure he does."

"Well I can't argue that. Except when I was there. I'll argue that till the day I die about what I learned from Jukey Johnson."

"Listen, James, it's not my function here to be purposely contentious, but the fact is I served in the marines in World War Two. I was on Okinawa. Went ashore in the third wave, and when it was over I walked up the ship's ladder under my own power. I have no idea how I survived. Nearest I came to being wounded was that I nearly lost my toes from foot rot. But my perception of that reality on that island for those who fell all around me is that death or mutilation in modern warfare is absolutely random. It has not the slightest rationality to it. No amount of study or wisdom or insight or intuition will keep you alive if you happen to be standing where the bullets are flying or the shells are exploding. It's simple physics, understandable to the average high school kid, but how those physics are applied, why one man dies, another loses both arms, another his eyes, another goes insane, and yet another doesn't suffer a scratch—it's totally irrational."

"Yeah, okay. I get what you're sayin', but see, I told you before, I couldn't let myself believe that. I would never've lasted a week if I'd let myself believe that. I would've been . . . I mean, I would've been paralyzed with fear. I don't know how many times I saw it happen. The first day, when I got dropped off in my unit's base camp, it was at a place called Cu Chi, and right after I got off the chopper, I could hear these boom boom, and then again two more, boom boom, and then a couple seconds later three more, and this guy, he was walkin' toward me, when he heard the first two he just dropped, right into this big puddle, and he just curled up and started cryin'. And they were way off, these noises, I could see the smoke from them, but they were at least a couple hundred meters from us, way out there. But this guy was just a pile of clothes in the middle of a puddle.

"And this colored guy walked up, asked me for my orders, and when I tried to hand 'em over, I had to wait till he pulled this guy to his feet and then he looked at my orders and told me to help him take this guy to the aid station, and then he took me back to his area and introduced me as an FNG. But I'll never forget the way this colored guy was lookin' at everything, his eyes, they never stopped movin', they were constantly scannin' everything, me, everything behind me, the guy in the puddle, I said to myself, hey, this guy knows somethin'. And I found out real soon, sure enough, he knew everything, man. And I mean everything."

"So he survived. And you did too by learning what he knew. So you think that, uh, you perceived that as the way you survived."

"No. He didn't survive. I mean he survived Nam. But after his tour was over, he went on leave back to Mississippi, and some cracker ran him down with a truck, broke both his legs, crushed his pelvis, broke coupla vertebra in his lower back. He's in a wheelchair. I mean, he survived, he's alive. But he can't walk."

"You stay in touch with him?"

"Try to. Call him every month or so, see how it's goin'. That wasn't random either."

"Excuse me? How so?"

"This cracker thought he was with some civil rights workers. Thought he was there to stir up some trouble, you know, it was like two, three weeks after Martin Luther King got shot. But he just happened to pick that time to take his leave, that's all. Fact was, those civil rights workers, I mean, they were bustin' his balls about bein' in the man's army, over there killin' his Vietnamese brothers and all that crap. So this cracker sees him talkin' to those people, he's in civvies, cracker must've figured he's one of them. And first chance he gets he runs him down."

"And you don't think that was random?"

"No, I think that's absolutely logical. 'Cause he told me, Jukey, straight out, he said arguin' with those civil rights kids, when they started trashin' him to his face, that distracted him. Made him forget where he was—just long enough to get hurt—I mean he said he forgot that he was in Mississippi and there were people there wanted to hurt him just as much as if he was in Nam. But it would've never happened to him in Nam, 'cause he expected Victor Charlie to be anywhere and everywhere. He'd've been in Nam he would've smelled that cracker comin' fifty meters away, believe it."

"How do you explain that the man in the truck singled him out? You don't think that was random? Why didn't he crash his truck into all of them while they were arguing?"

"You'd have to ask him. So okay, I guess, alright, you could make the case that was bad luck. But I keep tellin' you, I couldn't let myself think like that. I would never have been able to move if I'd let my mind get full of thoughts like that. I saw guys, I mean, they'd get under a mortar attack, be fine for a while, then just stand up, start screamin'. Guaranteed dust-off time, physical or mental, one or the other. And you can't tell me one's any better than the other. They're just different, that's all."

"Psychological death is the same as physical death?"

"Hey, I went to see this guy in the VA hospital in Pittsburgh, you know, the one off Washington Boulevard there?"

"I know where it is. Three days a week, I work there."

"Oh. Well, anyway, I heard this guy was there. He was a good guy. I got to know him better than most, maybe 'cause he was from Pittsburgh. But he was an okay dude. Funny. Reliable. Always did what he was supposed to. Nobody had to tell him anything twice—for about eleven months. Then he got short. Thirty days. All of a sudden, he just couldn't stand the thought that he'd get dusted off when he was that close to goin' home. I mean, he just got that thought in his mind, and, man, he was finished. Paralyzed. I mean literally. Couldn't eat, couldn't brush his teeth, couldn't do anything. Finally, I didn't have any choice, I had to take him to the aid station, and the dude just wigged out there, man. Went after a medic with a scalpel. We finally got him in a jacket, they shot him full of morphine, MPs put him on a plane back. And he's been in the hospital ever since. When I went to see him, he didn't know me from a cheeseburger. His mind was alphabet soup. He's never gonna get outta there."

"And you equate that with being dead?"

"He's breathin', but if you call that livin', forget it."

"And you think this is because he let himself think wrong."

"No question. Why was he fine for eleven months? Suddenly he gets short, I mean, hey, if you last long enough to get short, you're gonna get the short-timer's attitude. Everybody does. I had it too. But it just exaggerated everything I knew, just made me double my concentration on what I was doin' and how I had to do it. Jukey used to say, emotion starts with a thought, and fear starts with a wrong thought. I refused to let myself think wrong."

"Yet you came out of your vehicle and used your baton like a lance. Rammed it into a man's kidney without identifying yourself as a police officer, without—according to the report I read—without so much as one word of warning."

"Uh . . . you got me there, what can I say?"

"I don't want to have you anywhere, James. I want you to tell me, and I especially want you to tell yourself—what you were thinking at that moment—that's why you're here. This is the wall we run into every time we get to this point. How many times have we been over this, is that your question? How many times have you been here? And how many times have you refused to answer when I ask you why you didn't identify yourself?"

"I wanted him . . . I wanted him to know . . . I was thinking I wanted him to know what it felt like to be on the receiving end of that."

"Oh come on, James, you aren't Superman, it's not your job to go around avenging injustice, delivering retribution on behalf of the downtrodden. Life is not a comic book. You took an oath to serve and protect. You took all the courses, passed all the tests, passed your probationary period with exemplary behavior, got outstanding fitness reports from all your teachers, all your training partners. I've read your records a dozen times. Then suddenly you see a father beating a son, and you forget how to speak? Suddenly you can't summon the brainpower to identify yourself as a police officer? Suddenly you can't remember the word *freeze?* Suddenly you find yourself with only one possible option to stop this beating? Suddenly the only way you know how to stop this beating is to take your baton and, without one word of warning, ram it into this man's back and rupture his kidney? Are you seriously asking me to believe that's what happened here? This, from a man who endured twelve months in Vietnam under the extreme stress of guerrilla warfare, who survived that warfare by controlling his mind, by refusing to allow himself to think a wrong thought? This man—you—you're trying to tell me now, that when you put your hands on that baton, that was your thought process?"

"Pretty stupid, huh?"

"No, James. Not stupid. Intelligence is not the issue here. Evasion is the issue here."

"You tellin' me I'm supposed to know why I was thinkin' that way? I thought you were the one supposed to do that."

"James, please, everything you've told me so far tells me you calculate everything you do. We've been going at this now for how many months? Eleven?"

"Yeah. Next report I write for Balzic will be number eleven."

"And how many times have we been over what you learned from Jukey Johnson?"

"I don't know, fourth, fifth, it's all startin' to, uh, blend in, run together, one session sounds, looks, I don't know, like the rest."

"You think this is the fourth or fifth time? Are you serious?"

"I don't know, I said."

"I don't know, I don't know, please, James—stop whining and think! We've been going over this since the third month. Comes up at least once every session. And how many times have I asked you, for example, how old you were when you made the decision to be a soldier?"

"Four, five, I'm not sure exactly."

"Well I ask you again: how old? Do you remember?"

"Not exactly, no. Pretty young though."

"And I ask you again, do you remember what prompted it?"

"Yeah. What I told you before. What I keep tellin' you. Probably just took a beatin' from one of the Guinnans. Or all of 'em."

"Well what was your thinking like then?"

"I don't know."

"Well did you just say to yourself, for example, that when I grow up I'm going to be a priest, so I can hear the Guinnans' confession? So I can give them absolution, so they won't have to feel guilty for tormenting me—is that what you were thinking?"

"You kiddin' me? Priest?! Hear their—get out. Say their funeral mass maybe."

"Well if you weren't thinking that, perhaps you were thinking you might grow up to be a soldier? Were you thinking, if I become a soldier I can learn how to defend myself against my enemies, so when these Guinnans pull this crap, I'll be able to defeat them, did you think something like that?"

"I doubt that's what I was thinkin'. But it might've been somethin' like that. Maybe it was, I'm not sure."

"And do you remember what you answer when I ask if you were influenced to make that decision by watching war movies? Or war shows on TV? Or reading about war?"

"And I'm tellin' you again, for the umpteenth time, whatever, I don't know. Maybe. But if I was, it wasn't anything specific. Nothin' I can remember anyway."

"Please. Stop with this nonsense about the umpteenth time. That's ridiculous. I just told you how many times we've discussed this issue."

"Alright, alright."

"And what do you answer when I ask if you were influenced by a relative? Your father perhaps, or an uncle? What do you say?"

"I say no. Because I wasn't."

"Because your father was not a soldier, correct? He'd never been a soldier. And you had no uncles or cousins or siblings, no one in your family, correct? Who was a soldier?"

"Correct."

"So who does that leave, James, tell me."

"What do you mean who does that leave?"

"Oh James, James, after your mentor Johnson—you're the second most calculating soldier in Vietnam—with whom did you equate the VC, the NVA? Who, James?"

"Uh, the Guinnans?"

"Alleluia, alleluia, the man has spoken. He recognizes, finally, that it was all about the Guinnans."

"Well . . . yeah . . . I guess."

"You guess?"

"Okay. So I don't guess. Sure. Those pricks . . . man, every morning, last thing I did before I left our house, I took a leak. And the last thing before I left school too, I made sure I didn't have any piss left in me. 'Cause the last thing I wanted was to let 'em see me piss my pants 'cause of how scared I was."

"And, uh, nobody defended you, nobody came to your defense?"

"Nah. My mother, you know, she tried. She went to their house coupla times, when I'd come home with my clothes messed up. They'd lay off for a couple weeks. Then they'd start in again."

"And your father? What about him?"

"My father, I told you, he had a heart condition. Congestive heart failure. He was lucky he could walk, you know, lucky he could still, you know, still be able to go to work. Had an office job. With the railroad. Down the repair yards. Then he died."

"And you were how old?"

"When he died? Fourteen."

"And what about your siblings? Did you have brothers?"

"No. Why you askin' me? You know I had two sisters. Both older. Fact, when he died, Lorraine, she was already married. Wasn't livin' at home anymore. And Louise, she was goin' to business school. Then she went to work for the state. For the Revenue Department. She still lives at home. Me too."

"Got a girl?"

"Had one."

"What happened?"

"She married this guy when I was in, uh, in Nam. My mother sent me the announcement . . . outta the paper, you know?"

"Never told you herself?"

"Nah. Apparently that, uh, that must've slipped her mind."

"How'd that affect you?"

"Not much. We weren't that close. Least I wasn't. Obviously she wasn't either."

"Was that another thing you refused to allow to affect you?"

"Yeah, I guess you could say that. Pissed me off for a while, but, uh . . . not for that long. I said we weren't that close."

"You wouldn't let it?"

"Yeah. Exactly. I had more important things on my mind right then. Fact, that was right in the middle of Tet. You know, the big NVA offensive? They were supposed to push us into the sea. With the whole population, they were supposed to rise up, kick our asses outta there. Load of shit that was."

"Excuse me?"

"Well, you know, every time somebody mentions Tet, they call it the Tet Offensive, you know, with the big capital O, like oh wow, the VC and the NVA, they put on this big offensive, they kicked our ass, changed the course of the war and all that. But that's bullshit. I mean, in our area, where I was, Tet was nothin' special. Around Saigon and Hue now, couple other cities, I guess it was, I don't know, but, hey, every book I've read since I've been back, they all say the same thing—after Tet, the VC was no longer an effective force. They got hammered during Tet. Now maybe the books I'm readin', maybe they're bullshit propaganda, I don't know. But everybody I talked to comin' home, and the whole year after I was back, when I was down Fort Jackson, everybody who'd been in the southeast in Nam there, and everything I've read, it wasn't us got our asses kicked during Tet, it was the VC."

"For somebody who insists he was nothing but a soldier, who was never interested in the politics, you're pretty vehement about the outcome."

"Nah. Well. Okay, I guess, yeah. But I don't like people who weren't there talkin' when they don't know anything about anything."

"Well I assure you, James, the Tet Offensive made quite an impression here. Whether it was a real victory or a propaganda victory, I'm not wise enough to say, but it certainly made an impression, all those TV images of Saigon practically under siege. I mean after all, that was the capital."

"So what? It was a civil war. During the Civil War here? I mean, where was Washington, huh? Right in the middle of enemy territory the whole war—I mean, wasn't it?"

"Yes of course, but it was never brought under siege the way Saigon was—"

"Well maybe Robert E. Lee shoulda thought about it. Maybe old Giap, maybe he didn't read Lee's memoirs—or if he did, maybe he didn't pay attention to them."

"For somebody who keeps insisting he doesn't know anything about the politics of war, you've certainly got strong opinions."

"Aw hell, that doesn't mean I know anything. The books I read, they're out there for anybody wants to read 'em. Just put what I read up against what I did and where I was, that's all."

"Let's get back to your father."

"What about him?"

"Did it bother you that he couldn't defend you? From the Guinnans?"

"Maybe. But I don't think so. I knew he couldn't do much in the way of physical stuff. So, no, I don't think that bothered me."

"So did that influence your thinking? About wanting to be a soldier—and not just wanting to be a soldier, but wanting to learn how to be the best soldier you could be?"

"I don't think it had anything to do with it."

"Don't you think you saw yourself at that time as being totally helpless? According to what you've said before, you were fourteen when your father died, so you were what, in ninth grade?"

"Yeah. Probably."

"C'mon, James, no probablies. You had to endure all or some of the Guinnans' torment for three or three and a half more years—after your father's death, right?"

"Yeah. Sounds right."

"Why are you being so hesitant? You know it's right, it doesn't just sound right."

"Okay, alright, it's right. What's your point?"

"My point? Oh really, James, c'mon, what're we doing here? What are you doing here?"

"I guess I'm supposed to be figurin' out why I didn't ID myself when I, uh, you know—"

"You guess?!"

"Okay, no guessin', yeah—"

"Listen, James, and listen carefully. What I'm telling you is, if you want to keep doing this job you say is the only other job you've ever wanted—besides soldiering—you're going to have to come to terms with what you did. And not only for your chief's comprehension, or for your City Council's comprehension, but much more importantly, much much more importantly, for your comprehension. Because, James, you're walking around with a bomb in your mind. And if you don't start talking about why it's there, it's going to go off again. Just like it did in that alley. And when it goes off again, and if you don't get it resolved here, it will go off again, you're gone. Not only gone from this job but very likely gone into prison. Because you were extremely lucky this time, James. I know you don't believe in luck, but even you, when you consider the ramifications of what you did, I mean, my God, James, you cannot deny—can you?—how lucky you are this guy had a really crummy lawyer? Or that he didn't die? People have died as a result of one kidney rupturing, James, it is not that remote a medical probability. Would you like me to arrange a meeting with a pathologist, huh? So you could hear for yourself how lucky you were?"

"No, thanks. You don't have to do that."

"Then talk, James. You want the bomb out of your mind, you've got to start talking. We've been shadowboxing around this issue for months—it is the issue, James. It's why you're here. And there's something else you should be aware of. You write a monthly report for Balzic? So do I."

"You think I didn't know that?"

"I'm sure you do now. Do you also know that he calls me after he reads them?"

"I'm sure he does."

"And are you sure what his reactions have been? To this point?"

"Well . . . knowin' him—and I'm not sayin' I do, understand? But I figure he's gotta start bein' a little, uh, a little impatient with the progress here. Or the lack of it."

"Bravo, James. Bravo. He signed you up for a year. We're in the eleventh month. He thought as sharp as you are, it wouldn't take half that long."

"What'd you say?"

"I said, sharp or not—and he is sharp—even the sharpest guy can get to be very dull when his perimeter looks like it's about to be breached."

"Is that what you think I'm doin'?"

"Yes, James, that's exactly what I think you're doing. We've talked about Vietnam, about soldiering, about growing up with the Guinnan brothers as your daily nemesis, a twice-daily torment, going to school, coming from school, more if they happened to catch you out and about after school. We've gone around and around and around this, and yet somehow, you don't seem to make the connection between the helplessness you felt every day for twelve years at the hands of the Guinnan brothers, who were much bigger, much stronger than you, and what you saw in this boy's beating at the hands of his much bigger, much stronger father—which provoked you to attack him. Without warning, James. An absolute no-no for a police officer."

"I don't know what to say."

"Oh James, look. You're a very bright guy. Everybody who was ever your superior whether in the army or in the police training classes you had to pass in order to be hired—you were tops in your classes, either first or second. Fitness reports from your training partners, they're unanimous in their praise and commendations. Yet here we sit, as we invariably do, after we have rehashed events I know almost as well as you do, here we are, both of us staring at this apparently impenetrable wall which you seem unable to recognize is there! Here's what it comes to, James, yes or no, you want to be a cop?"

"Yes. Absolutely."

"This is only the second thing you've ever wanted in life, correct?"

"Yes, correct."

"Then, James, listen to me. Imagine it's not me talking now, but your mentor in Vietnam, Jukey Johnson. Imagine it's Jukey sitting here telling you this: James, you want to stay alive as a cop? You've got to bring all your senses to bear on this one issue. Your sight, your hearing, your taste, your smell, your touch, all of them, if you want to stay alive as a cop in Rocksburg, James, you've got to bring them all to focus on this one issue—"

"I wanted to surprise him."

"You wanted to surprise him?"

"Yeah. I wanted to surprise him. I knew if I said anything he'd turn around. I wanted him to get hit without knowin' it was comin'. Like it was . . . like it was . . ."

"Like it was what, James?"

"Like it was God. Like it was the hand of God come down to strike him for what he was doin' to this kid."

"Like it was the hand of God . . . okay, James. Now we're starting to get somewhere. Now of course, all you have to do is explain to me—and to yourself—why you thought you were, at that particular moment, God's agent. Why you thought you were doing God's work, when everything I've learned from you about you says to me clearly that you are a man looking, not for faith, but for information. In all the months we've been talking here, you've never so much as mentioned the word *church*—until earlier today. When I suggested that you might've wanted to grow up to be a priest, the look on your face was contempt. In all your talk about combat, you insist it is not random, that luck plays no part, and you never say one word about prayer, in everything you've said about your twelve months in Vietnam, you never mention the word *chaplain,* yet suddenly when you start to talk about what you were thinking when you put your hands on that baton, you talk about surprise, you talk about making this man think it was the hand of God come down to punish him for his beating of a helpless child. James, explain please, if you would, because I am now really confused."

"I . . . I used to pray all the time when I was a kid. I prayed that God would kill them all, all the Guinnans, their whole family, mother, father, even their dog. Prayed all the time. When I was an altar boy in St. Malachy's, I'd be doin' what I was supposed to, bringin' the water and the wine and the wafer to the priest, standin' there while he was washin' his hands for communion, I'd be prayin', you know, hey, God, please, for me, just this one thing, okay? Please make the cocksuckers die. But he never did. And no matter how many candles I lit, no matter how many times I asked him, no matter what I did, the only thing I could do, uh, the only way I could stand the pain, was to know there was no pee in me so at least they wouldn't have the satisfaction of seein' me piss my pants. That was all I could do. So . . . uh, when my father died, I mean I really liked my father. I felt real bad for him 'cause he couldn't do the simplest things, he'd get all outta breath. But every day, man, rain, snow, sun-shine, whatever, he left the house, he walked all the way to the yards, he did his job, he made it all the way home. I respected that. I ad-mired that. Even though he couldn't help me, I never lost my re-spect for him. But when he died, when God took him to a better place this priest said, I said bullshit. He took my father but he lets the fuckin' cocksuckin' Guinnans live? I said fuck you, good-bye. That's the last time you're ever gonna see me. Never went back to church again."

"Okay. Okay. I follow that. That's very plain, very understand-able. So how did you get from there to the hand of God coming down to take this man by surprise? How do you get from there to you—you, James Reseta, who at age fourteen says fuck you to God, and then comes out of his MU with his baton without a word of identification of who he is but with his mind filled with the idea that he is to be God's instrument to take this man by surprise and punish him? How do we make that transition, James, you wanna ex-plain that? Because I'm very interested in that. And because you should be too."

"I been thinkin' about it. When I'm alone that's what I think about. When I'm alone that's all I think about."

"So why haven't you raised it here, why keep that to yourself?"

"Because I can't put it together."

"Excuse me?"

"I can't make it come out right—I don't even know how to say this, it's all mixed up. I know I'm nobody's avenging angel. That's the last thing I am—or wanna be. But when I saw that kid takin' that beating, I thought you motherfucker you. Don't you feel big, huh? Well how big you gonna feel when I swoop down on your ass like a hawk, like an eagle, an eagle on a fish, whoosh, clamp, you're in my claws, bingo, up and away, your ass in my claws and nothin' you can do about it, how you gonna feel then?"

"And what is this, James? Is this the calculated reaction of a po-lice officer to a crime in progress?"

"No."

"Then what is it?"

"It's the, uh . . . it's the emotional reaction of a boy."

"To what?"

"To somethin' that happened . . . a long time ago."

"No, James, not that long ago. You're twenty-three now. Five years ago, what was happening to you? Five years, James. What? Pick any day from your last year in high school."

"I was takin' a beatin' from Teddy Guinnan."

"Where?"

"In the locker room."

"Why? What was it about?"

"About? It didn't have to be about anything."

"No, James, think this through. C'mon, you're very close. Don't stop thinking now. What was it about?"

"It was about him, you know, just fuckin' with me. Humiliatin' me. Givin' everybody a laugh."

"So what was it about?"

"It was about him . . . him doin' what he wanted . . . with me."

"That's right, James. Which meant he had the what?"

"He had the power."

"Exactly, James. He had the power. To do what he wanted. Why did he have the power?"

"Because . . . I don't know, 'cause there was nothin' to stop him."

"Exactly. For no other reason than there was nothing, and nobody, to stop him."

"Right. So?"

"So? What do you mean, so?"

"So what's that have to do with me rammin' the guy's kidney?"

"James, come on, put it together. All your prayers—your unanswered prayers. All the times you had no one to come to your defense. And what have you wanted out of life? To be a soldier, to be a policeman. To belong to a military organization. To belong to a paramilitary organization. Put it together, come on, man! Yes?"

"I guess there's somethin' I'm just not pickin' up on here, I don't know."

"James, a very smart man once wrote that if you have a bulldozer, you don't need faith to move a mountain. All you need to know is how to operate it. You don't understand? You can't see? You can't connect that your time in the army, your time in the police, that what you were building was your own bulldozer? You don't comprehend that?"

"Well . . . you put it that way, yeah. Sure."

"What other way is there to put it, James, tell me."

"I don't know. That's as good as any. I guess."

"Stop guessing, James! It's your career on the line here. It's the job you've always wanted. It's the eleventh month. Your boss has given me one more month. After that, if in my opinion, you still haven't understood what you were doin', you're gone. I cannot, I will not, in good conscience recommend that you continue to be employed as a police officer. Whether you believe in luck or not, you are extremely lucky that that man didn't die as a result of your unprovoked attack—"

"Unprovoked?! Bullshit unprovoked! He was whackin' that kid with a piece of rubber hose, that kid was in the hospital for a week!"

"And his father was in surgery for three hours. And in intensive care for forty-eight hours. And his medical bills cost your employer's insurance company a sizable pile of moolah, James. And the loss of his kidney cost that insurance company another sizable pile of moolah. Do you want to discuss how lucky you are to have a boss who's on very good terms with the district attorney? Which district attorney chose not to prosecute you for aggravated assault? And how about the mysterious fact—dare we call it luck, huh?—that this story received almost no play in the local newspaper? To what do you attribute that, James, huh? A force of nature perhaps? Wanna explain that to me?"

"Why you so pissed off? Why you—I mean, you're yellin' at me."

"Am I? Really? Maybe it's because we're running out of time here, James, and you can't seem to comprehend that you are one lucky S-O-B. You committed a first-degree felony and all you got out of it was six months of administrative probation and twelve months yakkin' it up with me once a week. The DA doesn't prosecute you, your boss is on your side, he wants you to succeed, and I'm pullin' teeth to get you to see the root of this tree which bore this illegitimate fruit, so you can keep doing what you've always wanted to do. And what do you do? You sit here and talk about how you wouldn't allow yourself to be paralyzed with fear—by thinking wrong thoughts. We get right up on the thought process you were having at the exact moment you're committing this first-degree felony and you back away from it as fast as your mental feet can move—and you ask me why I'm yelling? Tell me, James, why do you think I'm yelling?"

"Guess you're frustrated—"

"Again with the guessing—of course I'm frustrated. Moses, Moses, burn this man a bush, maybe it will light up his mind!"

"Uh, am I . . . am I that dense?"

"No, James, you're not dense. You're just walking around denying a huge part of your emotional life. And if you don't stop denying it, it's going to bring you down, it's going to take you away from the job you want, the life you want. Put it together, that's all you have to do. Connect the dots. 'Cause if you can't do that, you can't have the life you want, it's as simple as that. Other people, with a greater responsibility, will prevent you. They will put up roadblocks everywhere you turn. And if that happens, James, I don't think you'll be able to deal with it."

"Why's that? What do you mean I won't be able to deal with it?"

"Because you give every indication that you've made no other plan. You act and think that because this is what you've wanted, and this is what you've got, then this is what you're going to keep just because you want to keep it. And if others stop you—and they surely will if you don't connect the dots here—I have serious reservations about how you're going to react. And I will have to make those reservations public. You may think you have no other choice. But I really do not have another choice. So start connecting the dots, James. We've got four more sessions. Stop running from the reality you understand better than anybody else in this world. . . ."

Reseta had brought a voice-activated tape recorder into his sessions with Stein. Normally, Stein would not have permitted himself to be recorded, but Reseta argued that he needed the tapes to write accurate summaries of the sessions for Balzic. He replayed them repeatedly while writing the summaries, and had also been replaying them at least once a year every year since October 1971, when his sessions had ended. He'd found out who, what, when, where, how, and why he was in those forty-eight hourlong sessions, and he'd been smart enough to know that if he listened carefully enough to Stein and to himself, he would know as much about himself as he could learn. When it came to himself, Stein had said to him in their last session, he was the smartest, coolest, most experienced, most observant person about James Reseta that anyone knew. What Stein had finally made him understand was that he had to stop playing footsie with himself. As long as he could summon up the will to tell himself the truth about himself, he'd be okay. He'd get to be the cop he'd always wanted to be, and to live the life he'd always wanted to live. But connecting those dots was a hump. A big one. One he almost hadn't gotten over. And if it hadn't been for Balzic and Stein, he wouldn't have gotten over it. He had been lucky as hell. First, there was Jukey Johnson. Then Mario Balzic. And finally Abe Stein. How lucky does any man deserve to get in this life? Reseta asked the question over and over in the twenty-three years since his last session with Abe Stein. And the answer every time was damn lucky. . . .

"Thirty? You 10-8 or what?"

"Thirty here. Roger that."

"What's your 10-20?"

"I'm north on South Main, just passing the Rocksburg Foundry."

"Thirty, 10-91."

"Roger that." Reseta turned to the channel that avoided the eavesdroppers. "What's up, Vic?"

"Where you been? How long's it take you to get to juvey hall and back? Friggin' car oughta be able to drive itself there."

"What, Smoley's on strike again? You lose your kolbassi connection? You want me to go mediate?"

"Very funny. Listen, the United Nations is goin' apeshit again. Go back up Rayford."

"Where's Canoza?"

"Never mind where Canoza is, just go."

"Aw balls, man, I backed him up last night. And where was Canoza, huh? After everything cools out, that's when he showed up."

"Just get there and back up Rayford, that's all."

"Did he call for backup?"

"No. I'm readin' his mind. Go back him up, capeesh?"

"Hey, I know you think 'cause the pope's a Polak it's okay for you to try to talk Italian, but it's not workin', believe me. You can't even pronounce that right."

"Just go—"

"I'm goin', I'm goin'. Is it party time—hat and horns, or what?"

"Just the lights, that's all."

"And where am I goin'—Franklin or Jefferson?"

"Jefferson. It's the Russkies versus the Polaks. And don't wake up Scavelli, alright? Rayford's already had grief with him today."

"What's this one about—dogs, trees, or parkin' spaces?"

"Who knows? Probably the full agenda—just get goin', alright?"

"These people, I'm tellin' ya, they oughta all be in therapy. Should have their own group."

"Well maybe you should tell 'em that. And maybe they might request you personally to be their group leader. How close are you anyway—aren't you finished with that yet? Thought you told me you were gonna be finished with that before Christmas."

"Nah, still six hours shy. Just the thesis, that's all. Oh man, listen to me, just the thesis. Shit, me writin' the thesis is like climbin' a mountain with roller skates on. Hate writin'. It was due before Christmas, talked my adviser into lettin' me put it off till the end of May, here it is the middle of April, I haven't even started it. All I have is a briefcase full of index cards."

"Oh how the times they are a-changin'. I can remember when all you wanted to be was a cop."

"Don't remind me."

"Well you don't write that thing, get your master's, that's what's gonna happen. And then you're really gonna be a miserable prick."

"Your vote of confidence is duly noted, Mr. Dispatcher."

"Speakin' of which, get movin', Rayford's callin' me again."

"Oh for Christ sake, I have been movin'. Whatta you think—I gotta park to talk? I'm Canoza now?"

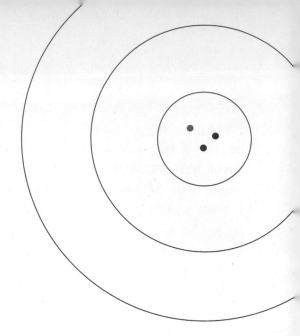

AFTER RAYFORD finished the unusual incident report, he sat for a long time thinking about what he'd just learned about the Scavellis from Stramsky. And then a phrase started running through his mind: sometimes for a cop compassion is a terrible thing. Where had he heard that? Probably from Reseta. Had to be. Man, that Reseta. There was one complicated dude.

Six years ago, when Rayford first joined the department, it took him no time at all to decide that Reseta was the coldest, most efficient grunt in the department. He was so cold, so efficient, some of the other guys called him Mussolini behind his back. And while there was no doubt that if you were headed into a nuisance bar you wanted Canoza beside you—or in front of you—there was also no doubt that when the truly sticky shit went down, the man you wanted beside you was Reseta. Reseta never got flustered, never forgot who he was or what he was doing or who he might have to be doing it to.

Word was Reseta had seen real shit in Nam. He wasn't one of those dudes mopping floors in the NCO clubs or driving a forklift around the supply bases. He had the medals to prove it. Not that he ever talked about them, but everybody knew he had a Purple Heart with two clusters, a Silver Star, and a Bronze Star. Even Carlucci,

that squiggly little detective who'd seen enough of his own shit in
Nam, told Rayford that Reseta had all the brains and all the gear to
be chief. But for reasons Rayford had never managed to get out of
anybody, Reseta, even though he'd passed the tests for sergeant, lieutenant, and captain, was still a patrolman.

And he wouldn't talk about that. Every time Rayford brought it
up, all the times he'd asked Reseta for advice about how to prepare
for the sergeant's test, no matter what or how Reseta told him to
study, when it sounded as though he might start talking about why
he wasn't a captain, lieutenant, or sergeant, he just wouldn't. It was
just not something Rayford could get him to talk about.

Rayford couldn't help thinking how weird that was, because he
couldn't wait to take the sergeant's test, and when he found out he'd
passed it, he couldn't wait to order the stripes and have a tailor sew
them on one shirt so he could wear it around his apartment and
check himself out in all the mirrors even before he learned that he
was actually going to receive the promotion. Which, three months
later, he still hadn't received.

Fact was, fully half the patrolmen in the department had passed
the sergeant's test. And a third of those had passed the lieutenant's
test. But of those the only two who'd passed the captain's test were
Carlucci and Reseta, and Carlucci kept saying Reseta was the
sharpest guy in the department. Even when Carlucci was acting
chief, before Nowicki got the job permanently, Carlucci said repeatedly that Reseta was way better qualified than he was—and test
scores didn't have anything to do with it. Carlucci said it was because of the way Reseta sized up every situation, every incident.
Carlucci said, "He prepares, man, that's all there is to it. I swear he
stays up nights dreamin' up situations just so he can be ready for 'em
when they happen. Prepares like nobody else. Always has, long as
I've known him."

But, whether he prepared like nobody else or not, for reasons of
his own Reseta hadn't wanted any of the promotions, and certainly
not the chief's job. Not that it had been offered to him. Carlucci

said the offer and the acceptance were both political and that was the one area where Reseta seemed weak. Seemed, Carlucci had emphasized, because he wasn't really sure that if Reseta hadn't made up his mind to be chief he couldn't have been as political as the job required, because he certainly had the mind and the character to learn how. "God knows," Carlucci said, "I don't have it."

But Rayford always had the feeling there was something else chewing on Reseta. He didn't know what, but something had changed in Reseta since 1993 when Rayford had come into the department. Something had happened. Even though there was a lot of talk about it when Reseta wasn't around, the talk was nothing but speculation. It was a particular incident, it wasn't a particular incident, it was the whole thing just wearing him down, it was him going to college two, three times a week, juggling his watches to match his class schedules, finally getting his B.S. in criminal science after fourteen years of night and Saturday morning classes. Then, without a word to anybody, he changed directions and started a master's program in psychology.

Weight-room talk was that nobody could keep that up for twenty-five years, that kind of intensity, staying in shape physically, keeping up with all the changes in the law, never losing your cool on the street. But more and more guys started asking Rayford if he was noticing that Reseta seemed to be running on empty—or running on caffeine. Weight-roomers got silly one day and voted him the Last Guy You Wanted Spotting for You in the Bench Press. Printed up a sign and hung it on the back wall of the john stall. Hung there for nearly a week before Reseta found it. They could hear him tearing it up and flushing it. He came out of the stall and never said a word. Just started his lifting circuit, like he'd done every Monday, Wednesday, and Friday for twenty-five years.

But Rayford couldn't help noticing it, mostly when they were running together, because that's when they talked. Or rather Rayford talked. He was under the impression that they could talk about anything and everything, but when he thought back about those conversations, he saw they were all one-sided. It was him talking out *his* problems, *his* collars, *his* patrols, *his* wife, *his* mother-in-law, *his* girlfriends, whether he should finish the B.S. he'd started in the air force. If Reseta said anything it was only to talk about what Rayford was talking about. Rayford hadn't realized how one-sided their conversations were until the other guys started on him about whether he was noticing how edgy Reseta was getting lately.

Patrolman Larry Fischetti came to Rayford and asked him straight out if he'd noticed any change.

"Why you askin' me, man?"

" 'Cause you're always with him."

"Always with him? Whachu talkin' about?"

"You run with him, you lift with him."

"That's *always* to you? That's maybe an hour and a half a week runnin', maybe three hours a week liftin'. Four at the most."

"That's what I'm sayin'. That's a lotta time to spend with one guy. You're not noticin' anything?"

"Noticin' like what?"

"Hey. Last week, he backed me up in a domestic. Guy had a knife, fillet knife, you know, for fish? Bonin' knife? Eight inches at least. It's dark, 2100, and here he comes, Reseta, outta the car with his hands empty. No flash, no baton. And he won't draw his piece. Just starts talking to the guy."

"So? Did he cool him out or what?"

"Yeah. Eventually. But that ain't my point."

"Which is what? Cooled the guy out, didn't he? What'd you want him to do, shoot him, bust his skull, keep shinin' his flash in the dude's eyes till he went blind or what?"

"Hey, Rayford, first fuckin' rule, which you know as well as me, you come outta the MU with all the necessaries, you don't come outta there sayin', hey idiot, wait a second, I forgot my MagLite, can't see what the fuck I'm doin' here, don't move till I go get it."

Rayford couldn't argue with that. Coming out of an MU with your baton and your flash at night should've been as automatic as breathing. All Rayford could do was shrug and say, sure, he ran with Reseta, he lifted with him, they backed each other up when the occasions arose, but he really couldn't say he knew Reseta any better than anybody else. He also pointed out there were weeks when Reseta was the same old organized, competent, confident Reseta again, cleaned and polished, in such good shape from running and lifting that during his annual physical his body fat content was in single digits. "And the only other motherfucker in this department can make that claim is me," Rayford said.

When they caught the same watches, Rayford and Reseta not only ran together and spotted for each other in the weight room, they also paired up in self-defense classes. That was when Rayford gained the most respect for Reseta, who, though he was nearly twenty years older, regularly and routinely handled Rayford with ease no matter what they were practicing: takedowns, come-alongs, edge encounters, gun encounters. Reseta was just enough quicker and just enough stronger to show Rayford that he was nobody to fool with physically, no matter what might be going on in his mind.

But still, Rayford couldn't deny that something about Reseta had changed. Maybe it was all those psych courses he was taking. Maybe he was just getting the short-timer's attitude. He never talked about retiring exactly, never talked about what he was going to do when he did retire, but more and more he seemed to be talking about how stupid it was to keep locking people up for screwing up their families when nobody seemed to be teaching anybody how to have a family in the first place, except for the religious nuts running for seats on school boards all over the county. "Those cretins think they got a pipeline to God, but I wouldn't let 'em raise my dogs—if I had any," Reseta said once. That was the most Rayford got out of him on that subject.

On the days when Rayford got around to pissing and moaning about his wife and his mother-in-law—and he usually got around to that subject at least once a week—Reseta had started telling him to tune into *Oprah* on Tuesdays because there was a guy named McGraw he should listen to.

So Rayford did. And then he was really confused. 'Cause this McGraw, who, according to Reseta, was some kind of hot-shit mind-man, sounded to Rayford like ninety-nine percent of the crackers he'd run into in Alabama. And when he'd told Reseta that the next time they ran, Reseta had said, "What, you listen with your skin now? You don't use your ears anymore? The man frequently talks about just the kind of situation you sound to me like you have. The one you talk about constantly? Like once a week? Like for the last six years? Pay attention to him, I'm tellin' you. Fact, you want, I'll buy you a copy of his book."

And two days later, Reseta showed up in the weight room with McGraw's book *Life Strategies: Doing What Works, Doing What Matters.*

"And don't just read it, you hear? There's a buncha tests in there. Take 'em. And I mean really take 'em, don't just screw around like they're some sex test in *Cosmo.*"

"*Cosmo?* You read *Cosmo?*"

"Like you don't. You'd be the first guy I ever knew didn't see one in a doctor's waiting room, didn't pick it up see if he couldn't find some new magic bullet in there on how to score."

"Oh well, doctor's office, yeah."

"I'm serious. Take the tests. Be surprised what you don't know about yourself."

"You think I don't know myself?"

"You know, when you let your voice get all screetchy like that, you sound like some crackhead from Monessen. I know you don't know yourself. Nobody knows themselves all the way. One way or another, we're all bullshittin' ourselves about something."

"My man, I don't know, watchin' *Oprah* and shit? You're payin' way too much attention to them psych books, man. Some people sayin' your reaction time is backin' up a notch."

"Oh is that right, huh? Not you though, right?"

"Not me. No."

" 'Cause I know a guy runs a gun range out in the township, he's got a timer rigged up to a strobe light, can tell you in hundredths of a second how fast your draw is. Wanna go? Little wager maybe?"

"James, man, it ain't about that, you know this ain't me talkin'. This is other people. I know you could whip a pit bull, man, give the motherfucker two bites head start. It's just . . ."

"Just what? Say it."

"Guys sayin' you come out the unit, man, forgettin' your gear."

"Oh I get it, this is Fish, right? First place, he never woulda started this shit with me before Carlucci's mother cracked his head open. He hasn't been right since. Anybody's reaction time changed, it's his. Now when he comes outta the MU, he's already got his piece out, doesn't wanna talk about nothing to nobody. Ask me, he oughta retire before he shoots somebody. 'Cause far as I'm concerned, the man is certifiably paranoid.

"Here's what it is, listen to this. He got pissed 'cause last week I talked this guy down. I swear, he was actin' like he wanted to dust him off, he was all itchy, you know? Just had that look. The guy hadn't hit anybody, hadn't cut anybody, hadn't even tried. Just beefin' with his wife, that's all, started rantin', grabbed the knife, ran outside. When I got there, Fish was ten feet away from him, got his light in one hand, his piece in the other, he's aimin' at the guy's chest, right at his heart, 'cause I came up behind him, I got on his right shoulder, I could see exactly where he's aimin'. And what's he wanna know? Where's my light, where's my stick, where's my piece—I told him, I said, Fish, just make sure you don't shoot either one of us, okay? And pay attention here, you might learn something. So, okay, I know I shouldn't've said that, 'cause I knew he was gonna feel like I was patronizin' the shit out of him, feel like I was comin' on all superior 'cause I had a plan. And meanwhile it's not like he didn't bring it up, you know?"

"You mean he said somethin' right then?"

"Yeah. Course he did."

"What?"

"What do you think? Started talkin' rules and regs, I said look, Fish, the guy has not made a move on anybody. When his wife called, she did not say she had been injured in any way. The guy grabbed a knife, he ran out of the residence, he didn't go after his wife, the wife didn't chase him out, he went out there on his own. That's a man who was lookin' to cool out. Poor bastard, he looked sheepish, embarrassed, ashamed. I started talkin' to him, what's he tell me? Just that day, that was the day he finds out his unemployment checks are done. Felt like king of the losers. Man wasn't gonna hurt his wife. If he was gonna hurt anybody it was himself. Felt like he couldn't take care of his family anymore. And there's Fish, ready to dust him off. And then he's gonna harp on rules and regs to me? Please, what the fuck. And this is why I'm backin' up a notch? On my reaction time? Double fucking please, okay? You take any of those tests yet?"

"Huh? What tests?"

"What tests. Jesus. The ones in that book I gave you. McGraw's. You haven't take a one of 'em, have you? See there? When I tell you somethin' might help you out, give you a book maybe could help you improve your family situation? What do you do? You turn into the point man for the rumor squad."

"Aw c'mon, man. It ain't like that and you know it."

"Yeah? Well, when you figure out what it's like, you be sure and come tell me, okay?"

"Man, James, stop. Just stop runnin' a minute."

"No, I'm not stoppin'. I'm not gonna defend myself to you or anybody else about bullshit rumors."

"Hey, man, look here. Six years ago I come in this department, I never saw you prayin', man. Last couple months or so, every time before you get in the MU, you're down on one knee, givin' yourself a cross and a Hail Mary or whatever, whatever you Catholics pray."

"Is that right?"

"Yeah that's right, don't tell me it ain't, I see your reflection in the car next to you. Don't be denyin' that, my eyes are twenty-twenty, man. This is new, man. You never used to do that. This just started, seemed like to me right after Christmas, you got spooked or somethin', don't try to tell me you didn't. Whyn't you just tell me what the fuck it is? I been tellin' you shit about me for years now, real personal shit I never tell anybody else, you ain't never said nothin' 'bout yourself."

"You just figure that out?"

"Yeah, I just figured it out, so I'm a slow-ass motherfucker, so what? Figure somethin' out, don't matter how long it takes, long as it's right."

"What can I say, you're an interesting guy. I like to hear what you have to say. About your family, your wife, girlfriends . . . your boy."

"Oh what the fuck, man, I'm a case study now?"

"Maybe."

"Man, don't fuckin' maybe me. Guys're talkin' shit on you. Even Carlucci."

"Carlucci?! Bullshit. I'll believe that when he asks me if I got a minute. Rugs doesn't trash anybody behind their back. Not his style."

"Awright, so, uh, all he said was, uh, you probably just 'got the short-timer's attitude, that's all. Happens to the best of us'—his exact words."

"Whoa, now there's an indictment for you. Carlucci say I'm *probably* a short-timer. Okay. Guilty as charged."

"What? You goin' quit? Hey stop, man, this is serious, c'mon, stop runnin', no shit." Rayford pulled up short and hollered after Reseta, "C'mon, man, stop, talk to me."

"Not today," Reseta said over his shoulder as he ran on, leaving Rayford straining to catch up. Every time Rayford got close enough, Reseta put it in overdrive and pulled away, staying just far enough ahead to make it impossible to talk. And after they stopped their run, Rayford continued to push him but Reseta just shook his head and said, "Not ready to talk about it."

"Well, tell me this at least. Somethin' happened, right?"

"Not recently, no."

"Well when? What?"

"Man, I'll say this for you. You are one persistent prick. Okay. Got a letter."

"A what? Letter? From who? What about, grad school?"

"I wish."

"Aw man, what the fuck, don't do this coy shit with me, huh?"

"Coy?! This isn't about coy, man. This is . . . this is heavy, okay? I don't know if I can talk about it."

"Hey you can't talk it out with me, what the fuck? I thought we were tight."

"We are. You're a good man. Let your dick do your thinkin' for you too much sometimes, and that's gonna come back on you sooner or later, but other than that, you're alright."

"Just awright, huh?"

"Yeah, alright. What's wrong with alright? Rather I said you were all wrong?"

"You know what I mean."

"Okay, I see your point. Uh, let me say it this way. When I was in Nam, I had a buddy . . . shit, buddy . . . that word doesn't begin to cover it. Not even close. Closest I can come to it is he was my rabbi, but even that doesn't do it, you know? The man taught me how to stay alive in the stickiest shit I ever walked through. Never steered me wrong, never busted my balls, never once got chickenshit with me. Then he went home on leave. This was '68, shortly after Martin Luther King got dusted. And, uh, and he just got totally fucked-up. . . ."

"How?"

"Got hit by a truck. Some cracker thought he was down there tryin' to stir up the race thing. Wound up in a wheelchair."

"This is what the letter was about?"

"Oh no, no. No, I knew about this . . . almost right after it happened."

"So what was this letter about?"

Reseta looked away, then hung his head, and pinched the bridge of his nose. "Man . . . don't even know if I can say it . . . aw fuck." He formed his right hand like he was holding a pistol and aimed it at his open mouth. Then he quickly turned his head away.

"Aw shit. When?"

"Christmas. Christmas Day. Wheeled himself out to this, uh, this shed behind his mother's house . . . she's who wrote me the letter."

"Aw shit, James, whyn't you say somethin', man? Fuck you carryin' this around for by yourself, man, this is some heavy shit. Couldn't tell me this? What the fuck? No wonder you're fucked-up."

"I am not fucked-up. Why you sayin' that? You think I'm fucked-up?"

"You ain't?! You ain't fucked-up?! Behint this shit? The man eats his gun? Your rabbi? And you think you ain't fucked-up behint this shit? Hey, James, you wanna lie to me, that's one motherfuckin' thing, but you lyin' to yourself, man. I look like I'm walkin' behint a long, white stick? Motherfucker, James, you need to talk this shit out, man, you can't be holdin' this shit back like that. Constipate your mind like that, what the fuck?!"

"You do have a way of puttin' things, Rayf. Ever think about clinical psychology, huh?"

"Oh would you listen to this? Now you mockin' me, man. I'm tellin' you, you in serious shit and you mockin' me, what the fuck."

"I am not mocking you, okay?"

"Well that's good you ain't, okay? Motherfucker, man, you been carryin' this shit—you been carryin' this load since Christmas?! Is that what you tellin' me? Since motherfuckin' Christmas? Fuck is wrong with you, James? I mean, seriously, who the fuck you think you are, huh? Fuckin' Jesus maybe? The Buddha? What, you think your heart made outta motherfuckin' stainless steel? Titanium?"

"No. It's way worse than that. I'm lyin' awake every night, plan-nin' how I can get down there."

"Down where?"

"Mississippi."

"That's where he was? Oh man, James, c'mon, man, don't even say that shit."

"Hey you asked me, remember? You're the one wants me to talk. Well I'm talkin' now, okay? I don't know why but I am. And I'm tellin' you what's goin' on. Every night, I wake up about three, three-thirty, same time every night. I'm right in the middle of this dream. Only there's no symbolism in it. I don't have to consult any of my textbooks to figure out what it means. It's plain as the back of my hand. I'm down there, I find this cracker, I cuff him, take him out some godforsaken road, pistol-whip that prick till he's semicon-scious, then I lay him out across the road and I run over the prick half a dozen times, back and forth, back and forth. 'Cause that's what I wanna do so bad sometimes I can't swallow water. I wanna go down there and find that cracker, run over him with a car. And when he's layin' there cryin' for his momma, then I just wanna empty a box of .22s into him, start at his hips and work my way up both arms, one bullet every minute, take forty-nine minutes before I get to the last one, and I save that last one for right between his eyes, and between every shot I get down there in his face, and I say, you feel that, motherfucker? Do you feel that, huh? That one—you feel that? That one was for Jukey. And so's this next one, you pile of pig vomit. You ruined a man on the best day of your life and on the worst day of his, you wouldn't make a pimple on his ass . . . that's what I'm carryin' around, Rayf. You want the truth, there it is.

"And this is me talkin' now, you hear? Me, the guy who's one thesis short of a master's in psychology. Gettin' ready to start on my Ph.D. in clinical psychology. And what am I thinkin' about? I'm walkin' around thinkin' how we don't do somethin' about the crazy-ass way we raise children in this country, I'm thinkin' about all the books I've read about our emotions, how our minds work on our

bodies, all the classes I've sat through, all the seminars I've partici-
pated in about how to manage anger, how to mediate disputes, how
to read people's body language and interpret their meanings in what
they think they're sayin' and what they're actually sayin' . . . and for
the last three and a half months, all I do every night is dream and
scheme about how to find this cracker and turn his legs into a pile
of bloody rags. I am, in the language of the trade I thought I wanted
to get into, I mean, what you see before you, Rayf, is one conflicted
motherfucker . . . I talked to that man . . . I didn't let thirty days
pass that I didn't talk to him . . . talked to him Christmas Eve . . .
didn't pick up one hint, one clue, one sign, one word, one thought,
one fuckin' eentsie . . . anything, man, that he was . . . that he was
gonna . . . do that."

"What, you thinkin' you coulda stopped him?"

"I don't know! Yeah! Maybe! What the fuck . . . I don't know."

"You say this shit happened in '68?"

"Yeah."

"And he made it till last Christmas? That's what, thirty years?
Thirty years in a chair? Damn. Man had some kinda guts, you ask
me. Somebody told me I was never goin' walk again? Much as I like
to run and shit? I'd be reachin' for my piece 'fore the sun went
down."

"Rayf? Excuse me, but this is not about you."

"I know it ain't. I'm just sayin' the man had a ton a guts. Motherfuckin' ton more than I'd have, James, that's all I'm sayin'. Jesus,
sentenced to a chair for thirty years? Damn!"

"Yeah. And the cracker that did it—"

"Yeah. What about him? That motherfucker, what'd he get?"

"Two to five, out in three."

"Out in three?! Woo-ee, that's some evil shit. Sometimes, James,
I swear, life is the motherfuckin' unfairest shit there is. But, James,
look at me, man. Look in my eyes now."

"Huh?"

"Look at me, James. You can't go there, you hear? You can have that dream all you want. You can be schemin' all you want, you can plan it out all you want, James, you can vis-u-a-lize it, man, see every motherfuckin' .22 go in that motherfucker's flesh, but you can't be doin' that shit, you hear me? You cannot do that, James."

"Why? Why's this prick different from all the slopes I killed in Nam? I didn't have anything against those people. I didn't know them from that utility pole over there. This prick, I hate him with every cell in my body."

"That was war, man, c'mon! Government said they was the enemy."

"Oh, Rayf, man, please. In Nam, you'd be out there diggin' up mines, tryin' to keep a road open, kids'd come along tryin' to sell you a can of Pepsi. That night, soon as it got dark, those same kids'd be out there helpin' their fathers plant new ones. And girls, girls that would spread their legs in the late afternoon? They'd cut your throat that night. I laid one for five dollars one day, two nights later I dusted her right before dawn. She made it to within three steps from my LP before I heard her."

"Your what?"

"Listening post."

"Well that's what I mean, man, it was war. It was official, signed, sealed, executive orders, presidential orders, congressional orders, whatever the fuck name they wanna put on 'em, you were there under orders, man, in uniform, under your flag. Didn't mean shit what the other guys was wearin' or who they was, kids, ho's, whatever. But you go down the old country, man, Mississippi? You ain't goin' be wearin' no uniform, you ain't goin' be marchin' under no flag. And don't tell me you don't know that. What you dreamin' and schemin' is murder, man."

"Wouldn't be the first."

"Huh? Say what?"

"Never mind."

"Wouldn't be the first? Man, what the fuck are you talkin' 'bout now?"

"Never mind, I said."

"Damn, James. Sometimes, I swear on my momma, if I knew where she was, if you ain't the complicatedest motherfucker I ever met, I don't know who is. Don't talk that shit to me if you ain't goin' explain it."

"You're the one wanted me to talk. I don't talk, you get pissed. I talk, you get pissed. Sorry I said anything. C'mon, let's go. Time to go to work."

"Oh yeah, now we just s'posed to go to work like nothin' happen. Right. Shit. Your man eats his gun, you dreamin' and schemin' you wanna dust the motherfucker that caused the problem from the git, then you tell me wouldn't be the first, and I'm just s'posed to go to work. Hi-ho, hi-ho, off to motherfuckin' work I go, like Grumpy, Sneezy and all the rest of them dwarfy motherfuckers. Got-damn, James, you call in sick from now on, I'm goin' come by your place every day you off, man, and your dago ass better be in bed. Better never come by your place after you call in sick and find you and your ride gone. 'Cause I'll know where you'll be, man, and you can't put that shit on me, you hear?"

"Don't worry. I won't be puttin' anything on you. Fact, from now on, we'll go back to the way we used to be. You tell me all about your problems, and I'll help you solve 'em. Whether you want me to or not."

"Aw, see there? There you go, mockin' me again."

"No I'm not. It's just it was a lot less of a hassle when you were talkin' and I was listenin'."

"You a motherfuckin' mockin'bird, James. I swear, man, sometimes you could piss Jesus off. . . ."

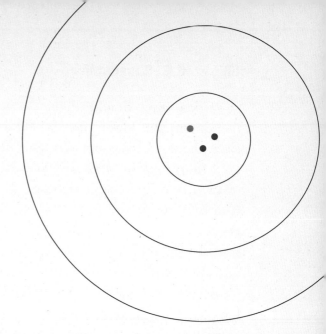

Sometimes for a cop compassion is a terrible thing—when did James say that? Why's that important? Why'd I think of that? 'Cause of the Scavellis or 'cause of those got-damn tests he's always tryin' to get me to take. No it's not, it's the got-damn Scavellis. Question is, were they fucked-up *before* their kids died? Or are they fucked-up *because* their kids died? And how the fuck am I supposed to know that? And what difference does it make anyway? If it slows you down when you have to bust a move, then James is right, compassion is a terrible thing for a cop. 'Cause when Scavelli got a shovel full of dog shit and is heading for the Hlebecs' house, what does it matter his kids died in a fire he started? Then is then, now is now, and no matter how bad I feel for him, I still got to stop his ass.

Oh man, I got to stop thinking 'bout the Scavellis. Hear that shit about that fire, their kids, all I see is my kid. Now how can your mind get so fucked-up so fast you hear about somebody else's kids dyin' in a fire and what you see is your kid fallin' out the smoke and flames—how the fuck does that happen? What shit goes on in your mind to make that picture? There was no fire when my kid . . . no fire when he fell. Just my ignorant-ass, ugly-ass, voodoo-believin' MIL. James tell me how he wanna go down the old country run over that cracker, he thinks I can't appreciate that shit. He don't know how many times I wanna throw my motherfuckin' MIL out the window. Aw, fuck he don't, told him enough times. Why else he always be tryin' to get me to take those McGraw tests?

McGraw. Help McGraw take a bite outta your mind. Oughta make a commercial outta that shit. Hi. McGraw here. And I need your help to take a bite outta yo' mind. All y'all needs to do is read my book, life's little strategies, doin' what works, doin' what matters. And be sure'n catch me on *Oprah* every Tuesday where I take a bite outta her mind and anybody else's mind wantsa sit there and be humiliated on national TV, tell the world how fucked-up they are. I'm humiliated when there's just me, Charmane, and the marriage counselor in the room. Let thirty million people in on how many pieces my shit is in? Not in this life. . . .

Rayford reached into his briefcase and found the steno notebook he'd bought for just this purpose, to take McGraw's tests and "be surprised," according to Reseta, "what you can learn about yourself."

Rayford had read just far enough into the book to get to the second test. He ran into a wall on that one, so he backed up to the first test and said maybe he really did have to write the answers down to see whether he was bullshitting himself or not. He wrote the test down first and studied it for a while to make sure he understood what the assignment really was. "Your first assignment is to challenge your beliefs right now, by listing in order of significance the top five things in your life you have simply failed to fully and completely admit or acknowledge to yourself."

Yeah, right. Like there's five things in my life I have not fully and completely admitted or acknowledged to myself. Let's see now, what would they be? Oh, I know, how's this for number one? I am an orphan. I don't know who my daddy was and my momma's been gone since I was seventeen.

Number two. I am a nigger. I have been told this in one way or another by every motherfuckin' honky I ever met. Not only am I a nigger, I am a schizophrenic nigger. I speak and think two languages. I speak and think nigger. And I speak and think honky. I can speak and think nigger with the best niggers. And I can speak and think honky with the best honkies—if there is such a thing as a best honky. Well, shit, there are some. Two at least. Balzic is one. And so is James. If they got bigotry in their bones, they hide it better than any honky I ever met. Course Balzic got two daughters now. Wonder how he'd be actin' if I asked one of them for a date. Assuming they looked good enough to take out in public. Though if they look anything like their mother, they should be awright. On the other hand, if they look like him, Lord have mercy, shame on their ass.

Number three. I have a boy child. I had a boy child. I hold my boy child in my heart every day of my life. I told James he couldn't be talkin' murder in Mississippi, but if I thought dropping my MIL on her head from the second floor would bring William Junior back, I would've dropped the bitch on her motherfugly head four years ago.

Number four. My wife wants to be with her mother more than she wants to be with me. If I murdered my MIL, would my wife come be with me? If God murdered my MIL, would my wife come be with me? When you die, you dyin' 'cause you dyin'? Or is God murderin' your ass? People murder one another, we lock 'em up, put needles in their arm—why don't we get pissed at God 'cause people we love die? Why don't we put God in jail? Why don't we put him on a table, belt his ass down, stick a needle in his arm, ask him if he got a statement he wanna make 'bout all the people he kills every motherfuckin' day. If I coulda got my hands on God the day I found that ambulance in front of my place I woulda said, motherfucker, pick—you or her. One of you motherfuckers goin' die today for this shit. And what do we hear from God's salesmen? Preacher say this be all part of God's plan, God got plans for William Junior. Ours not to question why, ours but to do and die. Yeah, right. Some motherfuckin' plan. Give me the child for nineteen months, take him back in one motherfugly second. That's a plan?

Not a sparrow falls that God don't see it, Momma told me that every day of her life. I said if he sees it fall why don't he be catchin' it? Why he wanna make it fall in the first place? Smart-ass. Little boy big mouth. Jivin' my momma about what she believe. Tell you true, Momma, I saw you tomorrow I'd fall down on my knees and beg you to forgive me for talkin' shit on what you believed. Shoulda slapped my face, what you shoulda done. Every time I got smart with you, shoulda slapped me upside my head. Last person on this earth I got a right to trash what they believe was you. But when you fell, Momma, what was God doin', huh? Standin' there watchin'? Sayin' whoops, what'd she fall over there for, I had the net over here. Was that what the motherfucker was sayin'? Is that a bird? Is that a woman? Is that a sparrow? Or is that Miss Rayford? And what little William goin' do now without his momma? Who goin' tell him when he come home from walkin' through Diablos' turf with his lip split and his shirt bloody that it goin' be awright, you just have to find another way home, little sparrow? Who goin' tell him that now, God? Motherfucker? Hey?! You listening?! Who goin' tell him where she buried, motherfucker? You seen her fall, you know why she fell, you know where she fell at, I guess that also part of your big plan, motherfucker—you goin' tell me someday so I can maybe go put a flower on her grave? Pauper. Indigent. Busted-out nigger woman and her teenage boy don't have the first dime's wortha no insurance, no nothin'. City of Pittsburgh buried her someplace. God knows where. 'Cause those motherfuckers won't tell me 'cause either they forgot where or else they never bothered to write it down. But God knows where, 'cause not a sparrow falls. Oh yeah, William, it's all part of the plan. Motherfucker just won't let me in on it.

Stop your monkey mind, William, and get back to the test. Number five. Last part of McGraw assignment number one. "What is it that you know in your heart is a problem not acknowledged or at least so painful that you avoid it?" Well now tell me, McGraw, what I need number five for? Ain't the first four enough? I need an-

other some-motherfuckin'-thing to add to my list? I don't think so.
I think the first four is about two more than I can carry as it is.

Rayford took McGraw's book out of his briefcase and turned to
dog-eared page 19. Oh listen to this, he said, I love this part, reading it in a whisper. "I would wager that whatever made your list is
at least in part a product of your own behavior. I also suspect that
the main difference between your problems and the more terribly
tragic situations we hear or read about is the result, not the behav-
iors that led up to it. For aren't the patterns in your life, and those
present in the more tragic stories, very likely the same? You've driven
a little too fast down a neighborhood street; you've left the kids unattended while you ran next door 'for a minute'; blah blah blah. The
'shocking stories' are often about people who have done the very
same things. But only because of a tragically different outcome, they
wound up in jail, or burying a child, or dealing with HIV."

No, motherfucker, it ain't *them* "burying a child," it was me.
And I don't care what you or Oprah say, that shit was not a product
of my behavior. I did not leave my child unattended. I begged Charmane, I begged her ass, don't be leavin' our child with that woman!
That woman don't be watchin' him! She be watchin' them motherfuckin' freak shows. I ain't goin' take the rap for this, no motherfuckin' way. William Junior's life is a product of my behavior.
William Junior's death is a product of the behavior of a stupid-ass,
ugly-ass, voodoo-believin' bitch think it more important to watch
idiots screamin', hittin', and spittin' on one another than to watch
the child her daughter put in her care, and if I'm lyin' I deserve to
be dyin'!

And what part of my behavior made me a nigger orphan, huh?
What part of this does Reseta think I don't know about me? What
part of my answer is goin' light up my mind so I can know me better, huh? And how the fuck is knowin' me better goin' get Charmane back?

Uh-huh! There it is. There's number five. That's the one I refuse
to admit or acknowledge. Finally got to it. Sittin' here in the MU,

thinkin 'bout the Scavellis. That's the one belongs to me. How long am I goin' bullshit myself she goin' come back? 'Cause she ain't goin' come back. Woman told me every way she know how. Say it in words, say it with every move she don't make. She picked. Got two choices. Her momma or me. And she sure as fuck ain't picked me.

Six years I been waitin' for her to show up. And six years she still ain't showed up. When that shitty little fact goin' sink in my burry head? I can piss and moan, bitch and groan all I want 'bout bein' a nigger orphan but the only thing really upset me about that is I don't know where my momma's buried. I know what cemetery, that's easy. But they don't mark the graves of indigents. Don't even know why that itches my mind, but it does and it's a motherfuckin' itch I can't scratch and I wanna scratch it so bad, it just won't leave me be. Can't do nothin' 'bout that 'cept get over it. 'Cept it just ain't right that nobody know where they buried her. Somebody oughta have a chart or a diagram or something somewhere, got-damn. That ain't right. And that ain't a result of my pattern of behavior either, you McGraw motherfucker you.

But Charmane stayin' with her momma? That's mine. I'll take that. Thing is, now that I take it, now that I admit it, now that I acknowledge it, what the fuck do I do about it?

He turned to the next page in McGraw's book that he'd dog-eared, the one where the second test was, the one that asked him to write a story entitled "The Story I'll Tell Myself If I Don't Create Meaningful and Lasting Change After Reading and Studying This Book," the test that had stopped him cold. Couldn't even read that test.

He looked down at the bottom of the page where McGraw had listed the excuses people used for not changing. Every place there had been the word *he* in the list, Rayford had crossed it out and printed *she* above it.

It was just too hard.
She doesn't really understand me.

That's all for other people.
I couldn't focus because of the kids and my job.
She's just too harsh; I need a more gentle approach.
My problems are different.
I need to read it again.
Until my spouse reads it, I'm just spinning my wheels.
I'm right and she's wrong.

At the end of the next paragraph was this sentence: "Instead of asking whether the way you are living, behaving, and thinking is 'right,' I want you to ask whether the way you are living, behaving, and thinking *is working or not working.*"

Got me there, McGraw. 'Cause sure as God made niggers what I'm doin' ain't workin', and everybody can say amen from now till everybody wake up the same color, she still ain't goin' leave her momma to be with me. Why in the motherfuck didn't I see that when I married her? Whole time we were in Alabama she didn't talk to nobody but her momma that I could see. Never once tried to talk to anybody else, never once struck up a conversation with anybody else's wife live on that base. What the fuck is wrong with me—I need a B-52 fall on my head? Wake up in the mornin' those two be talkin' like they ain't seen each other in twenty years, and keep that talkin' shit up all day. Damn near have to make an appointment to get some pussy, and this come as a surprise to me? That she don't wan' be with me?

What the fuck they be talkin' 'bout all the time? I don't know. Didn't never know. Ten years of this shit, may as well had my eyes fulla pepper spray, my ears fulla chain saws, I looked and I didn't see nothin', I listened and I didn't hear nothin'. How in the fuck could I've lived in that same trailer with those two women and not know that I was nothin' but a ticket to the commissary and the PX? That's all they did, talk and shop, shop and talk. They could try on more clothes and talk about tryin' on those clothes and what they bought and what they shoulda bought and why they didn't buy what they didn't buy than anybody I ever heard.

And why the fuck didn't I get that? Didn't talk to me about that shit. Charmane buy clothes, she didn't show 'em to me, didn't ask me how I liked 'em, how she looked in 'em. She put 'em on for her momma, asked her momma how she liked 'em, how she look. Fool! You didn't need a B-52 fall on your head, you needed a whole squadron of them motherfuckers fall on your head. Got-damn. Was I that stupid? Am I that stupid? Moth-ah-fuck-ah, *I am that stupid.* You don't see somethin' right under your nose for ten years, you one stupid motherfucker. So okay, McGraw, gotta give it to you, you done took a bite outta my mind.

And what excuse am I goin' use? How this story goin' end? What am I goin' be tellin' myself 'cause I didn't make any mean-ingful or lasting change? Ain't but one change I got to make. I got to divorce that woman, that's all there is to it. Payin' rent for those two? That's bullshit. I need proof I'm a fool, there it is. What was the name of that song? I'm a fool for love, was that it? Who sang that? You a fool for love, William. Double fool. You a fool for a pussy you ain't touched in six years, and you a fool for payin' rent on two places. Stop payin' her rent, see how fast she grab the yellow pages, find a got-damn shyster her own self.

"Thirty-one?"

Oh shit. "Thirty-one here."

"Thirty-one 10-91."

"Roger that." Oh shit. How long I been fuckin' the dog here?

"Thirty-one, you writin' a report or a book, what?"

"I'm 10-24 on that."

"What, the book or the report?"

"I'm 10-8, base."

"No kiddin', are ya? Think you could find some time to go cool out the mopes on Jefferson Street?"

Rayford sighed, squeezed his eyes shut, and rolled his head from shoulder to shoulder. Not those motherfuckers again. "What's the 10-20?"

"I tell you Jefferson Street and you have to ask? Where you think? It's the all-American boys."

"One of the wives call or somebody else?"

"The old lady across the street thinks they're gonna kill each other. They're on the sidewalk."

"I want backup from the go. Who's available?"

"That's a problem. Reseta's transporting a juvey. Canoza's, uh, he's gotta go pick somethin' up. So you're flyin' solo for a while. Just cool 'em out, that's all."

"Oh is that all? Yes sir, Mr. Dispatcher sir. I will 10-17 immediately and cool them out, yes sir. Thirty-one out."

"Watch your back, thirty-one. Base out."

I always do, Rayford thought as he pulled off the parking brake, put it in drive, and headed onto Miles Avenue and backtracked to within one block of where he'd been—how long ago? He checked his watch. Oh shit. An hour ago.

This time he was heading for Jefferson Street and the properties that abutted the Scavellis and the Hlebecs: the Hornyaks' backyard, which abutted the Hlebecs', and the Buczyks' backyard, which abutted the Scavellis'.

Rayford didn't know which of these combinations of neighbors was worst. God knows, the Scavellis and the Hlebecs had been beefin' about three times as long as the other two. And until about five years ago, the Hornyaks and the Buczyks appeared to have been good friends as well as good neighbors. Pete Hornyak and Joe Buczyk had played football for Rocksburg High School, guards on offense and linebackers on defense. Both went on to play college football at notorious football factories, but neither had graduated, not even with the kinds of degrees football factories notoriously dispense, such as physical education with an emphasis in playground supervision or recreation direction or summer camp administration or camp counseling, degrees that weren't even valid certificates of class attendance because the only classes they ever attended were taught by assistant coaches and their only textbooks were their playbooks and films of their games, their practices, and their opponents' games.

With banged-up knees, shoulders, and hands from playing sixteen years of football since the second grade through five years in college—through various dubious schemes tacitly approved by the bodies that were supposed to govern football played by pretend colleges—and having no marketable skills to speak of, Pete Hornyak got a job driving a truck for a furniture store, and Joe Buczyk got a job driving a truck for a building supplier. Twenty-five years later, Hornyak and Buczyk were both working for Home Depot, Hornyak selling flooring and floor coverings and Buczyk selling paints and painting supplies.

They each married the girl of their dreams, former drum majorettes for the Rocksburg Rams varsity marching band. Mary Falatovich became Mrs. Peter Hornyak, and Susan Syzmanski became Mrs. Joseph Buczyk. They bought houses next door to each other in the Flats, and for many years apparently happily shared beer and barbecues in their backyards, watched televised football in each other's basement game rooms, and even vacationed together in Atlantic City, New Jersey, or Ocean City, Maryland. Rayford had collected this information over the last six years from reading unusual incident reports and from talking to the patrolmen who'd written them.

He'd also learned that the Buczyks had two children, a boy, seventeen, a senior in high school, and a girl, fourteen, a sophomore. The boy was cocaptain of the football team, and the girl, like her mother before her, was a majorette. The Hornyaks had no children, apparently because either or both had some physical problem that prevented it; if they'd talked about this problem sympathetically with the Buczyks at one time, they certainly were no longer doing so. Fact was, their last confrontation became physical when Pete Hornyak accused Joe Buczyk of taunting him that if he was a man he could've had children. Buczyk denied it afterwards, but that didn't keep the blows from landing.

What started to spoil the friendship, as near as Rayford could figure out, was that approximately five years ago, the Hornyaks and Buczyks decided, whether by design or accident was uncertain, to get into the dog-breeding business. Mrs. Hornyak's mother died and left her daughter, among other things, a registered male Border collie, barely two years old. It so happened that the Buczyks had two female Border collies of their own, both duly registered with the American Kennel Club. Nature being nature and dogs being dogs, the two female Border collies soon dropped litters, seven pups each. Registration papers were filed, ads were placed in newspapers in Rocksburg and Pittsburgh, the Hornyaks got the pick of each litter and ten percent of the sale price, and the Buczyks sold twelve Border collie pups for a sum of money, the exact amount of which became the start of the dispute between them.

Now the Hornyaks had three Border collies, the father and two daughters, while the Buczyks still had their two females, the mothers of the only litters which had produced pups for cash. After the first couple of arguments about who had paid what to whom, the Buczyks, without discussing it with the Hornyaks, had their females spayed, thus ending the breeding business. And the friendship.

The other observable fact about these two couples wasn't anything Rayford could have put in any of his unusual incident reports, but it was something so obvious he'd have to have been blind not to notice. Rayford had long ago observed about white people that if you talked to a white woman long enough, sooner or later she'd start talking about what she was eating and why, whether she was on a diet, had been on a diet, was planning to go on a diet, or why this, that, or the other diet did or didn't work. He'd also observed that on the covers of any of the magazines white women bought out of the racks in the checkout lines in grocery stores there was guaranteed certain to be one headline on the cover about how to lose ten pounds in ten days or how to eat all you wanted while the fat melted off while you slept. Then there were those tiny books, the fat counters, the cholesterol counters, the Hollywood diet, the grapefruit diet, the high-protein low-carbohydrate diet, the low-protein high-carbohydrate diet, the soy diet, the vegetarian diet, right there in the little racks next to the *TV Guide.* Then there were the medical reporters on the local TV news, interviewing skinny doctors who raved about the obesity epidemic as though fat germs were carried by rats or mosquitoes and the whole population was in danger of being infected. The only black woman Rayford had ever heard making such a fuss about diet was the queen herself, Oprah, but even she in the last couple of years seemed to be backing up a notch on her obsession with weight.

When the Hornyaks and the Buczyks were going at each other, it was impossible for Rayford not to notice that Mrs. Buczyk and Mr. Hornyak seemed to be growing rounder and rounder, while Mrs. Hornyak and Mr. Buczyk seemed to be growing leaner and more muscular. The first time Rayford had responded to a call from Mrs. Hornyak about a tree problem—almost six years ago—the four of them seemed in fairly good shape. But over these last six years, Mr. Hornyak had put on at least fifty pounds, most of it around his stomach and buttocks. Mrs. Buczyk, on the other hand, seemed to have distributed her extra fifty pounds all over her body, from her cheeks to her ankles. And more than once Rayford had spotted Joe Buczyk sneaking looks at Mary Hornyak and Mary Hornyak sneaking looks back.

It was another chicken-and-egg puzzle, like the Scavellis. Were they screwed up before their kids died or did they get screwed up because they'd died? Were Susie Buczyk and Pete Hornyak getting fat before they started selling dogs? Or were they packing on the pounds because they were trying to eat their way out of the stress that had developed because they'd stopped selling dogs? And what was behind those sneaky little glances between Joe Buczyk and Mary Hornyak?

"You're imaginin' shit," Canoza said after the last blowup.

"No I'm not. Check 'em out, I'm tellin' you, there's somethin' cookin' between those two. I don't think it's about the dogs at all. Or the trees. Or the parkin' spaces. The dogs, the trees, the parkin' spaces, they're all just excuses. It ain't about where the cars are parked. Somethin' else is goin' on. I think two of those four want the cars parked in front of the other house."

"Ah you talk to Reseta too much, all that psychology shit."

"I'm tellin' you, next time—and guaranteed there'll be a next time—you watch those two. They're eyeballin' each other. That man is checkin' out her legs and behint, don't think he ain't."

"And what's she checkin' out?"

"Don't know that. But her old man's gut is so big, I'll bet she gotta tie his shoes for him."

"So what?"

"Hey, would you want that whale humpin' you?"

"I don't want any whale humpin' me. Or any guy either."

"Plus, that man's a heart attack walkin'. What if he has one on top of her? He collapse on top of her? She'd suffocate, man."

"Aw he just drinks too much beer, that's all. Eats too much pizza. And you think too fuckin' much. Course that would be funny."

"What would?"

"The headline. Fat husband fucked to death, crushes thin wife to death. Police suspect foul foreplay." Canoza thought that was hilarious.

"And you think *I* think too much? How long you been workin' on that one?"

"What, you think I didn't just think that up? I ain't as slow as everybody thinks."

"Yeah? Well think about this. You ready? 'Bout two weeks ago Reseta and me were runnin' along the old Conrail tracks, you know? And we saw 'em."

"Saw who?"

"Who we talkin' about? Joe Buczyk and Mary Hornyak."

"Aw you two fuckin' guys, you're seein' shit all the time, swear to Christ. You two, I'm tellin' ya, he's got your head so fulla that psychology shit, you don't know what the fuck you're seein' anymore. Besides, even if you saw 'em, say it was them—which I ain't, okay? But say it was. How you know they weren't just tryin' to patch things up?"

"I didn't say I knew what they were talkin' about. What I'm sayin' is they were alone. Their spouses weren't anywhere around, okay? And they were lookin' very chummy when we passed 'em."

"Aw probably wasn't even them, c'mon. How good a look'd you get? And anyway I been meanin' to ask you somethin' for a long time now."

"What?"

"All white people look alike to you?"

"Aw will you shut the fuck up—do all white people look alike."

Canoza threw his head back and howled and gave Rayford a playful backhand into his shoulder that nearly knocked him off his feet.

"Hey man, easy, what the fuck, you tryin' to bust my shoulder?"

"C'mon, just a little love tap."

"Oh yeah, real glad we're buddies and shit. You don't know your own strength, man."

"I been wantin' to ask you that ever since I met you. Just wanted to see your face, see how you'd react."

"Yeah? So?"

"It was worth it. Shoulda seen your face. You got really pissed there for about a half second—till you caught yourself. Wish I'da had a fuckin' camera, man, that was funny. You fuckin' spades make me laugh, no shit."

"Is that a fact? Us fuckin' spades make you laugh, no shit."

"Hey don't get all huffy, I meant that in a good kinda way."

"Did you now?"

"Yeah. Hey listen. When I was in Nam, know what I did? I ran the NCO club in Pleiku. Know why? 'Cause they needed a bouncer.

'Cause the fuckin' MPs got slower and slower respondin' to shit, know what I mean? So when I showed up, they said, oh man, here comes Big Stupe. Let's get him to run the fuckin' NCO club, nobody's gonna fuck with him. Well they didn't fuck with me but they sure fucked with each other. Believe me, I saw more shit, more blood than half the guys in the line outfits. And you know what most of it was? Shit between the whites and the blacks. Not the lifers. The FNGs, the ones that went through NCO School, Leadership School or whatever they called it, over there."

"The what kinda NCOs?"

"FNGs."

"What's that?"

"You were in the air force, you don't know what FNG means?"

"Just ast you, didn't I?"

"Fucking new guys. Get a couple stripes, go to that school, they'd come in with chips on their shoulders big as pizza pans. After about six months of that shit, I'd just walk up to 'em soon as they came in, I'd say all white people look alike to you? 'Cause if they do, just turn around and get the fuck out now. 'Cause those ones thought like that? Get three, four beers in 'em, man, they'd start woofin' and shit? Knives, pistols, bottles—I don't know how I didn't get killed in that fuckin' place. I did more hand-to-hand combat in there in one week than most grunts did their whole tours, and I didn't even get a fuckin' CIB out of it."

"A what?"

"Combat Infantryman's Badge."

"Wait wait—you wanted a medal for breakin' up bar fights?"

"Hey fucker, combat's combat, I don't care who it's against. You think you shouldn't get letters of commendation when you make a good collar just 'cause you collared Americans? Case you haven't noticed, you ain't collarin' Canadians. PDs hand out medals all the time, you get one you gonna give it back 'cause it wasn't in action against some fuckin' slopehead? Since when?"

"Oh yeah? Well there's an interesting point of view. So, uh, back to this other thing. Tell me, you ever ask the white guys if all black people looked alike to them?"

"Huh? Whattaya mean?"

"I mean did you ever ask the white guys? You said you asked the black guys if all white guys looked alike, but you didn't say anything about askin' the white guys if all black guys looked alike—"

"Hey, Rayford, c'mon, okay? I'm just bustin' your balls, that's all. I never asked anybody anything—whatta you think, I'm stupid? If I'da asked everybody came in the door somethin' that dumb, how long you think I woulda lasted, huh?"

"Oh. So was it really that bad? Between the blacks and the whites?"

"Hey, all I know about is when I was there, which was from June '69 to June '70. And there was a lotta bad shit between 'em then. You don't remember that time? Man, after Martin Luther King got dusted, whatever was here, it just got carried over there."

"You kiddin' me? I wasn't even born till 1969."

"Trust me. It was bad shit after King got dusted. Riots everywhere, man. But hey, even before he got dusted, there was bad shit in LA, Newark, Detroit, '65, '66, I don't even know all the cities where they had these riots."

"Yeah, I've read about 'em. Lotta people got killed by cops, they weren't just killin' each other."

"Course they did, whatta you think? Just like in Nam, lotta guys got dusted by friendly fire. That shit happens. Every war. And all these people all worked up about the MIAs, you know? You ask me, half those guys are deserters, and the other half got blown into so many pieces they couldn't even find their dog tags. Know how many MIAs there were in World War Two? I looked it up once 'cause I got sick of listenin' to all this bullshit about the MIAs in Nam."

"No. How would I know that?"

"Just thought you mighta read about it. Can't guess? Huh? Take a guess."

"Guess? Couple thousand, what do I know?"

"Aw what're you, shittin' me? Couple thousand, come on, Christ. Like between fifty and sixty thousand. All over Europe. Just fuckin' disappeared. Now how many of those guys you think traded some Lucky Strikes or Camels for some civilian's clothes and just sorta faded into the woodwork, huh? C'mon. I had uncles and cousins in that war in Italy, man, they told me. Fuckin' guys were buggin' out every day. You can only stand so much of that war shit, you know? Then you either go nuts and shoot yourself in the foot, or blow your thumb off, or start takin' your clothes off, shakin' your dick at your CO. We got this dumb-ass attitude in this country, everybody in Big Two was Audie Murphy or John Wayne or some shit."

"John Wayne was never in a fuckin' war. Only war he was ever in was in Hollywood, even I know that much."

"I know that. But not Audie Murphy. He was for real, man. Most decorated soldier in World War Two. He was a real fuckin' hero, that guy, way before he was a movie star. But what I'm sayin' is, for every Audie Murphy, there was ten guys never fired a shot. My uncle, he went through the whole fuckin' war in Italy, never fired his rifle once."

"Yeah, but which side was he on?"

"Oh that's fucking hilarious. Our side, you Bojangles mother-fucker you."

"Yeah, but can he prove that?"

"Same way you can prove you saw Joe Busy runnin' with Hornyak's old lady."

"Joe Busy?"

"That's what I call him. How you s'posed to pronounce all them z's and c's and y's? When he says it, it sounds like Bu-chek. I just say Busy. Fuck's the difference, I know who he is."

"And I don't, huh? 'Cause all white people look alike to me?"

"Now you got it. Right. Exactly right."

"Aw fuck you. Who's writin' this up, you or me?"

"Hey, I wasn't the first one here. This is yours."

Rayford remembered that conversation as if it had happened yesterday. In fact, it had happened only two weeks ago, right after he and Canoza had processed Joe "Busy" Buczyk for violating the statutes prohibiting assault and aggravated assault on Pete Hornyak.

And now here was Rayford again, pulling up to the curb across Jefferson Street from the Hornyaks' house. He left the light bar and engine on, pushed the foot brake, and put it in park. He reached for his baton and MagLite and got out, slipping them into their loops on his duty belt, and walked quickly across the street, stopping before he reached the sidewalk.

Hornyak and Buczyk were in each other's faces, each standing on his side of the property line which extended from between their houses out to the street. They were both inviting the other to cross the line as Rayford approached, saying, "Whoa down, folks, everybody just whoa it down here a second. Take a step back, please. One step back, c'mon, you can do it, I know you can."

Dogs were barking and howling in both houses. One of the Border collies in the Buczyks' house was scratching the aluminum storm door.

"I ain't afraid of you, Joe," Hornyak was saying.

"Well good for you, you ain't afraid of me. I ain't afraid of you either."

"Well that's good that nobody's afraid," Rayford said. "'Cause fear will mess you up, make you do all sortsa dumb stuff. What do we have here, gentlemen? Who wantsa go first?"

"Whatta we always have here?" Buczyk said.

"You tell me. You sayin' it's about the same thing as last time?"

"And the time before that and the time before that and how far back you wanna go, huh?"

"Okay okay, let's see if we can't find somethin' different about this time, okay? This time. Right here, right now, okay? Stay back, Mr. Hornyak, don't be edgin' up there."

"Tell him stay back!"

"I'm askin' you to stay back, sir. I'm asking both of you to stay back, awright?" Rayford had stopped about four paces equidistant from them. The light was fading. He guessed it would be dark in another thirty, thirty-five minutes. He glanced at his watch and saw that it was 1910 hours. So maybe he didn't have as much daylight left as he thought. Need to get these two off the street and inside their houses soon. Don't wanna still be out here after it gets dark. The dark would trigger the streetlight on the corner shortly, but even after that happened the two large maple trees in front of the Buczyks' house would cast the sidewalk in shadow where the two neighbors were facing each other.

"So, Mr. Hornyak, you wanna tell me what this is about?"

"He's an asshole, that's what."

"Any particular reason?"

"You want a reason? You were here two weeks ago—what, you forgot that already?"

"I didn't forget, sir. Just want you to explain to me, in detail if you would please, what's got you upset now?"

"I came outta my house, he was out here, I'm tryin' to mind my own business, I'm not sayin' nothin', right away he starts in—"

"I didn't start nothin', that's bullshit and you know it—"

"Whoa, Mr. Buczyk, you'll get your chance—"

"Yeah shut the fuck up!"

"Pete, please don't, okay?" came his wife's voice from their front porch. Behind her, a dog began scratching the inside of their storm door.

"Oh what, you gonna take his side again, what kinda shit is that, huh?"

"Whoa, Mr. Hornyak, lower your voice, sir."

"Don't tell me how to talk. If you knew what the fuck you were doin', he'd still be in jail. Why's he out anyway? You told me aggravated assault was a felony, fuck's he doin' out, huh? If that's a felony?"

"Hasn't been tried yet, sir. As I understand it, he's out on property bond, right, Mr. Buczyk?"

"Don't try explainin' anything to him, he doesn't understand bail, he doesn't wanna learn anything, thinks he was born knowin' everything—"

"Oh me, I'm the know-it-all, huh? Yeah, you, you go to the library, right, read up on this stuff? Is that what you're sayin' now? In a pig's ass, that's where you go to do your readin', don't give me that shit I don't wanna learn nothin', there ain't nobody on this planet with a harder fuckin' head than a Polak—"

"Watch it, Pete, don't start with that Polak stuff, huh?"

"Hey! My old man told me forty years ago, forty years ago he said—you listenin', huh? Forty years ago what he said about Polaks, he's still right! You fuckin' Polaks, you got the hardest fuckin' heads in the world. I argued with him, you hear me? Hear what I just said? I argued with my father about you. I said, nah, not my friend Joe, uh-uh, he's not like the rest of them, pure fuckin' concrete between their ears—"

"Oh I'm sure that's what you said—"

"Hey I'm tellin' you, you fucker you. I argued with my father for you. Got smacked in the face for it, that's what I got, defendin' you, you sonofabitch—"

"Easy, Pete, go easy, man, I'm tellin' ya—"

"Yeah yeah, that's what you said when I told you don't cut that tree down. Your exact words, I remember, go easy, man, don't worry, we ain't gonna take the whole tree down, just those branches up over our gutters, that's what you said."

"And that's all I did—"

"Bullshit that's all you did! You took every fuckin' branch off on your side of the tree. I told you just take the top ones off, but no, nothin' doin', not you, you gotta strip the whole fuckin' tree—"

"How many times I gotta tell ya it wasn't me? The kid was up the tree with his saw before I even knew they were here. I was in the cellar, I didn't hear the guy knockin'—"

"So the guy starts cuttin' before he even talks to you? You hear this shit? You see what I'm dealin' with here?"

"Lower your voice, Mr. Hornyak, I have no trouble hearin', sir."

"Well listen to what he's sayin'. What bullshit. No tree guy works that way, what're you talkin' about? Guy gets outta the truck starts cuttin' without talkin' it over first? Without seein' what you want cut, what you don't want cut? Don't give me that bullshit—"

"That was four years ago for Christ sake!"

"Aw fuck you, four years ago, what's that have to do with anything? Who cares how long ago it was? Look at the tree, look what the fuck you did to it. And don't try to give me that shit again about the kid goin' up there without tellin' you what he was gonna do, that's bullshit."

"See what I mean? He don't wanna listen to anything."

"Besides which, it still don't make any difference with your gutters. Still gotta go up there and clean 'em. Or pay somebody."

"And you still think those leaves didn't have anything to do with causin' that water to get up there under the shingles and freeze—"

"Aw here we go again with the ice under the shingles—"

"Why don't you wanna listen about the ice under the shingles? You never wanna listen about the ice under the shingles—"

"What're we gonna do now, go back to who's supposed to pay for your new roof now, is that it? I ain't payin' for your fuckin' roof, I don't give a shit what your roofer said, I don't give a shit what your lawyer said—"

"In the first place I never ast you to pay for the whole roof. I ast you to pay for about six square feet of shingles, that's all—and I didn't even ast you to pay for the labor, I had that covered—"

" 'Cause what you were sayin' was makin' no sense. It was like I got up on the top of that tree and purposely poured them needles and branches into your gutter. That was an act of God for Christ sake, why the fuck should I pay for that? I didn't do it. You think I tell the wind which way to blow?"

"You planted that tree—"

"Oh here we go. I planted the tree. And how the fuck did I know it was on your property? If you can remember anything, you

fuckin' cement-head, can you remember we didn't have the lots surveyed? Huh? You remember how we used to talk? You were the one
said friends don't needa get their lots surveyed, that was for assholes
didn't know how to get along with one another—"

"Mr. Hornyak, you wanna talk about now? Tonight? Why you
two are standin' here screamin' at each other?"

"Hey, cop, why you think there's all these Polak jokes, huh? You
think there ain't a reason for them? Everybody knows, everybody
got these fuckers pegged, you think we don't? Whole world knows
what fuckin' morons they are—"

"So what you're sayin', sir, is you're havin' a disagreement over
intellectual capacity, is that it?"

"Oh that's a good one, cop. That's a real good one. Go 'head,
bust my balls for me. He ain't enough aggravation for me, you gotta
show up with your wise fuckin' mouth and your big lips—"

"Mr. Hornyak, sir, you're real close to ethnic intimidation and
harassment, sir. I'm warning you, please go inside your house—"

"Oh and what about him, huh? What, you two gonna have a little chat out here, huh? What the fuck, I might as well get you two
a coupla lawn chairs and a six-pack? Pound of kolbassi maybe and,
uh, and, uh, my little kettle grill, huh? Some black Russian rye,
some horseradish, some Dijon mustard, huh, whattaya say? Oh I
forgot, Mr. Physical Fitness over there, you don't eat kolbassi no
more, huh?"

"Pete, c'mon, please, c'mon in, okay?" While Mary Hornyak was
pleading with her husband, one of her dogs was scratching and
whining by her leg. "Stop it! Get in the kitchen! Go 'way!"

"No I ain't comin' in," Hornyak said. "Surprised you ain't out
here comparin' calorie charts with Arnold Schwarzenefsky over
there—"

Oh-oh, there it is, Rayford thought. I don't get these people
cooled out, there's goin' be blood on the sidewalk again, got-damn.
Where the fuck is James? How long's it take to get a juvey into detention? And where the fuck's Booboo?

"Why don't you listen to Mary and go inside?"

"Hey don't you worry about Mary, huh? You let me worry about Mary, okay? You wanna count calories with somebody, Schwarzenefsky, go count calories with Susie, don't be tellin' me about Mary—"

"Maybe you oughta go inside take a look at yourself in a mirror before you go callin' names 'cause people wanna take care of themselves."

"Take care of themselves? Is that what you said? Is that what you and my wife are doin'—takin' care of yourself? That's what you call it now, huh? Takin' care of yourself?! No shit. Maybe you oughta start takin' care of yourself with your own wife—"

"What're you sayin', huh? You sayin' there's somethin' goin' on between Mary and me, is that what you're sayin'?"

Oh-oh. Reseta, man, come on! Where the fuck are you? Damn! This shit goin' get ugly any second here.

"Hey that's 'Mrs. Hornyak' to you, no Mary, I don't wanna hear no *Mary* shit comin' from you, and don't you pretend like you don't know what I'm talkin' about, don't be insultin' my intelligence. Your head might be made of cement, but mine ain't."

"Go inside, Mr. Buczyk—"

"No no, wait, I wanna hear this. You got somethin' to say, say it out, don't be hintin' and insinuatin' 'n'at, just spit it out—"

"Hey, everybody ain't as blind as you think. People got eyes, you know? Got ears too."

"What people? C'mon, who? Name one!"

"Mr. Hornyak, Mr. Buczyk, that's enough. Go home, please. I'm askin' you both, go inside your houses now. And stay there—"

"Pete, come on in, please? Good God, don't do this, please?" Mary Hornyak swatted at the dog. "Told you to get outta here!"

"Why you askin' me? Why don't you ask him, huh? That's who you really wanna come in there. Think I don't know that? Think I'm stupid? Blind? Deaf? Think I don't have any friends? Think my friends are all deaf and blind too? They're all stupid?"

"Oh Gawd, Pete, Jesus, stop it!"

"Stop what? What should I stop? I didn't start nothin', I ain't stoppin' nothin'. Anybody oughta be stoppin' anything around here, it's you and him! Think I don't know what's goin' on, huh?"

"Oh God, Pete, Jesus, how can you say that? We're not doin' anything!" Mary said.

"Easy, that's how I can say it. Easy! 'Cause that's what I'm hearin'."

"Who you hearin' it from? You ain't hearin' it from nobody, you're makin' this up!" Buczyk said.

"Makin' it up?! I'm makin' it up?! Is 'at what you think? Everybody, that's who I'm hearin' it from. Everybody!"

"Everybody? Everybody who? You ain't playin' softball this year, we had sign-ups last week, you weren't there. You didn't sign up with anybody, and you didn't bowl last year either. Asked everybody if they saw you, nobody saw ya once in Rocksburg Bowl—"

"You think that's the only place in this town to go bowlin'? Think the only people I know are people you know? Guys play softball? Guys you bowl with?"

"You don't go to the Legion anymore, you haven't been down there since two New Years ago—"

"I know plenty of people, I don't have to go to the Legion—"

"Where? That's what I'm askin'. Mary says you don't leave the house—"

"Again with Mary. Shut up about Mary I told ya!"

"Says all you do anymore is drink beer and watch TV—"

"Like it's any of your business what I do in my house. Except you want it to be *your* house, right? You think I'm just gonna move out so you can move right in, right? That's what you want, ain't it? Right? Well fuck you! I ain't movin' outta anywhere. You two *wanna take care of yourselves* you're gonna have to do it in your house. And what's Susie gonna say about that, huh? Bet she has some choice words to say about that, huh? Susie? 'Member her?"

"Pete! Stop it! For God's sake stop it!"

Just then Rayford saw the light bar reflecting off the Hornyaks' windows before the MU turned the corner onto Jefferson. He was hoping it was Reseta, but when the door opened and that mass lumbered out he knew it wasn't. And even though daylight hadn't faded enough to trigger the streetlights, Rayford could see from the way Canoza's shirt fit across his shoulders that he wasn't wearing his vest.

Well at least neither of these guys has shown a weapon yet, and maybe seein' Canoza might make them think about him instead of each other. But Canoza was backin' me up two weeks ago, and that didn't stop Buczyk from lungin' at Hornyak, catchin' him flush with that straight right. Course maybe he thought he'd just get one in and Canoza would stop it before Hornyak could get back up and throw some of his own. Hard to say. Let's hope the motherfucker remembers how it felt with Canoza kneelin' on his back pushin' his face into the sidewalk so I could cuff him. And if he doesn't remember that, maybe he'll remember how good it felt to post his house for the bond, just for the pleasure of that one punch. Motherfucker better remember somethin' bad about that, 'cause Hornyak is lookin' way too wild. Got-damn, James, where the fuck you at, man? She-it, now who the fuck is that hangin' back there? Between the houses?

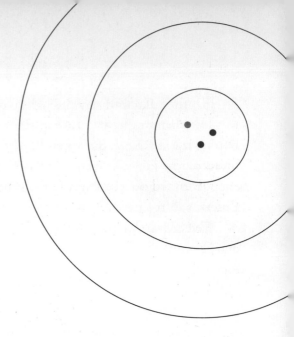

HEY! WHAT'RE you doin' here?" Rayford shouted at the face he saw peeking at him from between the houses. "Watch them," he said to Canoza as he skipped and sidled quickly around the Buczyks' Plymouth minivan.

"Go home!" Rayford shouted. He shone his MagLite on the face, and his jaw clamped. Got-damn you people. "This is none of your business. You don't go home now, you will go to Mental Health tonight, you understand me?"

"According to the prophecy, the coloreds—"

"No more prophecy crap! Go home!"

"Hey, tuzone, you don't tell us where we can be."

Aw shit, her too, got-damn! He turned the flash on her. "Mrs. Scavelli, I'm orderin' you and your husband to leave this scene now!"

"Scene? What scene? What's he talkin' about, scene?"

"Don't pay no attention to him, we ain't doin' nothin', we're just watchin', he can't tell us what to do."

Rayford strode quickly across the sidewalk and onto the grass separating the two houses. Nick Scavelli was to his left, Rose Scavelli to his right. Shadow cast by the Buczyk house made it seem almost night between the houses. They put up their hands and turned away as he aimed his flash first at him, then at her.

"Quit shinin' that thing on me!" Rose Scavelli said.

"I had enough problems with you already tonight to last me the rest of my life. I'm orderin' you to go home! Now! Or you're both under arrest!"

He turned over his right shoulder and called out to Canoza, "Get Reseta, tell him get here now."

"What for? We can handle this."

"Already had grief with these people today, shouldn't be here."

"Then send 'em home, I got these two covered, no sweat."

"Call Reseta I'm tellin' ya."

"Hoo-ha-ha, see? Not even other cops listen to you, tuzone," Rose Scavelli said.

"I know what that means, lady, stop callin' me that."

"You don't know nothin', all you know how to do is pull your gun," she said. "Wave it around in people's face, show off how you got a gun. Woo-woo, big deal."

"Turn around and go home now!"

"Stop shinin' that thing on me, I can't see."

"Go home, you can see all you want."

Rayford heard somebody coming, and turned to see Canoza walking fast toward him.

"Boo, what're you doin' here, get back out front."

"Hey, Scavellis, shuddup the both of ya, and get outta here before I take youns down the river and drown ya both—"

"Boo? Reseta here? Who's watchin' them?"

"Forget about them, they ain't doin' nothin'."

"Aw man, Boo," Rayford said under his breath, scurrying back to the front of the houses in time to see Hornyak pulling back his right leg and aiming a kick at Buczyk, who'd moved to where he could see what was happening with the Scavellis.

"Freeze!" Rayford shouted.

Too late. Buczyk howled as the kick landed somewhere on his right leg—Rayford couldn't see exactly where. He just saw Buczyk buckle to the right. Hornyak kicked him again in the other leg, and

Buczyk, howling and cursing, sank to his hands and knees, his eyes pinched shut.

Rayford's options buzzed through his mind. He jumped over Buczyk and swung his MagLite with both hands at Hornyak's chest, catching him in the left shoulder as Hornyak was ducking away to the right. Now Hornyak was howling and cursing.

"Freeze!" Rayford shouted again. Buczyk was now on his back, knees up, rubbing the backs of his thighs, rolling from hip to hip.

Hornyak was bending up and down from the waist, holding his left shoulder. "Sonofabitch! You broke my collarbone!"

"Goin' break the other one you don't back up and get on the ground! Get down now!"

"Mary? Maaaaaa-ry? Call an ambulance! Goddammit, Mary, you hear me?"

Rayford could hear other voices, shouting, snapping, and snarling at one another. He knew who it was but he wouldn't take his eyes off Hornyak and Buczyk to see what was happening with Canoza and the Scavellis. He kept glancing back and forth between Buczyk, still rolling on his back on the sidewalk, and Hornyak, who was still holding his left shoulder, still bending up and down from the waist, and now shuffling gingerly around in half-circles. Rayford stepped quickly back out into the street to keep both Buczyk and Hornyak in sight while staying three or four steps from both.

"Broke my fuckin' shoulder, you bastard—"

"Get down! Get down now!" Rayford shouted. He wound up as though ready to swing the MagLite again. Hornyak sidled back a couple of steps but remained standing. With his left hand Rayford aimed the flash at Hornyak's eyes and drew his pistol with his right.

"You don't get down now I'm goin' put one in your kneecap!"

"Aw that's right, threaten me, you fuckin' nigger. Gonna shoot? Shoot! Go 'head, see if I give a shit!"

"Last warnin'! Get down! Facedown on the ground! Or I shoot!"

"Owwww! Jeeee-sus fuck!" Canoza cried out.

Rayford turned quickly to see if he could see the reason for Canoza's cry of pain.

"Boo, what happened? Boo? Boo, say somethin'!"

"You stupid fuck!" Canoza shouted, hissing and groaning. "Oughta pinch your fuckin' head off. Jeeeeees-us Christ." He staggered out from between the houses with Rose Scavelli slung over his right shoulder, his knees wobbling, his face twisted up in pain. Then he straightened up and trotted across the street to his MU, where he dumped her back-first across the trunk, her head hitting the metal with a hollow thump.

Rayford was glancing rapidly back and forth between Canoza and Rose Scavelli and the two men in front of him. He heard Rose Scavelli's body and head hit the metal and heard her groan. He watched Canoza flip her over onto her face like she was no heavier than a magazine. That's when, in the light coming from the mercury lamp at the corner, Rayford saw the greenish handle of something sticking out of the top of Canoza's back, on the right side just below his neck.

Rayford kept looking back and forth between Canoza and Hornyak and Buczyk. He caught a glimpse of Canoza cuffing Rose Scavelli. When he turned back to glance at him again, Canoza was stuffing her into the backseat of his MU. She was limp. After he shut the door, Canoza tried with both hands to reach the thing that was sticking in him, but when he took hold of it with his right hand, as soon as he touched it he let out a howl and let go immediately. His knees buckled. Just as quickly he straightened up, turned, and started back across the street, muttering and cursing.

"Boo, what happened? You awright?"

"Stabbed me . . . sonofabitch . . . he stabbed me!"

Between the sounds of Hornyak and Buczyk groaning, moaning, and cursing, Rayford could hear someone going away from them, tripping and falling, crying out. He stuck the flash in his right armpit to switch on the radio attached to his left epaulet and momentarily lost Hornyak to the darkness.

"Base? Thirty-one here. Ten-forty-seven, officer needs assistance,

10-47, officer down, 10-47!" While he was talking he grabbed his flash and aimed it at Hornyak again. Hornyak, it seemed to Rayford, had moved much closer to him. He was now on the edge of the side-walk closest to the street.

"Last time, Hornyak, on the ground! Now!" Rayford aimed at the grass about a foot beside Hornyak's right knee and fired.

"Shootin' at me? You shootin' at me now you nigger bastard!"

"Next one's in your knee! Get on the ground! Get on the ground! Base, 10-16, what're you doin'?"

"Roger that, thirty-one. What's your 10-20?"

"Jefferson Street! Where you sent me! Canoza's stabbed! Two ac-tors on the sidewalk, one fleein' on foot. Where's Reseta?"

"Roger that, thirty-one. He's 10-17."

"Tell him move it!"

Rayford saw Canoza, walking much slower now, make it back across the street, hissing and grunting out every breath. Rayford could see Canoza's back wet over the right half of his shirt, the wetness as black as the shirt. His pistol handle and holster were also wet. As though in slow motion, one drop slid off Canoza's holster and fell to the street, bright crimson. Rayford couldn't tell what the thing was in Canoza's back, except it didn't look like a knife.

"Boo, you hear me? Can you hear me?"

"Yeah. What?"

"You okay, man?"

"Fuck no . . . got me three times, that prick . . . three times."

"Three?"

"Yeah . . . that's what it feels like. Oh fuck . . ."

Rayford had been swiveling his head back and forth, but heard movement and turned to see Hornyak taking a step toward him. Ray-ford didn't hesitate. He leveled the pistol on Hornyak's right knee and fired.

Hornyak hopped back across the sidewalk and fell hard on his tailbone, screaming and clutching at his knee.

"Thirty-one, who's firin', who's firin'? Thirty-one?"

"Me! I'm firin'! Now I need another 10-47. And got-dammit where's Reseta?"

"He's 10-17. Shoulda been there by now."

"Well he isn't! Wait wait, I hear the horn, I see lights reflectin' in the windows. Ah crap, it's the 47. Call Reseta, man, tell him get here! And Carlucci too. And the chief too."

"Roger that, thirty-one. Base open."

Rayford hurried to Buczyk's side. He was still on his back, holding and rubbing both his legs.

"You stay right where you are, you hear me? You move I'll put one in your knee just like I did him, you understand? Don't just nod, I wanna hear words!"

"I understand."

"Good!"

Canoza was now crossing the sidewalk and heading between the houses when Rayford rushed to his side and said, "Where you think you're goin'?"

"Get that cocksucker—"

"No you ain't! You goin' stay right here. You goin' get in that 47 and get your ass to the E.R. I'll get him, soon as Reseta gets here, don't you worry about him."

"All you're gonna do . . . you're just gonna collar him. I'm gonna take him down the river . . . drown his fucking ass."

"Shuddup, Boo! Shuddup a minute. You ain't goin' do none of that! Hey! You guys?" Rayford called to the EMTs now jumping out of the ambulance and scrambling for their gear in the back.

"Over here! Forget those two! Here's your work, right here."

Rayford moved around the other side of Canoza and held his left arm and patted his left shoulder. "That okay if I do that? Don't hurt, does it?"

"No. Why?"

"Don't wanna hurt you, that's all."

"How'd that old prick . . . how'd he move that fast . . . how'd he get me three times, old as he is . . . you figure that?"

"Didn't get you three different times," the ambulance crew chief said, coming up on Canoza's other side and taking hold of his right arm. "Just got you once."

"Huh?"

"It's one of those, uh, I don't know what you call 'em, three-pronged diggers or somethin'."

"Huh?"

"It's a gardening tool, you know?"

"Oh yeah, Boo, it's like a little rake, you know? Only with just three prongs, know what I'm talkin' about?"

"Hey fuck what it's called, okay? Just get it out!"

"Oh I'm not takin' that thing out, not here."

"Why not?"

"'Cause he's losin' enough blood with those prongs pluggin' up the wounds. Mighta caught a major vessel under there—"

"Yeah," said another EMT. "Can't tell how deep it is. I wouldn't touch it."

"Hey, you guys wanna talk about this later, fine. Get him in that wagon and get him up the ER, let those people handle it."

"Plus," the crew chief said, "God knows what's on that thing."

"Hey stop talkin' and start movin', huh?"

"Hey, Rayf? 'Member when you were a kid, huh? You get hurt? Your ma, huh? She'd kiss your boo-boo'n make it better, 'member?"

"Yeah. I remember." But at that moment he was just talking.

"Every time my ma tried . . . my old man'd say, don't do that . . . you're gonna make him into . . . into a sissy. Prick. Shoulda been married to Mrs. Scavelli."

Rayford took his hand off Canoza's back where he'd been patting him. His fingertips were wet and slippery. He wiped them on his trousers.

Canoza looked at Rayford and said, "I grabbed her up . . . was gonna grab him . . . carry 'em both back to their place . . . she got her hand loose, stuck her fingers up my nose . . . hada jerk my head back . . . and that's when that fucker nailed me."

"Man, he's huge," said the third EMT.

"Can you walk?" said the crew chief.

"What you askin' the man if he can walk for?" Rayford said.

"You wanna try puttin' him on a gurney? With that thing where it is? How much you weigh, Officer? What's your name?"

"His name's Robert Canoza. Patrolman Canoza. Twenty-five years in the department, did one tour in Vietnam. And if he hadn't showed up, that thing probably be stickin' in my back. So quit askin' him how much he weigh and get him goin' any way you can, awright?" Rayford didn't want to say that if Canoza had stayed on the sidewalk and watched Hornyak and Buczyk, he wouldn't be the object of all this attention now.

"Hey, it ain't like I . . . I can't talk myself, you know?" Canoza said. "Or like I don't know . . . who I am."

"Yeah, like you know who you are. Just like you remember to wear your vest."

"Oh man . . . Nowicki . . . he's gonna be . . . so fucking pissed."

"I doubt a vest woulda helped him. Not where that thing is."

"Hey, cut the talk, get movin'!"

"C'mon, let's go, guys. One on each side, one behind, c'mon. We're gonna need all the help you can give us, Patrolman, okay? What is it, Canoza, is that your name? I used to know some Canozas. Up in Norwood. Robert? Is it Robert?"

"Yeah . . . 'at's me . . . Ma'd try to kiss my, uh . . . my boo-boo . . . woo, man, startin' to get dizzy here."

"Hey, don't fall now, man, c'mon, couple more steps here, you can make it, c'mon. Hey, Patrolman? How about you get up in there, grab hold of his hand, huh? Wanna get up in there, take his left hand?"

Rayford hustled around them, stepped up into the back of the ambulance, and reached out.

"C'mon, give your partner your left hand, c'mon, stretch it out. Man, how much you weigh? You gotta be two-seventy, two-eighty, huh?"

"Ain't my partner . . . he was my partner he'da blown his head off . . . that's what a real partner woulda done."

"You were s'posed to stay on the sidewalk, man, watch those other two. Why'd you come around there anyway?"

"You don't know how to talk to dagos . . . takes a dago . . . talk to dagos."

"Oh you talked to 'em real good, didn't ya? Gimme your hand, c'mon, take ahold. C'mon, Boo—hey, you guys, everybody. On three, c'mon. One, two, three!"

With the EMTs pushing and Rayford pulling, Canoza lurched into Rayford and sent them both sprawling to the floor of the ambulance.

"Aggghhh, Jeeeee-sus! Owwwww, man, get off, get off! Get off me, owwwww!"

The EMTs clambered in and rolled Canoza to his left off Rayford, who immediately curled up, instinctively covering his genitals with his hands as though that would bring relief from the excruciating pain bringing tears and a rainbow to his eyes. He thought he was going to throw up. The pain rolled over him. There was nothing else. He was lost in it, swallowed by it, consumed by it. He passed out from it, awoke to it, and passed out from it again. He heard voices, coming to him from a long tunnel filled with thick white soup. He tried to roll another way but couldn't, rolled back, then slowly, slowly regained awareness of where he was while the pain turned from white-hot hammers to a viselike throb, throbbing more with each turn of the vise's screw, finally easing off slightly more as each second passed. It occurred to him that he might not die, when just moments before he'd been hoping he would die instantly.

He tasted his own tears, licked his upper lip and tasted mucus. "Man," he croaked, "fuck happened?"

"He landed on you with his, uh, looks like the handle of his nightstick there. Musta slipped around."

Rayford whispered, "If he ain't dead I'm goin' kill him."

"Oh, he's not gonna die from that thing. You okay?"

"No. Aw shit . . . man . . ." Rayford tried to pull himself up to a sitting position. One of the EMTs reached out to help him.

"Think you can stand up?"

"Don't know. Jesus . . . never felt pain like that in my life. Gimme your hand."

The EMT pulled and Rayford heaved himself up, where he doubled over immediately as another, different kind of pain shot out from his testicles.

"Motherfucker, Boo, when you get out the ER, I'm goin' shoot your ass, you hear?"

"What's goin' on?" Reseta said, sticking his head in the back. "Man, William, you don't look so good—hey what's wrong with Boo? Hey! Somebody! Talk to me!"

"Fuck you been, man? Long's it take you get a juvey down there?"

"Problem child, what can I say—what happened to you guys?"

"Motherfucker fell on me, somethin' stuck me right in my balls. Handle on his P-24 probably."

"Ow shit," Reseta said, wincing.

"Yeah ow shit. Better believe ow shit. Worst ow shit I ever felt. Nuts feel like they're in a vise and somebody's poundin' on 'em with a sledgehammer."

"Well what happened to *him?*" Reseta said, nodding toward Canoza, who was being wedged into a position so he couldn't roll once the ambulance began to move.

"Donchu worry 'bout him. He be fine—till he get out the hospital. Then I'm goin' kill his dago ass. Motherfucker. He'da stayed where I told him, none of this shit woulda happened."

"Coupla minutes ago, you were sayin' how if it wasn't for him, that thing would probably be stickin' in *your* back."

"Fuck's talkin' to you? And whatchu still doin' here anyway? Shoulda been gone already. Look out, James, back up, I need to get out this motherfucker."

Rayford stepped down, immediately doubling over, then trying to straighten up while walking gingerly on the balls of his feet.

"Man, I know that hurts. Got kicked there once."

"C'mon, let's go." Rayford hobbled and limped past Buczyk, who was trying to get up. "Who told you get up?"

"Huh?"

"Did I tell you get up? Get down! On your belly! Put your hands behind your back."

Buczyk obeyed without a word. Rayford cuffed him.

"Help me," Hornyak pleaded. "Help me. Somebody help me, please. Maaaaa-ry!"

"Shuddup!"

"Fuck you too, nigger."

"Wow," Reseta said. "The way you've improved community relations here, I'm impressed."

"Real funny, man. I want you to know I know how long it take to get to the juvey center and back. I made that trip a few times myself, case you don't remember."

"Where we goin' now?"

"Goin' grab up old man Scavelli."

"Huh? Why?"

"He stuck Boo, that's why."

"He stuck Boo?! Get outta here—that scrawny old man?"

"Yeah that scrawny old man. Boo grabbed up his old lady, put her on his shoulder, said he was goin' carry 'em both home, and he stuck him. That's what Boo said anyway."

They started between the houses. As they passed between the two back porches, Reseta's right foot shot out from under him and he went down hard on his right hip and holster.

"Shit!"

"What? What happened? You awright?"

"Aw man. Jesus Christ."

"What, what?"

"Slipped . . . dog shit. Awwww, man."

"What?"

"It's all over my shoes, my pants, my hand, holster, Jesus—that's it for these people. Everybody got a dog here's goin' to jail tonight, if I gotta fill out UIRs till tomorrow. Gimme your hand."

"Not the one with shit on it."

"Gimme your hand! Where's my flash? Dropped it. You see it?"

Rayford pulled Reseta up and shone his light around the grass. "There it is. C'mon, let's go collar this old prick. And watch your step, shit probably all over here."

They made it the rest of the way across the backyards without falling and came to the stockadelike wooden fence surrounding the Scavellis' backyard.

"Prick turned out all the lights," Rayford said. "You want the front or the back?"

"I'll stay here—unless there's no gate in this fence."

"Never saw a gate here," Rayford said, walking up and down the fence, sweeping his flash over it, finding no gate. "Course, I never been back here before."

"Hey, no gate, it's all yours, I'll take the front."

"Bullshit too, I ain't jumpin' no fence in the dark, uh-uh."

"So how'd he get inside then?"

"Who said he's inside? Went alongside the fence probably. C'mon." Rayford led the way to the end of the fence, then turned down the narrow bricked walk alongside the Hlebecs' house.

"These people have guns?" Rayford whispered. "You know?"

"If they do, they never showed 'em to me."

"Okay," Rayford said. "Here we go."

The narrow walkway led to the sidewalk on Franklin Street. As soon as they got to the sidewalk, Reseta turned his flash back along the other side of the wooden fence and whispered that he was going there to get to the back of Scavelli's house.

But as soon as he started up that path, somebody started whimpering and groaning on the Scavellis' front porch. Rayford turned his flash up on the porch and saw Nick Scavelli huddled by the front door, looking at his left shin, which was scraped raw and bleeding. Rayford shined the flash on his hands.

"It's him, James. Hey! Put your hands out where I can see 'em! Hold your hands out! Not goin' tell you again."

"Where's Rose? What'd you do with her?"

"Never mind about her, Mr. Scavelli, you're in a lot more trouble than she is."

"Lousy tuzone, go to hell."

Reseta shone his flash on Scavelli, went up the steps, and said, "Mr. Scavelli, well look at you, huh? You're under arrest, sir."

"Arrest," he said, as though trying to decipher the meaning of the word. "You want fries with that?"

"Aw here we go with the fries shit."

"I fell. Think I broke my leg. You saved room for dessert?"

"Saved room for what?"

"How 'bout a nice pecan ball? Piece a pie maybe, huh?"

"He know what he's sayin', you think? Or this just part of his act?"

"Right now I don't care. Turn him around and I'll cuff him. Listen to me, Mr. Scavelli. You listenin'? You make a wrong move here, you're gonna get hurt, you hear me? You stabbed a friend of mine. That makes me really angry. So you don't wanna get hurt, just turn around and put your hands behind you."

"Don't eat too much . . . save room for dessert . . . got all kindsa pie . . . banana cream, chocolate cream, apple, cherry, rhubarb."

"He's not gonna move, pull his ankles out and turn him around."

Rayford reached down and pulled Scavelli's ankles until the old man's back slid down his storm door.

It sounded to Rayford as though every dog on two blocks was barking and howling. So was Scavelli. He was barking. Like a dog.

"Now listen to him, Jesus Christ."

"Hey, Mr. Scavelli? Stop that and listen. You're under arrest for assault, aggravated assault, assault with a prohibited offensive weapon, assault on a police office, aggravated assault on a police officer, assault with a prohibited offensive weapon on a police officer, attempted homicide on a police officer. You have the right to remain silent—"

Scavelli interrupted his barking to say, "I fell down. I, uh, broke my ankle. Needa go to the hospital."

"If your ankle's broke, how come you didn't holler when I grabbed it just now?"

"Your ankle's not broken, you just scraped your shin. Hope you fell in somebody's dog shit."

"Speakin' of which, one of y'all's really stinkin', man."

Reseta blew out a sigh as he pulled Scavelli around, cuffed him, and continued advising him of his rights. "You have the right to an attorney. If you can't afford an attorney, one will be provided for you. You understand what I just said to you?"

"Gonna have any dessert today? Piece a pie maybe?"

"This ol' fart ain't goin' do a day, is he?"

"He will waitin' for his trial. After that, who knows? You stay with him, I'll go get my car."

"Hey, you got any plastic cuffs on you?"

"What for? Where's yours?"

"I didn't cuff the one I shot, he's—"

"Wait wait! *You shot somebody?* Who? When?"

"Hornyak. He was comin' at me—"

"You shot him?!"

"Yeah. What's wrong with you? Told you twice already, you didn't hear him moanin' and groanin' back there?"

"You shot him? Where?"

"On the sidewalk between his house and Buczyk's."

"No I mean where'd you shoot him, where on his body?"

"Hey! My ankle hurts. It's busted. I needa go—"

"Shuddup! Nothin' wrong with your ankle—where'd you shoot him?"

"In the knee. He was comin' at me. Wouldn't get on the ground."

"Oh man, why'd you do that—you just walked into a shit storm."

"Huh? Walked into what? Whatchu talkin' about?"

"Better pray he doesn't die. Get back there and make sure he's still alive. And get a wagon."

"I requested three already. Probably there now. Think I heard one right before I heard him moanin'. I know I did."

"Get back there, man, go on. I'll stay here. Go on, get goin'."

"Why you soundin' like that, man, you scarin' me."

"Rayf, I shot a guy in Nam. I'll tell you about it sometime."

"Thought you shot lotsa people over there."

"Uh-uh. This one was on our side. Get goin', man, show some concern."

"What? Show concern?! Fucker'da got up, next one was goin' in his heart. He started for me right after Boo got stabbed."

"Go show some concern, I'm tellin' you! It'll go a long way, believe me, EMTs see you. Don't argue with me, Rayf, just do it."

"I don't b'lieve this," Rayford said, but he didn't argue any more. He took off trotting on the sidewalk around the Scavellis' house, on Bryan Avenue. He wasn't going to risk slipping and falling in dog crap by going through the Buczyks' backyard.

When he got around to the front of the Buczyks' house, Bucyzk's wife and dogs were out on the sidewalk hovering over him. The dogs were licking his face and whimpering and whining. Rayford went out into the street to avoid them.

Another ambulance, its light bar going, was in the middle of the street, its back doors open. This crew of EMTs was preparing to lift Hornyak onto a gurney. Hornyak was hissing, moaning, and cursing Buczyk, his wife, the EMTs, and Rayford.

Rayford hurried to the foot of the gurney and asked how Hornyak was doing.

"That's the one shot me, the sonofabitch. Just standin' there, front of my own house, mindin' my own business, he shoots me. No reason, nothin'. No warnin', no nothin'. Just shoots me."

"How's he doin'?"

"Oh like you care?"

"I'm not talkin' to you, Mr. Hornyak, okay?"

"Oh listen to him now, now it's *Mis*-ter Hornyak. 'Fore he shoots me, it's hey, hunky, shuddup. Then he shoots me. I wasn't sayin' nothin'. Only one on the force, you ain't gonna be hard to find. And my lawyer's gonna find you, bet your ass on that!"

"Who's the crew chief here?"

"I am."

"You wanna step over here and tell me how he is?" Rayford stepped out into the street just as a minivan was pulling up. A teenage girl got out and ran to Joe Buczyk's side, calling out, "OhmyGod, ohmyGod, what's goin' on? What happened? Daddy?!"

The two dogs who'd been hovering around Joe Buczyk left him and ran to her, jumping on their hind legs, barking, wagging their tails. She stumbled over them and almost fell. "What's goin' on? What's happening? Mom? Daddy? Why you—why you got handcuffs on?"

"It's alright, everything's alright, don't get excited," Joe Buczyk said.

"You too, Buczyk," Pete Hornyak called out as he was being lifted into the wagon. "Lawyer's gonna find you too. Real easy!"

"Soon as we get him in, Officer, I'll tell you," the crew chief said to Rayford.

A city owned unmarked Chevy tried to pull around the minivan, backed up, and then pulled onto the Bryan Avenue side of the Buczyk house. A moment later, Detective Sergeant Ruggiero Carlucci came walking around the corner and up to Rayford.

"Whatta we got here, William?"

"Big mess is what we got."

"Okay," the crew chief said, after his crew had loaded Hornyak. "I can give you about thirty seconds."

"How's he doin', that's all I wanna know."

"Well, barring unforeseen complications, he's not gonna die, if that's what you're worried about. Course he's not gonna be walkin' real good from now on either. Went right through his kneecap, the patella."

"No artery bleedin'?" Carlucci said.

"Not that I could see, no. Guess it just missed the femoral. Gotta go, okay?"

"Yeah, get goin'," Rayford said.

"You shot him, right?" Carlucci said.

Rayford nodded.

"Any witnesses besides you?"

"Haven't asked anybody yet."

"What's his story?" Carlucci said, pointing with his thumb over his shoulder at Joe Buczyk. One of Buczyk's dogs came bounding out to where they were standing and jumped against Carlucci's leg, pushing him slightly off balance.

Carlucci bent down and gave the dog a scratch behind the ears and a rub on the chest. "What's up, doggie? Didn't happen to see the good officer shoot the bad man, did ya?"

Carlucci looked back at Rayford. "Canoza got stabbed, is that right?"

"Yeah."

"He alright? You know?"

"He was awake and alert when he left here, I haven't heard otherwise."

"So what's his story again?" Carlucci nodded toward Joe Buczyk.

"He was part of the original beef. Him and Hornyak, the guy next door—"

"I know 'em both," Carlucci said.

"Well they were beefin'—I still don't know what it was about this time. Then Boo showed up. Then the Scavellis stuck their noses into it. I told Boo stay on the sidewalk, watch these two, Hornyak and Buczyk there, and I go try to get the Scavellis to go home. Next thing I know Boo's standin' beside me, I ran back out here, and Hornyak's windin' up to kick him in the ass, Buczyk there. Gets him in one leg, then kicks him in the other one. He goes down, I'm tellin' Hornyak to back off, and then I hear Boo screamin' and cussin'."

"Wait wait, don't get ahead of yourself here. Why you got him cuffed? You gonna arrest him? Buczyk?"

"That's what I wanna know," said the teenage girl, obvious now to Rayford that she was Buczyk's daughter, though he'd never seen her before. She was pulling anxiously on the cuffs of her sweatshirt. "Why did you do that? If Pete kicked him, why did you put those on my dad?"

"At the time I had other problems, young lady."

"What's your name, miss?" Carlucci said, holding up his ID case for her to see.

"Janet. You gonna arrest him? My dad?"

"Not sure yet. How long've you been here, Janet?" Carlucci said.

"Just got here. Coupla minutes ago. Two maybe."

"People in that van there," Carlucci said, looking back at the minivan, "they friends of yours?"

"Yes."

"Do they live on this street?"

"No."

"Well how 'bout you tell 'em you're alright and there's nothin' to see here and they should go home, okay?"

"Okay," she said, and went across the street to talk to the driver. When she stepped away from the van, it started backing out onto Bryan Avenue and then turned and drove north away from the intersection.

Carlucci tapped Rayford on the arm, crooked his finger at him to follow, then walked across the intersection until they were well out of the hearing of the Buczyks.

"I'm only gonna say this once," Carlucci said, "so pay attention. I don't care what you did or why. But when I ask you a question about what you did or why you did it, don't lie to me. If it happened, don't leave it out, and if it didn't happen, don't put it in. Don't minimize anything, don't exaggerate anything, you got me? And don't think I won't find out what happened. 'Cause that's what I'm good at."

"Okay," Rayford said. "Uh, is this the beginning of the shit storm?"

"The what?"

"Reseta, uh, that's what he said."

"Well, you could put it that way, I guess. But here's the facts, just so you know what's comin' and why. And the only reason I'm tellin' you this is 'cause I know you're a smart guy. I know you passed the sergeant's test, and I know Nowicki's seriously been thinkin' of makin' you a detective 'cause he talked to me about it. He asked me what I think about ya. And I told him."

Rayford said nothing.

"You don't wanna know what I said?"

"Not right now, no. Right now I wanna know about these facts you said you were goin' tell me so I can know what's comin'."

"Okay. Right now what you gotta understand is, soon as you turn in your UIR, Nowicki's gonna have to turn it over to the Safety Committee on council. Twenty, twenty-one years ago, approximately, there was an officer-involved shooting, and everybody on City Council found out at that time there was no procedure for them to go through to investigate it, so they hada set up this ad hoc committee. You know what that means?"

"Yeah. For some special purpose or reason, right?"

"Right. Well, the local paper got hold of it and the Pittsburgh papers picked it up, and council got their onions crushed big-time about not havin' any special procedure, and so forth, and, uh, you know what happens when politicians get their onions crushed in public, they get all carried away, and so they wrote up this plan for this board of inquiry just for this one purpose, and that's to investigate officer-involved shootings. So what's gonna happen—"

"Who's on it?"

"Huh? I'm not sure now. Used to be the chief and the Safety Committee. But then that got changed and I don't know why so don't ask me. Tell ya the truth, council just shuffled committee assignments, so I'm not sure who's on what. But the mayor has the right to approve who's on it, that's for sure. Nowicki knows. Ask him."

"Okay. What's the rest?"

"The rest is, like I said before, don't lie. You lie, and you get caught in a lie, it won't matter what you did or why. All they'll re-member is you lied. And for them that'll be enough to can your ass. You got me so far?"

"Yeah."

"Okay. Then let's go find a witness, preferably one with good eyes and good ears. It'd also be good if they were reasonably intelligent and not too fuckin' nuts."

"You don't wanna interview me first?"

"I'll get to that, just let's see if we can't find somebody who saw you shoot him. Who called it in, the original beef?"

"Lady across the street."

"Okay. I'll take her first, you try the two wives, okay? Where's Re-seta by the way? Thought he responded to this. That's what Stramsky said. No?"

"He's with Scavelli."

"What's he doin' with him?"

"That's who stabbed Boo. Didn't I say that before?"

"Not to me you didn't. I just asked you if it was true he got stabbed."

"Well that's who it was oh shit."

"What?"

"She's in the backseat of his MU."

"Who?"

"Canoza's—Mrs. Scavelli. He put her in his MU. Right after he picked her up is when her old man stabbed him."

"After he got stabbed, he carried her to his MU? How'd he get her in the backseat if he was stabbed?"

"Ask him, I don't know, I just saw him do it, that's all."

"So she's still in the backseat?"

"Far as I know, yeah."

"Checked her out lately?"

"No. I had a few other things goin' on, you know?"

"Better check her out, see if she's okay."

She better be, Rayford thought as he trotted across the intersection and shined his flash through the window into the backseat. Rose Scavelli was sprawled across it.

Just as Rayford opened the back door and started to lean in, two other cars pulled up to the intersection. He waited a moment to see who it was. He recognized the driver of one car as a reporter for the *Rocksburg Gazette*. The other was obviously a photographer.

Rayford started to lean in and was overcome with the smell of feces. He recoiled, covered his nose, and reached in to feel for a pulse in her neck.

He couldn't find a pulse. "Oh shit," he said, moving his finger around on her throat, still trying to find one. "Oh lady, don't be dead, please don't be dead. Got-damn."

He backed up and shut the door and called out, "Hey? Detective? Sergeant Carlucci! C'mere!"

The reporter and photographer were starting toward him.

"Stop where you are!" Rayford called out to them. "This is a crime scene. I know we don't have the tape up yet, so you don't needa tell me that, but just stay where you are, we'll get to you in a little while. And no pictures till we say so, got that?"

The reporter and photographer looked at each other, started talking, but stopped and didn't make any move to get closer to anybody on the other side of the street.

Carlucci had just knocked on the door of the lady who called in the complaint. He backed up and looked at Rayford, who was waving his left hand toward himself as though urgently directing traffic.

Carlucci hurried toward Rayford. "What's up?"

Rayford leaned close to Carlucci and whispered, "Dead."

"You sure?"

Rayford nodded. "No pulse, no respiration, bowels emptied."

"Oh man. Oh shit, here we go. Okay, I'll call the coroner, you get some tape up. We're gonna do this the right way. You control the scene, tell Reseta get Scavelli booked and locked in, and then get back here fast as he can. Oh good, here comes Nowicki."

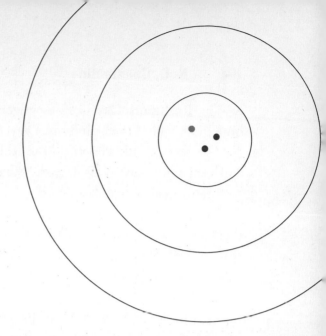

CARLUCCI SET his tape recorder in the middle of the table between himself and Rayford.

"Uh, before we get started here," Chief Nowicki said, "just so you know, the board of inquiry will be listenin' to this tape and the tape of your previous interview, and they'll be comparin' what you said then and what you say now with how you wrote it up, understand?"

"I understand," Rayford said.

"Okay, Rugs, turn it on, let's go."

Carlucci pushed the record button and said, "Second interview with Rocksburg PD Patrolman William M. Rayford—what's the 'M' stand for, by the way? Meant to ask you last time, I forgot."

"Milton."

"Milton?" Carlucci's eyebrows went up and he smiled. "You don't look like a Milton."

"You don't look like a lotta things you are. And you look like a lotta things you're not. Want me to name 'em?"

"Okay, sorry I brought it up. Second interview with Patrolman William Milton Rayford, shield number five two nine, in re case number ninety-nine dash four sixteen. Time is 1000 hours, Thursday, April 22nd, 1999. Interview conducted in room A, Rocksburg PD

Station, Rocksburg City Hall. Conducting the interview are Rocksburg PD Chief Nowicki and me, Detective Sergeant Carlucci."

Carlucci put his elbows on the table, laced his fingers together, and leaned his chin on his fingers. "We got some problems."

"Same ones we had last time?"

"Yeah. If anybody saw you fire the shot that struck Hornyak in the right knee, they're not willing to say so. I've interviewed them all twice. Chief Nowicki has also interviewed them twice, which you know, I believe, correct?"

"Correct, yes."

"Hornyak and his wife, Mary, Joseph Buczyk and his wife, Susan, Mrs. Marie Tomko, the lady across Jefferson from the Hornyaks who called in the original complaint, uh, the Jednaks, who live across from the Buczyks, as you know, were not home. The Hlebecs, who live behind the Hornyaks, also claim they were not home. Forget the Scavellis for the time bein', uh, the residents of 212 Jefferson, the Halupas, say they saw the first shot but, uh, ran inside and heard the second shot but did not see it. No point goin' over each name, but up and down both sides of the 200 block of Jefferson Street, they're all either deaf, blind, stupid, certifiably nuts—or they all ran inside after the first shot."

"Or they were all shoppin'," Nowicki said.

"And of course, as you know, Hornyak is sayin' it didn't happen the way you say."

"Which puts us in the middle of he-said he-said," Nowicki said.

"Well, what? Is the lady across the street, that, uh, Mrs. Tomko, what's she sayin' now—there was nothin' goin' on before I arrived? That made her call?"

"No, not at all. She's on the dispatcher call tape, she couldn't deny that even if she wanted to."

"Well it's good she's not."

"No no, she still says there was a beef between the two of them, she hasn't retracted any of that, and she still thought it was gonna get violent, and that's why she called. But just like the Halupas—and all the rest of them—she says the first shot, it scared the hell out of her, she backed away from the window, she heard the second one, but she definitely did not see it."

"Didn't even see the flash?"

"She says no," Carlucci said, shrugging. "And believe me, Patrolman, I've been up and down that street, and halfway into the 300 block even. Talked to anybody who might've had a clear field of vision there. So'd the chief here. We cannot find one other person who witnessed the second shot, or is willing to say so if they did."

"Great," said Rayford. "Fucking great."

Nowicki tapped Carlucci on the shoulder and motioned for him to turn the recorder off. Carlucci shrugged and turned it off.

"Hey, William, try to watch your language, okay?" Nowicki said. "That's not what we wanna hear when we play it for the board, you know? Back it up and erase it, Rugs."

"Hey, you wanna erase it, you erase it, I'm not erasin' anything. Somebody gets a hair up their ass, they bring a tape expert in and he finds out part of it's been erased, they'll have all our asses. Hey, leave it in, so he swore, so what? If I told you what I just told him, you wouldn't be swearin'? Better believe I would."

"Hey, Rugs, you keep forgettin'—why, I don't know but you do. Remember? Mrs. Remaley? That woman does not like swearin'. Why you keep forgettin' that, I don't know, but—"

"I'm not forgettin' anything about her. She's the idiot asked me why the man wouldn't obey the officer's order to get on the ground. And was it really necessary for the officer to fire his weapon. I told her that's the purpose of this inquiry, ma'am, okay? She's the pinhead we have to convince. Why you keep thinkin' I can't remember her, I don't know, but believe me, I remember her."

"You're sure that thing's turned off, right? 'Cause I don't know what's worse, 'fucking' or 'idiot' or 'pinhead.'"

"Let's just move on here, okay? I'm turnin' it back on now. Everybody ready? Here we go."

"Wait wait. William, indulge me. Watch your language, okay?"

"Yes, sir."

"Hey, everybody, I'm turnin' it on, okay?"

"Okay, okay."

"So, uh, Officer Rayford. Once more, in detail, as much as you can remember, tell what happened Friday, April 16th, 1999, at approximately between 1910 and 1930 hours."

"You want me tell it the way I wrote it up in my UIR?"

"No no no," Nowicki said, "don't tell it like you're fillin' out a form. Just talk it through, that's all."

"Okay. I got the call—but without referrin' to the UIR, I can't remember the exact time. I think it was 1910 hours, but don't hold me to that, it might've been later."

"Okay. Go 'head."

"Okay. I just finished writin' up a UIR on the Scavellis and the Hlebecs when I got the call. I was driving Rocksburg PD MU 31, and I approached 214 Jefferson Street from Miles Avenue. I was comin' from the west. I parked across the street, on the north side, and I approached two men engaged in a verbal dispute on the sidewalk between the houses, uh, that's between 216 and 214. I knew them both from previous responses to the same address. Joseph Buczyk and Peter Hornyak. Uh, Mr. Hornyak lives at 214 Jefferson, Mr. Buczyk at 216 Jefferson."

"Was either man armed—as far as you could tell?"

"Not as far as I could tell. I stopped walkin' about, uh, approximately three steps from the sidewalk, which, according to PD policy, is sufficient reaction distance."

"Where were they standing, approximately?"

"They were halfway between their houses. Looked to me like they were both makin' sure they were on their side of the property line."

"Which is imaginary of course," Nowicki said.

"Of course. There's no line there."

"No fence separating the properties, right?"

"Correct. No fence."

"What's between the houses?"

"Just grass."

"Could you see the grass in that light?"

"In that light? I don't recall. But I knew it was there. Saw it every other time I responded to that address."

"And these are typical city lots, right? Neither one is a double lot? And there's no vacant lot between 'em, is that correct?"

"That's correct. Typical city lots. Forty feet wide. Houses are twenty-six feet wide. Fourteen feet between 'em. Now 216 Jefferson, that's a corner lot. Forty-eight feet wide."

"But where the incident took place is between and in front of 216 and 214, correct?"

"Right. Correct. Between them. But not where I shot him, no."

"Where was that?" Nowicki said.

"After Mr. Hornyak kicked Mr. Buczyk, Mr. Hornyak ran backwards to the other side of his house."

"Okay, wait a second here," Carlucci said. "Back up. Before we get to that, go back to where you stopped in the street. Then what?"

"I asked them what the problem was. They never answered me. Never said what started that beef—that dispute at that time. Soon as I asked, they both started accusin' each other of startin' it. Especially Mr. Hornyak. And he was really upset with me because Mr. Buczyk was out on property bond for a previous dispute between them, which occurred, uh, two weeks before, on, uh, April 2nd, I believe."

"Before you go on, what did you have in your hands at that point? Had you drawn your service pistol at that time?"

"No. All I had was my MagLite. Had it in my left hand. I don't think I'd even turned it on yet. But I didn't draw my pistol until, uh, later."

"Okay. So go 'head."

"Well, Mr. Hornyak was really, uh, angry because I'd arrested Mr. Buczyk for assault and aggravated assault—I'd have to refer to my UIR of that incident to recall the exact charges, but the point is, Mr. Hornyak was seriously angry at me because he thought Mr. Buczyk should still be incarcerated for those offenses. He didn't understand why he was allowed to be home, when, as he put it, I'd told him I'd arrested Mr. Buczyk for a felony."

"Had you told him that?"

"I might have, I don't remember. Probably I did, but it doesn't stand out in my mind what I said or didn't say at that time. Didn't matter anyway, 'cause it wasn't up to me what Mr. Buczyk's bond status was. I tried to tell Mr. Hornyak that. So did Mr. Buczyk. But that just made him madder. Mr. Hornyak. Then they started in about who did what kinda research where and who thought he knew everything, I mean, it was just two so-called adults woofin' at each other like a coupla kids. I couldn't make sense with either one of them."

"What time was it? Approximately. And what was the light?"

"Not sure about the time. Mercury light on the corner in front of Mr. Buczyk's house hadn't come on yet. But there's two big maple trees in front of his house, so maybe I just didn't see it if it was on. But I'm sure by that time—no, I didn't turn on my MagLite till I saw somethin' movin' between the houses. I saw Nick Scavelli's face—well I didn't know it was him until I—wait a second, I'm wrong. Boo showed up before that—before I saw Mr. Scavelli. Patrolman Robert Canoza showed up to back me up, and he parked front-to-front with my MU across the street. He got out, he came toward me, asked me what was up, and that's when I saw Mr. Scavelli's face. So I had to turn my flash on, and I remember runnin' around—out in the street around Mr. Buczyk's minivan, his Plymouth. And uh, I, uh, shined my light on Mr. Scavelli and then I heard his wife sayin' something, and I shined it on her so I knew she was there too."

"Why're you sayin' it that way? You knew she was there too. She had to be there if you shined your flash on her."

"No, I know that sounds stupid, but I, uh, I already had one incident with them. Earlier. Mostly with him, Mr. Scavelli. Nothin' with her. And the Hlebecs. Uh, who live next door to him on Franklin Street. In fact, as I said before, I'd just finished fillin' out the UIR on that incident when I got called to respond to 214 Jefferson. And I've had way way too much, uh, well . . . I have myself taken Mr.

Scavelli to Mental Health three times in the past five and a half, six years. They keep him for the max permissible, uh, thirty days, and then he comes out, stays cool for a while, and then he, uh, he goes trippin' off to wherever he goes trippin' off to."

"This incident with Mr. Scavelli and Mr. Hlebec, would you describe that briefly? It's been reported by numerous witnesses you drew your service pistol and pointed it at both of them at various times, is that correct?"

"Correct. Yes. And I warned them that if they didn't shut up and get back in their residence, I would arrest them all. Well, I was drivin' by Mr. Scavelli's house. I'd just responded to an incident there the night before, April 15th. These people, I mean, the Scavellis and the Hlebecs, they been neighbors for twenty years, maybe longer, and this guy, Mr. Scavelli, he just goes off, starts harassin' 'em. Not just them, everybody on that block. But he's got it in for the Hlebecs 'cause he thinks it's their dog that craps in his yard.

"Comes outta his house with a hair-dryer, blow-dryer, sits in his truck, points it at cars goin' by, then he writes 'em up in his notebooks, wants me to arrest 'em. Points it at people walkin', does the same stuff, wants me to arrest them. And he does this kinda stuff to the Hlebecs couple times a week. Most of the time they ignore him, but April 15th, somebody smeared dog crap all over their doorknobs, and they accused him. So I thought I was gonna have to arrest 'em all that night, but finally I got 'em all cooled out, no arrests, no citations, got 'em back inside their houses, and then, April 16th, I'm drivin' by, routine patrol, and I see Mr. Scavelli with a shovel headin' for the Hlebecs' front porch. So I stopped him.

"And then Mr. Hlebec came home and they started in on one another. Then Mrs. Hlebec came home, and the only way I could get 'em cooled out and inside was to draw my piece and threaten 'em all with arrest. So apparently a lotta people came outta their houses and called the station, said I was wavin' my piece around. Which I wasn't doin'. I was in control, I knew what I was doin', I knew what I was sayin', but it was very, uh, frustrating, you know? Tryin' to get so-called grown-ups to quit actin' like kids. And Mr. Scavelli, he's done this sorta thing with every member of the department at one time or another, well, maybe not every member, I haven't taken a poll or anything. But the man's famous for this kinda stuff. Am I exaggeratin' this? You two been in this department way longer'n I have, am I exaggeratin' any of this?"

"Not as far as I'm concerned," Nowicki said. "I went to that address many times myself. Took him to Mental Health once, had to testify at his competency hearing."

"I never took him to Mental Health," Carlucci said, "but I went to their address when I was a patrolman and they lived up on the hill, in Norwood. At least twice. You're not exaggeratin', not from my experience. So, uh, you saw him. On the 16th I'm talkin' about now? Correct? You turned your flash on 'em, you knew they were both there, then what?"

"Then, the next thing I know, Boo, Patrolman Canoza, he's standin' next to me—but first I confronted them. I went between the houses and told 'em get outta there, go home. Then Canoza's there."

"And?"

"And I said what're you doin' here? To Canoza. Who's watchin' them? Meanin' Mr. Hornyak and Mr. Buczyk. And he said somethin' about they weren't doin' anything, and I turned around and went hustlin' back out to the sidewalk where they were. And just as I get there, Mr. Hornyak is kickin' Mr. Buczyk in the leg. The right one. And then he kicked him in the other leg."

"Which leg was he kickin' with?"

"His right one. And Mr. Buczyk goes down, and I jumped over him and swung my MagLite with both hands and, uh, I hit Mr. Hornyak in the left shoulder, not sure exactly where."

"Thought last time you said he went runnin' backwards to the other side of his house."

"Yeah. He did. And I was right after him. That's when I hit him."

"So he's now between his house and the Buczyks' house—is that what you're sayin'? Between 214 and 212?"

"Yeah. Correct."

"And what happened then?"

"I was tellin' him get down, get on the ground, and he was just hoppin' around, holdin' his shoulder, cussin' me out, sayin' I broke his shoulder, or collarbone. And then I heard Boo scream, Patrolman Canoza, and I'm tellin' Mr. Hornyak to get on the ground, and he's still hoppin' around, shufflin' around in, like, uh, half-circles, and the next thing I see, uh, I see Patrolman Canoza, he's carryin' Mrs. Scavelli over his shoulder to his MU."

"How's he carryin' her? Describe it exactly as you remember it."

"Uh, he's got his arm, his right arm around her knees and she's kinda slung over his right shoulder."

"Was she moving?"

"No. She . . . I'm not sure. She looked kinda limp."

"Was she saying anything?"

"No. Definitely no. She was not sayin' anything."

"But you're not sure whether she was movin', huh?"

"No. I mean her arms were movin', but I think that was from how Patrolman Canoza, was, uh, well, he was sorta staggerin', and her arms were, uh, they were sorta swingin'. Limp."

"And then what?"

"Well you gotta remember I was tryin' to watch him and watch those other two, so my head was goin' back and forth real fast, and then I see Patrolman Canoza set her down on the trunk of his MU, and she falls back and I hear her head hit the trunk, you know, with this hollow kinda whump noise. And that's when I see this thing stickin' outta his, uh, like right below his neck and to the right a little bit. Had this kinda greenish handle, but it was in a, uh, a goofy angle."

"Goofy how?"

"I don't know how to explain it exactly—I mean I didn't see it till later when I was holdin' him, but then was when I stuck my flash under my right armpit—no no, before that I'd drawn my piece. Oh wait a second, no—shit, before that I already fired the first shot I think. See this happened so fast I'm almost . . . it's like it was all happenin' together."

"Take your time, take your time, we ain't goin' anyplace here," Carlucci said. "I know it happened fast. Try to break it down, close your eyes, visualize it in slow motion if you can."

"Yeah. Well. I don't know if I can do that," Rayford said, closing his eyes, licking his lips, inhaling deeply, and sighing. "Okay. Lemme try. I had my piece in my right hand. Had my light in my left. Hornyak was back on the grass between his house and 212. He wouldn't get down. I kept shoutin' at him get down, get down. He just kept cussin' me. He was holdin' his shoulder. His left shoulder. And it looked to me like he was comin' closer. So I fired. Fired into the grass. On purpose. Missed him by a foot to the left of his right knee. He called me a nigger bastard. Right then, that's when I heard Boo scream, and I started shoutin' at him, you know, Boo, what happened, what happened, say somethin', and then he came out from between 216 and 214 with her over his shoulder, Mrs. Scavelli. Over his right shoulder he had her. No. His left.

"And after he set her down on his trunk, and I saw the thing stickin' in the top of his back, that's when I put my flash under my right armpit to turn on my radio and call 10-47, officer needs assistance, officer down, I don't remember what I said exactly—"

"You said all of that," Nowicki said. "It's on the tape."

"Yeah. Well when I was doin' that, and my flash was under my right armpit, I lost sight of Mr. Hornyak. I mean my flash, the beam was kinda goin' off to the left, and by this time it was dark and for just a split second there, I didn't know for sure where he was. So when I got the flash in my left hand again, it looked to me like he was way closer to me. And he was definitely movin' toward me. So I didn't hesitate. I fired. Leveled on his knee and fired."

"Then what?"

"Uh, well, he started hoppin' on his other leg, he was screamin', he was hoppin' backwards, and, uh, then he fell back, straight down on his, uh, his butt, his tailbone. His head bounced."

"He says it didn't happen that way."

"Hey. He can say whatever he wants. That's the way I remember it."

"He's sayin' you never told him to get on the ground—"

"Oh that's bullshit. And I don't care whether the people goin' hear this tape like swearin' or not. There's only one word for him sayin' that, and that's bullshit. I told him get down six, eight times at least. Told him get on the ground. Fired that warnin' shot. Told him he didn't get down I was goin' put the next one in his knee. There's maybe nobody saw me fire that second one, but Buczyk was there. He heard me. He had to hear me. I know he heard me, 'cause he wasn't layin' three, four, five steps at the most away from me—and I was yellin'. So what's he sayin', Buczyk? He sayin' I didn't tell Hornyak get down? And those other people, the ones ran inside after the first shot, they sayin' they didn't hear me yellin' get down? Before the first shot? Or before the second one? I ain't buyin' that, no way."

"Just tellin' you what he said, Patrolman," Nowicki said. "Didn't say anything about what they said."

"Well you said you both interviewed everybody twice, so what's Buczyk sayin'? One thing I know—if I don't know anything else—is he didn't run inside after the first shot. He was on his back, he was facin' the other way, away from me, but the man wasn't three, four steps away from me at the most. And I know he can hear. 'Cause after the first 47 came, and Patrolman Reseta and me was goin' go grab up Mr. Scavelli, I told him turn over and I cuffed him. He didn't have any trouble hearin' me then, and I wasn't shoutin' when I told him turn over. So what'd he say?"

"We'll get to that later."

"Wait wait wait, what do you mean we'll get to that later? You sayin' he's sayin' somethin' else? Different from what I'm sayin'?"

"I'm not sayin' that, William," Nowicki said, "I just think we got other things to cover here."

"Hey, I'm sure you do. But every so often here, I'm startin' to get the feelin' there's some bad vibes goin' around, like maybe I didn't do a righteous shooting. Just remember I had a backup, I wasn't there by my lonesome. Boo was there. You tellin' me Boo's sayin' something else?"

"Well, see, Canoza's got his own problem."

"Wait. What's that mean, got his own problem?"

Nowicki motioned for Carlucci to turn his recorder off again, which Carlucci did.

"You were the one reported her to Detective Carlucci. You said, uh, she—she bein' Mrs. Scavelli—she had no pulse, no respiration, and had emptied her bowels was I think how you put it, am I right, Detective?"

"Right."

"So I talked with the coroner this morning, and all he can determine is she died of a cerebral hemorrhage, but she's got this bump on the back of her head, and you're the one said you heard her head hit the trunk after you saw Boo set her down, right?"

"Right. That's what I said. So Boo got a problem from that?"

"We all got a problem from that. Coroner says it's chicken and egg, he can't tell whether the bump caused the hemorrhage or whether she had the hemorrhage before she got the bump. Plus, remember that reporter and that photographer you told to stay away from the scene?"

"Yeah. From the *Gazette*. But I didn't tell 'em stay away from the scene, I told 'em they couldn't talk to anybody until they cleared it with Rugs. He just got through tellin' me it was a crime scene, told me get the tape up, secure the scene, and that's what I did."

"Well maybe he didn't like the way you said it, I don't know. But apparently, after the first story, when Canoza's mug shot was on page one, he got some calls from a couple old ladies, this reporter. One in particular, who had what she considered was a very nasty encounter with Boo when he was poppin' a lock on her car. So since then he's been playin' this angle, you know, Mrs. Scavelli was an old lady and Boo was the officer involved, insinuatin' and implyin' that Boo maybe got some kinda head problem with old ladies—"

"Aw that's just bullshit."

"I know it's bullshit," Nowicki said. "But the DA called me and said he got called by the president of the local chapter of the AARP. They wanna make sure he isn't blowin' this off. They want him investigatin' Boo for these other complaints, and they want a full and complete investigation into the death of you know who."

"Full and complete," Rugs snorted. "Like they would know."

"Hey, Rugs, don't be takin' that attitude. We don't take this shit seriously, we're in trouble, I'm tellin' ya. Far as I'm concerned, the coroner could not've come back with a worse ruling. Now nobody's gonna be able to say what happened. And these geezers, hey, they think somebody's fuckin' with 'em, they start makin' calls, writin' letters, showin' up at the council meetings, they'll start bustin' everybody's balls. And the DA, don't think he doesn't know who votes. I guarantee every time a geezer calls him about this and wants to bitch, he'll take the call, don't think he won't."

"Wait wait wait," Rayford said. "Her fuckin' old man was the one stuck Boo with that thing that was covered with dog shit—anybody remember that? They just took him off the critical list yesterday. Monday, when I saw him, he was makin' no fuckin' sense at all. They had him full of the most powerful antibiotics they got, that's what the nurses told me—and we're gonna start runnin' scared 'cause some motherfuckin' reporter is speculatin' about Boo and old ladies? Fuck that!"

"I know, I know—"

"You know?! Hey, Chief, all due respect, but got-damn, man, every time we got some real shit in a nuisance bar, who's first one in the door? Who gets called out—whether it's his watch or not?"

"I know, I know, I'm the one who calls him."

"Well we goin' let him get hung out to dry 'cause some old lady lock her keys in her Toyota? I own Toyotas, man, I know how hard they are to pop the lock. Boo told me 'bout that one, she busted his balls big-time."

"He lied about his shield number to the other one."

"Aw, man, this ain't nothin' but chickenshit. Got-damn Scavelli, shoulda shot that motherfucker my own self. Like to see what the pres of the local AARP woulda said Scavelli smeared dog shit over all *his* doorknobs. Or when he's comin' at him with a shovel fulla dog shit. Or when he's pointin' a blow-dryer at him, tell him he's walkin' too fast. Deal with that shit night after night for a coupla years, then we'll see who he wantsa talk shit on."

"You know," Carlucci said, turning to Nowicki, "probably wouldn't be a bad idea you call the local president in, whoever it is, have a heart-to-heart with him. Sure wouldn't hurt. Maybe even let him read some of the UIRs about the Scavellis."

"Yeah. And get that reporter down here too, let him read 'em. Let him go talk to the people at Mental Health."

"Stop already, you know they're not allowed to talk to him."

"Off the record?" Carlucci said. "Why not? If you talk to the director up there first, clue him in."

"Wait a second," Rayford said. "There's some things I got to know. Hornyak get himself a lawyer?"

"Whatta you think?"

"Okay. Then does the physical evidence match up with me or with him—and don't bullshit me now, this I gotta know."

"Matches up with you," Carlucci said. "Shell casings ejected where you said. Blood started drippin' on the street edge of the sidewalk, and went back onto the grass where he fell. And we had to wait till Saturday to get a metal detector, but we found the one you fired into the grass. Just would be a whole lot better if we had a witness, that's all. Eyewitnesses stink, but, uh, for some reason people believe 'em, don't ask me why, I don't know. I was plannin' to talk to Buczyk again."

"Well I know he heard me, got-damn!"

"You got him for assault and aggravated assault on Hornyak from two weeks prior. Without a deal, would you wanna help you?"

"Well, screw it, kick it down," Nowicki said. "Tell him you talked to an assistant DA and he told you he couldn't make aggravated stick.

Tell him he cops to simple assault, you'll see he gets ARD, plus costs. First offense, right?"

"Yeah. Pretty amazing, considerin' how many times we been called there, but that's all it is for him."

"Well if he's lawyered up—"

"Told me he can't afford one, has to get a PD."

"Okay. Then get the PD in on it, see if his hearing improves or not."

"You can do that?" Rayford said. "Without talkin' to somebody from the DA's Office first?"

"That recorder's still off, right? You sure?"

"It's off, it's off, Christ." Carlucci stood and stretched. "We done here? Anything else?"

"Course we can do that."

"Well what's Hornyak goin' say?"

"Fuck can he say?" Nowicki said. "DA and the judge go along with the ARD, his civil suit's dead, he can't say nothin'. Okay, I'm done here, who's left? Reseta? Then we got to see if Boo's in good enough shape to talk. Okay, William. Anything else, we know where to find you. Second watch tonight, right?"

"Right."

"Well, hey, look at it this way: with her dead, him in Mental Health, and Hornyak on crutches, cruisin' the Flats oughta be a walk in the park tonight."

Rayford hung his head and shook it. "Don't care what you say, man, that place ain't never goin' be a walk in the park for me."

"Cheer up, William. It was a clean shooting. I know that, Rugs knows that, two-thirds of this board is gonna know that, especially if Rugs gets Buczyk to clean the shit and sawdust out of his ears. Then all we gotta do is make sure Mrs. what's-her-face doesn't get to one of the other two. Remaley."

"Who're the other two again?"

"Trautwine and Figulli," Nowicki said. "Trautwine's no problem, but Figulli? I don't know. She's got somethin' on him."

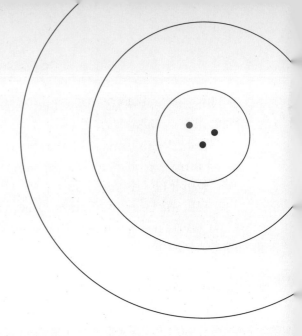

F IRST INTERVIEW with Patrolman Robert Canoza in re case number ninety-nine dash four sixteen. Place is room 421, Conemaugh General Hospital, Rocksburg, PA. Time is 1805 hours, Thursday, April 22nd, 1999. Present, in addition to Patrolman Canoza, are Rocksburg PD Chief Nowicki and me, Detective Sergeant Carlucci."

"Hey. How's it goin'?" Canoza said, his eyes puffy and red, his lips sticking together. He'd obviously just awakened from a nap. He was on his left side, propped up with two pillows behind his back, an IV drip in the back of his left hand. "Fuckers bring me anything to eat?"

"No," Carlucci said, shaking his head and turning the recorder off.

"I didn't know you were allowed to eat anything," Nowicki said.

"Aw listen to you, allowed to eat anything. Hope to fuck you both wind up in here real soon, like next week, so I can visit youns with empty hands. Didn't your mothers teach youns any better than that? Jesus Christ. I could die in here from the shit they feed you. Everybody works in that kitchen oughta be under arrest for fraud, pretendin' that shit is edible."

"At ease, at ease, what the fuck," Nowicki said. "I'll bring you somethin' tomorrow—"

"I'm hungry now! What's with the tape recorder?"

"Hey, Robert," Carlucci said, "try to focus, okay? We're here to ask you about the night you got stabbed, okay? Try not to think about food for a couple minutes."

"Hey, you try. I'm starvin' here. Least go get me a couple Hershey bars or somethin', Jesus, I'm tellin' ya—listen to what I had for breakfast today, no shit. They bring you like a half a cup a rolled oats, glass a skim milk, like six ounces of orange juice, fuckin' toast somebody put like a quarter-size glop of margarine in the middle of each slice, and fuckin' coffee so weak you could see the bottom of the cup— imagine me tryin' to survive on that, huh?"

"Hey," Nowicki said, "let me go down the coffee shop get this jaboney some candy bars or somethin'. Go 'head and start without me, I'll be right back."

"Kid who was in here with me? Didn't weigh one-fifty, he gets the same thing I get. Same fuckin' amount."

"Robert? Yo, Robert, you with me?"

"Huh? What? What?"

"Gotta ask you some questions about Friday, April 16th, you know? Case number ninety-nine dash four sixteen, you with me?"

"What questions? What's with the tape recorder I asked you."

"We got some problems, Robert."

"Which we you talkin' about? What problems?"

"You. Me. Us. All of us in the department."

"All of us? What problems?"

"For one thing, uh, Mrs. Scavelli? Remember her?"

"Exactly how could I forget her?"

"Well. Bad news there, pal. And try to take this a little more seriously, okay? By the way, you on any kinda pain meds right now? Morphine drip, Percocet, Percodan, anything like that?"

"Nah. Took me off all that stuff yesterday. I can have some of that Perco-stuff if I want it, but I hate it, I told 'em don't give me any more of that stuff, it just constipates the shit outta me. Two of those you need an enema. And it don't do nothin' for the pain anyway. Just makes you sleepy. Still fuckin' hurts and you can't shit, some fuckin' pain relief that is."

"So you're not on anything now—that you know of—that would interfere with your memory, right?"

"Just told you no, what do you want? Ask the nurses you don't believe me."

"Hey, Robert, another thing—try to watch your language, okay? We got a pain-in-the-ass committee to deal with and the chairman, chairwoman, chairperson, whatever, she doesn't like people swearin', okay?"

"What committee? Safety Committee?"

"No. Not the Safety Committee. An ad hoc committee to investigate Rayford's shooting."

"Huh? Rayford? He got shot? When?"

"No no no. No. He didn't get shot, he shot Hornyak."

"He shot Hornyak? When? He dust him off?"

"No he didn't dust him off. Shot him in the right kneecap. Right about the time Scavelli was stabbin' you with that rake."

"You're shittin' me. He shot him?! You're not shittin' me?"

"C'mon, I wanna turn this thing back on, okay? Stop cussin'!" Carlucci shook his recorder at Canoza.

"Stop cussin'? Why? I can't cuss I can't fuckin' talk."

"Stop, will you please? You don't cuss when you're talkin' to civilians. And I told you why. Pay attention here, c'mon. The woman Bellotti appointed to run the committee, she thinks swearin' is a sign of a lack of vocabulary, a sign of immaturity."

"Hey I got a vocabulary I'll put up against hers any day—whoever she is. I study vocabulary books all the time. Like she could tell me the difference between necrology and nephrology, huh? Or between oncology and ontology—"

"Not the point, Robert, c'mon, stop bustin' my balls here, please? We got problems I'm tellin' ya!"

"You keep sayin' that, I keep askin' what problems, you don't tell me what problems—"

"Listen up and I'll tell you, okay? First problem is Hornyak. We got lots of witnesses heard the shots. Lots of 'em saw the first shot. But if anybody saw the second shot, they don't wanna say."

"There were two shots? When'd this happen?"

"You sure you're not on pain meds here?"

"Now who's bustin' whose balls? I told ya no!"

"You tellin' me you don't remember hearin' two shots right around the time Scavelli was stickin' you?"

"I heard one."

"One?! Not two?"

"What, somethin' wrong with my vocabulary here? One is one, two is two. I heard one!"

"Yesu Maria. Think, Robert, this is important."

"I am thinkin'. But if *you're* thinkin', you know? *You?* You might remember I was havin' a little problem myself."

"I know you were. That's the other problem we got, you know? Mrs. Scavelli?"

"Yeah? What's up with her?"

"You gonna get serious now? 'Cause I'm turnin' this back on, you hear? It's on now, okay?"

"Okay, okay, so what's up with Mrs. Scavelli?"

"She's dead, Robert. Croaked out."

"Oh yeah? When? What happened? I was hopin' maybe I get the chance I could take her down the river and drown her ass—"

"No goddammit!" Carlucci said, jamming the stop button on his recorder so hard he broke the edge of his thumbnail. "Don't say shit like that, Robert, Jesus Christ, c'mon! Holy fuck, don't do that, please, okay? Givin' me a heart attack here."

"Why? What'sa matter? Stop talkin' in circles, Rugs, tell me what'd I say, huh?"

"Listen to me, Robert. We got a humongous fuckin' coupla problems here, okay? Number one, I told you about Rayford. Number two, after you carried Mrs. Scavelli up to your car—remember? You put her in the back, right? You do remember that?"

"Yeah yeah, so?"

"Well when Rayford went to check her out, she was dead, man, you capeesh?"

"Wait wait, fuck you sayin'—I killed her?"

"No! Nobody's sayin' you killed her. No."

"Why you hesitatin'?"

"I'm not hesitatin'."

"Fuck you ain't, I know when you're hesitatin'. What's goin' on? Somebody sayin' I killed that old witch?"

Carlucci squeezed his temples. "Robert, clean up your mind here, please? Start thinkin' like the police officer you are, will you please? We got an officer-involved shooting, that's Rayford. And we got an old woman found dead in your MU after you carried her out between the houses and put her in the backseat. Coroner says she died from a cerebral hemorrhage. He also found a bump on the back of her head. Rayford saw you set her down on the trunk of your MU and he says he saw her fall back and he saw and heard her head hit the trunk, okay? You startin' to understand the nature of the problems here?"

"Ohhhh man. Rugs, listen to me, I did not hurt that woman. All I did was pick her up, I was startin' to carry them both back to their house, okay?"

"Wait, I'm gonna turn this on now—"

"No no no no, don't turn it on yet! Just listen! Listen to me."

"Hey don't tell me what happened first, Robert, it's gonna sound like we been rehearsin' here."

"I'm not rehearsin', I'm just tellin' ya, c'mon. What rehearsin', what the fuck, listen to me here."

"Don't tell me till I turn this on, okay? And then remember that it's on, okay? Remember that it's on and watch your language, okay? Remember that you're a police officer and you got a good vocabulary. And, also, remember that you've had some problems with old ladies, okay?"

"Wait, hold it, why do I have to remember that? What's this shit about problems with old ladies? What's goin' on, Rugs?"

Carlucci told him about the reporter at the scene and about how that reporter had been called by the two old ladies whose car locks Canoza had popped, how their encounters with him had been, to put it mildly, something less than professional.

"Awwww man, I'm fucked."

"You're not fucked, Robert, listen to me. You just gotta start thinkin' like the police officer I know you are, okay? Are you listenin' to me?"

"I'm fucked, Rugs. They'll find out I lied about my shield number to that one lady, they'll find out I made that other one cry, now this. Aw fuck me. Goddamn Scavellis. It's dagos like them give dagos a bad name everywhere—and don't act like you don't know what I'm talkin' about, Rugs, 'cause I know you do. May as well eat my fuckin' piece right now—"

"Hey!" Carlucci shouted. "Stop that kinda talk right now! Don't you ever say anything like that again, you hear me! Eat your piece I'll smack you in the mouth you say that again! Put your brain in gear and stop feelin' sorry for yourself, we got problems to solve here, we don't have time for any of that eat-your-piece bullshit— you hear me?"

"Hey Rugs, coulda died in here, man. Doc told me it was touch and go for a while, with that infection, from that dog shit. All through me, man—"

"Yeah and it's over now, you're on your way back. No more coulda-died shit either, okay? I don't wanna hear none of that, you hear me?"

"You don't wanna hear somethin'?" Nowicki said, coming in with paper bags in both hands. "Tell you what nobody should hear, okay? You two shoutin' about what you been shoutin' about. Fuck's wrong with you two? Thought you'd have this thing wrapped up, I come down the hall, what am I hearin'? Two jaboneys shoutin' at each other about stuff no civilian should hear. There's nurses out there tryin' to pretend they're deaf, Jesus Christ. Oughta take you across the street to Mental Health, have a competency hearing for both you jaboneys.

"Here, Boo-boy, you wanted food, here's food. And don't thank me either."

"What is it?" Canoza said.

"What, if it's not on your diet you're gonna send it back? It's four cheeseburgers and two chocolate shakes. Think you can talk and eat at the same time so we can wrap this up? You did explain the problems, right, Rugs?"

"Yeah. But not only didn't he see either shot, he didn't hear the second one."

"Is that right? You didn't see either one?"

Canoza mumbled something while devouring the first of four burgers.

"Swallow. Then say it."

"I'm gonna turn this on now, you hear me? Both of you hear me?"

"Yeah yeah—you hear him, Boo?"

Canoza held up a finger and swallowed. "Don't call me that. Not on tape, okay? Especially not on tape."

Nowicki sighed and rolled his eyes. "Yes, Officer Canoza. I hear ya talkin'. Now can we get on with it, please?"

"Okay, Robert, here we go. Start with the dispatcher call."

"I don't care what the coroner says, I didn't hurt that woman. All I did was pick her up, and I started to turn around, I was gonna pick him up and he stuck me—"

"Officer Canoza, will you please pay attention to the questions as they are asked? And will you please restrict yourself to the specific answers to the specific questions—can you do that?"

"Yes sir, Chief Nowicki sir. I will do that. What's the question again?"

Nowicki groaned and said, "I gotta go to the john. Detective, please, I'm askin' ya, try to have this interview completed by the time I return, do you think that might be possible?"

Carlucci splayed his hands at Canoza. "Robert? You with me here or not?"

Canoza was nearly finished with the second burger. He was practically inhaling them. He nodded.

"Okay," Nowicki said, pausing at the door to look back. "Look at it this way, Officer Canoza. If you think of this as an infection it's as serious as your previous. Only there's no drugs for this one. So you have to serious up now, understand?"

Canoza finished the second burger and unwrapped the third. He nodded, held up the third burger, and saluted his chief with it. And took another bite.

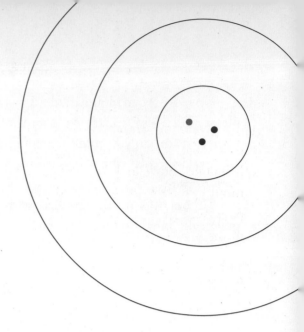

CARLUCCI TURNED on his tape recorder and said, "Third interview with Joseph Walter Buczyk, of 216 Jefferson Street, Rocksburg, PA, in re case number ninety-nine dash four sixteen. Time is 2016 hours, Friday, April 23rd, 1999. Interview conducted in room A, Rocksburg PD Station, Rocksburg City Hall. Present are Mr. Buczyk, his attorney from the Public Defender's Office, uh, would you state your name again, please, sir?"

"Minarcin. Theodore R."

"Uh, Mr. Buczyk's attorney is Assistant PD Theodore R. Minarcin. Also present is Patrolman James Reseta, Rocksburg PD, and I'm Detective Sergeant Ruggiero Carlucci, Rocksburg PD."

"Uh, excuse me," Assistant PD Minarcin said, clearing his throat, "but, uh, that's not the number of the case I was assigned."

"Huh? It isn't? What number you have?"

"Uh, ninety-nine dash four zero two."

"Oh, right right, I'm sorry," said Carlucci. "I said that other number so many times in the last coupla days, I got it on the brain. Sorry, you're right. Ninety-nine dash four zero two. Okay, now that we got that squared away, uh, well, see that other case, the number I just referred to—erroneously—that's what I wanna talk about now—in regard to Mr. Buczyk's case."

"I don't follow," said Minarcin.

"Well, uh, lemme see if I can explain it," Carlucci said, giving the young, anxious, weary assistant public defender the once-over. Minarcin didn't look old enough to have a driver's license, never mind to have graduated from high school, college, law school, and passed the bar exam. He looked like he was still buying his clothes in the boys' department.

"Your client here, Mr. Buczyk, was a witness to case number ninety-nine dash four sixteen."

"He was?" Minarcin turned to Buczyk and said, "You were?"

"Yeah. If it's what I think he's talkin' about. When my neighbor got shot? Remember? I told you about that."

"Oh yes, I remember now."

"Right, exactly," Carlucci said. "But every other time I've discussed this case with you, Mr. Buczyk—both previous interviews—I can give you the exact dates and times if you want—"

"Nah, I don't need the dates. I remember."

"Well you're gonna have to refresh my memory," Minarcin said.

"Right. Okay. Well in both interviews, Mr. Buczyk, you said you didn't know what Patrolman Rayford said before or between the shots he fired. I'm tryin' to remember now, did you say you didn't know, or you couldn't remember, or you didn't hear, which? I know I could get the tapes and play 'em again, but why don't you just say, okay?"

"I said I didn't hear him."

"Ah. Right. You didn't hear him. Uh-huh. Okay."

"Why're you sayin' it like that?" Minarcin said.

"Sayin' it like what?"

"Well I think, uh, I think I heard a little sarcasm."

"Sarcasm? Me? Oh no, uh-uh, I don't get sarcastic with people I'm interviewin'. Not when it's this serious, no way. I think you mistook my tone maybe—you think?"

"No," Minarcin said. "Maybe I did, but I don't think so."

"Okay so let me say it another way—you didn't hear him, right?"

"Right," Buczyk said.

"But you heard the two shots?"

"Right."

"Well was the first shot maybe fired right over your head, is that what interfered with your hearing there? A nine-millimeter goes off by your head, say within a couple yards, that could certainly mess with your hearing. I'm sorry—did you say somethin' interfered with your hearing? Or you just didn't hear? 'Cause if somethin' interfered with your hearing, then maybe I could understand why you didn't hear somebody who was standin', uh, less than two yards away from you, three at the most, why you wouldn't be able to hear him giving commands in a loud voice to somebody who was standin' maybe four yards from him."

"Maybe that was it."

"Maybe what was it?"

"Maybe the gun went off, uh, you know, real close to my ears."

"And so now you're sayin' that's why you didn't hear anything Officer Rayford said?"

"Could've been."

"Could've been?" Carlucci said. He turned the recorder off and said, "Okay, I'm turnin' the recorder off temporarily at this time, okay?"

"Why?" Minarcin said.

"Because I wanna give you both another possibility, another could've-been, okay? Or rather a could-be, huh? Could be if Mr. Buczyk's hearing comes back—and I've known several cases where people's hearing improved when they found out they weren't gonna have to do what they thought they were gonna have to do, huh?"

"What're you saying?" Minarcin said.

"I'm sayin' that if his hearing returns about what was said and who said it and how loud they said it in regards to, uh, case number ninety-nine dash four sixteen, I think some arrangements can be made in his regard concerning case number ninety-nine dash four zero two."

"Wait a second," Minarcin said. "Are you, uh, have you been authorized by anybody in the DA's Office? I mean, who said it was okay for you to be talking like this? Because it sounds to me like you're trying to make a deal here, and if that's true, uh, I'm not going to allow Mr. Buczyk to say anything until I see somebody from the DA's Office here—or somewhere, I don't care where—with a plea agreement. In writing."

"This is just preliminary conversation, okay?"

"Preliminary conversation? Is this a legal term now? Which you can show me from the *Rules of Criminal Procedure*?"

"No no, of course not," Carlucci said. "I just wanted to get together with you—"

"Is that thing still off?" Minarcin said, nodding toward Carlucci's tape recorder. "You didn't just accidentally turn it back on, did you?"

Kid's a lot tougher than he looks, Carlucci thought. I don't start duckin' and coverin' here, I'm gonna blow this, big time.

"Look, Mr. Minarcin, I'm not gonna try to tell you I talked to anybody in the DA's Office, because one call from you—"

"That's right, one call, right."

"And I'm not playin' the fool here with that, uh, I mean that preliminary conversation stuff, that was insulting and I'm sorry."

"Oh. Apology accepted, Detective. Now what's going on?"

"What's goin' on is ninety-nine dash four sixteen is an officer-involved shooting with, uh, as you can imagine, conflicting and contradictory statements made by the civilian who was shot and the officer who did the shooting, and Mr. Buczyk here, uh, he was arrested by the same officer who did the shooting, Officer Rayford, two weeks prior to the shooting incident. For this case, which you were assigned. I didn't say that very clear, so do you understand?"

"I understand better than I did a couple minutes ago. What you're saying is you think his hearing has been impaired by the fact of his arrest on these charges of assault and aggravated assault, correct? By the same officer?"

"Correct, yes."

"So just for my hearing," Minarcin said, "you have not discussed any possible reduction in charges with anybody in the DA's Office, is that correct?"

"Correct."

"Before addressing this subject with Mr. Buczyk or me, correct?"

"Correct again."

"And you're trying to find out whether Mr. Buczyk is open to the possibility of a reduction in charges before you go to anybody in the DA's Office, correct?"

"Yes, sir."

"Okay. I need some time with my client, please."

"You got it, sir," Carlucci said, picking up his recorder and leading Reseta out of the room.

Outside, on the way to the coffeepot in the duty room, Carlucci whispered, "Little fucker's a lot tougher than he looks."

"And you're a lot better at backin' up and coverin' your ass than you look."

After reaching the coffeepot and pouring his own and filling Reseta's mug, Carlucci said, "Hey. Nothin' says you know you're screwed better than sayin' you're sorry. Ever see this kid before?"

"No. Course, fast as they turn 'em over in that office, hey. What amazed me is how he looked, you know? Yeah. He first walked in, I thought angel food cake. But then he was lookin' at you like he was a mongoose and you were a cobra. An old one with a busted fang."

"You noticed that, huh?"

"Yeah. And a leak in your venom sack."

"Okay, you made your fuckin' point, I ain't that decrepit."

"On the opposite side of the table from him, you are."

"Okay, alright, forget that. I hear you're puttin' in for the gold watch. True?"

"Who told you that?"

"I don't know who. Coupla guys. True? Or not?"

"I think. Maybe." Reseta grimaced after he took his first swallow of coffee. He wiped his mouth with the back of his hand. "Who made this? Bet Stramsky did. You couldn't throw this down the drain, it wouldn't go. You'd have to take it to some garage, let 'em recycle it with the oil."

"So you're really thinkin' about it, huh? Retirin'? Any particular reason? Or just all of 'em?"

"All of 'em. Time to move on. Plus, uh, I guess, I don't know. Boo in the back of the wagon. You know. With that rake stickin' out of him. I mean if that skinny old guy could cause that much damage, Jesus. I don't know. You know?"

"Hey, it was touch and go with him for a while. That thing had dog shit all over it. Coulda been history for him. People with their dogs. Don't get me wrong, I like dogs much as anybody. But lettin' 'em run loose like that? Lettin' 'em shit everywhere, not cleanin' it up. Oughta be a fuckin' misdemeanor at least, you know? Nobody pays attention to that fuckin' ordinance. How many tickets you ever write for that?"

"Not enough. Should've written Hornyak and Buczyk about a hundred. Maybe then they would've built a fence. Course listen to me. When Rayford and I went to grab up Scavelli? I stepped in some. Right between their houses. Went on my ass, spent more than an hour the next mornin' cleanin' my shoes and my holster. Finally just had to pitch the holster, couldn't get the stink out. Cost me ninety-nine plus tax. So all the while I'm tryin' to clean it, I'm thinkin', would it've made any difference if it was nylon?"

"You had leather?"

"Yeah. Basket weave. Got in all those crannies. Couldn't get it out with a toothbrush and saddle soap, so like a genius I had this old suede brush. You know, with the bristles made of brass? So without thinkin', I made like two passes with that, put these big scars in it, man, just ruined it. I was so pissed. I wanted to go write those two idiots up—like it's their fault I ruined my holster."

"Who? Hornyak and Buczyk?"

"Yeah. Those fuckin' idiots. With their dogs."

"Whatta you got on now?"

"Holster? My original, can you believe that? It's fallin' apart. Split in three places. I was gonna go pick up a new one this morning, got stuck in a prelim, this jagoff's tryin' to defend himself on a hit-and-run DUI. I don't know where these people come from sometimes. That's why I bought the basket weave—'cause this one was fallin' apart. So instead of pissin' and moanin' about ruinin' my holster—which I'm responsible for, you know, wasn't anybody but me did that—I should've gone down there and written 'em both up. But I didn't. No. So I'm as bad as anybody about that. Tell you what, bet Nowicki starts a campaign about it."

"He already talked to me."

"He did? When?"

"Yesterday. Hey, let's go, Minarcin's wavin'."

Carlucci put his coffee mug down and led Reseta back toward the interview room.

"What'd he say? Nowicki."

"Said for the next three months we're gonna write up every dog-shit complaint, no exceptions."

"Oh man. See? That's why I know I should quit."

"Why?"

" 'Cause that makes me happy."

"You're gonna retire 'cause *that* makes you happy?"

"Hey, Rugs, when stuff like that starts makin' you happy, if you don't know it's time to quit, it's way too late for you, believe me."

"And here I thought all these years all you wanted to be was a soldier and a cop."

"I did, that's right. That's all. So I got my CIB, got a couple pages' wortha commendations, and I'm still askin' myself, am I a better man because of that?"

"Are ya?"

"Who knows? Somehow I doubt it."

They went into the interview room and Rugs resumed his seat across the table from Buczyk and his attorney, Assistant PD Minarcin.

"I called the DA's Office," Minarcin said. "They're miffed that you tried to do an end run around them."

"Mr. Minarcin, you know as well as I do, it didn't make any difference whether I talked to them before or after, nothin' was gonna happen without their approval."

"Yes I do know that. But in this instance, it seems to have offended their sense of protocol."

"Hey," Reseta said, leaning against the wall behind Carlucci, "all we're talkin' about here is kickin' one count of aggravated assault, we're not talkin' about blowin' up a federal building."

"Talk to them, don't talk to me," Minarcin said.

"We will," Carlucci said. "We have no choice. I just wanted to make sure you were open to the possibility that there might be another reason why Mr. Buczyk here is havin' problems with his hearing, okay?"

"Okay, I understand."

"Well, Mr. Buczyk, are you? You talked this over with your counsel, your hearing any better?"

"Maybe."

"Aw c'mon, Jesus. If anybody knows, you know that Officer Rayford gave half a dozen verbal commands and warnings before he fired those shots."

"Mr. Buczyk seems to me to be a perfect candidate for ARD," Minarcin said.

"You discuss that with whoever you talked to in the DA's Office?"

"I did."

"What's ARD?" Buczyk said.

"Accelerated Rehabilitative Disposition."

"What's that?"

Carlucci started to answer, but Minarcin held up his hand. "Allow me, okay? Joe, ARD is a discretionary program whereby first offenders are given an opportunity to rehab themselves, enter some kind of treatment or perform some kind of community service instead of being incarcerated. They're all different, depending on the trial judge, and the nature of the offense. The state likes it because it dispenses with a trial, the defendants like it because if they complete their program, whatever the judge sets up, they have their record expunged, and it's like they didn't do what they did. It's like their history didn't happen. You follow?"

"Oh. And what do I gotta do to get this, uh, this RAD?"

"ARD."

"Huh?"

"You said RAD. It's ARD."

"Oh. So what do I have to do, to, uh, to get this ARD?"

"May I answer?" Carlucci said.

"Be my guest," Minarcin said.

"Your hearing has to improve a hundred percent, that's all. And you have to say there was nothin' wrong with your ears whenever Officer Rayford's hearings start. And there're gonna be at least two of them. There's gonna be one in front of an ad hoc committee appointed by the Safety Committee to investigate this shooting. Then there's gonna be one in front of the Safety Committee, and depending on what happens in those, there could be one in front of the full council. And dependin' on how they rule, there could be a criminal trial. And dependin' on how that goes, there could be a civil trial, 'cause your neighbor retained counsel after he woke up from his surgery. So you have to remember, first, that what you said in your two previous interviews with me was that you didn't hear him, Officer Rayford. And people who wanna see Officer Rayford hung out to dry are gonna start bustin' your balls about what made you change your mind and what made your hearing improve, you get it?"

"I think so."

"Ever been cross-examined, Mr. Buczyk?"

"No."

"Then you don't know what it means to get your balls busted big-time. And they're gonna get busted big-time, believe me."

Buczyk shrugged and looked at his attorney, who shrugged back.

"Okay," Carlucci said. "I'm gonna turn this recorder back on now, and we're gonna start over, okay?"

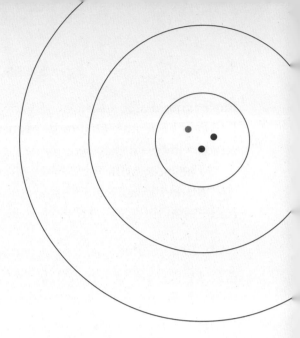

THE MEETING of this committee investigating the shooting of Peter John Hornyak, age forty-six, of 214 Jefferson Street, City of Rocksburg, Commonwealth of Pennsylvania, will now come to order. For the record, my name is Mrs. Anna Mae Remaley. I was appointed chairperson of this committee by Mayor Angelo Bellotti. Other members of the committee present are City Councilman Egidio Figulli, representing the Safety Committee and the Streets and Roads Committee, and City Councilman Thomas Trautwine, representing the Recreation Committee and the Electrical Committee. Counsel for the committee is Rocksburg City Solicitor Arthur B. Hepburg, Esquire.

"For the record, this hearing is being held in City Council chambers of Rocksburg City Hall. It's now ten minutes after 10 A.M., Monday, May 3rd, 1999. This inquiry is being recorded on audiotape. Should any participant wish to have the tapes transcribed, the costs will be borne by the participant who so wishes the transcription.

"My charge, as given me by Mayor Bellotti, is to lead the inquiry into the shooting of Mr. Hornyak on Friday, April 16th, 1999, at approximately 7:30 P.M. by Rocksburg Police Department Patrolman William Milton Rayford, shield number 529. Officer

Rayford resides at apartment 4A, 335 Detmar Street, Rocksburg, PA. For the record, Officer Rayford is thirty years of age and has served with the department for nearly six years.

"The shooting incident being investigated by this committee—"

"Madam Chairperson," said a tall, stooped, balding man in a rumpled suit. He raised his right hand as he stood.

"Yes?"

"Surely that's not the end of the exemplary performance of Officer Rayford you're going to enter into the record here today?"

"Uh, would you state your name and say why you are here?"

"My name is Panagios Valcanas. I'm an attorney, and I've been retained by Officer Rayford to represent him in this inquiry."

"And I take it you have something you wish to add to Officer Rayford's record, is that it?"

"Yes, ma'am, I do."

"Well I have no objection. Do I hear any objection?"

Councilmen Figulli and Trautwine shook their heads and said no.

"Then you may proceed, sir," Mrs. Remaley said brightly.

"Thank you, Madam Chairperson. I want it on record that my client, Rocksburg PD Patrolman William Milton Rayford, served four years in the United States Air Force, three years and nine months of which he served as a military police officer, either in training or on active duty. In that capacity, he served with distinction. He received six letters of commendation, two meritorious promotions, was awarded the Good Conduct Medal, and upon his honorable discharge was recommended for reenlistment. I wish it further added to this record that Officer Rayford, in his tenure with the Rocksburg PD, has served with no less distinction. He has received two letters of commendation, he's passed the sergeant's test, and is, pending the outcome of this proceeding, being considered for promotion to the rank of detective sergeant."

At that point, attorney Valcanas held up his hand as though to ask for a moment. He took out his handkerchief and sneezed strenuously three times. "Spring allergies, Madam, excuse me."

"Well God bless you, Mr. Valcanas, and thank you. The record will so note Officer Rayford's past service to his country and his ongoing service to this city."

"Excuse me, Madam Chairperson, I wasn't finished."

"Oh."

"Thank you. I just want to make it clear for the record that Officer Rayford has not been suspended by his superiors in the department for any reason related to this shooting, nor have they assigned him other, less rigorous duties pending the outcome of this inquiry. In other words, his superiors continue to demonstrate full confidence in his ability to perform his normal and routine duties as he has for nearly six years. And while they have questioned him rigorously on numerous occasions about the particulars and details of this alleged incident, they have in no way indicated that they doubt his capacity for truth and veracity. That's all, Madam, thank you."

"So noted, Mr. Valcanas," Mrs. Remaley said. She turned to the tall, paunchy, woolly-haired man to her far right and said, "Solicitor Hepburg, are you ready to proceed?"

"I am, Madam Chairperson."

"Do you have an opening statement?"

"No, ma'am, I do not. I think that the charge of this committee will best and most quickly be served if we merely question the witnesses."

"I could not agree more. Please call your first witness."

"Call Peter Hornyak."

Rocksburg PD Patrolman Lawrence Fischetti was guarding the door to council chambers. He opened it, pointed his finger at someone, beckoned that someone to come in, and then held the door as Peter Hornyak hobbled in on crutches, his right knee held at an angle by a soft cast.

Hornyak made his way to the chair positioned to the right of the committee's table. The chairperson asked him to raise his right hand and to place his left hand on a Bible Fischetti was carrying and asked him if he swore to tell the truth, the whole truth, and nothing but the truth, so help him God.

"I do," Hornyak said, and sat down with a thump and a wheezy grunt.

Solicitor Hepburg asked Hornyak to state his full name, address, and occupation. Hornyak gave his name and address and then said that he was presently on medical leave of absence from his job at Home Depot.

"And why is that, sir?"

" 'Cause my kneecap's shattered. I was shot by that cop sittin' right there," he said, pointing at Rayford, who was sitting in the front row of seats beside his attorney.

Valcanas raised his right hand, stood up in a kind of semi-crouch and said, "Madam Chairperson, before we get a minute further into this proceeding, I have to ask, what rules are we going to play by here? Are witnesses going to be allowed to editorialize, make unfounded accusations, as this witness just did here, and do I have the right to object to that kind of response? How're we going to do this, I mean, I fully realize this is not a court of law, but I think it is unreasonable to think I'm going to sit mute while a witness makes an unfounded accusation."

"C'mon, Mo, sit down," Councilman Figulli said. "You know your guy shot him, he knows he shot him, everybody knows he shot him, this ain't a trial, I mean, if your guy didn't shoot him, what're you doin' here?"

"That's an interesting way to phrase it, Councilman, but, uh, what I'm doing here—and counsel Hepburg knows what I'm talking about—is trying to determine if there's going to be any protocol to the introduction of evidence, as there is in a criminal trial. I want to know if that protocol is going to be followed here or just what the rules are here. Or are witnesses going to just yak away whenever they feel like it. Now either there's gonna be some coherence to this proceeding or there isn't. Because at this point, what I know, or what you claim I know, Councilman, or what you claim the mythical everybody knows, is irrelevant until such time as evidence establishing that has been introduced within the framework of this inquiry. Is this gonna be a free-for-all, or is there gonna be some rationale to it?"

"Counsel makes a good point," Hepburg said, turning to the committee. "Madam Chairperson, I would ask you to please inform the witness that he is to answer the questions and only the questions that are asked and not comment or editorialize in any way. If he does that, and only that, I'm certain we'll get to the facts of the incident with due dispatch."

"Well, I appreciate your concerns, of course, both of you," Mrs. Remaley said, "as long as you both understand that the committee reserves the right to question the witnesses when you've both completed your questioning. Is that understood? Mayor Bellotti gave me his word that my right to question any witness would not be obstructed by anybody in any way."

"Counsel?" Hepburg said, looking over his reading glasses at Valcanas.

"I understand," Valcanas said. "As long as the chairperson understands that I will object to her questions if I find them objectionable and that if I do we will find ourselves in the unusual position of having objections ruled on as to their merit by the interrogator who is being objected to—in which case I have no idea to whom I can appeal her ruling. Which is a question I meant eventually to ask, that is, who is the next higher authority in this matter?"

"Well that would have to be the full Safety Committee of City Council, wouldn't it?" Mrs. Remaley asked. "Mr. Hepburg, isn't that what you think? I mean who else would it be?"

"My question is not so much *who* it is, Madam Chairperson," Valcanas said. "My question is whether any ruling made here by this committee, or any member thereof, whether any ruling can be appealed to *somebody*, that's what I'm asking. *Who* that somebody might be is of secondary importance, from my point of view."

"Well I don't see the distinction there, but, uh, why not—Mr. Hepburg, do you agree? I mean we are going to submit our report to the Safety Committee, and it's my understanding they will have their own ruling on our findings, and the, uh, the full council will eventually rule, won't they?"

"And I am to understand that any ruling, by any of these committees, that any and all rulings and findings can be appealed eventually to the Court of Common Pleas?" Valcanas said.

"Mr. Hepburg?"

"I don't see why not."

"Fine," Valcanas said, resuming his seat. "I just wanted it on the record. Nothin' like knowin' where you can go if you don't like the show."

"Excuse me?" Mrs. Remaley said, eyebrows arched ominously.

"I beg the committee's pardon for my levity," Valcanas said.

"Levity? You think that was funny? What are you implying? You implying this is nothing but a show? I hope that's not what you're doing, Mr., uh, Mr.—"

"Valcanas, ma'am. Do you want me to spell it?"

"Mr. Valcanas—no, you don't need to spell it, I've heard of you. But I want to assure you this is anything but a show. An unarmed citizen of this community was shot and permanently injured by an armed officer of this community's police department, and I find nothing funny about that—"

"Objection, ma'am. Strictly speaking, we still have no evidence that anybody shot anybody—"

"Why the man's sitting right there, he walked in here on crutches, the only answer he was allowed to give before you interrupted him was he said he'd been shot by the officer sitting next to you, what more evidence do you need?"

"Oh, Madam Chairperson, I need a lot more than that. The witness's assertion is not evidence, it's merely an allegation. You see,

I was not present when the alleged shooting occurred, and if I might make an assumption here, I doubt that you were either, and furthermore, what I see in the witness chair is a man, with crutches, wearing a soft cast on his right leg, but all I've heard so far is his allegation, number one, that his kneecap was shattered by a bullet, and, number two, that my client fired that bullet, but since I'd never seen this witness until just a few moments ago, I have no way of knowing his capacity for truth and veracity. In other words, Madam Chairperson, while it seems obvious to me you've accepted the witness's story in its entirety before he's even had a chance to tell it in any detail, I must say that I am somewhat skeptical by nature and that I require more than a mere allegation by a witness of unknown character that an event happened the way he would like you to believe it happened. I apologize for taking up so much time with my objection."

"Why you sat right there when I called this committee to order, this inquiry to order, and I said specifically that, uh, that Mr. Hornyak had been shot—"

"That you did, Madam. But that was merely *your* assertion—"

"Merely my assertion? Why the whole town knows this!"

"I've lived here all my life, Madam, and I know no such thing."

"Well you're just being a lawyer, that's all! You're just trying to get your client off no matter what!"

Valcanas cleared his throat and quickly swallowed his smile. "I've never heard it put quite that way, Madam, but, uh, I agree, yes, I am just being a lawyer. And if my client is going to be tried here on politicians' assertions and allegations, then you can bet everything you own that I will get my client off no matter what. Or die trying."

"I beg your pardon, I am *not* a politician!"

"You were appointed by a politician, Madam, it amounts to the same thing—"

"I'll ignore that because we have proof—overwhelming proof I might add—that your client shot Mr. Hornyak!" Mrs. Remaley said, her face reddening. "Your client's own written report, for God's sake, of what happened, and . . . and, there are medical reports, there are reports from emergency medical technicians who took him to the emergency room, and reports from the doctors who operated on him—"

"So you say, Madam, so you say. But as yet none of these documents have been introduced as evidence. Neither you nor any member of this committee has thus far presented one shred of evidence—"

"Because you won't sit down and shut up—"

"I object to your tone and diction, Madam—"

"And I object to you standing up every time anybody says anything and objecting to everything that anybody's trying to do here!"

"Counsel," Valcanas said to Hepburg, "perhaps you could ask for a long recess and introduce Madam Chairperson to the *Rules of Evidence*—"

"Don't you patronize me, I know what you're trying to do—"

"I'm trying to make sure my client gets a fair and impartial hearing according to the *Rules of Evidence* codified by the legislature of this commonwealth over the past couple of centuries, not to mention his rights under the federal Constitution—"

"Don't mention anything else, you're out of order! Sit down!"

"Once again I object to your tone and diction, Madam."

"I don't care what you object to, sit down!"

"I believe now the record shows that the committee chairperson apparently believes she has been appointed queen for the duration of this inquiry—"

"Oh that's enough out of you! Officer? Officer? You in the back there?"

"Yes, ma'am?" Patrolman Fischetti said.

"Remove this man!" Mrs. Remaley pointed her finger at Valcanas.

"Excuse me?"

"Remove him! He's out of order!"

"Madam Chairperson," Counsel Hepburg said, walking slowly toward her. "You can't do that, ma'am."

"What? Why not? Who says I can't? That man's contemptible! He's doing everything he can to obstruct this inquiry!"

"Uh, Madam, he's defending his client—"

"Defending his client?! He won't let anybody get a word in edge-wise! Anytime anybody says anything he's raising his hand and ob-jecting. We're not going to get anything done that way—"

"Indeed you're not, Madam," Valcanas said.

"There he goes again! I want him removed! Officer, I'm order-ing you to remove this man!"

"Uh, I was, uh, I was just supposed to call the witnesses, ma'am. And hold the Bible," Fischetti said. "I don't think I'm allowed to re-move a lawyer, uh, least that wasn't in my orders—"

"Is everybody here trying to thwart me?!"

"If you're not going to play by the *Rules of Evidence,* I certainly am," Valcanas said.

"You're contemptible!" Mrs. Remaley said, standing up and shoving her chair back. "You're in contempt of me! We'll just see about this, I'm calling a recess, I'm going to see the mayor, we'll just see what he has to say about this. But for the record here—you want things on the record, mister? Well you put this on your record. I want everybody here to know I think you're in contempt of me!"

Valcanas laced his fingers together, put them behind his head, and leaned back in his chair. He watched Mrs. Remaley stomp out of the room, then looked at Rayford and winked.

Rayford leaned close to Valcanas's ear and whispered, "Uh, was that what you meant when you said you were gonna get her flus-tered? 'Cause she looked a lot more than just flustered to me, I mean, uh, she looked seriously pissed off."

"What I was doing was get on that tape that I have a right to ap-peal any ruling or finding here and also that she doesn't have a clue what she's doin'. And, if I do say so myself, I succeeded admirably. So now you can sit back, relax, enjoy the show. I guarantee she's gonna give me another ground for appeal every time she opens her mouth. The more she screws up, the closer we get to a judge. One with enough common sense to declare any finding by this committee null and void. Excuse me, I gotta take a dump. Don't let her start without me."

"Don't let her start? Why's she goin' listen to me?"

"Just stand up and say you have federal and state constitutional guarantees to have counsel present—and keep sayin' it till I get back. Be polite. Be firm. Just don't let her intimidate you. Gotta go."

Valcanas was back in plenty of time. The recess Mrs. Remaley called to settle the issue of her authority dragged on for ten minutes. Then fifteen. Then twenty. When she reappeared she was followed by the mayor himself, who stopped just inside the door and made some signs to Councilman Trautwine, who told Valcanas that the mayor wanted to see him.

Valcanas whispered to Rayford, "This oughta be good for at least one laugh," and took a while ambling back to the mayor.

Rayford turned around and watched the mayor leaning in close to Valcanas's ear and talking with many gestures for nearly two minutes. Valcanas never said a word. The mayor patted Valcanas on the shoulder a couple of times and gave him a serious smile and several nods. Valcanas turned and walked back to his seat, stood there a moment collecting himself, and then said, "Is the recorder back on?"

"It is now," Councilman Trautwine said.

"Are you going to object to something else again?" Mrs. Remaley said.

"No, ma'am, I just want to say for the record that Mayor Angelo Bellotti has asked me to go easy on you, Madam Chairperson, so we can get this matter behind us, because he said, just a minute ago, at the back of this room, and I'm quoting him exactly here, you don't know your ass from a ham sandwich, end quote."

"What?!" Mrs. Remaley said. "Why you miserable old goat—"

"Object to your tone and to that sobriquet, Madam."

"We'll see about this," Mrs. Remaley said, jumping up and knocking her chair back so that it rocked precariously on its back legs before settling forward again. She stomped out of the room again, with Valcanas calling after her, "Is this still part of the first recess, or is this a new one—does anybody know?"

Councilman Figulli came around the committee table to Valcanas and bent over and whispered, "Hey, Mo, Jesus Christ, you made your fuckin' point, whattaya want? The sooner you shut up and let her finish what she wantsa do, the sooner we all go home—and don't you fuckin' dare pull that shit on me you just pulled on Bellotti, you prick. 'Cause you do? Behind your office there? I'll find leaks in your gas line, your sewer line, your water line, I'll have your parkin' lot tore up for two, three months. And I'm also sure code enforcement will find a few things wrong with your office john, you hear? So stop fuckin' with her, she's a big enough pain in the balls without you bustin' her chops every coupla seconds."

"As usual, Egidio, your eloquence is inspiring. It moves me to try to reach common ground with the chairperson. Uh, there is one thing though. It's rumored that you and Mrs. Remaley are related in some way, could that be possible? She wouldn't be your wife's cousin, would she?"

"See? There ya go, ya prick, you can't leave well enough alone, always gotta be nosin' around, now you're tryin' to bust my balls, and I'm tellin' ya, don't do that."

"Egidio, how could a man of your persuasive powers allow this to happen? Seriously, you couldn't talk her out of this? You couldn't tell her what was gonna happen every time she opened her mouth? Looks to me like one of you is carrying a large debt. Or a large grudge. Want me to speculate?"

"Aw c'mon, Mo, for Christ sake, just let her alone, please?"

"No can do. Every time she demonstrates through her ignorance that she's runnin' a kangaroo court here, I'm gonna spank her. For me to do any less would make me ineffective counsel, and it'd be easier for me to grow hair than do that. So you wanna get this farce over with, take a little control here yourself, tell your counsel the next witness he oughta call is Joseph Buczyk."

"Oh what, he's talkin' now? Since when?"

Valcanas sighed and shook his head. "What the hell do you do all day besides ride around in a city truck and look for potholes? Course he is. DA signed the plea agreement at least a week ago. Sometimes, Egidio, I swear you pols communicated better when you used to pound on hollow logs with sticks."

"Yeah yeah. So no shit now, he signed a deal?"

"Why would I make that up?"

"Aw, this is such bullshit. What a waste a time."

"Not to mention actual Yankee dollars."

"Huh? What're you talkin' about, Yankee dollars?"

"Well you don't think I'm going to bill my client for defending him against this ridiculous attempt to besmirch his character, do you? The minute this farce is history, I'm going straight to the court-house to sue the city to pay my fee and expenses. And you know how those closet Republican judges love to bust your Democratic balls."

"Oh you would, wouldn't ya? Christ. Lemme go talk to Hep-burg."

Valcanas stretched and whispered to Rayford, "I do believe we might be out of here in time for happy hour at Mr. P's."

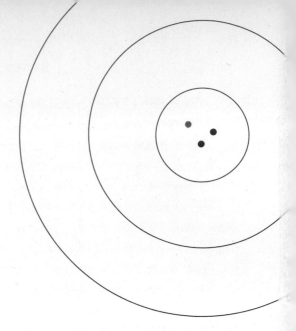

WHEN HEPBURG finished questioning Peter Hornyak, Valcanas stood and walked to the far right of the committee's table to put them between Hornyak and himself. Valcanas pursed his lips for a moment and said, "It's your testimony, is it, that Officer Rayford never ordered you or commanded you to get down or get on the ground?"

"Yeah. That's my testimony."

"And you also said you have no idea why he shot you, right?"

"That's right."

"You were just standing there in front of your home, correct?"

"Correct."

"Minding your own business, correct?"

"Correct."

"And Officer Rayford just drove up, parked his police vehicle across the street from your house, and without warning, without reason, without provocation from you, he just opened fire?"

"That's right."

"Fired two shots, correct?"

"Correct."

"Missed you with the first one, correct?"

"Correct."

"And struck you in the right knee with the second, correct?"

"Correct."

"Mr. Hornyak, before Officer Rayford arrived, what were you doing?"

"Uh, nothin'."

"You weren't having a verbal dispute with one of your neighbors, specifically a Mr. Joseph Buczyk?"

"We were just talkin'."

"Just talking, huh? No dispute though, right?"

"Right."

"Amiable conversation. About the weather perhaps? Or about baseball perhaps?"

"Somethin' like that."

"So then, how would you explain why one of your neighbors, specifically a Mrs. Tomko, who lives directly across the street from you, how do you explain that she's on the Rocksburg Police dispatcher's tape recording of the second watch at approximately ten minutes after 7 P.M. on Friday, April 16th—how would you explain her call to the police station that you and Mr. Buczyk were involved in a loud argument which she feared was going to escalate into violence?"

"She's old, you know how people get when they get old."

"She's old? How old is she, do you know?"

"Old enough to get Social Security, I know that."

"How do you know that?"

" 'Cause couple days before the end of the month, she's always out there lookin' for the mailman."

"And that's what makes her old?"

"No. Not just that."

"What then? What makes her old? You said before, I believe, you know how people get when they get old, isn't that what you said?"

"Yeah."

"Well what do they do that makes them old?"

"You know, they don't know what to do with themselves. So they start nebbin' in other people's business. Watches too much TV, thinks everything that happens on TV is gonna happen to her, so she calls the cops about every little thing."

"So—not to put words in your mouth—but if I understand you, you're saying she had no reason for calling the police at that time, that you're aware of, correct?"

"Correct, that's what I'm sayin'."

"Uh-huh. I see. Uh, have you ever had a problem, any kind of problem with Mr. Buczyk, say, like two weeks previous to April 16th?"

"I don't know what you're referrin' to."

"Let me refresh your memory. On Friday, April 2nd, at approximately 6:45 P.M., on the sidewalk between your house and Mr. Buczyk's house, did he not strike you in the face with his fist?"

"I don't remember."

"And wasn't he arrested by Officer Rayford for striking you with his fist?"

"I don't remember."

"And wasn't he charged by Officer Rayford with assault and aggravated assault upon your person?"

"I don't remember."

"I see. A man strikes you with his fist. A police officer, namely Officer William Rayford, the man seated there in the first row, that officer arrests the man who struck you, takes him before a district justice, charges him with violations of Title 18, all of which is now a part of police and judicial records, and you don't remember any of this, is that what you're saying now?"

"Right. That's what I'm sayin'."

"Mr. Hornyak, have you been having any trouble recently remembering things?"

"No."

"Have you recently been examined by a doctor, a GP, or a neurologist, or a psychiatrist, or a neurosurgeon?"

"No."

"Would you remember if you had?"

"Yeah, course I would. I'd remember that, if I'd been to a doctor, yeah."

"So no one in the recent past, say in the last six months or so, no duly licensed medical practitioner has said to you that you suffer from any brain dysfunction, is that correct?"

"Brain dysfunction?"

"Yes. Any kind of dementia, say as a result of a cerebral-vascular incident, a stroke, or perhaps suspected Alzheimer's disease, anything like that?"

"No. I think I would remember if somebody told me that."

"I see. Just a couple more questions, Mr. Hornyak. Have you retained the services of an attorney?"

"Yeah. Why?"

"That was my next question. Why? Why have you hired an attorney?"

" 'Cause he's lookin' into things for me."

"What kind of things?"

"That's between him and me. He told me whatever we say between us stays between us, that's the law."

"He told you that your communication was privileged, didn't he?"

"Yeah, that's what he said it was. Privileged."

"I'm gonna go way out on a limb here, Mr. Hornyak. Are you and your attorney planning to sue the city and Officer Rayford?"

"That's none of your business."

"Because what you and your lawyer have talked about is privileged communication, right?"

"Right."

"So it would be wrong for me to assume that you have a pecuniary interest in the outcome of this inquiry, is that correct?"

"A what kinda interest?"

"Money. A money interest."

"I don't know what you mean."

"I mean that if you and your attorney did decide to sue the city and Officer Rayford for the pain and suffering you've endured as a result of that gunshot wound to your knee, the outcome of your suit against the city and against Officer Rayford to a large extent will be determined by the outcome of this and subsequent inquiries, if there are any, that's what I meant. You understand me now?"

"Oh yeah. I understand."

"And do you agree?"

"I guess, yeah. No, wait, wait a second—hey, that's none of your business."

"Nothing further, Madam Chairperson."

Mrs. Remaley picked up several stacks of manila envelopes and folders. She slapped them down on the table emphatically as she read off their contents: "I'm introducing into evidence the unusual incident report filled out by Officer Rayford on Friday night, April 16th, 1999, in which he writes clearly that he shot Mr. Hornyak. Do you have any objection to that, Mr. Valcanas?"

"No objection, Madam."

"I'm introducing into evidence the reports filled out by emergency room doctors Kim and Marino from the Conemaugh Hospital ER after treating Mr. Hornyak on Friday, April—"

"No objection, Madam—"

"Would you at least have the courtesy to let me finish?"

"Of course, Madam. My apology. Please finish."

"I'm introducing the ER doctors' report of treatment of Mr. Hornyak for a gunshot wound of the right knee on Friday night, April 16th, 1999, at approximately 8:30 P.M."

"No objection, Madam."

"Thank you very much, sir. I'm now introducing the report filled out by the surgeons who operated on Mr. Hornyak—"

"Madam Chairman, at the risk of raising your ire again, I think I could save you time by saying that I have no objection to your introducing any written report made by any police officer or doctor or emergency medical technician relating to this shooting incident."

"Well my God, man, what was all that hullabaloo about before?"

"To use your own words, Madam, that was just me bein' a lawyer."

"Oh is that so? Well, Mr.-you're-just-being-a-lawyer, I'm going to read every one of these documents into the record—"

"That isn't necessary, Madam, I assure you. All you need do is identify them and give them an evidence number, I've seen them all, and I'm sure counsel Hepburg has too."

"Well aren't you two just the most wonderful little lawyers?"

"I object to your tone and diction, Madam," Hepburg said.

Valcanas bowed his head and hid his laughter behind his right hand as he pretended to rub his eyes.

"You two make me sick."

"Objection," they both said.

"Oh shut up for God's sake and let's get on with this."

"Objection to tone and diction," Valcanas said.

"Objection," Hepburg said.

"Overruled, both of you! Call your next witness, Mr. Hepburg!"

"Aren't you gonna finish entering, identifying, and numbering those documents as evidence? Before I call—"

"He said I didn't need to read them!"

"Yes, Madam, he did. But you still have to enter them as evidence, identify them, and number them in order for them to be part of the record."

"Oh for God's sake, I wish you two would make up your minds."

"I think it's safe to say, Madam, that we have," Hepburg said.

"Was that a snide remark? Is that what that was? I think I know a snide remark when I hear one, and that sounded like one to me."

"Hey, Anna Mae," Councilman Figulli said, "you wanted to do

this, will ya go 'head and do it already, huh? C'mon, Jesus, you keep this up, we're gonna be here till Friday."

"Excuse me?! Councilman Figulli, I'm warning you to remember who you are and who I am. In case you forgot, you're just a member of this board of inquiry, but I'm the chairperson. That means I'm in charge."

"How could I forget that? Mother a God," Figulli said, dropping his head into his hand as his elbow hit the table with a thump.

Mrs. Remaley glared at Figulli while he turned his head away from her and closed his eyes. When she was satisfied that he'd been duly impressed by her remarks, she summoned counsel Hepburg to join her some distance behind the committee table where she questioned him about something. Apparently she was asking how to introduce, identify, and number documentary evidence, because when Hepburg came back around to the front of the table that's what she did, turning her glare onto Valcanas while talking slowly and enunciating carefully each word. Finally, she was done. She then excused Hornyak and ordered Hepburg to call his next witness.

"Call Joseph Walter Buczyk."

Hornyak and Buczyk passed each other without a glance between them.

After Buczyk was sworn, and with Hepburg leading him along the same chronological path he had led Hornyak, Buczyk contradicted Hornyak in every way. Where Hornyak insisted that Rayford had not ordered him to "get down" or "get on the ground," Buczyk said he clearly and distinctly heard Rayford order Hornyak to "get down" or "get on the ground" at least four times before he fired the first shot and at least that many times before he fired the second.

When Hepburg asked Buczyk how close he was to Rayford when Rayford was giving those commands, Buczyk said that Rayford had jumped right over him as he was rolling around on the sidewalk and was never more than two or three steps away from him.

When Hepburg asked what was happening before Officer Rayford arrived, Buczyk said Hornyak had been "ragging and agitating me" for almost twenty minutes.

"What about?"

"Anything. Everything. Whatever he can think of. He's just real pissed off at me—"

"Hey!" Mrs. Remaley shouted, picking up her gavel and banging it hard on the table. "You watch your language, mister. Any more talk like that and you'll be in a lot more trouble than you are now!"

Buczyk stared at her, his chin dropping. "What'd I say? Huh? I say somethin'? What?"

"Oh don't you play innocent with me, you get your mouth out of the gutter and back where it belongs, mister! I'm warning you!"

Buczyk splayed his hands and looked at Hepburg, who approached him, leaned in close, and whispered for a moment. When Hepburg backed away, Buczyk was shrugging and shaking his head. "That's profanity? I didn't know that was profanity. Man, I heard Dave Letterman say that."

"Well if he's who you're going to use for a role model it's no wonder you don't know what's proper language anymore. Don't tell me what you hear on TV, mister, because if it were up to me, all the TVs in the world would be at the bottom of the ocean, where they belong. And if that's where they were, I have no doubt our children would know how to read. And don't you dare pretend you don't know what you said, and there'll be no more of that."

"Okay, yes, ma'am," Buczyk said, wide-eyed. "Where was I?"

"You were saying what you and Mr. Hornyak were doing before Officer Rayford arrived. You were saying, I believe, that he was ragging you, I think that's your word, and I asked you what about."

"Oh. Yeah. And I was sayin'—well I can't say that anymore. So, uh, he's just real real, uh, mad at me. I mean, we used to be buddies. You could almost say like best friends. Not almost. We were. Then we made the mistake of goin' into business together, and it's been all downhill ever since."

"What kind of business?"

Buczyk sighed. "Aw, man, do I have to? I don't really like to think about that. It still hurts, you know? Be accused by your best friend you cheated him."

"Briefly, Mr. Buczyk, you don't need to go into great detail."

"Uh, we bred our dogs—I mean we hadn't planned to breed 'em, it just sorta happened, and then we thought well, why not, it happened, let's make some money offa it, you know? And so I sold the pups. He was supposed to get the pick of two litters and ten percent of what I got for sellin' the rest. And that's what started it all, that's when he accused me of holdin' out on him, cheatin' him."

"How long ago was this?"

"Like five, maybe six years ago."

"And have there been other incidents between you two?"

"Over every little thing, whatever you can think of, if it was possible to start somethin' over it, he started somethin'. Where the property line was, where the tree branches grew, where the leaves fell on the ground, where the leaves fell in the gutters, whose leaves fell in whose gutters, whose dog was . . . uh, doin' their business in whose yard, whose car was parkin' in whose space on the street, where you were supposed to put your garbage cans on the sidewalk, whether the property line ran all the way out to the curb or whether it stopped at the sidewalk, and if it stopped on the sidewalk on which side of the sidewalk, the side closest to the house or the side closest to the street, you name it, man, he started somethin' about it."

"Any of these arguments become more than just verbal? Say like in the recent past? The past month or so?"

"You're referring to when I got arrested, right? For assault?"

"Yes I am."

"Well I did."

"Explain further, please."

"He said somethin', I said somethin' back, he said somethin' else, I don't really know what started it, it just went back and forth, he started bringin' up everything he was . . . uh, he was mad about. And then finally I just lost it and popped him one, I probably shouldn'ta done it, but, uh, hey, everybody has their limits, I guess, I don't know. Then somebody called the cops, and that cop right there, uh, Officer Rayford, he showed up, and Hornyak started hollerin' he wanted me arrested, so he arrested me. Took me in front of a magistrate—"

"District justice, do you mean?"

"Yeah. District whatever. Justice. And he went along."

"Who? Mr. Hornyak?"

"Yeah. And soon as the officer said everything he had to say, he was in that magistrate's face. Hornyak, you know, sayin' he wanted me locked up, practically screamin' I was a nutcase, I was a danger to the community, I was this, I was that, all kindsa nonsense. It was really humiliating. Next thing I know, I'm in the county jail 'cause I can't pay the cash bond, and I was goin' through *that* humiliation. Body cavity search, man. Talk about humiliation, lemme tell ya, there it is. Make you take your clothes off, and man, they, uh, they look everywhere—"

"You watch it, mister," Mrs. Remaley said.

"What? What'd I say, I didn't say anything wrong—did I?"

"Well forget about that search business and get on with it!"

"Yes, ma'am. Well, uh, the next day when I met my public defender, I found out why the bond was set so high. 'Cause it turned out Hornyak worked in that magistrate's election campaign. I never knew that. Anyway, had to put my house up to get out, property bond. For some reason I don't show up when I'm supposed to I could lose my house."

"You planning not to show up?"

"No no, I'll show up believe me, I'm just sayin', I could, you know? It could happen. All 'cause I popped him one. Didn't break nothin', his nose, or his jaw, didn't even loosen any teeth. Just cut the inside of his mouth a little bit, that's all, Jesus—uh, sorry. Sorry, ma'am. Won't slip again, promise."

"Slip, yeah. Last warning, mister. One more slip like that, it's going to cost you big. I have the authority to fine you, don't think I don't. And don't think I won't use it."

"Promise I won't, ma'am," Buczyk said, trying to remember what he'd been saying. "Oh. He didn't even need stitches. Is 'at worth somebody's house? Just 'cause you worked in somebody's election campaign, you can do that to somebody? Man!"

"When did this incident happen?" Mrs. Remaley interrupted Hepburg.

"Friday, April 2nd, two weeks to the day before the last one. The one where he got shot."

"And are you now awaiting trial on those charges?" Hepburg said before Mrs. Remaley could interrupt him again.

"Yes—well no, not anymore. I mean I was, but I pleaded guilty, so there's not gonna be any trial. Just a sentencing hearing, that's all."

"Uh, Mr. Buczyk, I have only one thing further to ask you, and that is, for some time in the early part of our inquiry, you were, uh, to say the least, uh, reluctant to testify, do you recall that?"

"Yes I do."

"And yet here you are now, testifying. Were you given some inducement to testify?"

"Yes I was."

"Would you explain that to the committee, please?"

"I was wondering if you were going to get around to that, Counselor," Mrs. Remaley said. "I was beginning to think maybe you weren't. Because I'm very anxious to hear this myself. Let's hear it, mister. I want to know exactly who you talked to and what they promised you."

"Uh, ma'am, I don't know why you keep talkin' to me like that, I don't think I ever did anything to you—"

"Mister, quit your sniveling and answer the question."

"Whew, wow. Uh, well, uh, the advice I got was, uh, I knew some things maybe certain people might wanna know. So I held back. I didn't say anything until, uh, you know, my lawyer said it was okay to say it. He said I say it to the right person I could probably get one of the charges thrown out."

"I knew it!" Mrs. Remaley said, throwing back her shoulders and lifting her chin. "I knew that's what happened. The curse of American justice—plea bargaining!"

Valcanas covered his laughter with phony coughing.

Hepburg cleared his throat several times before asking, "And is that in fact what happened?"

"Yeah. The cops brought it up first—"

"The cops?! I knew it!" Mrs. Remaley said.

"Madam Chairperson, I beg your pardon, but would you please let the witness finish his answer?"

"Well tell him to talk faster! I want to hear this as much as anybody in this room! More!"

"Talkin' as fast as I can, ma'am. Uh, where was I? Oh. And then I, uh, I talked with an assistant district attorney, and then I signed a plea agreement."

"Assistant district attorney? Which one? I want his name!"

"Madam, please?"

"Which one?"

"Ma'am, I don't know his name, I'm terrible at rememberin' names. All I know is, he said, uh, in return for my testimony about what happened that night, I would, uh, I mean they would throw out the one charge of aggravated assault and they would guarantee I would be placed in ARD. And I'd get no jail time for the other charge, uh, the simple assault."

"Nothing further, Madam Chairperson."

"Well I have something further," Mrs. Remaley said.

Hepburg, who'd resumed his seat, stood again and said, "Uh, excuse me, Madam Chairperson, but I think it's Mr. Valcanas's turn."

"He can wait, I'm not going to sit around while he pours sugar all over this thing—"

"Objection as to tone and diction, Madam."

"Overruled. Sit down."

Valcanas sat back down and once again covered his face with his hands to hide his laughter.

"So you made a deal to testify here, is that right, mister?"

"Yes, ma'am."

"So what's this AR whatever you said? AR what?"

Hepburg stood and started to explain it.

"I wasn't asking you, I was asking him."

"I think I can explain it better than he can."

"Says you. Sit down. I want him to explain it. I want to know why every time one of our investigators tried to talk to you, mister, you had nothing to say, and now all of a sudden you can't stop talking—I want to know exactly how that happened?"

"I told you. The detective told me—"

"Which detective? From the city? Or from the county?"

"The city, I guess. Yeah, it was the city. We were here, this is City Hall, right? This is where we were. He had an Italian name, Carlotti or somethin' like that."

"A city detective? Are you absolutely certain? Do you know what you are saying?"

"Yeah. I think. Why?"

"A *city* detective? The first time anybody mentioned a deal to you, it was a *city* detective? In City Hall, in this building we're in now? He's the first one who offered you a deal?"

"Yeah. He's the first one I remember."

"Officer? You in the back? Go find this detective, this Carlotti."

Fischetti had been daydreaming. He stiffened and said, "What? Excuse me?"

"Wake up! Go find this detective, this Carlotti whoever."

Councilman Figulli barely lifted his chin off his fist and piped up, "It's Carlucci, Anna Mae, Carlucci, it ain't Carlotti."

"Well I don't see his name on our witness list. Either one of those names. Why isn't it? Does somebody want to explain that to me? And when you're through explaining that—whoever wants to try—would somebody please explain why a city detective is investigating a city patrolman? I was told distinctly by the first assistant district attorney—and by the mayor—that county detectives were the ones going to do the investigation into this. It's ridiculous to have a city detective investigating this shooting, it's a gross conflict of interest, my God, can't anybody else here see that? We're going to be a laughingstock. I can see the headlines now, for God's sake. This is worse than embarrassing, it's infuriating!"

"Aw calm down, Anna Mae, Mother a God, you're hysterical, for Christ sake."

"How dare you talk to me that way! You of all people, you think you can use that kind of language with me?!"

"That ain't profanity, Anna Mae, that's me prayin'. You know, like Jesus, please make her calm down."

"Don't you get snotty with me, Egidio. You of all people. And furthermore, you—you're on the Safety Committee, are you telling me you knew this investigation was being conducted by a city detective? And I suppose that little fact just slipped your mind, is that it?"

"Relax, will ya? Will you relax? The county guys didn't wanna have nothin' to do with it. It's a city matter, the city should investigate it, whattaya think. If you had a TV, you might learn somethin'. If you watched *NYPD Blue,* you'd know that every time their cops do somethin' wrong, you think they have somebody else come in and do the investigatin'? They have guys from, uh, whatta they call it, IAD, Internal Affairs Division, that's New York cops, Anna Mae, they come in, they don't bring outsiders in. County detectives, Mother a God, what'sa matter with you? Matter with you, what'sa matter with me—what was I thinkin'?"

"This is not a TV show, you moron! Why Julie ever married you is one thing; how she stayed married to you after she actually heard you talk is something Jesus himself couldn't explain."

"Aw that's it, I'm outta here," Figulli said, jumping up and heading for the back door. "You wanna play big-shot crusader, fine. You can just go right ahead and play without me, I ain't puttin' up with another second of your crap, see you later, alligator mouth."

"This meeting's still in session, you can't walk out! You come back here! Come back here, Egidio, you're out of order! Stop him, Officer! Stop him!"

Fischetti shook his head as though to clear webs of confusion away. Before Fischetti could react, Figulli was by him and out the door.

Valcanas leaned close to Rayford and whispered, "I've been practicin' law so long, God, I honestly can't remember when I started. But this? I've never seen anything remotely like this. Gilbert and Sullivan couldn't've written this."

"Who?"

"Guess I'm not gonna make happy hour at Mr. P's after all."

"Who'd you say before? Gilbert and who?"

"Never mind. Coupla dead white guys. Probably wouldn't think this was funny at all. Probably just me. And the more I think about it, the more unfunny it gets—oh God, there she goes, stompin' out again. See, if we were in Jerusalem, Palestine, the West Bank, someplace like that, at least when we left here today we could leave with some hope that somebody might think she was important enough to assassinate. Where are all the terrorists when you really need one?"

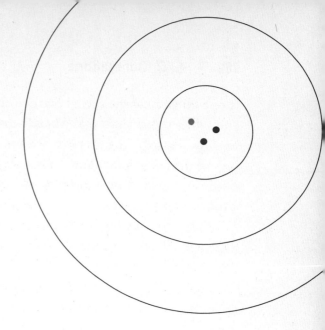

VALCANAS WAVED Hepburg over and led him off to a corner of the room.

"Hep, we gotta do something."

"You're telling me? Jesus, I knew it was gonna be bad after my first meeting with her, but I didn't know how bad."

"Well, listen, how would you feel if I called the DA, got him to explain the facts of life to her?"

"Oh hell, do it, I'll dial the number for you, except it's not gonna work. Woman's a fanatic. Absolutely, positively, irrevocably convinced plea bargaining is a plague, the curse of the system, it's what's destroying all our judicial values, you name it, whatever cockamamie theory anybody ever had about our courts, she's got it all boiled down to no more plea bargains, that's what'll fix it. What's the matter, Mo, you look like you don't remember who she is."

"I don't. Should I? Who is she?"

"Hell, man, she's the head case who ran against Failan for DA three, four elections ago—can't remember which one myself—you remember now?"

"I must've had a couple thousand too many martinis, no, I don't remember her—oh wait. She the one ran against him and isn't an attorney?"

"Now you got her."

"Oh for Christ sake. Well hell, it doesn't matter, we've still gotta do something about her. Hep, I'm open for suggestions—I may as well be pro bono here, but I don't wanna go broke over this nonsense. I thought one morning, two witnesses, once Buczyk got through we could wrap it up in the afternoon with the forensics."

"Silly you. Anybody needs to go behind the woodshed for this, it's Figulli. She was his idea."

"Well what the hell's he think he's accomplishin', walkin' out? Just multiplied the misery. Listen, unless you got a better idea, I'm callin' Failan. He owes me a couple. And I'm gonna suggest to him as strongly as I can that he and Bellotti and you and I sit her down and explain the facts of life, I mean, Christ, this keeps goin' the way it's goin', there's no tellin' how long she'll drag this out, now that she thinks she's got a soapbox. I'm surprised she agreed to keep the doors closed."

"Didn't. She lost, two to one."

"Should've known," Valcanas said, patting all his pockets. "Now where the hell'd I put my cell phone?"

"Here," Hepburg said, pulling his out. "Use mine."

"Thanks. Wait, what kinda lever we got? If she's not gonna listen to reason, we gotta have somethin'. What's she got on Figulli?"

Hepburg shrugged. "If I knew, believe me, I would've used it before now."

"Gotta be somethin' ugly or he'd've never gone for it. Think Failan knows?"

"Anybody knows, it's Bellotti," Hepburg said. "Way he works, he wouldn't have played along without knowin'. Tried to pump him after that first meeting, he just smiled and waved me off."

"Then he's who we need to talk to. We all stand on his shoes at the same time, he'll talk. I'm callin' Failan, you go get Bellotti, tell him this happy horseshit's gotta stop—huh? Oh hello, darlin', it's Valcanas, let me talk to your boss . . . no, on his private line, please. Thank you."

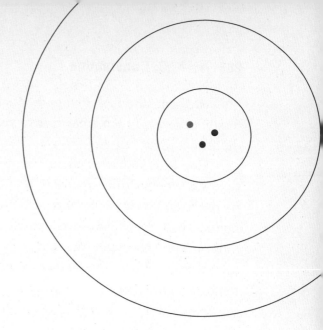

THEY WERE in Mayor Angelo Bellotti's office, they being Conemaugh County District Attorney Howard Failan, City Solicitor
Hepburg, Panagios Valcanas, Mrs. Remaley, and the mayor.

Failan was, as usual, glad-handing everyone, using his most pen-
etrating, most sincere eye-locking gaze, and saving the best for Mrs.
Remaley.

"Anna Mae, can't tell you how good it is to see you again, we
don't see each other nearly enough, how've you been?"

"Mr. District Attorney, we have some problems—"

"Just last week, Marlene said to me, Howard, we have to have
her over, and I said, well what's stopping you, Marlene, pick up the
phone and call her—whattaya think she's gonna do, turn down din-
ner! Not the Anna Mae I know—"

"Well I'm sure Marlene has better things to do, Howard—"

"Oh, what're you talkin' about, c'mon. I said, my God, Marlene,
what's the problem? Call the woman, she's one of my favorite people, brings out the best in me, I can't get away with one little thing
with her around, and that's what I need, Anna Mae. I need people
like you to keep me sharp, keep me honest. You know what I miss?
Huh? I miss those debates, Anna Mae, I really do. I loved those,
goin' around the county, you and me, all those fire halls? All those

buffets? Remember? All that god-awful rigatoni, boy oh boy, I can hardly believe it's been what, twelve years now? You know what we did, Anna Mae?"

"Howard, I'm having some real problems here—"

"We brought the democratic process to the people, that's what we did. And if you ask me that's exactly what's missing in American politics these days. These presidential debates they put on TV, why those people who stage them, they should've followed us around back then, we'd have shown them a thing or two about how to take the democratic process deep into the grass roots—"

"Howard, I was promised that your detectives were going to investigate this shooting."

"What? What promise? Why who made that promise? Not me, Anna Mae. I never told you county detectives were going to investigate anything, who said I did? Did somebody say I did?"

"Leo Harvey did, Howard."

"Leo? We talkin' about the same Leo Harvey here? My first assistant?"

"Well I certainly am."

"Oh, Anna Mae, I think you must be mistaken about that, I don't think Leo would've taken it upon himself to make a promise like that, no, he doesn't have the authority to make that kind of scheduling commitment. I think somebody's trying to steer you wrong, stir up something between us. Why don't we sit down here and talk this over—Angelo? Ho, Angelo, you got any coffee? How about we get some coffee in here, huh? Some Danish maybe? How about some Danish, Anna Mae—say, have you eaten lunch? Why I'll bet you haven't even had your lunch yet—Angelo, forget the coffee, call the Courthouse Café, tell 'em send us over lunch for—uh, how many we got here? Five? Six?"

"Howard, I don't need lunch, I need to get this thing straightened out—"

"Anna Mae, you know what Churchill said once? Right in the middle of World War Two? When hell itself looked like it was droppin' out of the sky and fallin' on London—know what old Winnie said? He said—and I think I'm quoting him correctly here—he said, 'There's nothing so bad it won't look better after lunch.' Now maybe that's not an exact quote but you certainly get the idea. Whatever problem you have here, you have got to admit it's not German V-2 rockets fallin' out of the sky on us, is it? So now what's the problem?"

"I'm trying to tell you, Howard—if you'll let me!"

"Oh, Anna Mae, I love it—don't you just love this woman? You fellas, I'm jealous, I'm tellin' ya. You're in there lockin' horns with this firebrand, boy oh boy, don't tell me she won't keep ya sharp. What're you gonna have, Anna Mae—listen, they make the best chicken salad on sun-dried tomato focaccia you ever tasted—that's what I'm gonna have, Angelo, tell 'em put at least one of those in the box for me. Anna Mae, their chicken salad's better than Marlene's—now don't you tell her I said that, but it is, I'm tellin' ya."

"Oh for God's sake, Angelo, order me one too—"

"Attaboy, girl," Failan said, beaming expansively. "Rest of you fellas'll probably order something positively boring like ham and cheese on rye, but that's 'cause you don't know what you're missing. I swear, Anna Mae, most guys in this town, they've got the taste buds of pubescent boys. Stick a pizza or a cheeseburger in front of them, that's the extent of their culinary curiosity. Course if it wasn't for Marlene, I'd be just as bad. She's the one keeps expandin' my culinary horizons, believe me—"

"Howard, you think we could talk about what's bothering me while we're waiting for the food?"

"Why, of course, Anna Mae. Let's get to it. What's on your mind? But I hope it's not about me breakin' a promise I never made, now is it? Tell me it's not about that, because I promise you right now, right here in front of all these witnesses, I never gave Leo Harvey authority to commit to havin' our detectives investigate this shooting, that's just not something I would've done—and I further promise you that Leo would've never—"

268 • K. C. Constantine

"Well somebody did, Howard! Now I don't want to call you a liar but either it was you or it was somebody who claimed to be speaking for you—"

"Anna Mae, just slow down now, take a deep breath—"

"I don't need to take a deep breath, Howard—"

"Yes, you do, Anna Mae, yes, you do—"

"I don't need instruction on how to breathe, Howard, I've been doin' that for a lot longer than you have—"

"And that's what's got me a little worried here, Anna Mae, your face is starting to get blotchy—"

"Oh stop pretending you're worried about my health, Howard, and tell me—no, forget that! You get Leo Harvey down here right now. You get him down here in front of me and everybody else in this room, 'cause I want to hear him tell me to my face he didn't promise me you authorized two county detectives to investigate this shooting—"

"Anna Mae, I couldn't do that even if I wanted to. Harvey's tryin' that Stillton kid that shot his mother's boyfriend, he doesn't have time to come down here—just listen a minute."

"No, I'm not going to listen to anything except him saying he didn't make that promise to me—"

"Just listen, will ya? Will ya just listen a minute?"

Mrs. Remaley folded her arms across her ample bosom and started shaking her head from side to side. "I'm not going to listen to you spin your way out of this, Howard, I won't be satisfied until I see Harvey telling you, me, and everybody in this room he didn't make that promise to me, that's all I'm going to listen to—"

"So you think I'm down here tryin' to spin my way out of this, do you?"

"You're the best spinner in this county, Howard, why would I think you'd be doing anything else?"

"Well now lemme tell you something, Anna Mae—"

"No, let me tell you something first. If this isn't straightened out, Howard, if you try to give me the spin here, I'm going straight to the *Gazette* and you know what the publisher thinks of me, Howard—"

"I know he financed most of your campaign against me, Anna Mae, I know that for sure. But—and I hate to be the one to tell you this so long after the fact—but he backed you not because he was in love with you, Anna Mae, but because he was in serious hate with me. He would've backed anybody was runnin' against me. And if you call the other candidate in that race, I think he'll tell you that his campaign was financed by the same guy who financed yours."

"Well if that isn't just like you to try to turn that around—"

"Well how's this, Anna Mae—and this has absolutely no spin on it, it's as straight as I ever throw anything. You just accused me of makin' a promise I never made and then breakin' it and then lyin' about it, and you did that in front of all these fellas here. You tried just as hard as you could to make me look like a fool. Anna Mae, I haven't been DA of this county for almost four terms because I'm a fool."

Failan turned to Bellotti, Valcanas, and Hepburg and said, "Fellas, how 'bout you give us a couple minutes here."

"Nothing doing," she said. "Anything you can say to me in private you can say in front of them, I don't have any secrets."

"Uh-huh. Okay. Fine. You want 'em to hear what I've got to say, that's fine with me. Fact is, Anna Mae, you *don't* have any secrets. You've never had a thought you kept to yourself, not in your entire life. If you thought it, you found some way to get it said. Well, I have to admit, there are some people that find that utterly charming. Hell, I heard one of your campaign groupies say one time that one quality was enough to make you positively charismatic. And I thought, well, yes, your so-called inability to tell anything but the truth does appeal to some people—the monomaniacs, the ones who think the world's all this or all that, whatever their particular flavor.

"And when you decided to run against me, well, I remember thinkin', say what you want about this woman, she's got 'em. Big as basketballs and solid brass. You'd have to. I mean, Jesus, to run for district attorney and not be one? I've asked everybody I know and I've researched it every way I can, but, Anna Mae, as far as I can determine, you are the only person in twentieth-century Pennsylvania to run for the office of district attorney without bein' an attorney."

"This is what you're going to talk about, Howard? My campaign against you?"

"Yes, Anna Mae, that's exactly what I'm gonna talk about."

"That was more than twelve years ago, Howard. Water under the bridge—"

"No no, Anna Mae, it's not water under the bridge, it's why you're here now, it's why you tried to make a fool out of me in front of these fellas, it's 'cause you didn't get it then, and it's 'cause you still don't get it now. When you ran against me and you said that all the office required was administrative abilities, that anybody who knew the basics of office management could do the job, I mean, you got me off my butt and into action. I loved it, I loved havin' the chance to get out there and explain why this job wasn't just any office manager's job. I loved goin' around the county explainin' what I did and what it required and why everybody oughta be concerned about who the DA was and what he was about."

"Howard, for God's sake get to the point, will you please?"

"My point is, Anna Mae, you didn't have the first idea what's involved in the job. And every time you started ranting about how plea bargaining was the plague that was going to grind American justice to a halt, I loved explainin' why, without plea bargaining, American justice *would* grind to a halt. And every time I did, you sat there, in all your smug theoretical righteousness, and never heard one word I said."

"Wrong, Howard, as usual. I heard every word you said—"

"May've heard them, Anna Mae, but didn't understand a goddamn one."

"Don't use that language with me—"

"Horseshit!"

Mrs. Remaley covered her ears and turned away, but Failan

grabbed her hands, pulled them away from her ears, and slid around in front of her.

"Just great, Anna Mae, you can call me a liar when I wasn't, you can accuse me of breakin' promises I didn't make, but I have to watch how I talk to you?! Horseshit! Double horseshit! Listen up, lady! I know what you're pissed off about and it isn't any promise about my guys doin' your work for ya. You're pissed because as soon as that guy, whatever the hell his name is, Buczek or Buski—"

"Buczyk," Hepburg said.

"Thank you. Him. Yes. You're pissed because the second our office agreed to plead him into ARD, your grand inquisition here went poof! And you can lecture everybody till their ears turn black and fall off about how you don't like plea bargaining, but without that kind of arrangement in this instance, Anna Mae, a good cop who did a clean shooting—if it were up to you—that good cop would lose his job. Now you can spin this thing down to the *Gazette* office if you want to, but you're not gonna change the fact we got corroborating testimony from the only witness—"

"The only witness who had a whole lot to gain—"

"Exactly! Of course he had something to gain. What the hell's so wrong about that?"

"And just happens to tell the same story as the cop—"

"No he doesn't—"

"Which tells me they rehearsed the whole thing—"

"Oh rehearsed my ass. I've read both their statements, Anna Mae, I've listened to the tapes of the interviews—not that I don't have a whole lot of other things to do—"

"Why take such an interest then, Howard, tell me that?"

"Because of you, Anna Mae. Because you were on your high horse again."

"Me? You got interested just because of me?!"

"Ask Leo, Anna Mae, about the bet I made with him. Ten bucks against a dime—which he owes me—'cause I bet him the day after the shooting you'd be bustin' Figulli's hump to get appointed to the board of inquiry. That's why I took an interest, my God, you think I wouldn't? With all your cockamamie theories?"

"Is it a cockamamie theory that private citizens should just shut their eyes when one of them gets shot by a cop?"

"Oh Christ, Anna Mae, come on, if you're gonna go to bat for a cause, at least pick a case that warrants an inquiry. This doesn't even come close—"

"Two witnesses practically tell an identical story, one of them is the shooter and the other one's getting a slap on the wrist in return for his testimony—"

"You forget the forensics, Anna Mae, and you also forget that the victim's statement is flatly contradicted by the forensics. The man said he was standing on the grass between the houses when he was shot—on the other side of the sidewalk opposite the street. Blood splatter doesn't lie, Anna Mae. Hornyak's blood was found on the curb, indicating clearly that where he took the bullet is not where he says he took it. And the shell casings ejected from the cop's service pistol were found to be exactly where they should've been found if he was standing where he said he was when he fired. Now if anybody's makin' up a story here, it isn't the cop and it isn't Bu, uh, Bu-whatever."

"And what you're forgetting, Howard, is who found all this forensic evidence. This case, this shooting by a city policeman, was investigated by a city detective! A Carlotti somebody, who conveniently can't be found to appear before my board—"

"Anna Mae, you're wonderful, you really are—"

"Don't you dare start that smarmy crap with me, Howard, I'm—"

"Smarmy crap? If you think what I'm gonna say is smarmy crap, you better suspend judgment for a couple minutes here, Anna Mae, because what I was about to say is that, even though nobody made a promise to you to have our detectives do your work for ya, that's exactly who did it anyway."

"What are you talking about?"

"Anna Mae, you're the perfect example of the ideologues who never let facts get in the way of their propaganda. Don't you know that the city of Rocksburg has no crime scene investigators?"

"What do you mean?"

"It doesn't, Anna Mae. There are only two crime scene investigating teams in this area. One of them is based at Troop A Barracks of the state police and the other—ta-ta! It's based in my office. And do you wanna venture a guess which of those teams did the forensics on this shooting?"

It took a long moment for the implication of what Failan said to sink in. "You are insufferable, Howard. You are despicable."

"Oh I'm probably a lot worse than that, Anna Mae. 'Cause even though nobody made any promise to you that my guys would do any of the work, you got my guys anyway. 'Cause the city detective—and his name's Carlucci by the way, not Carlotti—as soon as he finished doing what he could do, he immediately called my guys."

Mrs. Remaley's face was pinched with anger. "You knew this and you just let me go ahead anyway?"

"Oh no, Anna Mae, this isn't mine, this is all yours. That forensics report, my guys not only signed it, they typed their names and identified themselves just as fully as they have to do every time they submit a report, no matter which department requests their services. I knew you wouldn't bother to read those names. You have no interest in details, Anna Mae. Never did. You're all theory, through and through."

"And you're rotten through and through. You could've saved me all this."

"Oh no doubt of that, I could have indeed. But you know how people say it's bad for your health to carry a grudge, how they say it's way harder on you than it is on the person you've got the grudge against? Believe me when I say I agree with them. It is way harder to carry a grudge. Anna Mae, I tell you with every molecule in my body, you have no idea how deeply I felt the grudge I've been carryin' against you. You have no idea how hard I looked to find a suitable way to even up with you, for what an insult it was, not only to me, but to my office, and to every district attorney in this commonwealth, I don't give a damn what party they represent. When you took out that ad in the *Gazette* and announced your candidacy and said you didn't have to be an attorney to hold the office, that was one thing. But when you said all it took was the skills of an office manager, that just pissed me off to my bones. I vowed to myself that one day I'd even up with you for that. And I'm very relieved—finally—to say I think I just did."

Mrs. Remaley didn't say a word. She picked up her large, black, leather purse and her large, black, leather briefcase and marched out of the room, head held high.

There was an awkward silence for a few moments, then Valcanas cleared his throat and said, "Well, Mr. Mayor, if motions are in order, I move you declare this inquiry over."

"Not so fast, not so fast. I instigated this damn thing, the least you can do is give me a written report—or at least tell me you're gonna give me one, somethin' I can show the paper when they get around to askin' what happened. God knows, none of us wantsa look any more ridiculous than we are—least I don't. If I were you guys, and I was tryin' to make somebody pay for this, I'd make Figulli write the damn report. There's nothin' he hates worse, and you ask me he deserves all the pain you can give him."

"Well then, Mr. Mayor, I think it's incumbent upon you to appoint yourself chairman pro tem and get this thing wrapped up," Hepburg said.

"Yeah, you would. Okay, let's do it."

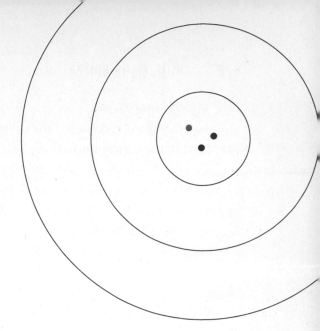

Rᴀʏꜰᴏʀᴅ ᴀɴᴅ Reseta were running at the Rocksburg High School football field. Once every couple of weeks, instead of running along the Conrail tracks by the river or running through town, they'd run a lap around the quarter-mile track at the football field and then take the bleacher seats two at a time up and one at a time down, do another quarter-mile, and then run up and down the bleachers again. It was Rayford's idea, and he was always trying to get Reseta to do it because it was the one way Reseta couldn't keep up with him. Going up the bleachers would cause the piece of shrapnel in Reseta's butt to stick him, and coming down jarred his back—though he didn't complain about it—and he'd have to push himself extra hard to catch Rayford when they got on the flat.

When they started their cool-down walk, Rayford said, "Know what I never ast you?"

"What?"

"Happened to that kid?"

"What kid?"

"Irish kid. One you was haulin' ass down the juvey center."

"When?"

" 'Chu talkin' 'bout, when? Second worst night of my life."

"Gone. Man, it's hot. Supposed to be this hot for May?"

"Gone? Gone where?"

"Gone, wherever gone is, I don't know. Children's Bureau found his foster family, sent him back to them, then he took off again."

"So he never had a lawyer momma? Or doctor father?"

"Maybe he does, I don't know. But there's no doctors or lawyers in the foster house. Just another foster family. Four other kids in the house. Apparently he was the only one didn't like their rules."

They walked a lap, wiping their sweat, drinking water.

"Still ain't goin' tell me what happened with you in Nam, are ya? When you shot that guy, huh?"

"No, and if you don't stop askin' you're gonna run by yourself from now on."

"Well why'd you tell me I was headin' for a shit storm after I shot Hornyak? And why'd you look like you looked?"

" 'Cause you were. But you got through it. Without any help from me no matter what I looked like. So forget about it."

"Sometimes I don't know why I even talk to you."

"You have to talk to me, nobody else likes you."

"Oh if you ain't the fucked-uppest motherfucker I ever knew— what happened to your face, you goin' tell me that?"

"If I told you, you wouldn't believe me anyway, so why should I?"

"Look here, man, you got one cut under your nose, you got 'nother one on top a your right eye, and you ain't goin' tell me what happen?"

Reseta stopped and faced Rayford. "If I tell you, I want your blood oath on your shield this stays right here."

"Ow, that bad, huh?"

"Wipe that smirk off your face, this is serious. I want your word—"

"Okay, okay, got-damn. It stays here."

"I, uh, I been on this med. For, uh, depression."

"Depression? You? You mean like the real shit? Not some-woman-stole-your-furniture-and-wrecked-your-ride kinda depression? The chemical shit?"

"Yeah the chemical shit."

"Since when, man? Whyn't you say somethin'?"

"I am sayin' something, you gonna let me say it or not?"

"Yeah yeah, say it, man. Sorry. Shit."

"You know, since, uh, since after Christmas."

"Oh. Yeah. Your man in Mississippi."

"Yeah. It got real bad around the middle of March, end of March. So, anyway, had to do somethin', I couldn't keep on like that. Went to see this GP, he prescribed this med. For a while it worked real good. Then it started messin' with my sleep."

"Messin' how?"

"Started havin' these dreams, man. Awful. So bad I'd wake up, two, three, four times a night. Be so tired in the mornin', it was like I hadn't slept at all. I was runnin' on caffeine."

"Yeah, man. We noticed that."

"We? Well, yeah, I'm sure everybody did. But not as much as I did. Started forgettin' things. Simple stuff, basic stuff. Come outta the unit, forget my baton, my flash, started screwin' up my UIRs. One day Nowicki chewed me a new one. So I got the dose adjusted, worked okay for a little while more. Then it started again. The dreams."

"Like what kind?"

"Okay. I'm gonna tell you the last one. And this is how I got these cuts. You can laugh, I don't care, but you can't tell this—"

"Already swore, James, I said I wouldn't, what the fuck?"

"Alright. Here it is. I'm on some kinda campus. College campus somewhere. There's shit everywhere. Human shit. It's impossible to walk without steppin' in it. I'm short, I'm fat, and I'm wearin' a basketball uniform—"

"Basketball uniform?!"

"Just listen, okay? Some guy's leadin' me to this field house. I'm supposed to win this basketball game, everybody's cheerin' me. The game's goin' on right then, it's bein' played while I'm bein' led into the field house. And I'm supposed to win this game, but not because I got great basketball skills . . ."

"What then?"

"It's, uh, it's because I fart—"

"Say what? 'Cause you fart?"

"Yeah, just listen, willya?"

"Okay. 'Cause you fart. You goin' win the game 'cause you fart—"

"That's right, it's a dream, alright? When I fart, I emit this noxious gas, really nauseating odor. It's so bad people can't stand to be anywhere near me. So what I'm supposed to do is get in the game, get under the basket, and fart, and the other team, they're gonna wanna get away, and our guys are gonna get all the rebounds, and that's how we're gonna win."

"Well if your farts are so bad, why're your guys, I mean, how come they don't try to get away?"

"I don't know. That wasn't clear. All I know is the person who's leadin' me into the gym, he's arguin' with somebody about what to feed me to produce the foulest smell. Somebody tells him that I love kolbassi and the garlic in it will make me fart more. And worse—"

"You told me one time you don't like kolbassi—"

"It's a dream, okay?"

"Oh. Okay. So then what?"

"I mean this is all serious, this is as though life itself depends on the outcome of this game. And as we're about to enter the field house, the entrance, it's lined with the longest turds I've ever seen, ten, twelve, fifteen feet long. It's very hard to avoid them. And I notice how much they resemble kolbassi. I think maybe they are kolbassi—"

"Oh man you ain't goin' tell me you wind up eatin' shit—"

"Stop interruptin' me, will ya?! It's a dream."

"Please don't tell me you—"

"Shut up, will ya! I don't eat shit, okay? But somebody comes runnin' up, they're slippin' and slidin', and they got one piece of grilled kolbassi on a tree branch. Everybody's cheerin'. They're sayin', yeah, that'll do it, feed him, feed him, put him in, put him in, they're chanting, and the noise is ferocious, it's deafening. And then I hear these girls talkin' about how fat I am, how short I am, how it's ridiculous to think I'm gonna help the team win because they say I can't play at all—"

"Oh I've seen you play, James, and they're right, you can't—"

"Will you shut the fuck up and let me tell it? You wanna know what happened to my face, I'm tryin' to tell you."

"Okay, go 'head, go 'head."

"So I'm insulted by these girls. I become determined to play well, that if they put me into the game I'll win it not because of my farts but because I play well. And then I'm in the game, I get the ball, I attempt a shot and I'm fouled. I go to the foul line. I'm so in-experienced at basketball I have to ask the ref if I'm standing in the right place. And he tells me yeah, so I try to bounce the ball, you know, dribble it a couple times to relax myself, and its surface, the surface of the ball is like the top of a muffin—"

"The ball's like a muffin? A muffin?"

"Yeah, a muffin. Don't ask me what kind. And it's very heavy, the ball. I don't know if I have the strength to make the shot. But I try. The ball barely makes it to the front of the rim, but it bounces straight back to me. I don't hesitate. I shoot and I make the basket. On the inbound pass, the ball's rollin' loose on the floor. I'm deter-mined to get it. Like it's the most important thing in the world for me to get that ball. So I dive for it. And I wake up, my nose is bleedin', my eye's bleedin', my elbow's throbbin'. I dove off the fuckin' bed—"

"Oh man, you dove off the bed?!"

"In my sleep, yeah. To get the ball. Face-first into the table be-side my bed."

Rayford tried not to laugh, but couldn't help himself. He dou-bled over and stamped his feet.

"See, you think that's funny—"

"I can't help it, James, it is, man. That's the wildest shit I ever heard."

"Well it ain't funny to me. That's the kinda dreams I've been havin' since about two weeks after I started on this med. Can't remember the last time I had a good night's sleep."

"Well, believe this, I started dreamin' 'bout playin' B-ball that bad, I'd flush that shit in a heartbeat."

"Yeah? Me too. Except the depression's a whole lot worse."

"Well I'd either get me another pill, man, or another pill-roller, one or the other."

"I thought so too. For a while. But I don't know. I think these dreams're tellin' me it's time to pack it in. Move on with my life."

"Shit, James, you been sayin' that for how long now?"

"No. I mean it. I mean what's this dream about, huh? Me tryin' not to step in shit. Human shit. Me tryin' to get in the game. And the people want me in the game, they want me in there not 'cause I'm good but 'cause I emit this gas that's so noxious it drives everybody away. And that's what I've been doin', long as I can remember. The Guinnans, Victor Charlie, the Scavellis, the Hornyaks, the Buczyks, man, that kid, the runaway. Then the night I saw you and Canoza in the wagon, you were holdin' your nuts, that thing was stickin' outta Boo, and the next thing I knew, I was on my ass 'cause I stepped in dog shit. Enough's enough, man, how long can you keep tellin' yourself you're helpin' people when all you're doin' is tryin' not to step in their shit?"

Rayford shook his head. "You put it that way, man, maybe it's time for you to be gone. But I think you're wrong. I think you helped a lot more people than you think you did."

"Yeah? Name one."

"Me."

"Oh right, yeah, I helped you a lot."

"You did, man. Gave me that book. Made me take those tests. I got to the second one, that one that goes, what you goin' tell yourself if you don't make a change in your life? And soon as that inquiry bullshit was over, I talked to my lawyer, you know, Valcanas?"

"Yeah?"

"Told him my situation, told him I cut off my wife's rent, and he told me he'd do my divorce for a hundred and fifty bucks. So I said go on and do it, man. So see there? If you hadn't given me that book, I wouldn't've done that. *Life Strategies: Doing What Works, Doing What Matters.* Ol' Phillip C. McGraw. Man done made me take a bite outta my life. So see there? Wasn't for you, I'd still be messed up."

"Oh you think you're not, huh?"

"Oh, I'm 'onna pay you a compliment, you goin' talk shit on me. Awright. Well see here, motherfucker, when I go to bed, I sleep. And if I'm dreamin' B-ball, you can believe when they put me in the game it ain't 'cause I can fart, it's 'cause I can shoot, and I ain't shootin' no motherfuckin' muffins either. B'lieve that."

"Aw you're so fulla shit. What time is it?"

"Time to go to work. Time to collar some non-pooper-scoopers."

"See there? That's what I mean? After twenty six years, that's my mission now?"

"Yes it is, my man. And you don't soon get you a new holster, you keep showin' up with that funky-ass thing a yours, Nowicki goin' shit a hat and make you wear it. Worse than Boo, man."

"Can you imagine how bad he'd be on Boo if he'd've got stuck any lower on his back? Where his vest should've been?"

"Aw Boo man, that dude—what can I say? He is seriously fucked-up behint that."

"You would be too you were sweatin' a coroner's inquest."

"Hey, I sweat my own thing, man, remember? Inquest, inquiry, whatever—"

"Trust me, Rayf. The coroner is no Mrs. Remaley. That man asks hard questions."

"Well you ask me, it look like pilin' on, man. I don't think Nowicki was right, suspend Boo's ass on top a him lookin' at that in-quest? Which I don't even wanna think 'bout it, man," Rayford said. "Excuse me while I put on my honky voice. I don't even want to think about it, sir."

"You better think about it. 'Cause you're sure as hell gonna get asked about it."

"Just wish I hadn't said what I said."

"Well you said it, so just keep on sayin' it. Whatever you do, don't change it now."

"Wasn't plannin' to. Just . . . just feel shitty, that's all. For Boo. 'Cause every time I go over it, you know? What I said? Sounds like what I said was he slammed her down. And her head went whump! I can't think of how else to say that."

"Well did he slam her down or not?"

"No. She just kinda fell back down. Like she was out already. Or maybe even dead already—"

"Hey don't speculate, Rayf. Don't say anything except what you saw and heard. You do that, you might make detective sergeant yet."

"Whattaya mean *might*? Already made it. They just ain't give it to me yet."

"Tell you what. When I get my Ph.D.? I'll give you the first month's therapy free. One hour a week, you can come in and vent how they're screwin' you around on your promotion. Should have my office open in about three years."

"Hey, motherfucker, I don't get those stripes by Labor Day, I'm goin' re-up in the air force."

"Yeah, right. That's you, off into the wild blue yonder—"

"No shit, man. I mean it."

"You're gonna be wearin' Rocksburg black for the next twenty years, who you tryin' to kid?"

"I'm tellin' you, man, no stripes by Labor Day, I'm gone."

"Uh-huh. C'mon. Time to collar some non-pooper-scoopers. Jesus, twenty gazillion years of human evolution and this is the best I can do?"

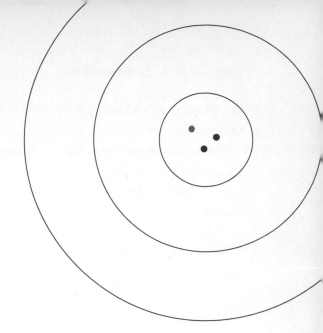

RAYFORD WAS cruising the Flats. It was 2215 hours when he'd pulled in for gas and a coffee refill at Sheetz's. And when he passed the Rocksburg National Bank their sign said the temp was 81 degrees. That was a half hour ago. Fifteen minutes to go on his patrol, and the air flowing in his windows was gluey with humidity and the raw smell of storm sewers clogged from yesterday's daylong downpours. The Conemaugh River had risen more than two feet in the last twenty-four hours, and the gutters in the Flats were still rushing with muddy water. At least it had quit raining.

For most of his patrol yesterday, Rayford felt like he was back in Alabama during hurricane season. The only good thing about it was that the weather had kept the civilians inside—except when they were in their doorways anxiously eyeballing the water backing up out of the storm sewers. So he was spending his patrol tonight, like last night, mostly in the service mode, calling the fire department to start cars and pump out cellars.

Rayford liked service much more than protection these days, especially when he cruised the Franklin, Jefferson, Bryan, and Miles block. That's when, during some part of his patrol, he'd see Joe Buczyk doing part of his ARD by driving Pete Hornyak to and from his medical appointments or shoveling up dog crap before he cut the grass, in both their yards, or like tonight, hosing the mud off Hornyak's sidewalk.

It helped even more that Nick Scavelli was still in the Mental Health Unit, though it was almost a sure pop he was going to be transferred to Mamont State Hospital once it was determined he was incapable of aiding in his defense for stabbing Canoza. Rayford learned on the sly from a female aide who worked in Mental Health that all Scavelli did all day was ask people if they'd saved room for dessert.

"Asked him, since when you get dessert with breakfast? He just said if you ain't gonna save room for it you ought to eat it first. And that's all he says. Doesn't know what day it is."

Cold as it sounded, Rayford had to admit it helped him as much as Canoza that Mary Rose Scavelli was dead and buried and that Coroner Wallace Grimes had ruled her death a result of natural causes.

"That sound they heard in Pittsburgh was me sighin' in Rocks-burg," Rayford told Canoza after he reported back to work. "Thought sure your ass was gonna get nailed 'cause of what I said."

"Piece a cake," Canoza said, but Rayford knew he was blowing smoke.

Because Chief Nowicki allowed Canoza to serve his suspen-sion—for not wearing his vest—while on medical leave, Booboo showed up for work wearing his vest and had been wearing it every day since he'd come back, and not even once did he have to be re-minded to put it on.

And most of all, as far as Rayford was concerned, it helped that he'd had a private, intense discussion with Nowicki the day Canoza returned to duty, at the end of which Nowicki swore on his shield that Rayford would be a detective sergeant by Labor Day or he'd know the reason why, which satisfied Rayford enough to call Reseta at home just to tell him, "I told you so."

Rayford was pondering all this as he was passing the Scavellis' house when something to the right of the porch steps caught his eye, and he hit the brakes, backed up, and parked. He saw a sign that said "House For Sale" that he knew hadn't been there yesterday. He tried to recall what Stramsky had told him about the Scavellis and their two children who had died in the fire in their house on Norwood Hill. He thought Stramsky had said they had had no other children, but this sign wasn't a legal notice put up by anybody from the city or the county. It was a sign somebody had bought in a hardware store with a white space at the bottom for a phone number. But the Scavellis must have a relative somewhere, Rayford thought, or who else would be able to make a claim on the property in order to sell it?

Rayford got out of the MU to check the sign to satisfy his own curiosity, but there was something not right about the sign. He couldn't put his finger on it, but there was something goofy about it. He read it a dozen times, thinking there had to be something weird with the phone number, because what could be weird about the words "House For Sale"? When he was looking at the number for about the tenth time again and stretching his memory to make some association with it, something else caught his eye: a flame through the window in the cellar. It looked like a cigarette lighter. It was gone as quickly as it had appeared, and he wondered if he was seeing things.

A moment later he saw what was obviously the glow of a cigarette.

Some motherfucker's squattin' in this house. Just when tonight looked like it was goin' be a lovely night of sweet service, some motherfucker got to pick this place to squat. She-it, this ain't no squatter. This is some diddy-bop think he found a cool place to smoke.

Rayford tried to remember where all the doors were in the Scavelli house as he stepped back on the sidewalk to call the base on his epaulet radio. He knew there was a door out of the kitchen in the back of the house and another one on the south side facing the Hlebecs' house. He thought those were the only two, but he walked around the north side of the house to make sure. He found no doors but he did find two block-glass windows, one with a clothes-dryer vent in it.

Satisfied that there were only the three doors, he went back onto the sidewalk and called for backup for a possible burglary.

Two minutes later Reseta pulled up with no lights or siren.

"What's up?"

"Somebody smokin' in the cellar. Probably some kid."

"Try any of the doors?"

Rayford shook his head. "Just checked to make sure there wasn't one on the north side."

"So there's just the one in the back and one in the side, right?"

Rayford nodded.

"Okay," Reseta said. "I'll take the back."

"Ain't goin' in, are ya?"

"Hell no, I'm just gonna rattle the door and holler. Damn Scavellis. Dead or locked up, still can't get away from 'em."

Rayford heard Reseta announcing his presence by hollering and pounding on the kitchen door, then drew his nine and turned his MagLite on, his gaze darting from the front door to the side door and back.

A few seconds later, the side door inched open, and somebody started tiptoeing toward Rayford, who brought his MagLite up alongside his nine, blinding the burglar, and shouted, "Freeze! Police! Get on the ground! Now! Get down!"

The tiptoer threw up his arms to ward off the light, then spun around and ran smack into Reseta, who caught him by the arm and put him on the ground with a hip toss. Rayford rushed to assist Reseta, and in a moment, the burglar's hands were cuffed behind his back and Reseta was patting him down. He found nothing, then rolled him over.

"Oh man, look here. Look who we have here."

"Who?"

"My little Irish runaway. Little Billy Arbaugh. Remember him?"

"The one split from his foster home?"

"None other. So this is where you're livin' now, huh?"

"Fuck you."

"Every time you run, Billy-boy, you're goin' right back there, don't you know that? Till everybody gets tired chasin' you, then it's the next step up the penal ladder."

"You can take me back but you can't make me stay."

"Well if you're gonna run, hotshot, why don't you really run, huh? You think comin' down here to the Flats is runnin'? From Maplewood? What is that—two and a half miles?"

"Whatta you care, fuck-face? Ain't none of your business."

"More and more, kid, I wish it wasn't. But it is. So get up."

Reseta took one arm and Rayford the other and they tried to pull him up but he went limp.

"Aw, c'mon, kid, don't pull this crap, c'mon, get on your feet, you're just makin' it harder."

"You think I'm gonna make it easy for you to take me back there, you're fulla shit. Those pigs, all they feed us is rolled oats. Oughta be arrestin' them, not me."

"Rolled oats?" Rayford said.

"Hey, that's one for the Children's Bureau to figure out."

"Oh yeah, like 'em fuckers give a shit."

"Well it's their job, kid, not ours."

"Why don't none of you fuckers believe me? I told the fuckin' judge, that guy down the juvey center, teachers, guidance counselors—"

"Told everybody what?" Rayford said.

"Don't listen to him, Rayf, he's gamin' us."

"What'd you tell everybody, huh?"

"They're starvin' us to death. Those fuckers took out big insurance policies on us."

Reseta started dragging the kid toward the sidewalk. "And there's black helicopters gonna fly 'em to Brazil after they cash in."

"Big fuckin' joke to you, huh? Littlest kid in the house, he's seven years old, he don't weigh thirty pounds. Look at me, look how skinny I am. If I didn't find this place, eat the food here, I'd be dead now. They won't even let us drink water, they're tryin' to kill us, I'm tellin' you. All you gotta do is go there, see for yourself, you don't believe me."

"Whattaya think, James? Think we oughta check it out?"

"Children's Bureau, Rayf, that's their job, you know? Don't listen to this kid, all he's done from my first contact with him is lie. He's a pro, I'm tellin' ya."

"Wouldn't hurt to check it out, would it?"

"Hey, I went to the house, remember? I saw the other kids. They're not starvin'! But you wanna check it out, be my guest, it's your collar anyway, you got here first. I'm goin' home, try to get some sleep."

That said, Reseta let go of the kid's arm and headed for his MU.

Instead of slumping as Rayford expected him to do, the kid straightened up. "You gonna check it out, huh?"

If this kid was a liar, he was Oscar material.

Rayford started to lead the boy out on the street, but there was Reseta standing by his MU, one foot still on the street. "Hey, Rayf, I don't wanna see you do somethin' dumb, okay?"

"Yeah? So?"

"So think, man, c'mon. Foster children? Big policies on their lives? Husbands, wives, ex-husbands, ex-wives, yeah, but foster kids? Don't take this wrong, Rayf, okay, but the only reason you're even thinkin' about checkin' this out is 'cause of your own baggage, man."

"What baggage? What're you talkin' about?"

"Aw, man, c'mon, I have to spell it out?"

"Yeah. I think you do 'cause I don't know what you're talkin' about."

"Rayf, for six years, man, when we run what do you talk about? Huh? Subject comes up once a week at least."

"You lost me. What?"

"How old would your boy be now, huh? You hear about a seven-year-old boy maybe bein' mistreated, your nose gets wide open. C'mon, Rayf, this kid's a pro. You wanna check somethin' out? Go inside. C'mon, Nowicki's gonna make you detective sergeant, go on in, look around, tell me what you see."

"And look for what exactly?"

"I'm not gonna tell you, you're the one wants to be a detective. Just go on in, let your intelligence be your guide. Go on, I'll watch him."

"Don't listen to him, man, he's just like everybody else, nobody gives a shit."

"Shut up, kid. Okay, I'm goin' in," Rayford said, and after Reseta took charge of the boy Rayford went in the same door the boy had come out on the side of the house.

He went in and turned on the light to the cellar. He went down the steps and found the floor covered with at least six inches of putrid water with opened, empty cans floating everywhere and many others visible just below the water's surface: pink salmon, sardines, tuna, peaches, pears, applesauce, baked beans, chocolate pudding, cola—the boy had been eating and drinking his way through the Scavellis' pantry and throwing the empties down the steps where their residue was mixing with the backed-up sewer water.

Rayford didn't see anything else that caught his eye, so he went back up the steps, turned out the light, and went into the cramped, messy kitchen. All the cupboard doors were open, and there weren't too many cans still left on the shelves. What immediately caught Rayford's eye was the heaps of mail and newspapers scattered across the small dining table near the refrigerator and on one chair and on the floor underneath the table. The boy had apparently been amusing himself by going through the Scavellis' mail every day and reading their daily paper.

Well you want to be a detective, Rayford thought, you better find something here. Reseta sounds too damn sure of himself. What's he think I'm gonna see that'll make me know the kid's lying?

Rayford fingered through the stacks of envelopes and papers. Among all the utility bills and advertising circulars, he found Social Security checks for both the Scavellis. The delivery dates on them showed they'd each been in the house at least a week. If the kid was the pro Reseta insisted he was why hadn't he tried to sell them to somebody old enough to cash them? Surely with that much time on his hands the kid would've thought of that. Maybe he didn't trust anyone old enough to try cashing them. Or maybe nobody he'd approached had offered him a satisfactory way to share the money. Nah, this isn't what Reseta wants me to find.

Well what then? Rayford kept pushing the papers around, first the bills, then the advertising circulars, then the newspapers. It was the newspapers that finally attracted and held his gaze. There was something about them, but he wasn't sure what. Then it became so obvious he laughed out loud. The ones on the table were all the same section of the paper—not sports, not world, national, or state news, not food, and not entertainment. The only news that interested this kid was the section devoted to "local" news. At the bottom of that stack was the front-page story of Nick Scavelli's assault on Canoza and Mary Rose Scavelli's death. And each succeeding paper in the pile was open and folded to the follow-up story the next day. The kid had picked this house because he knew from the daily paper nobody was coming back here to live, and he could stay as long as the canned food held out. Now how did Reseta know that? What the hell did he see that I didn't?

He turned off the lights and went back outside.

"Okay, James. So how'd you know, huh?"

"Look at the sign."

"What, the For Sale sign?"

"Yeah the For Sale sign, look at it."

"I did. That's what made me stop. I know there's somethin' wrong with it—aw man. I don't believe it."

"See what I mean? Kid's a pro. Every word's a lie, and then he busts your balls on top of it."

"Hey, I didn't put that sign up there, I don't know nothin' about that sign."

"Yeah, right. Gimme him, James, go on home, get some sleep."

"I'm tellin' ya, I don't know nothin' about that sign—"

"Shut up and get in the back here! Had me goin' with your bullcrap about starvin' kids. Can't believe I didn't recognize that number."

"You gonna tell this?" Reseta said, trying not to laugh.

"You tell this I'm goin' tell your dream."

"Oh man, you have to tell—one of us has to tell this! It's too good not to tell. I promise I won't tell that you didn't recognize the number, okay? But we have to tell, man, it's too good—tell you what, let me go grab up the sign—"

"Aw no, James, nothin' doin', it's my collar, it's my sign, I'm takin' the sign, that's evidence, that's probable cause, man—"

"How could that be probable cause if you didn't recognize the number?"

"The sign itself was enough to make me stop, I didn't have to recognize the number, I knew the situation here—"

"Ohhhh, you knew the situation, I see. That's why you're gonna make detective sergeant. You recognize the situation, so you didn't have to recognize the number for the courthouse, I get it."

"Awright, James, have your fun, go on and laugh all you want, man, but hand it over, it's my evidence, c'mon."

Reseta handed the sign over. "I'm givin' you twenty-four hours, Rayf. If this story's not all over City Hall this time tomorrow night, I'm tellin', man."

After he'd restrained the boy's legs, Rayford put the sign in the front seat on top of his gear bag.

"Know what, James? You can tell the whole thing far as I'm concerned. 'Cause there wasn't any reason for me to recognize that number. Anybody I need to call in the courthouse, I know their number there. I don't b'lieve I've called that switchboard number more'n twice in six years, man, so go 'head and tell it all, I ain't scared to look a fool. This ain't goin' touch me at all, man, go on and tell it, shit."

"Aw now see? You gonna be like that, Rayf, I'm not gonna have any fun at all."

"Hey, how long you guys gonna keep yakkin', huh? I needa take a piss, let's go if we're goin'."

"Shut up, you little Irish prick," Reseta said, "before I whack you in the shins."

"And you talk about my baggage," Rayford said.

"Yeah, but the difference is, I understand my baggage. You didn't even know you were carryin' any till I explained it to you."

"Talk trash on me all you want, James," Rayford said, laughing hard, "I will not be touched. You can talk me a shit sombrero, man, that will not be me wearin' it—wait, wait, hold him a second."

"Why?"

Rayford got a couple of green plastic garbage bags out of his gear bag and spread them across and over the front of the backseat.

"Okay, kid, you need to pee, go right ahead but now you won't funk up my vehicle."

"You think I'm gonna piss my pants?"

"Wouldn't put it past you. Put the courthouse number on that sign, wanna play everybody for a fool, be just like you to try to funk up my vehicle. Now shut up and get in. Watch your head. And swing your legs out."

Rayford attached the nylon restraining strap to the boy's legs, then shut the door on the other end, got behind the wheel, started the engine, reported in to base where he was headed and why. Then he waved to Reseta and pulled away from the Scavellis' house, heading south toward the juvey center.

" 'Bout time," his prisoner said.

"Shut up, kid," Rayford said, glaring at him in the mirror. "Put the courthouse phone number on that sign, think you a real wise guy—"

"I didn't put that number there."

"You didn't put the sign up either, did ya? And you weren't livin' in that house, were ya? Or eatin' all that food, or throwin' all those cans down the cellar steps either."

"I don't know what you're talkin' about."

"Yeah, right, you don't know anything. Well here's what I know, kid. You did at least one thing right today. You served as a bad example for a police officer. Me. William Milton Rayford. Patrolman. Soon to be detective sergeant. And I hope somebody has sense enough to make you clean up that house."

"I'm not cleanin' it up, I didn't dirty it up."

When Rayford stopped at the light at the intersection of Main and Broad, he looked at the kid in the mirror and thought, my beautiful little boy is dead and your lyin' ass is alive. Just one more thing God got to answer for.

"What're you waitin' for, there's nobody comin'! Go through it, I gotta piss I told ya!"

"Everything you say is a lie, kid, why should I believe you got to pee?"

"Oh you think you're real fuckin' smart, don'tcha? Fuckin' nigger you."

"Smart is relative, kid. Everybody's smart about somethin', everybody's ignorant about somethin'. The lesson for you to think on tonight is you're the one in the backseat. Maybe you oughta start askin' yourself how many times you wanna ride back there."

The light changed and Rayford drove on, thinking, if that's the lesson for him tonight, what's the lesson for me? Got to learn how to not let liars like him touch me with his lies. Got to get a whole lot smarter about my baggage. And I damn sure got to memorize the number of the courthouse or I'll never be able to shake this. Only chance I had was to tell it first. And that's gone, 'cause soon as James get back, I know he's goin' tell Stramsky. Got-damn . . . goin' live with this for the next twenty years. . . .

And why's the PO still delivering mail to that address? And why's the paper still being delivered? Okay, so if the kid was taking

the mail out of the box every day, I can understand why the mailman wouldn't get wise, but the paper? Don't the people there read
their own news? Guess not. Somethin' else for me to learn. . . .